SPACE WOLF

THEY HAD ALMOST crossed the gallery when Ragnar heard a familiar melodious yet sinister voice ring out behind him.

'Where are you going, puppy? Do turn around, please. I want to look at you, for I never like shooting anyone in the back.'

Ragnar recognised the voice. It belonged to the Chaos Marine who had taunted Sergeant Hengist. Slowly he turned around. He had half expected to see a full squad of dreaded Chaos Marines and a horde of nightgangers. All he could make out was a solitary figure.

'Madok!' he spat. Ragnar noticed that some of the icons on the Chaos Marine's armour were glowing, doubtless with malign energies. The hairs on the back of Ragnar's neck prickled. Was there a cursed spell being cast here?

'You remember. I'm flattered. That's good too. When your soul reaches hell, you will be able to tell everyone who killed you.'

A WARHAMMER 40,000 NOVEL

SPACE WOLF

By William King

A BLACK LIBRARY PUBLICATION

First published in Great Britain in 1999 by
Games Workshop Publishing
Willow Road, Lenton,
Nottingham, NG7 2WS, UK

10 9 8 7 6 5 4

Cover illustration by Wayne England

A CIP record for this book
is available from the British Library.

ISBN 1 84154 106 0

Set in ITC Giovanni

Printed and bound in Great Britain by
Omnia Books Limited, Glasgow

See the Black Library on the Internet at
http://www.blacklibrary.co.uk

Find out more about Games Workshop
and the world of Warhammer 40,000 at
http://www.games-workshop.com

PROLOGUE
ASSAULT ON HESPERIDA

ALL AROUND the buildings burned. Ragnar strode through the maelstrom of battle, shouting commands to his men.

'Brother Hrolf – I want two krak missiles into that forward emplacement now! The rest of you form up and prepare to storm in as soon as the door is blown.'

Acknowledgements filled the earbead linking him to the comm-net. He raced from the doorway where he'd been sheltering to a huge block of fallen masonry some twenty metres closer to his objective. Enemy laser blasts melted the concrete behind his heels but, even in his powered armour, he moved too quickly for the heretics to get a bead on him. He threw himself into a crouch behind the rubble and waited for a moment.

The thunder of heavy ordnance filled the air. Somewhere off in the distance he could hear the howl of Thunderhawk engines and the multiple sonic booms as they slowed their speed down from the sub-orbital. Even as he watched, bright yellow contrails pierced the leaden clouds and the gunships hove into view. Missile clusters detached themselves from their wings and hurtled groundwards to smash into the heretics' positions. He checked his weapons with the precision born of a century of experience, took a deep breath, intoned a prayer to the Emperor and waited.

He was aware of everything. The beat of his primary heart was regular. His body was already healing the minor cuts and grazes he had taken from shrapnel. He could feel a slight nick on his face closing itself. His senses, far sharper than those of the human he had once been, kept up a steady flow of information on the battlefield around him. From nearby he could smell the comforting presence of his battle-brothers, a compound of hardened ceramite, oil, the flesh of Fenris and the subtle markers which told they were not quite human. More than that, he could pick out the faint pheromone traces of anger, pain and well-controlled fear.

He checked his armour to ensure the integrity had not been breached. Here and there were a few scuffs where shrapnel had bounced from the hardened ceramite of the carapace. In two spots he found blisters on the paintwork that told of the fleeting kiss of a lasgun beam. In one spot there was a distinct chip on the shoulder pad where a bolt pistol shell had torn through the raised rim. Nothing serious. The servo-motors that powered the mighty combat suit were currently operating at 75% efficiency, idling on most systems to save power. The suit's built-in auto-sensors informed him of faint traces of pollutants, contaminants and a residue of the neurotoxins that the heretics had used in their surprise attack on the loyalist forces when they began their rebellion.

Nothing much to worry about, praise Russ. His body's ability to metabolise poison was barely needed to deal with them. He had known poisons strong enough to give him headaches and muscle spasms and dizziness while his body adapted to their presence. These ones were nowhere close to that potency. All in all then, things did not look too bad. If truth be told, he was enjoying the situation. After a month of meditation in his cell back in the Fang and a week cooped up onboard one of the great Imperium starcruisers en route to this minor war, he relished the action. It was hardly surprising really: it was what he had been born to do, and what he had trained for. His entire life had been a preparation for this moment. He was, after all, an Imperial Space Marine of the Space Wolves Chapter. What more could he possibly ask from life than this? He had a loaded boltgun in his hand and the Emperor's enemies before him. In this life, there was no greater pleasure to be found than performing his duty and ending the lives of those sorry heretics.

The masonry at his back shuddered. Chunks of stone clattered off his armour. Someone had hit his cover with something heavy, a rocket perhaps or a very heavy bolter shell. Not that it mattered. He knew from long experience that the metal-reinforced concrete could take it. He studied the chronometer readout superimposed on his field of vision. A minute and four seconds had passed since he had given his orders to Brother Hrolf. He guessed that it would take two minutes for Hrolf to get into position, and another ten seconds for him to line up his shot. That was more than enough time for the rest of his force to get themselves into position. In that time, it was impossible for the heretics to chip away at his cover unless they brought far more firepower to bear than they were currently using.

It was a thought that had apparently occurred to the enemy commander too. Ragnar could hear the sound of monstrous tracks coming closer. He knew that they must belong to an enemy vehicle. The Imperial forces had just begun their drop from orbit with the Space Wolves as a spearhead. It was far too early for any Imperial armour to be on the ground. The logical conclusion was simple. Whatever was approaching was not friendly. A call on the comm-link soon confirmed this.

+Force Ragnar. Enemy Predator tank approaching your position. Do you wish assistance? Over.+

Ragnar considered for an instant. At this point, the Thunderhawks' air-cover was needed more elsewhere, to support troops still in the critical stage of landing under enemy guns. He did not want to draw their help away from his battle-brothers. Particularly not to deal with a single enemy tank.

+Ragnar here. Negative. We will deal with the Predator ourselves. Over.+

+Message received and understood. The Emperor watch over you. Over.+

Ragnar considered his options. He could hear the tank's approach, smell the acrid chemical fumes of its exhaust. Concrete was crushed under its treads as it moved. He could request Brother Hrolf with the squad's heavy support weapon to blast the tank but that would mean cancelling the attack on the bunker while Hrolf moved into a new position, and Ragnar doubted that there was any need for that, certainly not when he could deal with the tank himself.

He checked his belt compartments. Everything was in place. Healing drug syrettes, grenade dispensers, repair patches. He tapped the grenade dispenser and a krak grenade dropped into his hand. That would do. He glanced out of his cover and saw the long snout of the Predator's gun barrel coming around the corner. Moments later the whole tank hove into view. It was a standard design for an Imperial tank but instead of the neat patterns of the Imperially aligned planetary armies it had been hastily sprayed blood red, and a crude eight-armed Chaos symbol had been painted on the side in yellow. Ragnar bared his teeth in a snarl at the sight of that hated emblem. It was the sign of daemon worshippers sworn to overthrow everything Ragnar had fought to uphold his whole long life, and just the sight of it brought the animal ferocity that was so much a part of his Space Wolf nature bubbling to the fore.

He raised himself to his feet, measuring the distance between himself and the tank with a practised eye. No more than a hundred strides, he guessed. The distance was closing fast as the tank rumbled forward. He could see that the turret-mounted bolters were already swivelling to bear on him. His position had been flanked. It was just as well that he had decided to abandon it anyway.

The servo-motors of his armour whined as he raced across the open ground towards the tank. Once again lasgun fire dogged his heels, but as he had counted on, the gunners were too surprised by his sudden break from cover in the direction of the tank to target him swiftly. The tank's gunners obviously couldn't believe their eyes either. Tracer fire ripped the air over his head targeted on a spot behind him. The gunners' efforts were half-hearted. They seemed to have reckoned that he was going to be ground to pieces beneath their onrushing vehicle. Ragnar intended to swiftly prove them wrong. They would pay for underestimating one of the sons of Leman Russ.

He rushed directly at the tank. It swelled swiftly in his view. Even though he had often marched beside such vehicles or clung to their side as they carried himself and his battle-brothers into the fray he was surprised by how big this one looked now. He smiled. It was always different when you actually had to fight with one of these things. The gap between him and the Predator closed quickly. The air thrummed with the vibration of its engine. The exhaust stink became near-overpowering to his nostrils. The flickering lasgun fire came ever closer to his heels.

At the last second he threw himself to the right, putting the Predator between himself and the fire from the enemy bunker. He reached out and lobbed the first krak grenade between the drive cogs and the tracks they were linked with. The charge was shaped and the fuse was set for three seconds. Plenty of time for Ragnar to set another charge.

When they exploded, whole sections of tread were blasted away and drive cogs began to grind to a halt as the power train failed. A huge section of track flapped free and almost hit Ragnar. Only his lightning-swift reflexes, keyed to superhuman keenness by the stress of battle, enabled him to duck beneath it. Just as well, really, since he guessed the sheer force with which the articulated metal segments were moving would be enough to take his head clean off.

Robbed of the power of one set of treads, the Predator began to rotate slowly on the spot. The tracks on the other side were still working and pushing it forward but it was not going to go anywhere except in circles. Ragnar was glad of that. Since the turret was already beginning to swivel in the direction of his squad it was time to move to the next phase of his plan.

With a mighty leap Ragnar sprang onto the side of the Predator just above the track guard. He landed easily, ceramite boots ringing against the hull, and raced forward, hoping to Russ that no one inside the tank had yet realised what was going on. He could hear the muffled bellowing of orders and confused shrieks from within so he guessed they had not. Good. They would never realise what hit them. He raced forward to the turret and saw that the hatch was closed. A pity, Ragnar thought, but nonetheless it was what he had expected. In the close quarters combat of a city fight no tank commander was going to go around with his head exposed. Still, it was foolish for them to have advanced so far without close infantry support. It would have been far more difficult for him to do what he planned in the presence of armed warriors. He guessed that the tank had come as quickly as possible in response to a desperate plea for help from the bunker. Well, he would make sure the heretics paid for that mistake.

He reached down and grasped the handle on the top of the turret with both hands then braced himself. He strained with all the strength of his enhanced muscles and tugged. Nothing happened. He threw more and more power into the servo-motors of his armour until the muscle fibres were almost overloaded and the maintenance readouts superimposed on his field of vision were far into the red. Slowly at first, with an awful grinding sound, the hatch began to come away from its hinges. Ceramite buckled under the terrible strength of the Space Wolf. Ragnar almost overbalanced as the hatch cover came free in his hands.

There was a rush of foul air from within the tank, and Ragnar recognised the stink of mutation. Truly these heretics had paid the price of swearing allegiance to their dark masters. He tossed the hatch cover away and grabbed a frag grenade from his belt dispenser. He looked down into the interior of the tank. A quick glance showed him hideously altered mutant faces looking up at him. One was blotched with monstrous red warts each ending in an eye. The other had melted and run as if made of candle wax. The mark of their evil was plain upon them, their exterior selves had been altered to match their inner corruption by the evil powers they worshipped.

One of the mutants reached for his holstered pistol. By the look of blind panic on its face, Ragnar knew that the creature had worked out what was going to happen next. Nor was it wrong. Ragnar dropped the grenade into the open hatch and leaped away. Even as he did so he grasped another grenade and lobbed it with unerring accuracy back into the opening on the turret's top. It was just possible that the mutants might be able to find one grenade as it rolled about within and lob it clear. He knew they would not be able to get both.

The tank was still between him and the bunker. He whipped out his weapons. In the side of the Predator a hatch had half opened. One of the crew, realising what was happening, was trying to get clear. Ragnar kicked the hatch closed and sprang away again just as two enormous blasts shook the tank. A fountain of blood and flesh jetted up through the turret top. Ragnar moved quickly now for cover, knowing that it was all too possible that the drive systems of the tank would go up in the explosion.

Fortunately the inhabitants of the bunker were distracted by the fate of their support vehicle and he dived into the cover of the rubble in which he had previously crouched just as a wracking explosion tore the mighty vehicle to pieces. Huge chunks of metal armour were twisted outward by the blast of the exploding power plant. Oily black smoke twisted skywards from the remains.

Just at that moment the sound of another explosion assaulted Ragnar's ears. He knew that Brother Hrolf had hit the door of the bunker with the missile launcher. Ragnar sprang up, noting with satisfaction that the plasteel entrance had been blasted completely off its hinges by the force of the explosion and that the flanking force of Space Wolves was already moving into position from either side. Even as Ragnar watched Brother Snagga threw himself flat, wriggled on his belly under the firing slot of the bunker and lobbed a handful of microgrenades through the entrance. Explosions and screams of pain were his reward. Within seconds two Space Wolves had entered the bunker. Shots rang out as they finished off the survivors.

Ragnar smiled revealing two huge wolfish fangs. The gleam of triumph appeared in his yellowish dog-like eyes. Another victory was his. At that moment, he caught the faint gleam of sunlight hitting glass somewhere off to his right. Instinct told him to throw himself flat but he was already too late. Even as he sprang, the sniper's bolter shell, rocket-powered and armour piercing, was ripping towards him too quickly to be avoided. All his leap did was get his body partially out of the way. The shell which had been aimed directly at his heart exploded instead within his chest. Pain blasted through his body. Messengers of agony raced along his nerve endings. He fell forward into a molten lava pit of torment.

'DON'T WORRY, Brother Ragnar,' he heard a voice from the far distance say. 'We have you.'

Ragnar wondered about that, wondered if they were not too late. Already the voices sounded as if they were coming from the top of a huge well. It seemed to him that he was falling downwards, towards the cold hell of his people, there to be greeted by all his family and his friends, and all the old enemies he had sent there himself. It was odd, he thought, that he should be dying so far from home, so long after he had expected to die. There was something comforting about this strange sensation. He knew what to expect. He ought to. After all, he had died before.

Icy clarity possessed his spirit. His memory flooded back. His soul ventured back through the centuries. Remembering.

ONE
THE SEA OF DRAGONS

'WE'RE ALL GOING to die!' Yorvik the Harpooner screamed, glaring round, his eyes wide with fear. Lightning slashed through the sky of Fenris, illuminating the man's tormented face. Sheer terror made his shout audible even above the roar of the wind and the thunder of the waves against the ship. The driving rain running down his face looked uncannily like tears.

'Be silent!' Ragnar shouted and slapped the terrified man across the cheek. Shocked at being hit by a youth barely old enough to have the down of manhood on his cheeks, Yorvik reached for his axe, his fear momentarily forgotten. Ragnar shook his head and glared at the older man with his cold grey eyes. Yorvik stopped, as if realising where he was and what he was doing. They stood in full view of all the warriors on the prow of the ship. Attacking the son of his captain would gain him no credit in the eyes of the gods or the crew. The flush of shame came to Yorvik's cheeks and Ragnar looked away so as not to embarrass the man further.

Ragnar tossed his head to get his mane of long black hair from his eyes. Squinting through the lash of the wind and the salt-spray of the storm-tossed sea, Ragnar silently agreed with

Yorvik. They were going to die unless a miracle occurred. He had been going to sea since he was old enough to walk, and never had he seen a storm this bad.

Sullen dark clouds scudded across the sky. It was dark as night even though it was noon. Spray billowed as the prow of the ship cleaved through another enormous wave. The dragonhide of the deck echoed like an enormous drum with the force of the impact. He struggled to keep his balance on the constantly moving deck. Even over the wind's daemon shriek, he could hear the creak of the ship's bones. It was only a matter of time, he decided, before the sea killed the vessel. It was a race to see whether the force of the waves smashed the *Spear of Russ* into a thousand pieces, or whether it simply stripped the cured dragonhide from the ship's skeleton and left them to founder and drown.

Ragnar shuddered and not just from the chill, sodden wetness of his clothing. For him, as for all his people, drowning represented the worst of all possible deaths. It meant simply sinking into the clutches of the sea daemons, where his soul would be bound in an eternity of servitude. There would be no chance of earning his place among the Chosen. He would not die with spear or axe in hand. He would not find himself a glorious death or swift passage to the Hall of Heroes in the Mountains of the Gods.

Looking back along the rain-lashed deck Ragnar saw that all the massive warriors were as frightened as he, though they hid it well. Tension was written on every pallid face, and visible in every blue eye. Rain matted their long blond hair and gave them a hopeless bedraggled look. They sat huddled at their benches, useless oars held at the ready, massive dragonskin rain-cloaks thrown around their shoulders or flapping in the wind like the wings of bats. Each man's weapons lay beside him on the soaking deck, impotent against the foe that now threatened their lives.

The wind howled, hungry as the great wolves of Asaheim. The ship plunged down the far side of another enormous wave. The dragon tooth on its prow smashed through the foaming water like a spear. Overhead, the sails struggled and flexed. Ragnar was glad that they were made from the purest dragongut; nothing else would have survived the storm's rending claws. Ahead another massive mountain of water loomed.

Somehow it did not seem possible that the ship could survive it crashing down on them.

Ragnar cursed in fury and frustration. It seemed that his short life was over almost before it started. He would not live even to see his entry into manhood next season. His voice had barely broken and now he was doomed to be lost at sea. He shielded his eyes and gazed out into the storm, hoping to catch sight of the longship of his kinfolk. They were nowhere to be seen. Most had likely gone to the bottom. Their bodies would become food for the dragons and the kraken, their souls would provide thralls for the daemons.

He turned and aimed an angry glance at the stranger who had brought them to this. There was some satisfaction in knowing that if they died, he would too. That is if he were not a sorcerer, or some sea daemon in disguise sent to lure the Thunderfist folk to their doom. Watching the way the old man stood on the water-covered deck, fearless and unafraid, that seemed all too possible at the present moment.

There was something supernatural about this gnarled ancient. He looked strong as a warrior in his prime despite all the furrows age had ploughed in his brow and he held his balance better than many a seafarer half his age despite the white in his hair. Ragnar knew that he was a sorcerer. Who but a sorcerer would wear the pelts of those enormous wolves around his shoulders and that strange metal armour encasing his entire body, so unlike the leather tunics of the sea folk? Who but a sorcerer would carry all those strange amulets and charms around his person? Who but a sorcerer could offer his father and their kin enough ingots of precious iron to attempt the near suicidal passage of the Sea of Dragons in this, the Season of Storms?

Ragnar saw that the stranger was pointing at something. Was this some sorcerer's trick, he wondered, or was the stranger casting a spell? Ragnar turned to see and felt his mouth go dry with fear. Lightning flared once again. In the flash Ragnar saw a huge head had broken from the waves next to the ship, almost as if the stranger had summoned it. A nightmare face filled with teeth the size of daggers loomed above them. The long neck flexed and the head descended searching for prey. It was a sea dragon, and no mere hatchling but a full-sized monstrosity, large as the ship, stirred from the sea bottom by the fury of the storm.

The thunder spoke its angry words. Death struck an arm's length from Ragnar. He felt the wind of its passage as the huge jaws of the dragon closed on Yorvik. Great fangs pierced the tough leather of Yorvik's armour as if it were paper. Bone gave way. Blood gouted. The screaming man was lifted into the air, arms flailing, the harpoon dropping from his fist. A sneer curled Ragnar's lips. He had always known Yorvik was a coward and now he had proof. He would find himself a place in the cold hells of Frostheim. The dragon bit down and gulped and part of Yorvik disappeared down its throat. The other part splattered down on the deck near Ragnar. The rushing waves cleansed him of blood and bile.

The warriors swarmed from their benches, raising their axes and their spears in defiance. Ragnar could tell that in their hearts they were glad. Here was a quick death and a heroic one, fighting a monster from the depths. To many it must seem as if Russ had answered their prayers, and sent them this beast to grant a great doom.

The enormous head began to descend once more. At the sight of it, several of the warriors froze. As if it had been sent to weed out cowards, the beast struck them down, biting them in two with its rending fangs. Other Thunderfist warriors lashed out at it with their weapons. Axes bounced futilely from the heavy armoured scales. A few spears bit deep into flesh but the creature paid as much attention to them as a man might pay to a pinprick. The pain merely goaded it to greater fury.

It opened its maw and let out a terrifying bellow, audible even over the thunder of the waves. The sheer volume of it paralysed all the warriors. They froze as if overwhelmed by a sorcerer's spell. Ragnar could see that the creature had reared half out of the water. Its enormous length towered over the boat. It had merely to fall forward and its huge bulk would break the ship in two.

Something snapped within Ragnar. His anger at the storm, at the gods, at this enormous beast and his cowardly kinsman bubbled over. He reached down and picked up the harpoon Yorvik had dropped. Not pausing to think, not pausing to aim lest fear of those enormous dripping jaws should freeze him, he threw the harpoon directly into the creature's eye. It was a good cast. The bone-tipped spear flew true and buried itself up to the shaft in the dragon's eye.

The monster pulled itself up still further, screaming in rage and pain. Ragnar thought he would be deafened by the chill evil of its cries. He was certain now that he was going to die, that the entire ship was going to be smashed to flinders by the enraged beast. Then he heard another sound, a stuttering roar that came from the back of the ship. He risked a glance at the stranger and saw that he was the source of the noise.

The ancient had drawn some kind of massive iron icon from his side, which he held aloft and pointed at the beast. A searing blast of fire spurted from the end of the holy charm along with the roaring sound. Looking back at the dragon Ragnar could see that huge gaping wounds were stitched across its torso – testimony to the strength of the stranger's magic. It opened its mouth to scream in pain and the stranger raised his talisman still further. A hole appeared in the roof of the dragon's mouth and the top of its head exploded. The creature tumbled backwards to vanish beneath the waves.

The stranger threw back his head and laughed. His booming mirth drowned out the sound of the storm. Ragnar felt a shiver of superstitious fear. He could see that two enormous fangs jutted downwards from the stranger's mouth. He bore the mark of Russ! In him flowed the blood of the gods. Truly, he was a sorcerer or something more.

Crouching low on the deck, keeping his balance easily despite the motion of the ship, Ragnar turned and moved back towards the helm. Spray ran down his face like tears. When he licked his lips he tasted salt. As he moved past the stranger, a huge wave broke over the ship. He felt the pressure of tons of water and floundered. The force of the wave lifted him clear of the deck and send him tumbling. In the waves' fury he could get no clear view of where he was. He simply knew he was going to be swept overboard and carried to his doom.

He growled with rage and restrained fear. It seemed that he had survived the dragon's jaws only to be taken by the sea daemons. Then iron-strong fingers clamped on his wrist. Enormous strength fought against the power of the sea. Then the water was gone. In a moment Ragnar floundered on the deck, saved by the stranger who had banished the dragon.

'Be still, boy,' the sorcerer said. 'It is not my destiny to die here. Nor is it yours, I think.'

So saying the stranger turned and strode away to the prow of the ship. He stood there gazing forward like some elder god. Filled with fear and a strange superstitious reverence, Ragnar made his way to the place where his father stood. Looking up he saw understanding there.

'I saw it, my son,' his father shouted. Ragnar knew no further explanation was necessary.

As IF THE killing of the dragon had broken an evil spell, the sea began to calm. Mere hours later, it was as smooth as glass and the measured beat of the oarmaster's drum was the only sound save the quiet sloshing of the waves against the ship's hull.

The stranger still stood at the prow, as if keeping guard against the daemons of the sea. He scanned the far horizon, shading his eyes with one gnarled hand, seeking something only he could see. Overhead the sun beat down. It was not the pale small sphere of winter. Now it was a huge fiery orb that filled the sky with its golden light. The Eye of Russ was fully open, surveying his chosen people as they endured the terrors of Fenris's long hard summer. The remaining water steamed from the decks under its gaze.

The warriors were quiet. Awe had overcome them. There was none of the usual chat and boasting that one would normally hear from those who had survived such a terrible storm. There was none of the mirth or the singing either. Ragnar's father had not ordered the ale cask broached in celebration. A reverence that was close to terror seemed to have taken hold of the crew.

Ragnar could easily understand why. They had seen the stranger dispatch a dragon by the power of his spells. With a blast of his magic he had destroyed one of the terrors of the deep. With his gaze he had pacified the storm. Was there nothing he could not do?

Still there were questions here, Ragnar thought. If the stranger were so powerful why had he needed to hire their ship, paying in precious iron and promising more, to get to his destination? Why had he not used sorcery? Surely he could have used his mastery of the runes to summon a skyship or a winged wolf to carry him to his goal. Was there some sinister ulterior motive to this journey?

Ragnar tried to dismiss this thought. Perhaps the sorcerer had earned the enmity of the storm daemons and could not fly.

Perhaps his lore mastery did not run to control of such runes. How was Ragnar to know? He had no knowledge of spellcraft, nor had anyone he knew, except the Thunderfist's old skald, Imogrim, and he had looked on the stranger with superstitious awe and refused to say anything of him, except to tell his people that the stranger must be obeyed.

Ragnar doubted that even the superstitious awe that surrounded the stranger like a cloak would have made any of his people undertake this voyage if the skald had not recommended it. Their destination, the island of the Iron Masters, was shunned by all the sea folk except during the season of trade, during the spring. The last spring had ended over five hundred days ago and the trade time was long gone. Who knew how the mysterious smiths of the islands would welcome strangers now? They kept themselves to themselves mostly and defended their mines of precious iron the way a troll guards its hoard.

Still, Ragnar wondered, if the stranger had demanded to be taken, even without his handsome payment, could they have refused him? Ragnar doubted that even the entire village of brave Thunderfist warriors could stand against the magic the stranger had shown. Ragnar doubted that their weapons could even pierce the second skin of metal that surrounded his body.

There was something fascinating about the old man, and Ragnar longed to talk with him and question him. The stranger had saved him and spoken to him and surely that must mean something. Even so, Ragnar stood rooted to the deck. The idea of talking to the sorcerer was more intimidating than facing the jaws of the dragon.

He remained frozen for a moment then mustered all his resolve. Don't be foolish, he told himself. You have not even thanked him for saving your life. Silently Ragnar walked forward. Cautious as a man stalking a wild goat, he advanced towards the prow of the ship.

'What is it, lad?' the stranger asked, without turning, before Ragnar had even got within ten paces of him. Ragnar froze in shock. Here was yet more proof of the stranger's sorcerous powers. Ragnar knew that he had moved quietly. His feet had made no sound on the deck. He was considered a great hunter among his people. Yet the stranger had known he was there, and he was Ragnar, without even turning his head. Ragnar felt assured that he must possess something akin to the second sight.

'I asked you a question, boy,' the stranger said, turning to face Ragnar. There was no anger in his voice, just authority. He sounded like a man who was used to having his own way. There was something odd about his speech too. He spoke very slowly, and his accent was antiquated. It reminded Ragnar of the way the skald would speak when quoting the epics of Russ and the All Father. It seemed to Ragnar that this old man might have stepped straight from one of those sagas. There was a quality about him that one of the old heroes might possess.

'I wished to thank you for saving my life, jarl,' Ragnar said, using the highest term of respect he knew. There was something strange about the old man's face, he realised. It was long and feral, the nose was huge with massive flared nostrils. The leathery skin sunken over his cheeks gave him an even more wolf-like appearance. And what was the significance of those three studs set into his forehead, Ragnar wondered? And how had they got there? Among his own people, he could think of no way of doing such a thing that would not result in gangrene and the spirits of infection setting in.

'It was not your time to die,' the sorcerer said and returned to scanning the horizon. How could the stranger possibly know that, Ragnar wondered.

'What are you looking for?' Ragnar asked, astonished by his own temerity. The stranger was silent for a while, and Ragnar feared that he was not going to answer. Just then the sorcerer pointed. Ragnar could see that his finger was shod in metal, and reflected the sunlight. He looked at what the stranger was pointing to and caught his breath.

Ahead of them mighty peaks rose over the horizon, a great battlement of spears that pierced the clouds. The walls of the peaks were white and something like ice glittered along their slopes even where they flowed down into the sea.

'The Walls of the Gods,' Ragnar said and made the rune-sign of Russ over his breast.

'The peaks of Asaheim,' the stranger murmured softly and smiled to reveal those enormous fangs. 'I must have been your age when I first saw them, lad, and that was well nigh three hundred years ago.'

Ragnar looked at him open-mouthed. The stranger had all but admitted that he was a supernatural entity. No man of

Fenris, not even the oldest greybeard, lived more than thirty-five years.

'I am glad I had the opportunity to see them again this way,' the stranger said, sounding like one of the old men of the village did before he went off to chant his death poem. The stranger shook his head and grinned down at Ragnar with those alarming fangs. 'I must be getting senile, to babble so,' he said.

Ragnar said nothing, merely looked at him and then at those distant mountains.

'Run back and tell your father to change course. Bear to starboard and follow the coast. We will get to our destination the sooner.'

He said it with all the force of a prophecy, and Ragnar believed him.

FOR THE NEXT two days they sailed along the coast of Asaheim. Two days of quiet seas and cold winds, and a stillness broken only by the crash of huge chunks of ice falling from the mountains and drifting out to sea.

This was indeed Asaheim to the north of them, the place where the great icebergs were birthed, the frozen land from which the icy floating mountains came. Overhead, mighty sea eagles soared and occasionally the men spotted the spouts of the great orca herds as they rose from the cold, pure waters. They passed the mouths of great fjords, places of astonishing beauty, and sometimes saw the stone villages of the people of the glacier perched high on their slopes. They rowed swiftly then, for the folk of the fjords were fierce, some said troll-blooded, and were rumoured to devour their prisoners rather than taking them thrall. Such a fate made even the sea daemons' clutches seem tempting.

During the whole time they passed the coast, the stranger never left his post at the ship's prow. At sunset he stood there limned by the Eye of Russ's dying rays. At dawn he would still be there, as the daywatch arose. Ragnar talked with the night watch and was not surprised at all when they told him the stranger had not slept. If he felt any weariness, the stranger showed no sign. His eyes remained as clear and bright as they had the day of the battle with the dragon. Ragnar had no idea why he watched, he merely felt glad that the old man did so. While he stood guard, Ragnar felt that no evil could touch them.

Then once more the land fell away behind them, and they were on the open sea. The weather remained favourable. The stranger sniffed the wind and pronounced that the sea would remain quiet until they reached their destination. As if afraid to disobey him the sea complied.

After two days at sea, they saw smoke ahead of them, and fires lit the night sky. The men prayed to Russ in superstitious awe, but were afraid he would not hear them. They knew they were entering an area sacred to the fire giants, and here Russ and the All Father held little sway.

The next day, as they approached the islands, Ragnar could see that they were afire. Their tops blazed. The molten orange spittle of the fire giants ran down their black sides and sizzled and steamed as it entered the water. The roaring of the imprisoned giants made them shake.

Filled with trepidation, Ragnar approached the sorcerer once more. He was reassured to see that the ancient showed no signs of fear, merely a quiet pleasure and a certain sadness, like that of a man who has been enjoying a journey and is not looking forward to its end.

'They say Ghorghe and Sla Nahesh are imprisoned within those islands,' Ragnar said, repeating something he had heard the skald say after the spring trading. Despite his fear, he was excited. Never before had he sailed this far with his father. 'They say that Russ bound them there when the world was young.'

'Those are evil names, lad,' the sorcerer said. 'You should not mention them.'

'Why?' said Ragnar, for once undaunted by the stranger. His curiosity overcoming his reverence. The stranger looked down at him and smiled. He did not seem displeased by the question.

'Those are the names of great evils, born in a place millions of leagues away, and many millennia in the past. Russ did not bind them. No one could. Not even the Emperor – the All Father himself – in the days of his glory.'

Ragnar was not surprised to be told of their age. After all, Russ had fought them in the dawn ages before he had banished his people from Asaheim. He was surprised to be told that they had been born millions of leagues away. It was a distance he could not conceive.

'I thought they were the children of the dragon goddess Skrinneir, of her marriage to the dark god, Horus.'

'And that is another name you should not speak, lad. For you have no idea of its true significance.'

'Will you tell me its meaning then?'

'No, lad, I will not. If it is your destiny to know such things, you will find them out soon enough.'

'And how will I do that?'

'By dying, laddie, and by being reborn.'

'Is that how you gained your great wisdom?' Ragnar asked, annoyed by the stranger's response and surprised at the sarcasm of his own tone. To his surprise the stranger merely laughed.

'You have courage, youth, and no mistake.' He turned from Ragnar and gazed out to sea. Ahead of them dark clouds rose, and the sea was stained an oily black. To the west, the mountain shook, and a huge jet of fire emerged from its tip.

'The Fire Mountain is angry today,' the sorcerer said. 'It is a bad sign.'

TWO
THE TEMPLE OF IRON

'By Russ, have you ever seen anything like it?' Ulli asked, awe evident in his words. Ragnar looked at his Wolfbrother and shook his head. He was forced to admit that he had not.

The harbour was vast and strange, a huge cleft in the black cliffs which led to a massive lake enclosed by a black beach. There was room enough there for a thousand dragonships to dock at once without it ever being crowded, and Ragnar knew that during the trade time it was so. People came from all across the great ocean to barter for axe heads, spear points and all manner of metal goods.

It was not the sheer scale of the harbour that held Ragnar's attention so raptly. It was the buildings that surrounded it. The smallest of them was twice the size of the great long hall back home, which was the largest structure Ragnar had seen in his whole life. Much more strange was the fact that they were built from stone.

Stone, thought Ragnar and shuddered. It was near inconceivable. What if one of the great earthquakes came and sent them tumbling to the ground? Would not everyone inside be crushed to bloody pulp by the avalanche of falling rock? Those huge soot-blackened structures were death traps. Everyone knew it

25

was only sensible to build a house as you would build a dragonship – from dragonhide leather around a frame of dragonbone. Or for sacred structures you might consider using precious wood, though it might burn if an oil lantern got tumbled in the quake. Ragnar had seen such things happen. Everyone had. The islands of Fenris were unstable and had been since before Russ had led his chosen people here.

It was madness to build out of stone but these people had. And not just from stone piled upon stone, the way you might make a drystone dyke. No, these buildings were made from huge blocks of dressed rock, carved into perfect cubes and placed in interlocking patterns. And judging by the great layers of soot encrusted on the buildings and the blackened moss on their sides, these structures were ancient. They looked old, weather-worn, like the most ancient runestones in the great ring atop Thunder Mountain. And the skald claimed those had been there since the dawn of time.

It was not just one huge building but there were hundreds of them, some large as hills. Through the roofs of others protruded mighty chimneys from which black smoke belched and giant flares of flame gouted.

'They have tamed the fire elementals,' said Ulli. 'They are great magicians here.'

It certainly looked that way, Ragnar thought. These people assuredly did not fear fire either. They must be mighty magicians indeed, not to fear the trembling of the earth or the threat of fire. And how had they built these enormous halls? Did they use magic to sing the stones into place? Or did they make their captive daemon thralls do all the work? The power and skill at work here was awe-inspiring.

Still, Ragnar was not sure he would have liked to live here. The air tasted foul and acrid with the same chemical stink that came from the tanneries back home, only magnified and a thousand times worse. Billows of soot like black snowflakes drifted through the air and settled in their hair and clothing. The water was an odd colour, black and viscous-looking in some places, in others coloured red or green by effluents belched out of the black pipes that ran all the way to the harbour.

'Bones of Russ,' Ulli breathed. 'Look at that!'

Ragnar glanced in the direction indicated by Ulli's pointing finger and saw the most amazing thing. It was a tower built all of iron, one of the most precious of metals. It rose from the water's edge. Looking at it closely, Ragnar could see the construction was odd. It was not solid. It was like a latticework of metal beams, like the skeleton around which a hall would be built. Except that here there was no dragonhide stretched around it. The frame was open to the air and to the elements, and you could see the intricate machinery it enclosed.

There were huge cogwheels and great metal arms that rose up and down in a regular rhythmic movement like the pulsing of a great heart. Black stuff, liquid and slimy, bubbled from pipes on the tip of the tower and rolled down long tubes to be gathered in wooden vats around the base. Small figures moved around constantly shifting the vats and emptying them with buckets. It was at once the oddest, most impressive and most baffling structure Ragnar had ever seen.

'Why do these people not fear the quakes?' Ragnar asked Ulli, more just to air his curiosity than because he expected any answer.

'Because they have no need to, laddie,' said the voice of the sorcerer. 'These islands are stable and have been for centuries. They will be for many more.'

Ragnar's mind rocked. The concept was awesome. A land which did not constantly shake and quiver like a leashed beast. A place where there was no threat of the earth opening and swallowing you. A haven from the greatest and most commonplace of all the disasters that afflicted Russ's people. Could the inhabitants of these islands really be so blessed? Another thought struck Ragnar, the natural thought that would occur to any of his war-like people.

'Then why has no one taken them away from the inhabitants? The clans would kill to own such a safe haven. How have these people survived for so long without being overwhelmed?'

'You'll see soon enough, laddie. You'll see soon enough.' The stranger shook his head and seemed to be trying to contain his mirth.

'STATE YOUR BUSINESS, strangers, or prepare to die!' The islander's voice was harsh and guttural and there was menace in every word. It was amplified by the metal bullhorn he held in his hand that made it sound even flatter.

Ragnar gazed in wonder at the ships that had moved out from the island to meet them. Suddenly he felt very afraid. Truly here were vessels of great sorcery. The ships had no sails and were made of metal. How was it that they did not sink like stone? And what propelled them? Bound fire elementals? Perhaps that was why smoke billowed from the chimney at the rear of the ship. Such a thing seemed like an affront to the sea daemons but quite obviously it worked. Perhaps some odd pact had been made…

Before Ragnar's father could reply, the sorcerer bounded up onto the prow and extended an army in greeting. 'Tis I, Ranek Icewalker. They have brought me here at my request. I would have speech with the Ironmaster.'

This announcement set off a flurry of activity on the decks of the metal ship. Several figures huddled together in consultation before the speaker raised his bullhorn again. 'Word is that Ranek is dead. Are you some sea-ghost risen from the waters?'

This question sent a shiver of horror across the decks of the *Spear of Russ*. Ragnar could hear men move uneasily on their oarbenches. The sorcerer's great booming laugh roared out over the water. 'Do I look like a ghost? Do I sound like a ghost? Will my boot feel like that of a ghost when I kick your arse for your impudence?'

There was answering laughter from the deck of the other ship. 'Then come ashore, Wolf Priest, and be welcome here. Bring your companions and we will feast.'

The strange ship performed a manoeuvre that seemed super-natural to Ragnar. Without turning it reversed direction and began to move backwards to the shore, all the while keeping the dragonship in sight. The beat of the oarmaster's drum made the *Spear of Russ* spring to life as it made its way to dock.

RAGNAR FOLLOWED the Wolf Priest, if that was his title, through the streets, uncertain of quite why he was doing so, but determined to accompany him and ask questions for he never knew if he would get another such opportunity in this lifetime. The rest of the crew had gone to wait in a dockside tavern or scattered to wander the streets. Ragnar was on his own with the sorcerer.

Ragnar walked through streets covered in cobbled stones, through a maze of sooty buildings and cramped alleyways. The air tasted foul with the smell of smoke and acrid alchemical odours. The people were strange and new to him and talked in a dialect he did not understand. Many seemed small and hunched and undernourished. They were clad in tunics and britches of drab grey and brown and they carried no weapons. They collected scraps in the streets and hurried along bearing burdens and performing errands. Even here, on these islands rich with metal, there was poverty.

The rulers of the island were fewer and richer. All of them were garbed in metal armour and all of them carried blades of steel in scabbards of dragonhide leather. They were tall men, well-made, with dark skins and brown eyes. They nodded to him with distant politeness as he passed, and he responded in kind.

'Why are you following me, boy?' the Wolf Priest asked.

'Because I want to ask you questions.' The old man shook his head but he smiled, revealing those frightening fangs.

'It's always questions, questions, at your age, isn't it? Ask away.'

'Why did you come here? Or really, why did you pay us to bring you here? Could you not have used your magic instead?'

'I have no magic, boy. Not in the sense you mean.'

'But your talisman – the way you killed the dragon – it...'

'It was not magic. The "talisman" as you call it was a weapon, like an axe or a spear, only more... complicated.'

'A weapon?'

'A weapon.'

'You are not a magician then?'

'Russ forbid, no! I know some you would call magicians, boy, and I would not change places with them for all the iron on these islands.'

'Why?'

'They bear a terrible burden.'

Ragnar was silent. It seemed evident that the old man would say no more. Ragnar was absolutely certain that Ranek's iron talisman represented a powerful magic, whatever the Wolf Priest might say. They trudged on through the streets, past open shopfronts. Looking inside Ragnar could see that they were workshops filled with forges. The shadows of their interiors were brightened by the glow of red-hot metal. He could hear the clang of hammer on anvil and knew that it was in these places that the goods of the Iron Masters were made.

'You haven't answered my first question,' Ragnar said, astonished by his own temerity.

'I'm not sure I can in a way that you would understand – or that I ought to.'

'Why not?'

The old man's booming laugh echoed down the alleyways. Ragnar saw everyone turn to look at them, then make the sign of the hammer and look away.

'You're not easily discouraged, are you, laddie?'

'No.'

'Fair enough. I was on a mission. There was an accident. My vessel was destroyed. I needed to get back here and make contact with my… brethren. To cross such an enormous distance quickly I needed your father's ship, and for his aid he will be rewarded.'

'What was your mission?'

'I cannot tell you that,' Ranek said in a tone which brooked no argument.

'Was it for the gods?'

'It was for *my* gods.'

'Are not all gods the same? Everyone on the islands worships Russ and the All Father.'

'So do I, but in a different way from you.'

'How can that be?'

'One day, laddie, you may find out.'

'But not today?'

'No. Not today.'

They walked into a huge square atop the hill. It was rimmed around with massive buildings. Each was so broad as to seem squat even though it towered ten times the height of a man. The walls were carved in an odd fashion. Each of the massive stone blocks was carved with interlocking cogwheels. Metal pipes flowed in and out through the stonework, like clusters of huge worms emerging from the earth and plunging back in again. Soot blackened the walls, and from the pipes effluent had leaked in the past, staining the walls beneath with great blotches the colour of rust. From within came the sound of monstrous engines at work, a clattering and a banging as if giants struck furiously at enormous anvils. The smell of smoke and hot metal smote Ragnar's nostrils. He wondered whether he was the only person in the whole teeming throng that minded the noise and the stink.

They strode across the square to the largest of the huge structures.

'This is the Iron Temple,' Ranek the Wolf Priest said softly. 'And this is where we part our ways for now.'

Ragnar glanced up at the huge building. It was a squat, massive fortress but it dwarfed all the surrounding buildings. Arrow slits glared out from its walls like the eyes of a hungry beast. High atop the building was a great metal flower, as large as a dragonship. Ragnar could not begin to guess at its purpose.

Great metal-bound doors barred the way forward at the head of the ramp. Ragnar could tell by the smoothness and the indentations that many feet had passed this way over hundreds of years. Strange runes, most unlike any Ragnar had ever seen, were inscribed over its archway. Two sentries armed with metal tipped harpoons guarded the way. They seemed as if they were made of metal. Iron armour covered them like a second skin. Metal helmets guarded their heads. Shields of steel marked with the same runes as those above the door hung from their left arms.

'Are they your kin?' he asked Ranek. The old man's head swung swiftly to look down at him. The keen eyes bored in Ragnar's own. This close Ragnar realised how big the Wolf Priest was. He was considered tall and well-made among his folk but compared to this old man he was but the size of a child. Ranek was head and shoulders taller than he and would have been far more massive even without the odd armour that encased his body.

'No, laddie, the Iron Masters are kin only to themselves. There are no others like them on all the islands of the Great Ocean. They are a people apart.'

'I do not understand,' Ragnar said. 'With all this metal and all this… magic, why have they not sought dominance over all the world. Surely they could achieve it?'

'The Iron Masters seek dominance over nothing save metal and fire. Conquest is not their way. They fight only to defend themselves. It is part of the Ancient Pact.'

'Pact?'

'Enough questions, laddie. I must go.'

'I hope that one day we will meet again, jarl,' Ragnar said seriously. The old man turned and looked down at him. There was an odd look in his eye.

'I like you lad, so I will give you some advice. Pray that we never meet again. For if we do, it will be on a day of doom for you.'

Something in the old man's tone chilled Ragnar to the very bone. The words were uttered with all the force of a prophesy. 'What do you mean? Will you kill me?'

'You will know if ever it happens,' Ranek said, then turned and strode away.

Ragnar watched the old man stride up the ramp. As he did so, the great doors swung open soundlessly. He was greeted by a hunched figure garbed all in black robes, its face obscured by a metal mask. Ragnar watched him vanish into the gloom and then stood bemused for long minutes.

After a while he heard a humming grinding noise. The great flower on top of the building had started to move, to face away towards distant Asaheim. As he watched in wonder, its metal petals unfurled. In the centre lights pulsed eerily. Ragnar was not sure what this magic meant but he was sure it had something to do with the old sorcerer.

Left by himself in the huge square, something like panic seized Ragnar. He turned and hurried back to the docks.

THE DRUMBEAT sounded loud in Ragnar's ears as the *Spear of Russ* pulled out of the dark waters of the Iron Masters' harbour into the open sea.

He breathed deeply of the clean fresh air and smiled, glad to have left the foul and polluted town behind. The islanders may have been rich, he thought, but they lived in a way that seemed less healthy than the lowliest of thralls.

At the rear of the dragonship lay a cargo of iron axe and spearheads, wrapped all in dragongut to protect them from the corrosive effects of the sea. They represented huge wealth to the Thunderfist clan, and Ragnar was proud to have been part of the voyage that had won it. Still, there was something worrying about it too. He suspected good fortune, and he believed the old adage that the gods made men pay for their gifts. None of the others aboard seemed to share his concern. They sang cheerful drinking songs, relieved to be out of the harbour and no longer to have the Wolf Priest aboard. Much as they had respected and been in awe of him, his presence had damped all of their spirits. Now, they joked and told tales of the events of the voyage. They ate their salted beef jerky happily and drank stoops of ale with glee. Laughter echoed across the deck and it woke an answering joy in Ragnar's heart.

Suddenly there was a boom like thunder. Ragnar looked up in fear. There was not a dark cloud in the sky and no sign of a storm. There was absolutely no reason for the noise. His keen eyes scanned the horizon looking for the source. All around him the laughter stopped and he heard prayers being offered up to Russ for his protection.

There! In the distance, coming from the direction of Asaheim he saw it. It was little more than a black dot in the distance. It left behind it a white contrail like that of a meteor in the night sky, only this was broad daylight, and the trail was a white line written on the pale blue of the sky. Even as he watched, the dot turned and swerved towards them, and began to grow with appalling speed.

The curses and prayers grew louder, and men reached for their weapons. Ragnar kept his eyes fixed on the dot, wondering what it was. He could see now that it had two wings, like those of a bird, only they did not move. What sort of monster was it? A dragon? A wyvern? Some daemon conjured up by fell magic?

No, it did not appear to be anything like a living thing. As it came closer he could see that it was much more like one of those iron vessels in the harbour behind them. His mind reeled. Just as it seemed impossible that those things could float, it was surely impossible for this thing to fly. And yet it quite obviously was doing so. There was no way he could dis-believe his own eyes.

It slowed as it approached, losing some of the appalling velocity that propelled it across the sky faster than any bird. And the loud thundercrack boom had stopped, to be replaced by a wailing roar like the call of a thousand lost souls in torment.

The thing was flying low and he could see the wind of its passage was whipping up the sea below it, churning the waves to foam. It appeared to be coming right at them now, and Ragnar wondered whether they had done something to anger the gods. Perhaps this terrible apparition had been sent to destroy them.

It passed almost directly overhead. Looking at it from below Ragnar could see that it was some sort of metal vehicle, a winged cruciform with the shape of an eagle painted on its sides and wings. For a moment he thought he caught sight of windows in its front, and human faces looking out, but he dismissed that thought as a momentary aberration. Looking back as it passed he saw flames licked from its rear like the breath of a dragon. It screamed off into the distance towards the island of the Iron Masters and there it halted, great jets of flame belching forward. It hovered in the air above the Iron Temple for a moment and Ragnar watched breathlessly, not knowing quite what to expect. Half wondering whether it would destroy the town with its flames, half believing that he was about to witness some strange and appalling magic.

No such thing happened. The vehicle slowly settled on the roof of the Iron Temple. Everyone watched silently wondering what would happen next. No one spoke. Ragnar could hear his heart beating loudly in his chest.

Five minutes later the metal bird rose into the sky once more and hurtled back in the direction it had come. As it passed over them, it waggled its wings as if in salute. Suddenly, somehow, Ragnar knew that Ranek the Wolf Priest had found new transportation to take him wherever it was he wanted to go.

Everyone on the *Spear of Russ* was silent for hours afterwards.

THREE
THE FESTIVAL
OF PASSAGE

Ragnar smiled nervously. This was stupid, he told himself. He was a man now. He had taken his oath of loyalty to the ancestor spirits on the rune altar. He had his own axe and his own shield made of dragonhide leather stretched over a frame of bone. He had even started to grow his black hair long as befitted a Wolfbrother. He was a man now. He should not be afraid of asking a girl to dance.

And yet he was forced to admit that he was. Worse yet, he had no real idea of the reason why. The girl, Ana, seemed to like him. She smiled encouragingly every time he saw him. And of course he had known her for all the years of their childhood. He could not quite put a finger on what had changed between them, but he knew that something had. Ever since he had returned from the island of the Iron Masters all those moons ago something had been different.

He looked at his companions, the Wolfbrothers with whom he had sworn blood oaths, and it was hard not to laugh. They looked like boys pretending to be men. They still had the down of youth on their lips. They tried hard to emulate the swagger of the adult warriors and yet somehow it still seemed wrong. They looked like boys playing at warriors, not warriors themselves. And yet that was not the case. All of them had been to sea. All of them had pulled oars through storm wind's lash. All of them had aided in the hunting of the dragon and the orca. All of them had received their shares from the kill. Small shares admittedly but shares nonetheless. By the custom of their tribe, they were men.

Ragnar looked around. It was a late autumn afternoon and the weather was fine. It was the Day of Remembering, the first day of the last hundred-day of the year, the beginning of the short autumnal period when for all too brief a time the weather would be fine and the world would be peaceful. The Eye of Russ was growing smaller in the sky. The period of quakes and eruptions was all but done. All too soon, the snows would come and the long winter would descend on the world, as the Eye grew yet smaller. The breath of Russ would chill the world and life would become very hard indeed.

He pushed the thought aside. Now was not the time for thinking of such things. Now was the time for feasting, and making merry and betrothal while the weather was good and the days were still long. He looked around. The festive spirit possessed everybody. The huts were newly covered in fresh dragonhide. The wooden walls of the great hall were painted bright white and red. A huge bonfire stood unlit in the centre of the village. Ragnar could smell the minty scent of the herbs that would perfume the air when it was lit. The brewmasters were already dragging great barrels into the open air. Most people were still working but Ragnar and his friends were from the ships. This whole day was a holiday for them and they had nothing to do but loaf around dressed in their best. They had been kicked out of their huts so that their mothers could sweep and clean. Their fathers were already in the long hall swapping tales of the great battle against the Grimskulls. Somewhere in the distance he could hear the skald tuning up his instrument, and his apprentices beating out basic rhythms on the drums with which they would accompany him.

A long lean dog crossed his path and looked up at him in a friendly manner. He reached out and stroked it behind the ears, feeling the warmth of the fur already lengthening in preparation for winter. It licked his hand with a tongue as rough as sandpaper and then bounded off down the street, racing for the sheer joy of it. Suddenly Ragnar knew how it felt. He took a deep breath of the salt-fresh air and felt the urge to howl with the sheer pleasure of being alive. Instead he turned to Ulli, reached out, cuffed his ear and shouted, 'Tig! You're it.'

He turned and ran before Ulli had a chance to realise what was going on. Seeing that the game had started the other Wolfbrothers scattered, dashing among the huts and the busy people, sending chickens squawking skyward. Ulli raced after him, shouting challenges.

Ragnar turned on the spot, almost tripping from his own momentum as he did so and made a face at Ulli. His friend bounded towards him arm outstretched. Ragnar let him get almost within reach before turning once more and racing on. He ducked right and raced down a narrow street. He bounded left to avoid slamming into one of the brewers' barrels and as he did so, his foot slid on a slick piece of turf and he fell. Before he could recover Ulli was on him and they wrestled on the ground pitting muscle against muscle like playful puppies. They rolled over and over down the slope until they heard girlish shrieks and bumped into something. Ragnar opened his eyes and found himself looking up into Ana's long pretty face. She tugged her braid as she looked down at him and then she smiled. Ragnar smiled back and then felt his face flush.

'What are you two doing?' Ana asked in her soft husky voice.

'Nothing,' Ragnar and Ulli replied simultaneously, then burst out laughing.

STRYBJORN GRIMSKULL stood at the prow of the dragonship and glared ferociously at the horizon. He hawked a huge gob of phlegm into his mouth and then spat it contemptuously into the sea. Inside him he could feel the battle lust starting to build. He hoped that combat would come soon.

Ahead of the fleet lay the home island of the Grimskulls, site of their sacred runestone, the place from which they had been driven twenty long years ago by the accursed Thunderfists. Of course, that had been before Strybjorn had been born but that did not matter. He had grown up hearing all about the island's beauty and he felt that he already knew it. Its image was clear in his mind from his father's tales. This was the sacred land from which they had been driven by Thunderfist treachery all those years ago and which today, on the anniversary of their ancient loss, they would at last reclaim.

Anger at the interlopers filled him. He felt it as keenly as any of the survivors of the attack and the massacre when the Thunderfists had arrived from the sea to claim the land in force. Ten dragonships had overwhelmed the outnumbered Grimskull force while the vast majority of the warriors had been at sea following the orca herds. Those brave warriors had returned home to find their own land fortified against them, and their women and children enthralled by the Thunderfists. After a brief struggle on the beaches they had been driven back to their ships and out to sea, there to endure the misery of the Long Search.

Strybjorn shared their bitterness on that terrible voyage. The hopeless attacks on other settlements, the fruitless efforts to find a new home. He recalled the names of all those who had died of hunger and thirst and warfare as if they had been his own dead forefathers. He swore once more that he would avenge their spirits and appease their ghosts with Thunderfist blood. He knew it would be so, for had it not been ordained by the gods?

Had not Russ himself at last seen fit to reward the Grimskull warriors' perseverance with the prize. They had found the village of Ormskrik with the inhabitants half dead of the wasting plague and they had overwhelmed it, killing the men and enslaving the women and children according to the ancient traditions. And then they had settled down to brood and breed and recover their numbers. And all those long years they had never forgotten the site of the ancestral runestone.

For twenty long years they had planned and prepared. Sons had been born. The gods had smiled. A new generation had grown to manhood. But always the Grimskulls had remembered the treachery of the Thunderfists, and the mighty oaths of vengeance that they had sworn. Tonight Strybjorn knew those oaths would be fulfilled. And truly the gods did smile, for was not tonight the anniversary of the very day upon which the Thunderfists had attacked. It was only fitting that twenty years to the day they had lost their ancestral lands, the Grimskulls would reclaim them.

Strybjorn was proud of his folk. It would have been easy to forget. It would have been easy to sink into the comforts of their new land. Such was not the Grimskull way. They knew the value of an oath. They were bound to seek vengeance. They had bound their children to seek vengeance as soon as they were old enough to take their vows of manhood. When Strybjorn had become a Wolfbrother, he had sworn that he would never rest until the runestone was reclaimed, and he had watered the sacred soil of his ancestral homeland with foul Thunderfist blood.

He stroked his craggy brow with one broad strong hand, and shielding his eyes stared towards the far horizon. Soon he knew they would make landfall, and then let the Thunderfists beware.

RAGNAR WATCHED High Jarl Torvald light the great beacon fires. The burning brand arced onto the oil-soaked wood and the flames leapt high like daemons dancing. The smell of amber-gris and herbs billowed through the streets. The heat of the flames brought a flush to his face. He looked around and saw all the folk of the village had gathered around the bonfire and watched the chief perform his ceremonial duties.

Torvald brandished his axe. First to the north, towards Asaheim, and the great Mountain of the Gods, then to the south to the sea in defiance of the daemons that dwelled there. He raised the weapon high above his head, holding it with both hands and turned to face the setting sun. He let out a mighty roar and the whole crowd joined in, cheering and chanting the name of Russ, hoping to invoke the god's favour for another year, as they had done every year since Russ had smiled upon them and granted them victory.

Once the chieftain had finished and returned to the ranks of his warriors, the old skald Imogrim limped into the firelight and gestured for silence. His apprentices followed him carrying their instruments and softly began to beat time to his words.

Imogrim raised his harp and plucked a few chords. His fingers moved gently over the strings as he stood for a moment idly, seeming to compose his thoughts. A smile played over his thin bloodless lips. The firelight illumined every seam of his craggy face, and turned his eyes into deep caverns. The white of his long beard glistened in the flickering light. The crowd waited breathless for him to begin. All around the night was still. Ragnar looked around and caught sight of Ana. It appeared that she had been looking at him, for their eyes met, and she looked away, almost shyly, eyes cast down towards the ground.

Imogrim began to chant. His voice was soft and yet surprisingly resonant, and his words seemed to flow out in time with the beat of the drums. It was as if he tapped some huge spring of memory within himself, and it had begun to flow softly yet inexorably outwards.

He was singing the Deed of the Thunderfists, their ancestral song, a work which had been begun in the lost reaches of time, hundreds of generations ago, and which had been added to by every skald who had held the position since. It was Imogrim's life's work to memorise the song, and add to it and to pass it on to his apprentices as they would, in time, pass it on to theirs. There was an ancient saying that if the jarl was the heart of his people, the skald was the memory. It was at times like this that Ragnar understood the truth of it.

Of course there would not be time for the whole tale this, or any other night, so Imogrim contented himself with extracts. He alluded in passing to the most ancient times, when the people had sailed between the stars on ships built by the gods. He sang of Russ who had come and taught the people how to survive in the dark times when the world had shook, and old evils had entered the world. He told of the time of choosing when Russ had picked the best ten thousand warriors from all the clans, and led them off, never to be seen again, to fight in the wars of the gods.

He sang of the ancient wars, and all the mighty deeds of the Thunderfists. Of how Berak had slain the great dragon Thrungling and claimed a casket of iron and the hand of the thunder spirit Maya. Of how the great seafarer Nial had sailed around the world in his mighty ship, the Wind Wolf. Of the night when the trolls had come and driven the Thunderfists from their ancestral land.

He brought the tale up to date with the story of how Ragnar's father and his kin had found this island, ruled by the cruel and brutish Grimskulls, and had seized it in a day of bloody conflict. At this part of the song, some of those present had cheered. Others stared off into the fire as if remembering lost comrades and the brutal fighting of the past. And at last after long hours, the tale reached the present. Ragnar felt his heart lurch with pride as Imogrim told of their voyage to take the Wolf Priest Ranek to the island of the Iron Masters, and of how

Ragnar had speared the dragon through the eye before it was dispatched by the old sorcerer's magic.

He knew now that his name would live forever. For as long as his clan existed, his name would be recalled by the skald and his apprentices, and maybe even sung on high holy days and other feasts. Even after he had passed into the halls of the slain his name would live on. He looked over and saw the look of pride on Ana's face.

He was so thrilled that he paid little attention to the rest of the song.

HOW CONVENIENT of the Thunderfists to light a beacon to guide us, Strybjorn thought, looking at the vast flickering bonfire on the horizon. It gleamed brilliantly and its reflection, caught on the waves, seemed only to amplify the light.

At first Strybjorn had thought the beacon was some sort of warning sign, that the approach of the Grimskull fleet had been noticed, but there was no sign of any preparation for war. No warriors had assembled on the beach. No dragonships had moved to meet them. There had been some consternation as word had been passed around the fleet but so far nothing had happened.

Strybjorn had suspected at first that it might be some sort of trap. Yet more proof, as if any were needed, of Thunderfist treachery and cunning. Then word had been passed up the oar-benches that it was most likely the Thunderfists were celebrating the anniversary of their infamous victory, and gloating over the butchery they had so treacherously inflicted. Well soon they would know how it felt. The jarl had ordered them to make landfall at Grimbane Bay, out of sight of the village. From there it was but a short march to swift and final vengeance.

Strybjorn had felt himself swept up by the wave of anger that had broken over his kinsmen.

By Russ, how those Thunderfists would pay.

SOON THE SINGING was over and it was time to feast and dance. The jarl and his bodyguard led the way into the great hall. There the tables groaned under the weight of roasted chicken and new-baked bread. Mountains of cheeses towered over the trestles. Lakes of honey gleamed in their bowls. The smell of ale filled the air. The brewers were already filling huge jacks of it, and drinking horns were being passed from hand to hand.

Ulli grinned at him and passed him a leather tankard. Ragnar threw back the bitter-tasting brew like he had seen the old warriors doing. This was not the weak beer reserved for boys. This was feast day drink for warriors and it was strong and potent. The bubbles almost made him sputter and the strong bitterness of it surprised him. He held it down though and did not disgrace himself, downing the whole tankard in a few gulps to the admiring applause of his comrades.

Ahead of him he saw his father tipping back the great drinking horn and watched as the contents flowed inexorably into his mouth while the older warriors counted down from ten. The whole contents were gone by the time the count had reached five. It was a good time. As the horn was refilled and passed, the count started at five this time, but the new drinker was no match for Ragnar's father and did not complete his swilling until after the count was done. Sheepishly he passed the horn to the next warrior.

Ragnar made his way to the tables set for the Wolfbrothers and began to help himself to hot chicken and bread. The warm meat tasted wonderful. The juices ran down his chin and he wiped the hardening grease away with bits of bread before consuming them in turn. The ale had settled in his belly and he was feeling fine, if slightly fuddled from its unaccustomed strength.

Ulli let out a long howl followed by a belch. He looked meaningfully at Ragnar and then glanced over at the tables where the unwed girls were sat. Ragnar smiled and nodded, no longer quite so nervous. Soon it would be time to dance.

STRYBJORN HELPED the other warriors haul the dragonship ashore, beaching it on the sand. His muscles ached from the exertion, and his breath came in gasps. The ship was heavy even with the full complement of forty warriors tugging at it.

His feet were wet from the waves, and his britches were soaked up to the knee from when he had jumped down into the water. He felt slightly unsteady on his feet, and unused to the hard stability of land. Weeks at sea had him still compensating for the motion of the boat. Still he told himself it would take only a little time for him to get his land legs back and that was good, for he would need them soon for fighting and for killing.

He moved over to join his Wolfbrothers, youths like him eager to gain glory in this their first great battle, trying to carve out a name for themselves and to gain the eye of the jarl and of the gods. He offered up a prayer to Russ that he would fight well, and if he died, that he did so with his wounds to the fore and with the attention of the Choosers of the Fallen upon him.

Along the beach long lines of Grimskull warriors had begun to form up, weapons at the ready. Once assembled into their warbands, they began to move quickly and silently along the path towards the Thunderfist village.

RAGNAR WHOOPED and reached out to hook his arm into Ana's. He was drunk and he was happy. The dancers had formed up into long lines and weaved in intricate patterns to the music of the skald and his apprentices.

Ana smiled at him, face flushed, as they whirled around in a circle before returning to their respective lines one place down. In this way all of the youngsters got to dance with each other. It was a general reel. More personal dancing would come later.

From the distance he could hear the sound of singing and drinking as the elders continued their feast in the great hall. Slowly, the married couples were coming out to join in the dancing. Dogs barked. Geese honked. Goats bleated. The festivities stirred them up like nothing else could.

Suddenly the music stopped, as the skald and his lads broke off to quench their thirst with ale. Acting on impulse, Ragnar moved over towards Ana. They exchanged glances. Without speaking they moved off, arm in arm, into the darkness away from the hall. Ragnar could see that the girl's face was flushed. Her hair was in disarray. Her eyes seemed huge in the gloom and the torchlight. Ragnar reached out and put his arm around her waist, she did the same to him. They looked at each other and giggled like conspirators as they moved into the shadows of the huts.

Standing in the shadows, listening to the sounds of mirth from the village, Ragnar was aware that something important was happening here. He felt drawn to the girl by the same attraction that drew a lodestone towards the north. He told her this, expecting her to laugh. She looked up at him and smiled, lips parting slightly. He was immediately aware of her beauty and the soft warmth of her body against his. Without thought, he reached out and pulled her to him. Their lips met. Her arms came up behind his head to clutch his face from either side and to guide him.

After a long moment, they broke apart and smiled conspirator's smiles, then they returned to kissing.

MOVING ON silent padded feet Strybjorn and his Wolfbrothers approached the Thunderfist village. He was amazed. The fools were so overconfident they had not even posted a sentry. They had become soft living on the fat of Strybjorn's ancestors' land. Well, soon, he thought, they would pay for their mistake.

He knew that all around the village Grimskull warriors were taking up position. Soon seasoned warriors would slip over the palisade and seize the gate. Then Strybjorn and his kind would fall upon their besotted foes like wolves descending on the fold.

Nothing was going to stop them now.

'MAKE A WISH,' Ana said, rearranging her dress. Ragnar stopped buttoning his tunic and looked up in the direction she indicated. Overhead he saw a light in the sky. At first he thought as the girl had that it was a falling star but then he noticed the comet trail of fire that followed it. It reminded him of something else. At the moment, befuddled by beer and his recent embrace with the girl, he was not quite sure what.

In the distance dogs barked as if in response to the sight of the meteor fall.

He rolled over, grabbed the girl, and pulled her down to kiss him. She resisted playfully for a moment before joining him on the ground. He did not think he had ever been so happy as he was at that moment, but the thought of those flames falling downwards niggled at the back of his mind.

At last he remembered where he had seen something like them. They had been pouring from the exhaust of the skyship that had come to claim the Wolf Priest Ranek from the island of the Iron Masters.

What could be their significance, he asked himself lazily, before he stopped thinking altogether in the passion of the moment. He barely noticed it when the screaming began.

* * *

STRYBJORN HELD his axe firmly in his hand and raced through the open gate. All around him his Wolfbrothers pressed close, their eyes bright with anticipation, their mouths open. Strybjorn felt suddenly weak for a moment. He knew it would pass: this sensation always overcame him just before he encountered danger. It was like a sign his body was prepared for the encounter. He was suddenly aware of his breathing quickening, his heartbeat growing faster, the sweat on his palms making his axe difficult to hold. Along with his comrades he loped into the town. From up ahead, he could hear what sounded like music and dancing.

Suddenly, ahead of them were people. They were not Grimskulls. His every sense keyed up like a taut hawser, Strybjorn needed no more provocation. He lashed out with his axe. There was horrid sucking sound as the blade bit home and then was withdrawn. Strybjorn lashed out again, feeling warm blood spurt out of the man's body that fell at his feet. He pressed forward into the bodies. Strangely the music kept playing. Off in the distance a dog barked. As if announcing the attack somewhere overhead there was a boom like thunder.

'WHAT WAS THAT?' Ana asked, a look of fear appearing on her face. Ragnar disentangled himself from her and looked up.

'I don't know,' he said, and then suddenly realised that he was wrong. He had heard a thunderous sound like that before, when the skyship had first approached. Was this some sort of omen or sign? And what was that noise? It sounded like a huge brawl had broken out back by the long hall.

He pulled himself to his feet. Ana got up beside him. Holding her hand he made his way between the huts back towards the sound of the commotion. What he saw was worse than anything he had ever expected. Strangers were among the revellers. Huge burly men with dark hair. Their features were craggy and their jaws were massive. They looked almost trollish, and Ragnar recognised them instantly from the songs of the skald. It was as if they had stepped out of one of his songs. They were Grimskulls.

For a moment superstitious fear froze Ragnar. Had they returned from the grave to claim the souls of their conquerors? Was dark magic at work here? Could the dead have risen to take vengeance on the living?

As he watched he saw one brutal-featured youth, garbed like a Wolfbrother, hack down Ulli's father. The older man still looked befuddled by beer and surprise then he clutched at his stomach, trying to hold in the rope of guts that spilled forth.

'We're under attack!' Ragnar shouted, pushing Ana back into the shadows. 'It's a raid.'

In his heart of hearts, he knew it was no mere raid. Judging by the quantity of warriors present and the number of battle-cries he could hear coming from all around, this was a full-scale invasion intended to enslave or destroy his people. He cursed, knowing that the attack had come at the worst possible time, when all the warriors were drunk or dancing. And it was their own fault. They should have posted sentries. They should have been ready but they were not. The long years of peace had lulled them into a false sense of security such as no man of Fenris should possess. And now they were paying for it.

Anger and despair warred in Ragnar's heart. For a long moment he stood frozen, knowing that it was all hopeless. More than half the villagers were already dead or dying, smashed like rotting dragonbone by these terrible invaders. Their attackers were ready, fully equipped, in formation and fighting with a terrible purposeful discipline. The Thunderfists were unarmed, disorganised, confused and unable to do much more than be cut down like chickens being slaughtered.

Suddenly Ragnar knew that the doom of the Thunderfists was upon them.

FOUR
THE LAST STAND

'GET BACK!' Ragnar shouted, pushing Ana into the nearest hut. He knew that it would provide little protection for them, that soon the invaders might take a torch to all the buildings. Still, he wanted time to think, and he knew that without a shadow of a doubt there would be weapons inside better than the dagger at his belt.

Not quite understanding what was going on, Ana resisted, but he was stronger and he wrestled her indoors. He put his hand over her mouth.

'Be quiet if you value your life!' he told her and saw terrified knowledge appear in her eyes, swiftly to be followed by firm resolution. She was a true daughter of her people, Ragnar could see.

Screams and war cries filled the night, only slightly dulled by the tent's dragonhide walls. Inside it was gloomy. Ragnar fumbled frantically among the possessions until he found a shield and an axe. Swiftly he bound the shield onto his arm, and hefted the weapon. He felt a little better but he was still unsure of what to do. The things he had seen had already burned their way into his brain.

He recalled the look of horror on the face of Ulli's father. He remembered seeing old Horgrim lying in the dirt, the whole top of his head removed, the brains spilling out. He remembered the horrible pulsing wound in the chest of Ranald the brewer. Things that he had barely recognised at the time now burned into his mind. Wet tears ran down his face. This was not what he had expected. This was not the sort of battle of which the skalds sang. This was brutal slaughter of unarmed people by a deadly foe.

And yet some small rational part of his mind told him, this *was* battle. There were always dead and dying and terrible wounds. Sides were rarely fair. And such things always ended in terrible deaths for someone. The question was: what was he going to do?

Was he going to remain cowering inside this hut like a beaten dog, or was he going to step outside and face death like a man? He knew there was little choice. He was most likely going to die anyway and best to meet the spirits of your ancestors with your wounds to the fore and your weapon clutched in your cold dead hand.

And yet something stopped him from doing what he knew he must do. His eyes were drawn back to the frightened girl, standing dry eyed and pale faced in the corner. She wiped away her tears with the hem of her sleeve and tried to smile at him. It was a terrible grimace and he felt his heart would break.

How his life had changed in a matter of minutes. Less than an hour ago he had been totally happy. He and Ana had been together. Things seemed settled between them in the manner of the village. They would have been wed, had children, lived their lives together. Now that future was gone, as certainly as if someone had torched it. There was nothing left save blood, ashes, and perhaps the honourless life of a thrall, if he was spared. He knew he could not face that.

What was he to do? He could not stay. If he did, he would only be putting her life at risk. A brawl might break out, and angry men had been known to strike down innocent bystanders. Most likely she would be spared to become some Grimskull's wife or thrall. Such was the way of the world. The thought pained him more than he could say but at least she would live.

And still he could not go. The same magnetism that had drawn him to the girl earlier prevented him from leaving now. Instead he stepped towards her, put the axe down and reached out and touched her face, tracing the lines with his fingers, trying to memorise them so that he could carry them down into hell with him if need be. Of all that had happened in his life, she was the best. It tore at his heart now to know that there would be no more, that their lives were over before they had barely begun.

He reached down and pulled her to him for one last kiss. Their lips met for a long moment and then he pushed her away.

'Farewell,' he said softly. 'It would have been sweet.'

'Farewell,' she said, enough of a child of her people not to try to stop him going.

He stepped out into the burning night, into the howling chaos and madness. The next thing he knew a massive figure loomed over him, axe held high.

STRYBJORN STALKED through the night, killing as he went. He howled exultantly, knowing that the hour of his people's vengeance had come. The taste of blood was sweet in his mouth. He liked killing. He liked the feeling of power it gave him. He liked the contest of sinew against sinew, man against man.

And yet these Thunderfists were poor foes, barely worthy of Grimskull steel. They were drunk and ill-armed and seemed barely to understand what had happened. How had they managed to drive his warrior folk from their homeland, he wondered.

In the brief respite from the combat a thought struck him. Was it part of the penalty for living on these islands? Had the good life softened his ancestors, the way it had softened the Thunderfists? Had his people once lost their warriors' wits the way these sheep had? It was something he should mention to his father, he realised. It must never happen again. Would never happen again, when he became chief.

DESPERATELY RAGNAR parried his assailant's blow. The shock of the impact numbed his arm even though the shield absorbed some of the force. Ragnar aimed a counter at the man's head, only to have that parried in turn.

He punched with his shield arm, catching his assailant in the face. As the man reeled back off-balance Ragnar split his skull with the axe.

He looked around. His home was on fire. The great hall was burning. All was madness. Shadowy figures cut and killed in the gloom. It was like a scene from some hell. Women raced through the night, carrying children. Dogs worried at the legs of the invaders. A chicken flapped squawking through the night, its wings ablaze.

Where was his father, Ragnar wondered. Most likely at the great hall helping rally the warriors. If he was still alive. Frantically Ragnar tried to dismiss the thought but like a knife it sank in that by the end of this night, not only his father but every other warrior he knew, and most likely Ragnar himself, would be dead.

Still, there was nothing for it but to fight, no matter how hopeless the odds seemed. Every sense alert Ragnar raced towards the great hall, hoping against hope to find his father and the others alive.

ONCE AGAIN the strange howling passed overhead, and Strybjorn became aware that a huge winged shadow had fallen over the battlefield. He looked up and saw its burning comet tail passing low overhead. For a moment, the fighting stopped, and everyone looked up to gaze in awe and wonder at the sorcerous apparition.

'The Choosers of the Fallen!' someone shouted. Strybjorn was unsure whether it was Grimskull or Thunderfist. He only knew that whoever had spoken was correct. A shiver passed through him. The messengers of the gods were here. They judged the combatants. Now! At this moment, they looked down with their burning gaze to see whether anyone was worthy to join the great warriors in the Hall of Heroes. It was possible that this night someone would be borne living to the legendary mountain where the Chosen of the Gods dwelled in immortal splendour.

Strybjorn knew they would choose only the bravest of the brave and the fiercest of the fierce. Only the boldest were worthy of immortality. The names of the Chosen would live for eternity, sung by the skalds during the hero chants. Blazing ambition woke in his heart.

He knew now what he must do. Somewhere among these whipped dogs he must find foes worthy of his steel. He must find enemies worthy to be called the name and call them out in single combat. The Choosers did not appear for every battle; perhaps this chance would never happen again. It was possible that never again in his lifetime would there be physical tangible evidence of the presence of these mysterious beings.

He glanced around. The same realisation seemed to have touched every warrior regardless of clan. The Grimskulls sprang apart from their foes, giving them time to pick up better weapons. Strybjorn waited anxiously to see what would happen next.

IN THE LULL of the fighting Ragnar looked up and saw the sky-ship pass overhead. It seemed a lifetime ago that he had watched it from the deck of the *Spear of Russ*, although in reality it had been only two hundred days. Perhaps it was not the same ship. Perhaps there was more than one. Who but the gods knew about these things?

Slowly the thought bubbled into his mind that the Choosers must be present. Might be observing him at this very moment. Judging to see if he was worthy to enter the Hall of Russ. It was an oddly uplifting thought. It gave meaning to the savagery around him. Suddenly this was not simply a battle for survival but a test of honour and worthiness. Of course, all battles were supposedly that but at very few was there actual evidence of the presence of the gods' messengers. This was one such battle. It was possible for a man to step right from here into legend.

The massive burly warrior with whom he had been trading blows but a second ago looked at him, and something like understanding showed in his brutal grey eyes. They stepped apart. Ragnar backing away towards the rest of his kin around the blazing great hall, the Grimskull retreating towards his own lines.

Ragnar looked around to see who he could recognise. Ulli was there. So was his father, he saw with a sigh of relief. Jarl Torvald still stood, though his head was bleeding from a ragged cut. Even as Ragnar watched the warrior chieftain tore the sleeve from his tunic and bound it round his head. All of them exchanged strange haunted looks. All of them knew they were dead men. All of them knew it was only a matter of time.

Looking across at the assembled horde of Grimskulls it was obvious that they were now outnumbered at least five to one. Many of the Thunderfist warriors had fallen in the initial rush. There was no way they could hope to overcome so many, even if they proved much better warriors than their foes. And judging by the savagery of the Grimskulls that they had already witnessed such was not the case. Man for man they seemed equally matched – or perhaps even outmatched, Ragnar was forced reluctantly to admit.

Still, the appearance of the skyship had caused a change in the atmosphere of the battle. That much was obvious. The Grimskulls were holding back right now. They, as much as the Thunderfists, wanted to impress the celestial watchers. They had gone from seeking a slaughter to seeking worthy foes. A spark of anger flared in Ragnar's heart.

Now, they were prepared to fight honourably. Knowing the eyes of the gods were upon them they were prepared to grant their enemies a fair fight. A few minutes ago they had not been ready to do so. It hardly seemed fair or in keeping with the nature of true honour. A still small part of Ragnar laughed at his own naïveté. What was the point of protesting about the fairness or the unfairness of it? The gods would make their judgements in their usual inscrutable way, and they would not be fooled. He hoped.

Why should he protest? The Grimskulls were allowing him the chance of a worthy death even if they were foul hypocrites. And they were at least ensuring that the Thunderfists would take a few of their number down into darkness with them.

As it became obvious what was happening a few of the Thunderfist warriors raced into the blazing hall, returning with armloads of weapons and shields. The Grimskulls seemed quite prepared to let them do so, and to let their enemies prepare for battle.

There was a tension in the air now. It was quite palpable, as if the presence of the Choosers had generated its own electrical energy. Warriors limbered up swiping the air with their weapons. The Grimskull leaders were huddled, arguing among themselves over what to do – doubtless debating how to make themselves look best in the eyes of Russ.

Well, there were no such debates over here among the Thunderfists, Ragnar thought. Their duty was clear, to sell their lives as dearly as they could and to fight well and honourably before they died. There was no other choice.

From somewhere down the line he could hear the sound of a man crying. It sounded like Ranald Onetooth. This surprised Ragnar, for all his life he had known Ranald and he had always been a steady man, unflappable even in the face of the greatest of storms or the mightiest of orcas. By all accounts he had acquitted himself well in all the raids and battles he had taken part in too. In fact he had faced the Night Troll of Gaunt in single combat and emerged triumphant.

Why had his nerve broken now, Ragnar wondered. Of all the men present he was one who would have seemed most assured of the Choosers' favour. His bravery had been tested time and time again. Was it possible that a man had only a limited store of courage for his life, and when that was consumed his bravery failed? Or was it the presence of the Choosers themselves that had unmanned him? Knowing that the eyes of your gods were upon you might do strange things to a man, Ragnar thought.

Or perhaps it was the sure and certain knowledge every Thunderfist warrior now had, that soon they would be judged and know their ultimate fate. It was one thing to enter a battle or a storm or any other danger knowing that you might live by dint of luck or the favour of the gods or your own strength or skill. It was another knowing beyond any shadow of a doubt that your life would soon be over.

Ragnar inspected his own soul and found that there was fear there but it was not overwhelming. He was nervous and he was excited in an odd way but he was not terrified. More, there was an anger in him, and a thirst for vengeance on the Grimskulls for their treachery that made his fear seem like a small and insignificant thing. He felt himself on the verge of a towering killing rage. In his heart he was impatient to get to grips with his enemies, desperate for the killing to begin.

And he was forced to admit that a desire for the favour of the gods had nothing to do with this. He was sure that he would enter hell happy if he could take a Grimskull with him, and that his life would not have been in vain if he dragged down two. Knowing that his life was over, he had nothing left to lose. All that existed for him now was the chance to sell it dearly.

It was odd that in the course of one evening, a man could go through so many changes. He tried now to remember Ana's face, the face he had tried so hard to memorise only minutes ago, and found that he had no clear recollection of it now. A pity, Ragnar thought coldly. It would have been good to take the memory of something beautiful into the afterlife.

The Thunderfist warriors had finished arming and stood ready. The Grimskulls seemed to have chosen their warriors now. They faced each other across the shadows of the burning square. For a long moment they eyed each other with fear and hatred. Then all eyes were drawn to a massive figure that had emerged from the shadows. It was a monstrous burly man, clad in metal armour with an enormous wolf pelt thrown around his shoulders.

Ragnar felt a shock of recognition. It was the Wolf Priest who they had carried to the Iron Masters' isle those few short hundred days ago. Suddenly and with a surge of fear Ragnar remembered the Wolf Priest's final words. This had indeed been a day of doom for him. It seemed Ranek was a seer as well as a wizard.

Everyone stood now waiting to see if the Wolf Priest would intervene but he did nothing, merely surveyed them all with his blazing eyes. At that moment, Ragnar saw with utter clarity that there was something inhuman, or perhaps more than human, about Ranek. Whatever had happened to him, it had set him apart from the run of humanity, and turned him into something that was quite monstrous.

There was no fear in him. He stood there with utter confidence in his own invulnerability like a man watching children squabble, not someone standing on the edge of a battle between fully grown and fully armed warriors. It was as if he knew nothing could harm him, as if he could kill them all without effort should they annoy him. Remembering how he had dealt with the sea dragon Ragnar did not doubt that this was true.

Another thought entered his mind. Ranek had arrived with the skyship. He was no mere sorcerer. He was one of the Choosers of the Fallen, a representative of the gods themselves. The same thought seemed to have struck all present as they watched the firelight reflect off the Wolf Priest's shining armour. A feeling of awe came over everyone present. They knew they stood in the presence of something supernatural.

The terrible ancient watched them impatiently, as if waiting for them to begin. Ragnar suspected that his presence had intimidated all the warriors. For a brief moment, left to their own devices, they might conceivably stop fighting. Then the old man gestured for them to continue. The two forces steeled themselves like wolves preparing to spring into combat with each other, and then leapt forward into battle.

STRYBJORN FELT a thrill pass through him as the massively armoured ancient strode from the shadows. In his heart of hearts he knew that this was one of the Choosers, a being who could grant him immortality and an eternity of endless battle if he so chose. His eyes were drawn to the armoured figure like iron filings to a magnet. There was a sense of awesome power about the Chooser that filled Strybjorn with envy and longing. He wanted to share that power, to be able to stand amid carnage with the same certainty. He wanted to own something of the same pride. He knew that here was one compared to whom the greatest of the Grimskull warriors was but a clod. Whatever it was the old man had, he wanted it. He resolved there and then to perform like a hero in the coming battle or at least to die trying. If he got a chance. He was not in the first wave of warriors to go into single combat with the Thunderfists.

He glanced over trying to guess the numbers who remained and saw that one of the Thunderfists, a youth about his own age, was looking at the old one with recognition written on his face. Was it possible that he knew the Chooser? No. That could not be. It must simply be that the death madness was on him. Strybjorn did his best to memorise the youth's face. He was suddenly possessed of an unaccountable dislike of him, and he fervently prayed the lad would survive the initial battle so that he could kill him himself.

At the old man's signal the Grimskulls charged.

RAGNAR DUCKED the blow of a huge burly warrior. He swung his axe up and caught the man through the chest. Bones splintered, blood and entrails billowed forth. He turned just in time to duck the sweep of another Grimskull's weapon and then to his horror felt himself immobilised.

The dying man had reached up from where he lay in a pool of his own blood and grabbed Ragnar's leg. He seemed determined that his slayer would die with him. Pinned in place by his strength this suddenly seemed all too possible. The second Grimskull lashed out at him and Ragnar barely managed to block the blow with his shield. Impaired by the drag on his leg it was all he could do to keep his balance. He launched a counterblow sending his assailant leaping back. In the moment of respite he decided to take an awful risk. There was no way he could survive pinned in place as he was. He needed to break free. For a brief moment, he risked taking his eyes off his unwounded attacker, looked down and aimed a blow at the wrist of the arm that held him.

It came off cleanly, the sharp axe biting through flesh and bone and sinew. Hot blood soaked Ragnar's leg. The dying man let out a scream like the damned. Ragnar leapt aside barely in time to avoid his new assailant.

As the man swept past, Ragnar lashed out with his axe, catching him a terrible blow on the back of the neck. The axe cleaved through the vertebrae, and the man's head came half off the stump of the neck. Not yet knowing it was dead, the corpse ran onwards for a few strides before tripping over the handless man and falling to the blood-soaked earth.

Ragnar straightened himself and bounded forward, lashing left then right with his axe as he went. His first blow caught a surprised warrior on the temple and cleaved through his skull. His second blow was parried by a small, squat Grimskull warrior. With blazing speed he and Ragnar exchanged a flurry of strokes. A surge of pain lanced up Ragnar's arm where the man's spear point bit deep. Ragnar's return blow sent the man toppling forward into hell.

Ragnar was surprised by how well he was fighting. Everything seemed to be happening in slow motion. He fought with perfect co-ordination and a speed he had not known he possessed. His mind was crystal clear, cold as a snow-fed mountain stream. He felt strong and fast and he barely felt the pain of his wounds. Of course, he had heard that this was how it sometimes was from the older warriors, and he knew that he would pay for the wear and tear of battle on his body later. Right now, at this moment, he felt invincible.

A swift glance around told him how misleading that feeling was. There still seemed to be an endless horde of Grimskull warriors. As one fell another leapt forward, keen to get into battle. The Thunderfists were accounting for themselves well now but more than half of them were gone. As he looked around Ragnar saw his father dead upon the ground. He gazed skywards with sightless eyes, hands still wrapped around his axe, two dead Grimskulls at his feet.

Horror took a grip on Ragnar's heart. This was the man who had raised him alone ever since his mother had died. He had been there for as long as Ragnar could remember, a pillar of indomitable strength. It simply was not possible for him to be dead. Cutting foes down like chaff as he went, Ragnar forced a path to where his father lay. The young Thunderfist squatted down over the body and reached out to touch his father's brow. The flesh was already cold. Touching the throat, Ragnar found no pulse. Grief filled him and for a moment he was paralysed by it.

A Grimskull raced towards him. Ragnar watched him come. Grief hardened to something as cold as his father's corpse. The need to kill welled up within Ragnar's soul. The Grimskull moved so slowly that he seemed to be wading through molasses. Ragnar could make out every detail of the attacker, from the wart on the back of his left hand to the notches in the bright steel of his blade. Everything had a fatal clarity to it. He could see by the way the man was limping that he had twisted his leg earlier but it was not slowing him much. He watched as the man drew back his axe for the swing that would decapitate Ragnar. It was as if the whole thing were happening to somebody else.

Then past the attacker's shoulder he could see the old man, the Wolf Priest Ranek, watching him. There was something in the old man's eyes. It might have been compassion, it might have been contempt. Ragnar could not tell. Those wolf-like eyes were impossible for a mortal like Ragnar to read. And yet the gaze broke the spell that held him. Cold rage and hot hate filled him. He erupted into action, springing forward from his crouch under the incoming blow and cannoning into his assailant.

He lashed out, kicking the man in his already wounded leg and sending him tumbling off-balance. As he fell Ragnar split his skull like matchwood and advanced into the ranks of the Grimskulls, killing as he went.

Now he fought like a god. Nothing could withstand him. His hate and his anger drove him to new heights of speed and ferocity. He knew no fear. He lived only to kill and he did not care now whether he lived or he died. In fury he clove through the Grimskulls like a dragonship through a stormy sea. Anything that got in his way was chopped down.

Somewhere in the madness a blow from a Grimskull axe split his shield. He killed the man who had the temerity to do this and caught his spinning axe as it fell. With a weapon in each hand he stormed forward like a whirlwind of death, killing everything within his reach. He lost count of the number he slew after he put down the twentieth. He became used to the look of fear and horror he saw in the faces of the men who faced him. It was the same sort of look you might give if you confronted a daemon. Ragnar did not care; at this moment, he felt like a daemon. Maybe one had possessed him. If that were the case he welcomed it, as he would welcome anything that allowed him to kill Grimskulls.

For a moment, it seemed like he might turn the tide of battle single-handed. The Thunderfists rallied behind him and formed a flying wedge, ploughing through their foes, heartened by Ragnar's skill and strength. But it could not last. One by one his kinsmen fell. Nothing could maintain the terrible superhuman level of ferocity that Ragnar possessed. He bled from dozens of small cuts. His strength was sapped from absorbing dozens of numbing blows. He slowed, became conscious of pain and once more returned to the level of being human.

STRYBJORN SLASHED down another Thunderfist and tried to locate the youth he had seen earlier. He was nowhere in sight, and must have moved to some other part of the battlefield. It was unfortunate. Still, Strybjorn had managed to get the old man, the one who bore a resemblance to the youth. He had put up quite a good fight for a Thunderfist. Strybjorn was proud of himself. Now that the Thunderfists had regained some spirit they were turning into quite worthy opponents, and he had killed five. He felt quite certain that he had felt the Chooser's eyes upon him as he had done so. He had picked his foes well.

All had been warriors in their prime. All had been skilful and all had fallen to his axe.

Once more the sheer joy of bloodshed filled him. He realised that he was as happy as he had never been in his short hate-filled life. The act of slaying brought him more pleasure than food or sleep or ale. It was sweeter than honey or the kisses of a maiden. In dealing death, a man gained power equal to that of the gods. Or perhaps not, perhaps there was something sweeter than this, something known only to the Choosers and their masters. Strybjorn certainly hoped to find out.

Now it was time to find his chosen prey. It was time to kill again.

WEARINESS OVERTOOK Ragnar. He felt himself slowing. Strength leeched from him. Speed was lost. He blocked a blow from a Grimskull warrior, stepped back out of the way of a second swing. The edge of the axe tore his tunic, and left a bloody weal on his chest. He let the axe pass, stepped in, and chopped a huge chunk out of his attacker's axe with his second weapon. A blow from the right sent the man to his ancestors.

Behind him were many more Grimskulls. It seemed that for every one he killed two more stepped forward to take their place. Not that it mattered to Ragnar. He was intent only on killing, on making them pay for killing his father and stealing the life he should have had with Ana. He knew that when he strode into the cold hells he would be greeted by many that he had killed, and that knowledge made him glad. He was only sorry that he was not going to be able to kill them all, and that he could not maintain the killing rage that let him overpower so many.

A flurry of blows overwhelmed the next two assailants and then Ragnar knew his strength was spent. He had burned his strength up in this battle like a fire consuming wood. There was nothing left to use. He was fighting now only on instinct and reflex. His blows lacked the killing power they had once had, and then he came face to face with the man he felt sure was going to kill him.

It was a Grimskull youth he had noticed earlier. A youth of about Ragnar's age with a cliff-like brow and an enormous underslung jaw. He smiled savagely revealing teeth like mill-stones. There was a look of blood-crazed madness in his eyes that Ragnar knew must match his own. Briefly they paused to confront each other. Both sensed that in this meeting they felt the touch of destiny.

STRYBJORN GAZED at his chosen prey. At last he had found him. He had found the youth who had left such a trail of destruction through Strybjorn's kin. He had found the target he had singled out earlier for destruction, the one who had seemed to recognise the Chooser.

He did not look like much, just another slim, broad shouldered Thunderfist lad with an unusual mane of black hair, but Strybjorn did not underestimate him. He had seen first hand the havoc this youth had wreaked. Well that would end here. It was Strybjorn's destiny to slay this great killer and thus win the approval of the gods. This meeting had been fated long ago, of that he felt sure.

'I am Strybjorn,' Strybjorn said. 'And I am going to kill you.'

'I am Ragnar,' the Thunderfist youth replied. 'Go ahead and try.'

RAGNAR SAW THE look of hatred in the Grimskull's eye, caught the flickering glance that said he was about to attack, and ducked back as Strybjorn struck.

The Grimskull was fast, no doubt about it. Ragnar barely managed to deflect the blow with his axe, let alone get out of the way. And as he did so, Strybjorn followed through, bashing him from his feet with a blow of his shield. The shock of the impact sent stars flickering before Ragnar's eyes. He tumbled backwards and corpses squished under his weight.

Already the Grimskull's axe was descending in a blazing arc. Ragnar barely had time to roll aside. Blood sprayed over him as the axe bit into the dead body below with a sound like a butcher's cleaver hitting a side of beef. Ragnar lashed out with his boot, trying to kick the Grimskull's legs out from under him, but his foe leapt over the blow and brought his axe down once more. This time Ragnar managed to get his left axe in the way, but he was awkwardly positioned and the force of the impact drove his weapon back at his chest along with the Grimskull's blade. He winced with pain at the impact, and felt his own blood begin to flow over his chest.

Strybjorn raised his axe for another blow. Ragnar rolled again and scrambled to his feet, diving forward just in time to avoid another blow. He sprawled his length on the ground once more and then rolled to his feet. He found himself facing another Grimskull warrior. The man had raised his blade for a killing strike.

'No, leave him! He is *mine!*' he heard Strybjorn bellow from behind him. The second Grimskull paused in surprise. Ragnar took advantage of his confusion to smash his axe into the man's ribs and then turned just in time to parry Strybjorn's blow. The force of the impact this time did more than just numb his left arm. He felt something give in his wrist, and a flash of searing agony blazed up his arm. The axe fell from his nerveless left hand. Strybjorn's thick brutal lips twisted upward in a grin of triumph.

'Now you die, Ragnar Thunderfist,' he snarled.

Ragnar met his grin with one of his own and lashed out with his remaining weapon. The blow was quick, faster than the Grimskull's and Strybjorn barely had time to react and duck back out of the way. The razor-sharp axe cut into his flesh and raised a huge flap of skin. Blood started to dribble down into Strybjorn's eyes. He shook his head to clear it away.

Ragnar stepped back to admire his handiwork, knowing that if he was patient the advantage now lay with him. Blood from the cut would soon blind his foe, and then Ragnar could kill him at his leisure.

The same thought had obviously occurred to Strybjorn who let out a bellow of brute rage and charged forward like an angry boar. The flurry of blows he launched came close to overwhelming Ragnar but somehow he managed to give ground without taking more than a few nicks. He realised as he did so, though, that it was hopeless. Strybjorn's attack had driven him backwards into a huge semi-circle of Grimskull warriors, each of whom was eager for a chance to avenge the slaughter of his kin. There was no way to defend himself from them and from Strybjorn at the same time.

Instantly he came to a decision. He would make certain that he would take one last foe with him into the darkness. Leaving himself totally open, he braced himself for the killing blow then sent his axe hurtling forward. He felt the weight of death in it, even before the blade bit home. He knew his assailant was doomed. It smashed into Strybjorn's chest. Ribs cracked, entrails spilled forth. Ragnar felt a moment of satisfaction that his vengeance had been achieved then felt a surge of bright agony in his own chest.

With a reflexive killing strike Strybjorn had sent his own weapon deep into Ragnar's breast, then his kinsfolk advanced to finish the job. Wracked with agony from the flurry of blows, Ragnar tumbled forward into the darkness in which he knew death waited to welcome him.

FIVE
THE CHOOSER
OF THE FALLEN

Ragnar floated in an ocean of pain. His whole body burned. He ached in a way that he would not have believed was possible, endured agony that he was certain no mortal was meant to endure.

So this was hell, he thought. It was not what he expected. It was not cold. There was only pain. Where were the others he had slain. Why were they not here to greet him? Where were the judges of the dead? Where were his father and his mother and the rest of his kin?

Through his pain he was aware of a terrible sense of disappointment. He had not been chosen. He had not awoken at the great feast table in the Hall of Heroes high on the Mountain of Eternity. He had not proven worthy enough. He was diminished. The thought struck him sourly and then he was aware of nothing more.

Once again he was aware of the agony but it appeared to have lessened. There was a strange thumping sound in his ears and the roar of a mighty wind. Slowly it came to him that the thumping sound might be his heart and the wind might be the rasp of his breath.

Then it was as if pokers of red hot fire burned his chest, in every place where he had taken a wound. He wanted to scream but he could not open his mouth. He could make no sound. He felt as if needles of ice were being driven into his skin, and a thread of molten lead was being used to stitch his wounds.

Hell, he thought, was a place of torment. Blackness. Silence.

IT WAS COLD NOW. Ice surrounded him, clasping him in its chill, burning grip. This was more like it. This was what the skalds and the old songs had told him to expect. This was the place of endless chill where the lost souls wandered before all memory faded and they were absorbed once more into the primal stuff of the universe.

But where were the other restless dead, he wondered. And why could he not see? There were no answers. He drifted in the endless immensity for aeons then consciousness left him once more.

HE WAS GETTING WARMER. His body shook. Pain and heat seemed indistinguishable. They wrapped him like a cloak, like a shroud. He seemed to be shivering. He felt very tired. His whole body ached. He felt like his spirit had wandered a long way, and was devoid of all strength now.

Yet he was still aware of himself. He somehow still existed in whatever solitary void he occupied. He was aware only of the pain and of his own memories but he was aware. It was something to cling on to. Just as he made this decision, he felt the knives begin to cut once more, and fell into the long darkness of oblivion.

A WEIGHT LIKE that of an island pressed down on him, smothering him. He could not breathe and for the first time felt the lack of air. He was conscious of his limbs but they seemed too heavy to move. He was aware of his eyelids but he could not open them. It seemed to him that somewhere, a long way away, someone was calling his name.

Could it be the dead, he asked himself, already aware that it was not.

He forced himself to try and remain aware. He tried to open his eyes. It was like straining with an infinite weight. He knew now how Russ must have felt pitting himself against the awesome strength of the Midworld Serpent. The task seemed beyond him, and yet he would not allow himself to give up.

He focused all his willpower on the task of opening his eyes. They resisted him as firmly as the earth of a grave might resist the struggles of a dead man. He did not stop trying, would not allow himself to give up. He forced himself to go on.

Pain lanced through all his limbs once more but he did not let it distract him. Was that sweat running down his brow? He did not know, for he could not raise his hand to mop it away. All he could do was put all the strength of his life into trying to open his eyes. It should have been a trivial task for a man who had fought in such a mighty battle as he had but it was not. It was the hardest thing he had ever done.

He made himself think of his father and his mother and his friends. If he could open his eyes he could look upon them once more. He would be able to see into the land of the dead. The thought was frightening but what else could he do? He was there now. Sooner or later he would have to confront it, and he was not a coward. He knew himself well enough now to know that this was true.

Why then was he reluctant? Why did he feel this strange fear in the pit of his stomach? Was he frightened to look out on the unknown or was it that he feared looking on those he had loved once more, and explaining himself to them? He forced himself to continue and was rewarded with a brief glimpse of light.

Suddenly the darkness was split with a flash of blue and white. This was not what he expected at all. He forced himself to keep trying, to open his eyes to their fullest extent and slowly it dawned on him that he was looking up at a sky exactly like the sky of Fenris. Truly the afterworld was not what he had been led to believe it would be. He felt a little cheated.

As if the sight of the sky was a signal, other sensations flooded into his brain. He became aware of the scent of the earth, the song of the birds, the distant crash of waves on the shore. Then came the bitter smell of ashes, the smoky smell of burning and the bittersweet stench of human flesh on a funeral pyre.

Something soft was beneath him. He felt grass being crushed beneath his fingers as they bit into soft moist earth. He was aware of pain and a strange numbness that distanced him from it, in the way that the beer had separated him from the world, only this numbness was a thousand times more potent than alcohol.

A huge grizzled head came into view. Cold blue eyes, like chips splintered from the dome of the sky, glared down into his own. He recognised the seamed worn face. It belonged to Ranek, the Wolf Priest, the Chooser of the Slain.

'So you have followed me here,' he wanted to say but the words came out an unrecognisable gurgle.

'Don't try to say anything, laddie,' Ranek said. 'You have travelled a long way. It is an enormous journey back from the land of the dead to that of the living, and it's not one many men are given to make. Save your strength. You are going to need it.'

He said something in a language that Ragnar did not recognise to someone who was just outside his field of vision. Ragnar felt a pain biting into his arm, and then something cool as glacial meltwater flowed into his veins, and consciousness left him once more.

HE CAME AWAKE suddenly and instantly this time, aware of the sun on his face and the caress of the wind's fingers on his cheek. He felt well rested. He felt very little pain. He tried to sit up. It was an enormous effort but he managed it. He could see that he was naked. Instinctively he raised his fingers to probe where Strybjorn's axe had bitten into his chest. To his surprise he found only the faintest trace of a scar and an area of tenderness that gave him pain as he probed.

Looking down he saw a fresh pink scar and a yellowish area that looked like an old bruise. There were other scars and other bruises all over his chest, and he did not doubt that he had more on his back. What was going on here, he wondered. He saw that he lay close to the massive skyship. Looking around he could see what appeared to be the remains of a burned-out village.

It was odd; the afterworld bore a startling resemblance to the real world. Only some things were not quite correct. Where the Thunderfist village should have been was a collection of ruins. The roof of the tumbled down great hall still smouldered. Down by the beach funeral pyres burned.

Groups of living women and children were being herded into dragonships that lay out among the waves.

Slowly it dawned on Ragnar that perhaps he *was* in the world of the living. He remembered the great battle with the Grimskulls, and the fires that had burned then. His home village would look like this after such a battle, he was certain.

Or perhaps this was some new and unknown hell conjured by daemons. Perhaps it was a place intended to show him the consequences of the Thunderfist defeat. Certainly the scene was mournful enough to be that.

He heard heavy footsteps crunching across the turf behind him, and turned to look up at Ranek. The old Wolf Priest studied him with knowing eyes. 'You are back among the living, laddie,' he said. It wasn't a question.

'Am I? Are you not one of the Choosers of the Slain?'

The old man's booming laughter echoed out over the rubble. Several distant figures turned to look at him as if startled. 'Always questions, eh? You haven't changed much, boy.'

'I'm not a boy. I gained the robe of manhood days ago.'

'And what days they were, eh? Well, you distinguished yourself on the field of battle. I'll say that for you. You're a fighter, laddie. I haven't seen such carnage since the time of Berek and that was… well, that was a long time ago.'

'So you are a Chooser then?'

'Yes, laddie, that I am. But not in the sense you think.'

'Then in what sense are you one? Surely you either are or you are not.'

'One day, if you live, you will understand. The universe is not nearly so simple as you believe. You will find this out soon enough.'

'If I live?' Ragnar looked down at where the wounds in his chest should have been in wonder. 'Surely–'

'Surely you have already been dead? Is that what you were going to say? Yes, you were. Dead or the next best thing to it. Your heart had stopped beating and you had lost a lot of blood. Your body took a lot of damage but not enough. Our healer got to you before brain death could occur, and what ailed you was not beyond the power of our… magic… to fix.'

Ragnar was sure he had muttered another word before he said magic but he had never heard the word before and it made no sense, but that was only to be expected of wizards. They spoke in riddles and nonsense. Still, his words gave Ragnar hope.

'You can bring back the dead? Then my father–'

'Your father is beyond our aid, laddie,' Ranek said. He gestured towards the distant fires.

'Why didn't you help him when you helped me? You could have done it.' Ragnar was ashamed that grief kept his voice from being totally level.

'He had not proved himself worthy of our aid or our interest. You have. You have been chosen, laddie.'

'Chosen for what?'

'You'll find out soon enough, if that is your destiny.'

'You keep saying that.'

'I keep saying it because it is true.'

The old man showed his fangs in that disturbing smile. 'Now you belong to the Wolves. Body and soul, you belong to the Wolves.'

RAGNAR RAISED himself to his feet, unsteady as a new-born kid. He tried to put one foot in front of the other to walk but he found himself reeling and staggering. Almost at once, he overbalanced and the ground rose to meet him. He was slammed into the earth with painful force.

He did not let it stop him: pushing against the ground with both hands he rose to his feet once more. This time he managed a few more steps and before he could fall he stopped himself and stood upright, swaying. He felt nauseous. His stomach churned. He felt dreadful but at the same time he felt a huge sense of relief.

He was not dead. He was among the living. For whatever mysterious reasons they might have, Ranek and his fellows had chosen to spare him. Indeed, it appeared that in some way they had chosen him. Though it was not quite like any of the hero tales he had heard, still he had been picked out.

They were mighty mages indeed. They had healed his wounds. They had brought him back from the dead. Or had they? Was this some kind of foul sorcery such as the sea daemons were said to practise? Had they taken his soul and bound it into his corpse using dark wizardry? Would his body soon begin to rot and decompose? He turned to face the Wolf Priest.

'Am I dead?' he asked. It was an insane question, he knew, but Ranek looked at him with what appeared to be understanding, and perhaps even sympathy.

'As far as those people down there are concerned, yes, la[?] You are among the slain. You will depart from this place [?] to return. Your destiny lies elsewhere now, among the endless ice, and perhaps among the stars.'

Ragnar thought he saw Ana being pushed out onto one of the dragonships. Suddenly he knew beyond a shadow of a doubt that he had to get to her. He began to move towards the beach, staggering like a drunkard. He half expected Ranek to try and stop him but the Wolf Priest let him go.

Ragnar had no idea how long it took him to reach the beach. He knew that when he got there he was panting as hard as if he had run twenty miles over sand. He saw the Grimskull warriors all turn and look at him. There was wonder on their faces and horror. They made the sign of Russ over their breasts and continued to wade out into the sea and clamber on board their ships.

Ragnar tried to follow them but the waves beat against him and he fell. The water closed over his head and began to fill his lungs. He rose to his feet and started to splutter. He tried to push on out once more but a powerful hand closed on his shoulder. He turned around swiftly and lashed out with his fist. Agony shot up his arm and it felt as if he might have broken his fingers.

'Ceramite will not yield to naked flesh, laddie,' Ranek said, lifting him as easily as if he were a puppy, despite his struggles. 'You'll only break your hands if you keep that up.'

Out on the waters, the drums had begun to beat, oars splashed into the water. The dragonships began to pull away from land.

'Where are they going?'

'They are returning to their homes with their new chattels, laddie. They will not live here now. After the battle they believe this island will be haunted. I imagine that your seeming resurrection will only give credence to that viewpoint. This will be a sacred site before long. Of that I have no doubt.

'And then they will forget. Men always forget.'

Ragnar watched as the ships breasted the waves and wondered whether that small figure who seemed to be waving to him was Ana. There was no way to tell now, and he doubted that he would ever find out.

Ranek set him down on the beach and he waved back anyway, wondering whether the salty moisture in his eyes was tears
or merely the spray of the sea.

RAGNAR STUMBLED back towards the hill on which the skyship
lay. He tried to fix the village in his memory, for he believed
Ranek when the man said that he would never come here
again.

He passed the torn hut near the tumbled hall which had
been Ulli's home. Ulli was dead now, he knew. He must have
died with his father during the battle and he had not been
selected by the Choosers. It seemed impossible that he would
never see Ulli again, but it was the case. The friend he had
played with throughout his childhood was gone. All of them
were.

Ragnar remembered playing tig and kickball and fight-the-
monster over this very land. If he listened hard it seemed he
could hear the phantom voices of those lads playing but of
course it was nonsense. That was all in the past now, gone,
never to return. It was as cold as the ashes of the burned-out
hut.

Ragnar passed the spot where his father had fallen, and he
pushed that thought from his mind. There would be time to
deal with it later. Right now it was just too immense a concept
for him to deal with. If he even allowed it to touch his conscious mind he felt sure that rage and grief would devour
him.

He consciously avoided the place where his father's hut had
been, the only home he could ever remember save for the deck
of the *Spear of Russ*. His wandering steps pushed him out to the
edge of the village. He knew it had been a mistake moving
through the remains. The memory and the horror were too
fresh to be dealt with. He just wanted to get away. As fast as he
could, he walked towards the skyship of the Choosers.

AS HE APPROACHED the ship Ragnar noticed another body lying
on the ground. It was on some sort of metallic stretcher and all
manner of translucent tubes seemed to be buried into its flesh.
All of the tubes connected to a metal device that sat like a great
spider on the youth's chest. Fluids gurgled through them. Odd
runes pulsed in harsh reds and greens.

As Ragnar got closer he saw that it was Strybjorn, th
Grimskull with whom he had fought. It appeared that the
Choosers were working their magic on him too, and slowly the
realisation dawned on Ragnar that this could mean only one
thing, that Strybjorn too had been chosen. Hatred and cold
fury tore at Ragnar's bowels.

It seemed that the enemy he thought he had killed had
escaped his doom. Thinking of the way the Grimskull youth
had slaughtered his kin, remembering the look of hatred on his
face as their fight began, Ragnar wondered whether the gods
were mocking him by sparing his enemy, just as they had
spared him.

Without thinking he reached down and picked up a large
stone. He fully intended to take it and bash Strybjorn's brains
out, then smash the strange mystical device that clung to his
chest. He did not know whether it would work. Perhaps the
Choosers would be able to raise him from the dead again.
Perhaps their magic was that potent. Ragnar had no idea but he
fully intended to find out. He stalked closer to the recumbent
form of Strybjorn with murder in his heart.

He looked down on his intended victim. Strybjorn looked
fierce even in repose. His huge jaw and beetling brow made
him look like a primitive savage. Ragnar felt a terrible sick joy
clutch at him as he raised the rock. At that moment he did not
care what the Choosers might think. He did not care whether
he might be defying the will of the gods. All he cared about was
revenge. And he fully intended to take it.

Exultation filled him as he sent his arm arcing down. He
grinned in expectation of the moment when the rock would
collide with Strybjorn's head and turn his skull to jelly. It never
connected. Steel-strong fingers encircled his arm, stopping the
blow instantly. Ragnar's attempts to move it were as futile as if
he had tried to lift a mountain.

'By Russ, laddie, you're a fierce one,' said Ranek's voice. 'A
natural killer right enough. Still this one is not for you. He has
been chosen as well, and he is not yours to slay.'

'I will see him die,' Ragnar said, a terrible earnestness in his
voice.

'Where you are going, laddie, you well might. On the other
hand, it's equally possible he will watch your end.'

'What do you mean?'

'You will find out soon enough. Now go! Get into the Thunderhawk!' The old man gestured towards the flying ship. Filled with trepidation, Ragnar clambered inside.

THE INTERIOR OF the skyship looked like nothing Ragnar could have ever imagined. The floors were all of metal. The walls were likewise, save where small circular crystal windows allowed one to look out. The seat into which he had been strapped was made of some odd musty leather. Unknown runes flickered on panels near his head. Strange roaring noises made the entire vessel shiver as it strained to fly.

Ragnar fidgeted. The new garment the Wolf Priests had given him felt odd. It was a one-piece tunic all of grey that clung to his body like a second skin. Over his heart was a picture of a wolf's head, the sign of Russ. The garment covered all of him except his head. It was made of some fabric the like of which Ragnar had never encountered before. It stretched to fit him yet was light and breathable. It did not feel clammy but only slightly warm. While wearing it Ragnar felt like he might be able to walk through a blizzard without feeling the cold, which was odd, for the fabric was no thicker than the finest calf gut.

Suddenly the whole vessel shook. The roaring noise increased in pitch and volume. He was pushed down into the seat. Looking through the window he felt a brief sickening sensation as the land receded below him. It was unnatural watching the island fall away, as the skyship escaped the clutches of gravity and leapt into the sky.

Everything became smaller. He could make out the ruined village lying there like a child's toy. He saw the beaches that stretched around the island come into view. Slowly they rose above the height of the hills and the skyship gained forward motion.

Looking at the interior once more Ragnar could see the whole deck had tilted as the prow of the ship faced upwards. He glanced out of the window once more and saw that they were gaining forward motion as well as height and that his home island was already shrinking into the distance. Down on the sea he caught sight of the ships of the Grimskull fleet ploughing through the waves, and once more wondered about the people he knew who were upon them.

Then grey mist gathered around the skyship and the vessel began to shake. Fear clutched at Ragnar as he wondered whether the wind daemons were going to pluck them from the sky or whether some evil magic had them in its clutches. Then it slowly dawned on him that they were passing through the clouds.

No sooner had this thought struck him than they emerged into bright sunlight and the shaking stopped. Below him Ragnar could see an endless ocean of white, cut through occasionally with patches of blue. It came to him that he was looking down on the tops of the clouds, glancing upon a sight that it was given to few mortals to see. For a moment he felt a surge of wonder and gratitude.

The skyship continued to rise. Ragnar was still being pushed back into his chair. He felt as if a giant fist were pressing down on him and threatened to flatten him. He glanced around at the others and saw that the flesh of Ranek's cheeks was being pushed back as if by invisible fingers. What new sorcery was this, he wondered, too amazed to feel afraid. Whatever it was it did not seem to trouble the old man, he merely grinned and gave Ragnar a thumbs-up sign.

Ragnar glanced back through the window and saw that it was dark outside and stars were visible. Below them was a gigantic hemisphere, so big that its curve filled most of the view. It was mostly blue and white but here and there mottled patterns of green were visible. It came to Ragnar that perhaps he was looking down on the world globe and that the blue was the sea, the white was the clouds and the green was the land.

The pressure on his chest eased up with amazing suddenness and he felt himself begin to rise out of the chair. It seemed like only the straps restrained him. He felt as if his body had no weight for a moment, a strange and not unpleasant sensation. The noise of the ship had ceased and the silence was eerie and almost deafening.

Suddenly weight returned. The nose of the skyship tilted downwards and the orb of the world grew until it filled the entire field of vision.

Once again the ship began to shake. Looking out of the window Ragnar could see that the tips of the wings had started to glow cherry red like coals on a fire. A surge of terror filled him. Was the whole ship about to be consumed by magical flames?

Were the sky daemons angered? He risked another look at
Ranek. The Wolf Priest had his eyes shut and looked utterly at
peace. Ragnar fought for control for a long moment then
decided not to worry. Perhaps the blazing wings were merely
part of the spell that kept the skyship aloft. It was all beyond
his comprehension. Certainly Ranek did not seem at all troubled. As long as no one else seemed worried he resolved not to
worry himself.

The skyship continued to shake for long minutes. In a way it
reminded Ragnar of sledding downhill in the dead of winter.
Then once more the skyship roared to life. There was the sensation of enormous amounts of power being applied. The
pressure on Ragnar's chest returned as the vehicle began to
decelerate.

The stars disappeared. The sky went from deep black to shadowy to deep blue to blue. The clouds rose to meet them and
they plunged down into the misty void once more. The whole
ship tilted sickeningly like a boat caught sidelong by a wave
then it righted itself and for the first time Ragnar caught sight
of the land below them.

It was immense: a shattered landscape of rock and mountain, of lichen and snow. The horizon seemed far off. Huge
glaciers wriggled through the peaks. In all that distance, there
was no sign of life. It seemed as dead and alien as the surface
of the moon. The skyship raced on over the bleak endless
immensity unlike anything he had ever seen before.

'Asaheim,' he heard Ranek murmur.

The land of the gods, Ragnar thought, and wondered what
awaited him there.

SIX
THE CHOSEN

'YOU HAVE ALL been chosen,' Ranek said, gazing down from the Speaker's Rock at the newcomers. The enormous piece of stone jutted up like a fang; part of the tip had been chiselled away to make a podium. The whole stone had been carved so that the part facing the audience resembled a snarling wolf's head. 'And now you are all wondering why.'

Ragnar stared beyond Ranek at the distant mountains and shivered. Yes, he was wondering that. He looked around at the others. From the expression on their faces he could tell they were all thinking the same thing. Their eyes were glued to the figure of the old Wolf Priest with a near fanatic intensity.

There were nearly two score others present beside himself. They had been assembled on the flat ground at the edge of the village at first light in order to hear the Wolf Priest speak. All of them wore the odd tunics that Ragnar had worn on the skyship, and many of them showed bruising and scars on their faces and hands that told Ragnar that they had been subjected to similar healing to that which he had undergone. Ragnar shivered again. The air was cold, and his breath emerged in a cloud. He noticed the strange quality that the light had here in the mountains. Everything seemed brighter, and the air seemed unnaturally thin and clear. He felt as if he could see much further than ever he could on the islands.

'You have all been chosen by me, or by a Wolf Priest like me, because we saw the possibility that you might be worthy to join us. I emphasise the word "might".

'Firstly, though, you will have to unlearn many things. You have been told that you have to die to join the heroes of Russ in their long hall. In some cases, for some of you, this has proven true. You were dead and we brought you back through our magic. Others among you have been brought here while you were still alive. It makes no difference. Be aware of one thing.

'There will be no more second chances. If you die here, you die. Your spirit will step into the beyond and go to join your ancestors. And be aware of another thing – if you die here, it will be because you are not worthy to belong among heroes.

'In this place, at this time, you are being given an opportunity to prove that you are worthy to stand among the greatest heroes of our world. You will be given the chance to show that you are suitable to be among the chosen of Russ, to join the companies of the Wolves.

'Right now, you cannot understand what an honour that is, or what a weight of responsibility it may one day force you to carry. For now you will have to take my word for it. It is no small thing you are being asked to do. It is no small task you are being asked to undertake. In times to come it may lead you into terrible darkness, to face the most wicked of foes, in places beyond your ability now to imagine.

'You may be called upon to stand between humanity and its ultimate enemies, to fight against monsters terrible beyond the descriptions of legend. It may be that you will stand beside Russ himself in those final days when the forces of evil arise to destroy all that exists. All of this may be – if you prove yourself worthy.

'We offer you a task worthy of heroes. And the prize is not tawdry. If you are successful you will gain a life far longer than any normal mortal's, and powers as great as those of any demigod of legend. You will travel beyond the sky, to the furthest stars, and fight in battles that will test the measure of any warrior. There will be opportunities for glory and for honour and the respect of those whose respect is worth something.

'If you prove yourself: then power, glory and immortality. If you fail: death everlasting. These are the paths before you. From this day, from this minute, there are no others. You will either triumph or you will die. Do you understand me?'

Ragnar looked at the Wolf Priest. There was no friendliness and no compassion in him now. This was the sorcerer he had first met on the *Spear of Russ* what seemed a lifetime ago. The old man seemed to have grown huge in stature and was wrapped in a cloak of awesome presence. His words had the force of a prophet's and burned their way directly into Ragnar's consciousness. They were at once frightening and inspiring, and even though Ragnar did not understand much of what he had heard, he sensed the importance the Wolf Priest put in what he was saying, and that made it important to Ragnar too.

'Do you understand me?' the old man repeated.

'Yes,' a score of voices responded in unison.

'Good. You are now aspirants to the Chapter of the Space Wolves. When you understand the meaning of that, you will understand the greatness of the honour being offered you. Now, let me to introduce you to Hakon. He is the man who will teach you what you need to know, and judge whether you are worthy to live or die. Listen to his words carefully, for they mean life or death to you now.'

The Wolf Priest gestured to a newcomer who strode up onto the platform and regarded them with bright wolf-like eyes and a contemptuous smile. Ragnar studied the man's face closely. It was narrow and almost skeletal. The flesh seemed too tight, drawn taut by the dozens of scars that turned his cheeks into a patch-work quilt of flesh. His hair was grey and held in a long pony-tail. His face was dominated by huge eyes, a huge blade-like nose and thin, cruel lips. He looked like a predator, like a wolf given human shape, and right now he was looking at the assembled youths in the way a wolf might look at a flock of sheep. There was nothing whatsoever reassuring about his cold gaze.

Having performed the introduction, Ranek vaulted down from the platform without any further ceremony and strode off back towards the village. Ragnar noted that Hakon did not climb onto the rock himself. Instead he moved around to stand in front of it. The huge stone wolf head appeared to glare over his shoulders, and it was hard to tell which looked more savage, the carving or the man.

'Welcome to Russvik, dogs! I doubt you will survive here. As you heard, I am Hakon,' the newcomer said. 'I am Sergeant Hakon. That is my title. You will use it. Or, by Russ, I will tear off your limbs like a small boy tormenting flies.'

Ragnar stared at the speaker and fought down an immediate feeling of hatred. Sergeant Hakon was a terrifying figure but at that moment Ragnar felt nothing but loathing for him.

Hakon was tall and strong. Like Ranek, he was much taller than a normal man and would have been far broader even without the gleaming armour that encased his body. Like Ranek he had the same fangs visible when he smiled, which was often and cruelly. Like Ranek he carried many small talismans of obvious mystical significance. He had a huge sword with serrated edges, a mystical weapon of the type Ranek had used to dispatch the dragon, and various other accoutrements. Neither his armour nor his fetishes were as ornate as the Wolf Priest's but they were quite visibly of the same manufacture and must have come from the same forges.

Ragnar wondered where those were. Looking around he could see no sign of any foundries or smithies. All he could see was the small fortified camp with its huts built of wood and stone so unlike the buildings back home. Or back where home used to be, he corrected himself. Now there was no place to go back to.

'You may believe you have been chosen. You have not! You have been chosen to prove that you are worthy to be among the Chosen. Looking at all of you sorry swine I doubt that any of you are. I think the Wolf Priests have made a mistake and brought me a litter of stupid, useless foolish piglets. What do you think?'

No one was stupid enough to reply. Hakon's voice was harsh and guttural. The tone was a permanent sneer and an affront to their manhood. Back in the Thunderfist village such a manner would have resulted in Hakon being called out to duel. Here, it appeared he could speak in whatever manner he chose. Despite his loathing Ragnar doubted that there was anything any of the newcomers could do. Hakon was armed and they were not, and that was not even counting any magic that he might choose to employ.

'None of you have any guts, eh?' Hakon said. 'All spineless are you? As I suspected. Not a man among you.'

'You are armed and we are not,' said a voice that Ragnar was surprised to hear was Strybjorn's. He was shocked that the Grimskull had dared to speak when no one else had.

'What's your name, boy?'

'Strybjorn Grimskull, and I am not a boy. I have passed through the manhood rite.' A snarl twisted Strybjorn's thick, brutal lips. Anger flared in his cold eyes.

'Strybjorn Thickskull more like. Are you stupid, boy?'

'No.' Strybjorn took a step forward, his fists clenched. There was a sharp intake of breath from the assembled aspirants. No one could quite believe the Grimskull's temerity.

'Then why do you think I would need weapons to deal with an insolent puppy like you?'

'Wouldn't you? You talk big for a man standing there in armour carrying a blade. Maybe you wouldn't be quite so tough without them.'

The sergeant smiled as if he had been hoping someone would say this. He strode forward until he was looming over Strybjorn. The Grimskull was tall and strong but Hakon was much taller and much heavier. His smile revealed those uncanny fangs. Conflicting emotions surged through Ragnar's mind. It looked as if the Grimskull had made a terrible error and that there was the possibility that Hakon might kill him. Ragnar didn't mind the Grimskull's death so much as the fact that he would not be the one to slay him. Still, there did not appear to be anything to be done about that right at this moment.

The sergeant pulled his blade from its scabbard and raised it high. Strybjorn did not even flinch. Ragnar was forced to admit that the Grimskull was brave – even if he was foolish. Hakon drove the blade into the ground in front of Strybjorn. It stood there quivering, point first, down in the turf. Ragnar could see that the weapon was strange and complicated-looking. Serrated blades were fitted round its edges and the blade itself appeared to contain a complex mechanism.

'Pick it up, boy,' the sergeant said. 'Use it – if you can. You will be armed and I won't be.'

For a moment Strybjorn looked at Hakon. He seemed confused and a little shocked. Then the light of bloodlust appeared in his eyes and a brutal smile twisted his thick lips. He reached out and grabbed the hilt of the massive weapon. He tugged at it, obviously expecting to lift it as effortlessly as the sergeant had. No such thing happened. The blade refused to budge. Strybjorn grasped it with both hands. The muscles on his neck stood out like taut guy ropes. His biceps bulged. His face turned red. Eventually, with much effort, he pulled the weapon free of the ground.

'Too heavy for you?' Hakon sneered. 'Perhaps you would like something lighter? I have a knife here.'

With a roar of incoherent fury Strybjorn threw himself forward, bringing the blade arcing down towards the sergeant's unprotected head. Given the weapon's weight and Strybjorn's obvious strength and speed if it connected there was no way the sergeant could survive. And it seemed to be about to connect. The blade moved through a whistling arc and the sergeant made no attempt to deflect it or get out of the way. Then suddenly, just as it seemed his skull would be smashed, Hakon was no longer there. He simply stepped back and the blade passed through where he had been less than a tenth of a heartbeat before.

'You use the blade like a woman, boy. You could not split sticks. Try harder!'

Strybjorn roared and swung the blade at waist height. His face was red and contorted with fury. He obviously did not like being mocked. Ragnar stored this fact away in his memory in case it might prove useful later, for the inevitable day when he got the chance to take his revenge.

Once again Hakon waited until the last moment and then simply leapt into the air. The momentum of the blow carried the blade beneath him. He landed easily on the ground as Strybjorn almost overbalanced from his stroke.

'You're clumsy, boy. I'll give you one last chance if you have the courage to take it. But be warned it will go ill for you if you fail.'

Strybjorn aimed high this time, swiping sideways at the sergeant's head. The sergeant ducked and allowed the clumsy swing to pass over him. He stood there for a moment grinning nastily and then he struck. Keyed as he was to the slightest movement, still the blow happened almost too swiftly for Ragnar to follow. Hakon lashed out with a fist. It connected with Strybjorn's jaw with a sickening smack. The Grimskull toppled backwards, unconscious before he hit the ground. The weapon fell from his hand. Hakon picked the tumbling blade out of the air without any apparent effort, catching it one-handed and then holding it aloft.

He touched a stud on the handle and suddenly the weapon erupted into sorcerous life. The blades around its edges began to move round and round, accelerating so swiftly that they became invisible. All of the newcomers watched appalled as Hakon moved the blade through the air, waiting to see what the sergeant would do. Was he going to decapitate Strybjorn and use his head for a trophy? It seemed all too possible.

The dirt which had clung to it from where it was driven into the ground sprayed outwards. After a few moments Hakon touched the stud again and with a nerve-wrenching screech the blades stopped moving. Hakon inspected them fastidiously, obviously making sure they were clean before returning the weapon to its scabbard. Then he strode over to the unconscious form of Strybjorn and looked down on him contemptuously. Ragnar could see that the Grimskull's chest was still rising and falling. He did not know whether to be pleased or disappointed.

'"Thickskull" was right,' Hakon said. 'That punch would have broken the head of any man who did not have the skull of an ox.'

In an explosion of nervous tension all the newcomers began to laugh. Ragnar was surprised to hear himself join in. Hakon's glare swiftly silenced them.

'You'll all be laughing on the other side of your face in a few minutes. You two carry him down to second long hall and then report to the forges. The rest of you follow me. It's time to see you're all properly equipped.'

THE NEWCOMERS walked silently through the little village of Russvik behind Sergeant Hakon. They passed over the ditch that ran outside the wooden walls surrounding the place and through the open gate. Guards armed with spears looked at them from wooden watchtowers on either side of the entrance.

Ragnar looked around at the buildings in surprise. This was his first real chance to study them closely, and he saw how different they were to the ones amid which he had grown up. Here the main building material was not dragonhide and dragonbone. It was wood, and stone and thatch. Some of the buildings were loghouses: squat square structures made from the trunks of dead trees and roofed over with turf. Others were made from stones set one on top of the other like those used to make drystone dykes on the islands. These too were roofed with turf. Both sorts of buildings had holes cut in the roofs to act as chimneys for the woodfires within.

The streets themselves were all of mud. Pigs rooted amid the garbage and chickens fluttered squawking around makeshift coops. There was something oddly homely about the presence of these domestic animals. They reminded Ragnar a little of home. What did not were the odd carvings that marked all the junctions. These were made from wood, and all of them represented wolves, rearing, stalking prey, snarling, leaping. All of them were beautifully made, and all of them were strangely lifelike. Ragnar had no idea what the runes carved on them meant but he was sure they possessed some mystical significance.

The streets were filled with young men, all carrying weapons, all going about their business with an air of calm competence that none of Ragnar's group possessed. They looked at the newcomers with a mixture of pity and contempt as they passed. Here and there other older warriors garbed like Hakon were visible. These were treated with wary respect by all who encountered them.

Some of Ragnar's group looked at the stone buildings with a wide-eyed wonder that told Ragnar they were islanders like himself but that, unlike him, they had never seen the island of the Iron Masters.

It was all too strange. Russvik occupied a long valley, beside a deep blue lake. On either side were towering mountains on a scale unlike anything Ragnar had ever seen before. These peaks dwarfed everything around them, made all the works of man seem insignificant. It was almost as if this location had been chosen deliberately to make the newcomers feel small. Perhaps it had, Ragnar realised. Perhaps this whole process was designed to make them feel utterly insignificant.

He had no idea why that might be, but he could definitely see how it was possible. The location, the Wolf Priest's speech, Hakon's manner were all of a piece. They told you that you did not matter, that you had everything to prove. Somewhere deep within himself Ragnar felt a small spark of rebellion kindle and catch flame. He was not quite sure what he was going to rebel against but he was sure he would find something, and perhaps even get to finish the hated Strybjorn into the bargain!

He looked around and tried to make eye contact with the others. Only one looked back at him and smiled. All of the others seemed to be lost in a reverie of their own. Ragnar was not surprised. There was much to think about. He had seen so many new things that it seemed hard to believe it was only one day ago that he had arrived here. He had spent some of the evening being quizzed by Ranek. All of the details he had given in answer to the Wolf Priest's questions had been entered in a huge leather-bound tome in the central hall. Then he had been subjected to a physical examination by those Ranek had referred to as Iron Priests. They had passed many odd-looking amulets over him, and inspected his body minutely as if looking for the stigmata of mutation. If the situation had not been so odd Ragnar would almost have been insulted. There had been no mutants among the Thunderfists. Any babe which showed traces of the mark of Chaos had been drowned at birth.

It had been dark by the time he had been allowed to go. He had been shown to a longhouse built all of logs. The interior smelled of pine sap. There had been some grumbling from those already there when he arrived. He had found a straw pallet, lain down and fallen asleep instantly.

It was only in the morning that he had caught sight of his companions and realised that Strybjorn was among them. He must have entered the hall after Ragnar had dozed. Whatever wounds he had taken in the battle had also been mended by the healer's magic. It made Ragnar's flesh crawl to think that he had spent the night under the same roof as a sworn enemy. An enemy he had already killed once! Ragnar spat on the earthen floor in disgust.

There had been no time to do anything about it though, for the Wolf Priest had arrived and led them all off to listen to his speech and meet Sergeant Hakon. There had not even been time to introduce himself to any of the strangers. Now more than ever Ragnar felt the oddness of the situation. He was surrounded by people from dozens of different clans. Under normal circumstances all of them would have been his enemies except if they met during one of the great festivals. Yet here none of them were armed, and none of them seemed at all disposed towards hostility right at this moment. Sergeant Hakon had given them much else to think of.

It also came to Ragnar that most of the others seemed to know where they were going. Certainly the two who had been ordered to carry Strybjorn away knew where they were taking him. This indicated to Ragnar that most of the young warriors had been in the desolate camp long enough to find their way about, and to have some idea what Hakon was talking about. He knew he was a newcomer here and for the moment Ragnar resolved that it was wisest to keep his mouth shut and eyes open.

They arrived at one of the largest of Russvik's wooden halls. Hakon strode inside and within minutes returned with a pile of weapons. Immediately he began to call out names. As each named youth strode forward Hakon thrust a spear and a dagger into his hand and then ordered him to return to the ranks.

'Ragnar Thunderfist!' Ragnar heard his own name called out and strode forward. The sergeant loomed over him. Until he had got close Ragnar had no real idea of how big Hakon actually was. Now he could see that the sergeant was the biggest man he had ever encountered, taller and broader even than Ranek. Ragnar could see too that the armour he wore was covered in small mechanisms such as the ones he assumed had made the blades on the sergeant's enchanted sword rotate. Ragnar's respect for Strybjorn's bravery – and foolishness – increased by a notch.

'What are you staring at, boy?'

'You, sergeant!' Hakon's blow was almost blindingly swift yet somehow Ragnar saw it coming. He threw himself backward with just enough force to lessen the impact. The force of the impact still sent him sprawling back into the dust but he kept rolling and came to his feet. It felt as if he had been hit with a blacksmith's hammer, sparks danced before his eyes but at least he was still conscious.

'You have good reflexes, boy,' the sergeant said, and tossed the scabbarded knife and spear to Ragnar. Ragnar managed to pluck them from the air and still keep on his feet. He saw that the others were looking at him with what might have been envy, or perhaps respect. For this, he felt a small surge of satisfaction.

The scabbard was leather. The steel buckle was in the shape of a wolf's head. Ragnar was amazed by the ostentation. In all his life, he had seen such riches only once, on the island of the Iron Masters. Amongst the folk of the islands precious steel was for blades, and spear points and tools. Maybe a wealthy jarl might possess a few iron armlets as transportable wealth but it was rare. He pulled the blade from the oiled leather scabbard and inspected it. The quality was of the finest, the edge was razor keen. The pommel was tipped with a small wolf's head identical to the one on the belt buckle. The spear shaft was of the finest ygra-wood. The point was needle sharp steel with not the slightest trace of rust. Small runes had been carved into the shaft. The whole weapon gave the impression of being well-used. Ragnar had a sudden vision of generations of newcomers before him using the weapon. He did not know whether he found that reassuring or not.

Hakon was speaking again. 'These are your weapons now. Look after them. They may save your worthless lives. And do not lose them and come running to me either. There will be no replacements. In the unlikely event of any of you surviving your time here, you will be expected to return them. If any of you die, the survivors are expected to bring back his weapons. Leave the corpse for the crows if you like – but bring back those blades.

'Now I am going to assign you to your Claws. This is your basic fighting unit. Every one of you in a Claw will train together, eat together, hunt together and most likely die together. When I call out your names step forward.'

Hakon called out five names Ragnar did not recognise. Five of the newcomers strode forward to stand before the sergeant. He gestured for them to move to one side and then called out another five names. Ragnar wondered if his name would be called but it was not. Five more names were called and then five more and still Ragnar's name was not mentioned. Soon only himself and three other youths stood there.

'Kjel Falconer, Sven Dragonfire, Strybjorn Grimskull, Ragnar Thunderfist, Henk Winterwolf.'

Ragnar looked at his companions. He saw a short sullen-looking youth, very broad and very strong looking. A fresh-faced boy who looked younger than anyone present and a tall freckled fair-haired lad with an open smiling face. His heart sank when he realised that he had been assigned to the same group as the Grimskull. Briefly he considered protesting but one look at Hakon told him that it would do no good. In fact, judging by the malicious smile twisting the sergeant's lips, Ragnar suspected that Hakon knew exactly what he was doing and how nasty he was being.

Still, thought Ragnar, the arrangement had its advantages. At least the Grimskull would be in easy reach for his revenge.

Hakon's disturbing smile widened. 'Take a look around,' he said. 'Look at your comrades. Remember each other's faces and know this – unless you are very, very special, and I don't think any of you are – at least half of you will be dead by the time you leave this place.'

Ragnar felt a shiver pass up his spine. The sergeant's words had the disturbing ring of truth.

OUTSIDE THE long hall the winds howled. It seemed as chill as the inside of an ice cave. The aspirants lay on their pallets and wished for a fire. There was a fireplace in one corner but no wood. Each of the groups had arrived together and taken pallets near each other. There was an empty pallet among Ragnar's group which had been reserved for Strybjorn. Ragnar lay on his back and stared at the ceiling and thought about the events of the day. More examinations. More speeches from Hakon. A lot of hard exercise. A meal of porridge and turnip and something that resembled pig fat.

'Old Hakon is a bit fierce, don't you think?' said a calm, pleasant voice. Ragnar looked up to see the freckle-faced youth he had noticed earlier was looking around and grinning at them all. His features were long and he had a small upturned nose that made him seem at once cheeky and cheerful. Long blond hair framed his face. He seemed insanely happy considering the circumstances. Ragnar could not help but smile back.

'Yes,' said Ragnar. 'A bit fierce.'

'I am Kjel of the Falconers.' Kjel extended his hand in a friendly fashion and Ragnar shook it.

'Ragnar of the… Thunderfists.'

'You don't seem very sure of that.'

'I am not sure that there are any Thunderfists any more,' said Ragnar simply.

'Like that, is it?'

'Yes.'

'I assume you were chosen after the battle in which your clan was…. harmed.'

'Yes.'

'It was a great battle?'

'It was a fierce and hard one. I'm not sure I would call it great. My village was burned. My people put to the sword. My girl–'

'Yes?' Kjel asked. He appeared sympathetic.

'I don't know.'

'Best forget her then,' said the squat brutal youth on the next pallet. He smiled as if he enjoyed being the bearer of bad news. Ragnar could see that his teeth were large and square and even. His nose had been broken and badly set. His reddish hair was cut in a style that seemed unusual to an islander like Ragnar, cropped short and to the skull. 'You'll never see her again. You'll never see anybody you know again.'

'There's no need to sound so pleased about it,' Ragnar said. The other youth shook his head and clenched his fist. It was not a gesture of menace though, Ragnar could see, more an expression of anger.

'By Russ's iron bollocks, I am *not* pleased about it! I am not pleased about any of this. I expected to join the Chosen, to enter the Hall of Heroes. Instead what did I get? Sergeant bloody Hakon and his bloody speech about how bloody useless we all are.'

'Maybe you should take that up with him,' Kjel suggested with a grin.

'Maybe I will. On the other hand, after seeing what happened to Strybjorn and Ragnar maybe I won't. At least not until I learn what makes him so different from the rest of us.'

'You think that something made him that way?' Ragnar asked with interest. 'You don't think…'

'It's just what I've heard round the camp but it seems the survivors of these little bands are taken away to some ancient temple and magic is worked on them. They are transformed into beasts or into men like Hakon and Ranek. By the Ice Bear's ivory droppings, I'm bloody hungry. When do you think they'll feed us?'

'You think Hakon is a man?' said the fourth member of the group, the one who looked too young to be there. Ragnar looked at him closely. His features were fine and he looked delicate and intelligent, more like a skald than a warrior. 'I mean, those fangs and everything.'

'He is surely not a ghost,' Ragnar said. 'Not the way he hit me today anyway.'

'I was amazed that you almost got out of his way,' the youngling said. 'I didn't think anybody could do that.'

'Ragnar didn't,' the surly one said.

'He almost did.'

'Which are you, Sven Dragonfire or Henk Winterwolf?' Ragnar asked.

'I'm bloody Sven,' the short squat one said. 'And, by the Ice Bear's sacred right buttock, you have a good memory.'

'I'm Henk,' said the youngest and rose to shake hands with them all. Ragnar clasped hands. So did Kjel but Sven merely lay there with his hands behind his head staring at the ceiling.

'That would mean the last of our bloody merry little band is Strybjorn Grimskull,' said Sven.

'Yes,' Ragnar spat. Even he was surprised by the venom which showed in his voice. Sven's grey eyes flickered right to look at him.

'You don't like him, do you, Ragnar? Why?'

'He was one of the scum who attacked my village.'

'That's not good,' said Kjel.

'He should be dead. I thought I killed him,' Ragnar said.

'You didn't do a very good bloody job then,' Sven said. 'Considering he's up and walking about – or at least he was until old Hakon knocked him into the land of dreams.'

'The Wolf Priests used their magic to heal him. They did the same for me,' said Ragnar.

'I think they may have done the same for all of us,' Kjel said. He pulled open his tunic to reveal a long scar running right across his chest and down across his belly. 'I don't think anyone could have survived the wound that put me here without magic.'

'How did you come to be here?' Ragnar asked.

'There was a battle,' said Kjel.

'I think that goes without bloody saying,' Sven sneered. Kjel shot him a disgusted look.

'I was with a raiding party going down the great glacier. We were looking for sheep to carry off–'

'Sheep!' snorted Sven. 'What were you going to do with them I wonder?'

'In the valleys a man's worth is measured by the size of his flocks.'

'I'll bloody well bet it is,' Sven said, his voice all innuendo.

'Anyway, we were ambushed by the Wolfsheads just as night fell. The battle was sharp and fierce. I must have killed or wounded about five of the Wolfsheads before one of them put his spear in me. I thought it was all over then but I looked up and I saw an old man looking down from the hillside just before the darkness took me. When I woke the same old man was there but I was in one of the flying ships on my way here. How about you, Sven – what feat of great heroism did you perform to be chosen?'

'I killed eight men in single combat.'

'Eight? At once?'

'No. One after the bloody other. They were all brothers. They killed my uncle and refused to pay weregeld so I called them out at the Allthing Feast. The Wolf Priest watched while I killed them and then he told me I was chosen.'

'You weren't wounded? You didn't… die?'

'Eight men died. Eight grown men and warriors. They died, not me. There wasn't a wound on me.'

'Truly Sven, you must be a mighty warrior,' Henk said.

'Truly,' Ragnar said dryly.

'You don't bloody well believe me?' said Sven suddenly. The light of violence flickered in his eyes.

'I never said that,' Ragnar. said 'After all, you're here aren't you?'

'And don't you bloody well forget it,' said Sven.

'What about you, Henk?' Kjel asked. The youngling blushed and seemed embarrassed.

'I fought with a troll,' he said. 'Killed it with my spear. It had killed my uncle and all his brothers and it was already wounded so it wasn't that great a feat.'

'The Wolf Priest must have thought so.'

'He would most likely have killed it easily if I hadn't.'

'Why was he there?' Sven asked.

'I don't know. Maybe our croft being on fire attracted his attention. Who can say?'

Ragnar looked at the youngling in astonishment. He had faced and killed the deadliest creature ever to walk the surface of Fenris after it had done for his family, and he talked about it as if it were nothing. Indeed he seemed embarrassed about taking the credit. Given their tales it seemed that all of his companions were worthy of respect. Even the Grimskull, perhaps.

There was a gust of wind and all eyes present turned to look at the open door. Sergeant Hakon entered, carrying the still unconscious form of Strybjorn. He stomped over to an empty pallet and dumped him unceremoniously on the straw.

'Best get some sleep,' Hakon said. 'You'll need all of your strength tomorrow.'

Without saying another word he walked around the room and snuffed the whale-oil lamps with his armoured fingers then he walked to the door again in the darkness, picking his way over recumbent bodies with no apparent difficulty. The door slammed shut behind him to announce his departure.

Silence fell over the long hall. Ragnar lay for a long time in the darkness wondering whether to take his knife and slit the Grimskull's throat. In the end he decided against it. He wanted his foe to be conscious when he killed him.

'That strange gurgling sound you can hear is my bloody stomach,' Sven muttered. 'By the balls of the Ice Bear, I'm bloody hungry.'

SEVEN
HUNTING

RAGNAR LASHED OUT with his wooden baton, catching Strybjorn on the eye. It was deflected by his thick, beetling brow and bounced back. 'The eye! My kill!' he shouted, backing away. The circling of watching aspirants roared their approval. Ragnar risked a glance at Sergeant Hakon to see whether he would confirm the kill.

The Grimskull snarled and struck out with his own wooden rod. The curved point caught Ragnar just below the ribs and sent all the air from his lungs. It was thrust home with all the strength and weight of the Grimskull's massive body behind it. This was knife practice and no blows were pulled. Hakon did not want them to get used to fighting against foes who did not strike as hard and fast as the real thing. The pain doubled Ragnar up and made him want to be sick. He felt barely able to stand. His senses reeled. All around him he could see the grinning, jeering faces of the other aspirants. They were arranged in a circle to watch the fight.

Strybjorn brought the baton cracking down on Ragnar's skull. Stars flared in the Thunderfist youth's field of vision. He let out a long grunt of pain and fell to his knees. He saw Strybjorn draw back his foot to kick him.

Suddenly cold, hard anger erupted from somewhere deep within Ragnar. He allowed himself to fall forward and at the last second wrapped his arms around the Grimskull's legs. With a heave he toppled Strybjorn over. There was a loud crack as his foe's head hit one of the rocks protruding from the soft turf. Ragnar allowed himself a triumphant snarl and crawled forward to straddle Strybjorn's body. He took his own wooden baton and placed it across the Grimskull's windpipe and pushed forward, fully intending to stop off the flow of air, and choke his foe to death. The crowd's cheering filled his ears; obviously they did not understand his intention.

Suddenly a cold, armoured hand grasped Ragnar's neck and lifted him off Strybjorn. Ragnar lashed out with the baton but it hit the hard carapace of Hakon's armour and broke. The sergeant looked down at him.

'Some unorthodox knife work there, by both of you. Still, at least you were fighting as if you meant it.'

He set Ragnar down on the ground and glanced over at Strybjorn. The Grimskull coughed, spluttered and glared over at Ragnar with eyes full of hatred. 'I won,' he gasped.

'No, you didn't,' Hakon said. 'Your last stroke would have disembowelled Ragnar, sure, but if he had been using a real knife instead of these curved bits of wood his last blow would have pierced your eye and gone into your brain.'

Ragnar allowed himself a grin of triumph. The cold clear mountain air tasted sweet with victory. He even managed to ignore the pain in his ribs. 'I still would have killed him with my return,' Strybjorn said sullenly.

'Maybe you would have at that,' Hakon said. 'You're fierce enough.'

He turned to the crowd and pointed at Kjel and one of the newcomers Ragnar did not recognise. 'You two! Come on! We don't have all day.'

Ragnar glared over at Strybjorn once more, knowing that he would have killed the Grimskull for sure, if Hakon had not intervened.

RAGNAR FELT HIS breath coming in gasps. The mountain air suddenly did not seem thick enough to sustain him. The early morning chill bit into his flesh. His heartbeat sounded loud in his ears. Sweat ran down his brow and stung his eyes. His long black hair was plastered to his forehead. His legs felt like jelly. The slope before him seemed endless.

'Come on!' Sergeant Hakon yelled. 'You can do better than this. This is just one little hillock.'

Kjel came abreast of Ragnar and managed a sickly grin. 'Easy for him to say. We're not all half goat and half wolf,' he panted.

'Save your breath for running,' Ragnar gasped out. 'Remember, last one to the top has to do it all again.'

'I'd better leave you behind then,' Kjel said and loped ahead, his long stride covering the broken ground swiftly. Ragnar mustered the last of his strength and charged on, thinking that Kjel had been right. The sergeant had made it look easy. He had started after them, but even in his heavy armour had swiftly overtaken the lightly clad aspirants. He had reached the top of the hill while they were only half way up and now he stood there, looking utterly unwearied and bellowing at them. What was his secret, Ragnar wondered.

'Come on! Run!' shouted Hakon. Ragnar risked a glance over his shoulder. A long way below them, in the low valley, he could see Russvik. It looked tiny from this height. They had covered an enormous distance so far. Seeing the small figures of his fellows strung out behind, he was grateful to realise that at least he was not last. And he'd better make sure that he stayed that way.

On shaky legs he stumbled wearily on towards the brow of the hill.

'WHO AMONG YOU can hunt?' Sergeant Hakon asked. About half a dozen weary voices answered in the affirmative. They were all tired. For the past week it seemed they had done nothing but hard physical exercise. They had run up to the top of the hills overlooking the camp so often that Ragnar felt as if he could do it in his sleep. They had chopped wood. They had run up the hill carrying a log of the wood they had chopped. Those who had not been fast enough for Hakon's liking were made to do it again and again until they collapsed with exhaustion.

They had done endless exercises which had contorted their bodies and pushed their physical endurance to the limits, leaving them gasping for breath on the cold ground as their muscles spasmed and convulsed. They had drilled with spear and dagger. They had been shown how to fight with the axes they used for chopping wood. They had thrown spears at straw men.

The bits that had involved fighting or practising to fight had been almost enjoyable, Ragnar thought, and he had excelled at them. He had always been chosen as the best in his group of five to face the best of the other Claws. It was something that seemed to rankle Strybjorn and Sven but there was nothing they could do about it. He had consistently bested them in practice. With weapons he was better than either. At wrestling they had repaid him for the knocks he had given them with the blunted weapons. Both of them were strong and quick and cruel.

Ragnar hoped that soon they would start practising with real edged weapons. Then there would be an accident and Strybjorn Grimskull would go to greet his ancestors knowing that Ragnar had sent him there.

'Surely more of you than that know how to hunt?' Hakon said with a sneer. The aspirants all looked at each other warily. They had learned not to make claims to the sergeant. It usually ended up with extra duties or a severe drubbing when their level of competence did not reach Hakon's exalted expectations.

'Well, if none of you know how to hunt, I suppose we will have to teach you. It's the only way you're ever going to see meat again.'

THE LITTLE BAND of hunters moved in single file up the long rocky path. Ragnar turned and looked back the way they had come. The chill wind whipped his long black hair around his face. The clouds scurrying across the sky seemed somehow closer than ever. At least, though, they were white and intermittent, not dark and heavy with the threat of rain. He sniffed the air and caught the scent of pine. Strangest of all to him was the absence of the salty sea tang he had known all his life.

Far below them, Russvik was visible as a tiny collection of huts surrounded by its wooden parapet and the deep ditch. All around them massive peaks loomed skywards. He was breathing hard. They all were. His thighs felt like jelly from the prolonged effort of climbing the steep slope. His knees felt weak. His face was flushed. It was a relief to see that none of the others looked any better.

All that running up and down the nearer hills started to make sense now. Ragnar doubted that any of them could have made it to this height without rest if they had not been prepared for it by the training. It was exhilarating though. They had come further in the past day than it had been possible to walk without going into the sea on Ragnar's home island, and they had barely seen a tiny fraction of this vast land. It seemed to go on forever. The pillars of the peaks seemed to support the dome of a sky that lay infinitely far above them. The clouds were greyish-white and pregnant with the threat of snow. Strange trees covered the hills. They had needles instead of leaves and cones of wood littered the ground beneath them. They had been taught that if those cones were open it was most likely going to rain. If they were closed the weather might stay fine. It was another part of the strange lore they had been taught in Russvik. Large birds nested in those trees. Sven had already suggested foraging up there for eggs but the others had wanted to push on, to find something bigger, a deer or a wild goat that they could take back and show off to the other Claws.

This was the first time Ragnar's Claw had been dispatched to hunt. It was considered an honour to be trusted beyond sight of Russvik on their own, which in itself was galling, a cutting insult to the pride of the fierce young warriors. None had dared to complain to Sergeant Hakon that they were being treated like children. Now, they were confident of their new found skills. They had spent many days being taught basic survival techniques. How to survive in the howling Asaheim blizzards. How to find their way by the stars alone. Ragnar had found the last quite easy, being used as he was to travelling at sea. Granted, the stars here in Asaheim were slightly different, but the constellations were the same. They had been taught how to light fires quickly and efficiently. How to make lean-tos from branches, to give them at least some shelter from the harsh elements. They had been shown the basics of tracking in the wilds. It was not all that difficult to master. They now knew to look for the places the beasts came to drink, and to keep their eyes open for tracks. They knew how to build snares for rabbits and hares and other small animals. Those who had never learned were taught how to gut an animal, strip off the pelt, slit the belly and let the entrails pour out. Once again Ragnar, who had been gutting fish all his life, found it easy.

Now, armed with their spears and shields and daggers, they had been sent out into the wilds. It was as simple as that. They were to go and they were not to come back until they had hunted fresh food to eat, or lost a warrior trying. It seemed that training to be a Wolf consisted of being thrown into the water, and then thrashing about until you learned to swim. To Ragnar, it seemed that the attitude of Hakon and the others back in Russvik was that there were plenty more initiates where they came from. It was Ragnar's duty to prove himself, and he realised that no one else would look after him now.

In fact, in some ways Ragnar was glad to be out from under the watching eye of Hakon. He was happy that the Claw had been sent out on its own. He knew that before this trip was over there was every chance that Strybjorn would have a fatal accident. Certainly he would if Ragnar had anything to do with it. He turned and looked back at the Grimskull and noticed without much surprise that Strybjorn was looking at him. Ragnar shivered a little meeting his enemy's burning gaze. It was all too possible that the Grimskull was thinking exactly the same about him. With a dull grunt, Ragnar realised that he was going to have to be careful out here in the wilderness. He could be the one who might fall from one of the cliff-side paths or find himself in the path of an avalanche if he did not watch out. Right now, though, he was in charge. Sergeant Hakon had decided that Ragnar was the one best suited to giving orders to the Claw. So far there had been not problems from Kjel or Henk. Only Sven and Strybjorn had grumbled.

Pausing in his stride, Ragnar looked up at the sky. The red sun was starting to sink in the west. The sky there on the far horizon was the colour of blood, crimson light filtering through the cloud canopy to give the mountains a distinctly sinister look. It seemed to Ragnar all too possible that this place could be the haunt of trolls or other more hideous and savage beasts. Tales of a creature called the *wulfen* had been rife in the camp over the past few days. No one was exactly sure who had started telling the horror stories, but if there was any truth in the tales of dismemberment and grisly death, then the wulfen was a beast to be feared indeed. Ragnar suspected that the scaremongering was probably the work of Hakon.

This dread creature was said to be a monster, part man and part wolf, and wholly fierce. Near invulnerable to normal weapons, the tales claimed. The stories spoke of a wulfen-daemon which crept into Russvik and carried off aspirants. No one was sure whether this was the case or not, although everyone knew that a few days ago an aspirant called Loka had vanished while on sentry duty. No one was sure whether he had simply deserted his post. It was possible that he had been spirited away by trolls or evil sorcerers. But somehow, tales of the wulfen had gone around. Hakon and the other leaders had armed themselves and gone off, following a trail that seemingly only they with their heightened senses could discern. If they had found anything they had not said. Ragnar guessed from the set of their shoulders and the grim expressions on their faces when they returned that they had not found anything. Their hunt had been in vain.

Now, in the gathering gloom, with such tales crowding in on his tired mind, Ragnar tried not to think of what monsters might lie in wait for them in this mighty mountain range. A few miles back they had passed a cave. It could have provided them with shelter for the evening but as if by common consent the whole Claw had walked past it without saying a word. None of them wanted to encounter what might already be sheltered in the cave. Chances were that there would be nothing, but who knew? There might be a troll, a wizard, a bear or a wulfen. Not even Sven or Strybjorn seemed inclined to go and find out.

Ragnar was glad they had collected firewood earlier. Eventually, with dusk well advanced, he chose a likely site to make camp. Nearby, a small stream tinkled down the slope, bringing them water. It ran down to the boulder-strewn shingle shore of a small lake at the far end of the clearing. The still, black waters looked as deep as the ocean, and Ragnar wondered whether it would yield fish for them to eat. For tonight, though, they would make do with what provisions they had, as night was drawing swiftly on. Ragnar ordered Kjel and Henk to begin to build the fire while Strybjorn and Sven collected branches to build a makeshift shelter for the night as they had been taught at Russvik. He himself wandered down to the stream and began to collect water. He wanted to take the opportunity to be apart from the others for a little while, and also simply to make time to study their surroundings.

Even in the gathering twilight, as he surveyed the wild hills, the rocky canyons and sweeping forests which stretched away for countless leagues in every direction, Ragnar felt certain that if it were not for the beasts and monsters that were said to haunt this savage land, a man could be happy here. He nodded silent approval at his own thoughts. Here, on the mountainside, there was space enough for a freeholding, there was water and there was wood. From what the others had said, such hills would make good grazing for sheep or goats. A man could raise a family here, live in peace. Perhaps even find a degree of contentment, an escape from hatred and strife. With that, Ragnar's thoughts returned to Ana, and he felt the now familiar sadness welling within his soul. Looking back up the slope at Strybjorn he felt sorrow turn to bitter hate. Ragnar was going to make the Grimskull pay. That was the one certainty in his life now.

Snarling, Ragnar plunged his waterskin into the stream angrily, almost as if it were the Grimskull's head, which he intended to keep beneath the surface until the flow of silvery bubbles stopped once and for all. As he forced the waterskin into the icy stream Ragnar gasped at the biting cold. The water was so chill it seemed to burn him to the bone. Within seconds his hands were numb. Forcing himself to endure the pain, Ragnar pulled the dripping sack up, and scowled at the distant peaks. This was meltwater, Ragnar realised, flowing from the snows of the mountains. It was colder by far than the stuff found in even the deepest wells of the islands.

Such thoughts abruptly reminded him that he was a long way from home. Not that he had a home to go back to.

Ragnar's harsh laughter echoed amongst the darkening shadows.

THE FIRE WAS BUILT. The shadows gathered around the lean-to. Strybjorn and Sven had put together a very serviceable shelter from the evergreen branches which they had ripped from the towering trees around the clearing. The cooking pot was filled with bubbling oatmeal, the only food they carried with them. Each had a sack of the stuff and some salt. It was not exactly appetising but it would be filling, once it had been ladled out into the wooden bowls which they carried in their packs.

Ragnar glanced around the fire, seeing the faces of his companions altered strangely by the flickering underlight. It changed the angles of their faces, made them seem subtly different. So did the setting. In the few days they had been in Russvik, Ragnar had become used to the camp. Even with its privations and hardships, it had somehow become the place he was used to associating with his new-found companions. Now they were somewhere else, yet another strange and different place and in some way, this changed them in his mind to different people. To strangers.

The full moon had emerged bright and welcoming. The wolf-face was visible on its surface, a great patch of shadow roughly the shape of a snarling wolf's head. It was said that Russ himself had put his pet wolf Greymane there to watch over his world until his return. As if in answer to the sight, somewhere in the distance came a terrifying howling, a sound of unsurpassable loneliness and hunger. All of the Claw looked at each other.

'It's only a wolf,' Kjel said with what was clearly meant to be an encouraging grin. It would have been a lot more convincing had the youth's face not seemed so pale in the moonlight. 'Russ knows I've heard enough of them. They used to worry our sheep something fierce in the valleys.'

'I'll bet that's not the only thing that worried your bloody sheep,' said Sven nastily.

'What do you mean by that?'

Before Sven could reply the wolf's howl was answered from the other side of the valley. The long wailing note echoed over the distance and drove thoughts of anything else from Ragnar's mind. It seemed to be the signal for a whole chorus of howls. From every peak, or so it seemed, huge wolves bayed at the moon.

'A pack is out hunting,' Kjel said.

'You don't say,' Strybjorn said.

'I would never had bloody guessed,' added Sven.

'That's enough,' Ragnar said testily.

'Don't worry,' Kjel said. 'Wolves rarely attack armed men. They won't usually come near a fire either. Unless they're starving or desperate.'

'I don't know about them,' Sven said, 'but, by the Ice Bear's blessed right buttock, I'm certainly bloody starving. If they come near me, I'll skin and eat them!'

'So what else is new?' Ragnar said. All the same, he had to agree with Sven. 'Henk, serve up the gruel.'

'Surely,' agreed the youngest aspirant, leaning forward and beginning to ladle the porridge into their outstretched bowls.

'In Russ's name, what I wouldn't give for a nice bit of fish,' said Sven.

'Or chicken,' said Strybjorn.

'Or mutton,' Kjel said.

The sound of the baying increased.

'It seems like the wolves agree with you,' Ragnar said. No one laughed.

IT WAS LATE. The sound of the wolves had receded into the distance. Perhaps they had found other prey, Ragnar thought. Or perhaps they were merely silently and stealthily approaching. From the makeshift shelters on the far side of the fire came the sound of snoring. It was loud and wheezing, a combination of a blacksmith's bellows and a hacksaw rasping on a log. It was almost enough to drive all thoughts of sleep from Ragnar's mind.

Ragnar stared outward away from the fire, as Hakon had taught them. No sense in ruining your night vision when you were on watch. He clutched his spear firmly in his hands, wondering what he would do if the wolves or some vile monster of the dark attacked. There was a strange eerie quality to this mountain night quite unlike anything he had known back home.

Perhaps it was the sense of vastness and emptiness of the mountains which somehow suggested there was a place out here for anything no matter how inhuman or evil to hide. Back on the island, Ragnar had felt it was possible to know virtually everything about the rocky outcrop his tribe had lived and died on. As boys, when they had gone camping, they were never far from the village, and had inevitably roamed across land which they had seen or played on a hundred times before. Here among the mountains, Ragnar felt that a man might wander for a hundred lifetimes and still not see everything. It was a frightening and inspiring thought.

Ragnar wondered, though, at how quickly he had adapted. Despite the strange and alien nature of the place, he recognised that he had swiftly become used to living in Russvik, to the faces of his new companions, to the life of training and harsh discipline. There were times now when his life on the islands already seemed like a dream, and all the people he had once known little more than phantoms. Had he really once strode the decks of the *Spear of Russ* during a storm? Had he once hauled nets full of fish from the sea? Had he watched orca harpooned and sea dragons slaughtered?

Intellectually he knew he had. In his heart, though, it was sometimes hard to feel it as real anymore. What was he doing here sitting on a mountainside in the dark, gazing into the gloom? He had no proper idea. He had no real notion why he had been chosen either. He had simply lived while others had died or been carried away into slavery.

That thought brought raw emotions screaming to his mind once more. He suddenly remembered the dead and the dying and the girl that might have been Ana being carried off by the Grimskull fleet. The knowledge that one of those responsible was lying snoring not twenty strides away made him want to shout with rage or take his spear and plunge it into Strybjorn's belly. He could almost picture doing it, almost feel the glow of satisfaction he would get as he bore down with all his weight on the worn shaft and drove the bright point of hardened steel home in soft and yielding flesh. Ragnar's lips curled into a snarl, and he was so tempted to get up and do it there and then – when he heard the soft padding of feet coming towards him. Instinctively he brought his spear up into the ready position, but a glance told him that the approaching shadow was only Kjel.

Kjel squatted down beside him. 'May as well end your watch,' he said. 'I can't get any sleep right now anyway with that pair snoring like thunder.'

'You sure?' Ragnar asked. 'You're not too tired?'

'Maybe if I get tired enough I'll be able to sleep later.'

Ragnar nodded but did not move. He was not tired himself and he felt like talking. He felt certain that unless they shouted neither he nor Kjel would wake the sleepers.

'This is a strange place,' he said eventually.

'This valley or these mountains?'

'This land. I have never seen anything quite like it. Any one of these mountains seems larger than the island on which I grew up.'

'They probably are, in a way. Or they might well be the same size at least.'

'What do you mean?'

'I've heard it said that the islands were once mountains that have been swallowed by the sea so that only their tips now stand above the waters.'

'That is a strange story.'

'It is part of an old legend. It is said that in the days before the coming of Russ there were many more lands, each as large as Asaheim, but then the Flood came and it rained for a hundred years and all the lands save Asaheim were drowned. It's said that sea daemons live among the ruins of drowned cities, each as large as an island.'

'Do you believe that, Kjel?'

'Why not? It may be true. On the other hand it may not. My people are not great seafarers. They live among the valleys beneath the great glaciers and spent their days making war and hunting.'

'I have heard the only time the people of the glacier take a ship out of sight of land is to visit the islands of the Iron Masters.'

'That is more or less true. Why would anyone want to sail out of sight of land anyway? The sea daemons would surely take them.'

'I have also heard that the people of the glacier are well… cannibals.'

Kjel laughed. 'Really? I had always heard it was the islanders that ate each other. Not enough food on those small islands.'

'There's always fish and orca meat,' Ragnar spat. He was angry at being accused of cannibalism. On the other hand, he had more or less accused Kjel of the same thing so what right had he to be offended? In the darkness, he grinned at the irony of their legends. At their ignorance.

'You were right about this valley though,' Kjel said. 'There is a bad feeling about it.'

'What do you mean?'

'I don't know. Something about it makes my flesh crawl. It's like there's something out there, watching us.'

'Wolves?'

'Maybe. Maybe trolls or nightgangers.'

Ragnar shivered. 'Have you ever seen nightgangers?'

'No, but I knew a man once who had. Twisted evil things they were, with glowing skin. They dwell in the old places beneath the earth, so it is said, and emerge to feast on human flesh. It is also said that they worship the dark ones of Chaos.'

'I've never heard of such things. We should not talk of them.' Ragnar made a protective gesture of warding against evil.

'You live on the islands. The sea is clean of such filth.'

Ragnar nodded. Despite the shiver of fear Kjel's words had caused he stretched and yawned. He was suddenly tired.

HE CAST HIMSELF down by the fire and fell into a haunted sleep. He dreamed of many strange and terrible things. He dreamed of the blind worms that swarmed on the ocean's bottom and gnawed at the roots of islands. He dreamed of twisted night-gangers, and monstrous wolves. He dreamed of a huge beast in the shape of a man but with the head of a wolf. The mere sight of it in his dream snapped him to consciousness and he sat up suddenly, glaring around with haunted eyes and a hammering heart.

Suddenly fear twisted his gut, for it seemed to him that there, just outside the firelight stood the creature of which he had just been dreaming. He shook his head to clear it, hoping that what he was looking at was just some simple after-image from his dream but it was not. It still stood out there, in the dark, and it was as real as Ragnar himself.

Ragnar froze for a moment and studied it. No. It was not exactly like the thing in his dream. It did not have the wolf-like head. Instead he could see that its body was monstrous and misshapen. Huge horned spikes protruded from its flesh, and added a jagged, spiky quality to the silhouette. Its head was massive, with a huge jaw and enormous protruding bat-like ears. Its eyes glowed with an eerie greenish light. Slowly it dawned on Ragnar that he was probably looking at a troll. A creature of the most evil and horrifying tales. And most likely a hungry troll, for it was slowly advancing towards the firelight.

Where was Kjel, Ragnar wondered, or whoever in Russ's name was supposed to be on guard? Not that it mattered much anyway. He was going to have to do something himself. Stealthily he reached out for his spear and shield, praying softly to Russ that the troll did not notice his movements.

He let out a slow sigh of relief once he had his weapons nestled within his fist, and rose quietly into a fighting crouch. In the firelight, he could see that the others still slept. Strybjorn and Sven snored loudly. Kjel lay by the fire. Henk sat facing out into the darkness, but the way his head lay down against his chest told Ragnar that the boy was asleep.

He realised that it was going to be up to him to distract the creature while his companions made ready. And he realised that he was going to have to do it soon. But hold, part of his mind whispered, perhaps if he waited the creature might take Strybjorn and work his vengeance for him. Ragnar's lips twisted in a sick grin. This was a good thought, part of his mind whispered to him.

No, he told himself. That was not the way to do this. He wanted to kill his foe himself, not slay the Grimskull scum by an act of treachery. And, anyway, there was no guarantee that the troll would take Strybjorn. It might take one of the others, and he had to admit that they were fast becoming his friends.

The monster was almost at the fire, and Ragnar knew that the time for action had come. 'Awake!' he bellowed. 'Awake! A troll is upon us!'

As he shouted he sprang to his feet, and launched himself forward in the direction of the troll. At close range, by the light of the fire he could see it better. He could make out the scaly, leathery lizard-like skin and the slime that dripped from it, glistening in the moonlight. The creature gave the impression of having recently been wet, as if it had just come from the nearby lake.

Ragnar closed the range quickly. The thing was even bigger and more terrifying close up. It was nearly twice as tall as Ragnar and much, much heavier. Its chest was as muscled as that of the biggest bear, and its webbed fingered hands were almost as large as his shield. Each finger ended in a dagger-sized talon. It opened its mouth and let out an ear-piercing bellow. Ragnar could see that its mouth was lined with row upon row of huge sharp teeth. He lashed out with his spear, hoping to pierce one of the large, bowl-like eyes, but the creature turned its head and Ragnar's blade merely grazed its cheek. To Ragnar's horror, even as he watched, the leathery skin began to knit itself back together with a hideous sucking sound. This does not look good, he thought.

The troll struck back at him. Ragnar ducked beneath a blow that would have torn his head off had it connected and stabbed forward at the thing's groin. He was rewarded with an eerie high-pitched screech that almost deafened him. The thing retaliated with another powerful blow. Ragnar raised his shield, angling it in an effort to deflect at least part of the impact. He guessed he was successful but still the force of the blow sent him tumbling backwards. He landed beside the fire and smelled the stink of burning hair as part of his black mane caught alight. The impact of the blow left him feeling dazed and weak but he pulled himself upright and glanced around to see what the others were doing.

All of them were awake now and had grabbed their weapons and shields. Even as Ragnar watched, Kjel drew back his spear and cast it. It flew straight and true, directly into one of the creature's huge eyes. Ragnar's heart leapt. That was a killing cast, if ever he had seen one. He waited for the troll to keel over and die, but it did no such thing. Instead, it reached up and grabbed the spear. Its clumsy attempt to pull the thing clear merely broke the shaft and left the blade embedded in its eyeball. Now it hissed in anger, like a giant serpent. The sound was petrifying.

Strybjorn and Sven leapt forward, spears stabbing. The keen iron blades bit into the troll's leathery hide. Greenish blood flowed forth for a moment but yet again the wounds began to heal unnaturally quickly. The troll reached forward and grabbed Sven with its massive hand. Ragnar could see blood flowing from where the talons had pierced Sven's flesh but Sven showed no sign of pain.

'Take this, you hell-spawned troll dog!' he shouted and brought his spear round and down into the tendons of the troll's hand. It bellowed in pain and dropped him. For a brief, terrible moment Ragnar feared that Sven was about to be trampled beneath the monster's huge feet but he managed to roll to one side. Strybjorn meanwhile had sprung forward and took the thing clean in the chest. His spear passed upwards under its ribs and buried itself deep in the chest cavity where a man's heart would have been. Other than screaming yet louder the troll gave no sign of toppling over. Could nothing stop this thing, Ragnar wondered? He began to know fear.

Then he noticed something else. Strange fumes were wafting out from the area of the creature's pierced stomach and the shaft of Strybjorn's spear had started to melt away. Of course, Ragnar remembered, in all the tales the digestive juices of trolls were supposed to be so acidic that they could eat through solid stone. Things were going from bad to worse. With a backhanded swipe, the monstrous beast sent Strybjorn tumbling through the air to crash to the ground almost ten strides away. That had to hurt, he thought. Under normal circumstances he would have been exultant over the Grimskull's possible demise but he realised that here and now they needed every single warrior. So far they had not even succeeded in slowing the monster down.

'We need to use fire!' Henk shouted.

'What?'

'We need to use fire. That's how I killed the troll last time. I managed to lure it into the blazing croft. Its wounds won't close if they are caused by fire.'

Slowly Henk's words pierced Ragnar's brain. That made sense. Fire was mankind's best defence against many of the horrors of the dark and he had often heard old Imogrim's tale of how the men of Jarl Kraki had driven off one of the monsters with flaming torches and arrows. He reached down and grabbed a brand from the fire, swinging it around his head to fan the flames. As the brand blazed up Ragnar returned to the fray, with Henk right by his side. Henk too bore a firebrand.

The troll was stooped down now, reaching for the recumbent Sven who, scrabbling desperately for a foothold in the stony soil, just kept the hideous monster at bay by jabbing frenziedly at its one remaining good eye with his spear. Ragnar raced up and waved the brand in the troll's face. It turned towards him with an almighty roar. Ragnar couldn't help but notice as its stagnant breath washed over him that it smelled like rotting fish. The stench made him gag. He lashed out with his firebrand and contacted flesh. It sizzled and burned and blackened but did not heal. Praise be to Russ, thought Ragnar, Henk had been right.

A blur of fire from the corner of his eye told Ragnar that Kjel had joined the fray. He could see the Falconer wielded a blazing bit of wood in each hand. Wherever he touched trollflesh, the thing burned and did not heal. The troll had turned now like a beast at bay. The brands confused it, and it was not helped by the blindness of one eye. Henk gave a shout of triumph and leapt forward to smite the monster across the face, leaving a great black weal.

'Take this, beast,' he cried and laughed victoriously. The troll's answering bellow drowned out his voice. It reached down and picked Henk up. Its talons bit into his flesh, severing the arm that held the torch. It pushed the boy's head into its enormous cavern-like mouth and then bit down. Blood gouted and Henk's scream ended as his head was severed and swallowed whole.

Ragnar stood for a moment amazed with shock. He could not quite believe that Henk was dead. One moment the youth had been there, alive and fighting. Now he was gone. Death had reached out and decapitated him. The terrible realisation filled Ragnar that the same thing could easily happen to him, that the troll, though wounded, was still a creature of vast power, and might quickly slay them all. It was obvious that the same thought had occurred to every other member of the Claw for they stood frozen, uncertain of what to do. The urge to turn and flee filled Ragnar but he knew that if he did so, the others would run as well, and that Henk's death would go unavenged. Worse yet, it was quite possible that the troll would overtake them and kill them as they fled. In a second of decision, Ragnar realised that, scared though he was, he was not going to run.

'Come on, you dogs!' he roared. 'Best die with your wounds to the fore, if you're going to die at all.'

The others responded to his cry. Sven clambered to his feet and began to stab the troll. Kjel closed in with his torch while Ragnar came on from the other side. Strybjorn had risen to his feet, and he too had acquired a firebrand. Surrounded on all sides by the hated flames, dazed and dazzled and in pain from its wounded eye, the troll turned at bay and fled, following the stream, still clutching Henk's headless corpse in its huge paw. Blood splashed into the icy waters, black in the stark moonlight.

Ragnar and the others followed it over the broken ground, brands blazing brighter as the air whipped past. It was a swift but vain pursuit. For all its vast size and lumbering appearance the troll's stride was much longer than theirs. It reached the waters of the lake and plunged in, leaving a trail of foam in its wake. Ragnar and the others halted at the water's edge and watched as it waded slowly out into the deep. At last its head vanished beneath the surface and it was gone.

'Do you think it drowned?' Strybjorn asked.

'No.' Kjel replied. 'Trolls can live beneath the water. Its lair is probably down there.'

'Can we swim out and kill it?' Sven asked.

'How?' Ragnar said. 'Torches won't burn underwater.'

'But it's got bloody Henk,' Sven replied.

'Henk is *dead*. And there's nothing we can do here now.'

Still they stood by the water's edge and watched until the sun came up. The troll did not reappear.

'What now?' asked Kjel.

'We go back to Russvik and recount what happened,' said Ragnar. He was not looking forward to that. After all, he was the leader of the Claw and Henk had been his responsibility.

All of them exchanged looks. Ragnar felt as if they should be accusing him but he saw nothing but sympathy in all of their eyes, even Strybjorn's. It was as if fighting on the same side in the battle with the troll had created some sort of bond between them. Ragnar pushed the thought aside. There would be a truce until they got back to the camp. Every warrior would be needed until then, for who knew what other horrors might emerge from the surrounding hills? Once they got back, though, it would be every man for himself, Ragnar decided. Particularly where Strybjorn was concerned. The Grimskull could keep his sympathy, Ragnar thought.

'You are certain that is what happened?' Hakon asked. Ragnar nodded. The sergeant looked at him appraisingly.

He made Ragnar repeat his description of the incident all but word for word, then was silent for a long moment. Ragnar stared off over the sergeant's shoulder, remembering the march back to Russvik. It had not been a pleasant one. All the time he had wondered about the fate of Henk. He had been filled with the uncomfortable thought that his friend's doom might so easily have been his own. Henk had simply been in the wrong place at the wrong time. With chill certainty, Ragnar knew that he could just as easily have been the one taken.

A glance at the scared and weary faces of his companions told him that the same thought had occurred to them all.

During the long march back to the camp, exhausted, they had all started at the distant howling of the wolves. Jumping at shadows, they had expected to fight and die then, but nothing had happened. Nothing except that the eerie wailing of the beasts seemed to shiver its way into their very bones and echo there like a grating voice of doom. Ragnar was sure it would echo through his dreams from this night forth, and that he would see there the troll and the wolves and the dead Henk all inextricably linked. He himself felt responsible for the lad's death and had said as much to Hakon when the sergeant had begun his interrogation. Hakon had merely looked impassive, neither approving nor disapproving, and let him continue to talk. Ragnar was conscious of the weight of his own failure and there were times when it seemed to him that he could see Henk's fresh young face looking at him accusingly. It was almost as bad as the sensation he had felt after the destruction of his village. He wondered how this could be – after all, he had barely known Henk, while he had known his clan all his life. Part of him suspected that he already knew the answer though. Among the Thunderfists he had been a follower, expected only to fight and die for his people. With his Claw, out alone in the wilds of Fenris, he had been a leader. He was responsible for the fate of the Wolfclaw he led. Perhaps that was what it was like being a jarl or a ship's captain. He was not sure he entirely enjoyed the situation, and for the first time in his life Ragnar began to get the inkling that rank and glory might not be entirely an unalloyed benefit.

'What are you going to do now?' Ragnar asked. 'Hunt the troll down?'

'Why would we do that?'

'Because it killed one of our people.'

'If one of our people was weak enough to allow himself to be killed it has done us a favour.'

'I don't think that is so.'

'No one asked for your opinion.'

'Are we finished here?' Ragnar asked in disgust. Hakon nodded. Suddenly feeling empty and drained, Ragnar rose from the chair and turned to go.

'Ragnar!'

He turned to glare at the sergeant and was surprised to see something like sympathy written on Hakon's stern features.

'Yes, sergeant?'

'It's never easy to lose a man. Believe me, I know.'

Ragnar nodded and left the hall.

EIGHT
TRIALS

'MORE TRACKS,' Ragnar said, shaking his head. He looked around the bleak landscape for any signs of ambushers. The woods about them seemed empty. The pine trees sloped away below. Crags blocked the way to the right. There was plenty of cover but nothing stirred. He felt no sense of impending danger. He wiped the sweat from his forehead, and tugged his hair from his eyes. The great stag had led them a merry chase, and they were a long way from the path that led back to Russvik.

'That's the fifth set this week,' Kjel said. He grinned. 'Maybe we're being scouted out.'

'Maybe,' Ragnar said. He looked down at the steaming corpse of the dead deer. Strybjorn had finished gutting it while Ragnar and Kjel inspected these new tracks. 'Try and be a bit more careful with the knife, Grimskull,' he added.

Strybjorn glared back at him. 'If you think you could do better, last of the Thunderfists, why don't you draw your dagger and come over here? Maybe I'll show you how to gut something more than a deer.'

Ragnar's hand went to the hilt of his dagger. Hot hatred filled him. Kjel, seeing what was happening, was between them automatically. Sven looked on, waiting to see what would happen.

111

'That's enough, both of you,' Kjel said. 'There's few enough of us now that Henk's gone. We don't need to lose another man. Not if there are others about and we have to fight our way back. And Strybjorn, remember, Hakon put Ragnar in charge.'

'Aye and much good it's done us,' muttered the Grimskull dangerously. Ragnar began to move forward but Kjel pushed him back. He noticed the imperceptible shake of the Falconer's head. Slowly his anger receded. Kjel's words were as much a reminder for him as for Strybjorn. It would not do for another of his warriors to be lost while he was leader, particularly not if he killed him. He found the thought almost funny, and the tension drained out of him. He contented himself with grinning maniacally at the Grimskull.

Sven and Strybjorn were already tying the corpse to the pole on which they would carry it back to Russvik. Ragnar did not find the sight of the red dripping meat as disturbing as he once had. He was used to it now, having hunted and gutted dozens of the magnificent creatures. Anyway, a dead stag was hardly the problem. The problem was these tracks.

Who did they belong to? Where were they coming from? They certainly appeared to be the tracks of something at least man-like, but having never seen the tracks of the wulfen or even nightgangers, Ragnar was prepared to be cautious. He could try and follow the tracks, and perhaps wander into an ambush. Most likely following the tracks would be a useless exercise. The fresh winter snows which drifted in blizzards on the higher ground would cover them before they got anywhere near the source and their prey would vanish like a wulfen in the night. Maybe very like a wulfen, Ragnar thought.

It seemed as if the rumours and legends about Asaheim were wrong though. Banishing thoughts of evil creatures tracking them for a moment, Ragnar could see that tracks were tracks, and that people of one sort or another probably did live here. These tracks did not belong to any of the aspirants at Russvik, that much was plain. There must be some other folk among the mountains. Ragnar felt that he did not need to ask himself whether they would be hostile or not. On the surface of Fenris it seemed as though the natural state of affairs was that all people were rivals and enemies. Thus had it always been. Thus would it always be. Russ had ordained it so long ago in order to keep his people strong.

That the track-makers would be warriors, Ragnar did not doubt. He doubted that they would be a match for the aspirants in strength of arms. Numbers though might be something else. He had learned enough tracking skills in the past few months to be able to take a good guess at how many had been in the group that passed near here: at least a dozen. The question now was whether the tracks which the others from Russvik had found belonged to this same dozen, or to another group of strangers. Ragnar resolved that he would report the matter to Hakon when he returned. There did not seem very much else he could do right now.

RAGNAR TRUDGED down the slope towards Russvik. Down below he could see the lights of the lanterns glittering in the long halls. He could see the flicker of sparks emerging from the chimney holes in the roof of the great hall where it bulked massive in the gloom. Unfamiliar stars filled the sky. The hooting of night birds filled the air. He could smell wood smoke and the loamy smells of the oncoming night. As always it seemed to him that as the light failed his other senses grew stronger to compensate. Somewhere in the distance a wolf howled.

He turned to look back over his shoulders to make sure that Sven and Strybjorn were still there. He could make out their shadowy outlines in the gloom, the dead deer still carried between them. Looking ahead he could see Kjel loping along in the dark, scouting the way. He was going to lose no more warriors from his Claw if he could help it. Not that it seemed all that likely now. In the months that had passed since Henk's death, his companions had grown nothing but harder and tougher. The regime of constant training and exercise had filled them out, made them stronger and fitter and faster than any islander lads Ragnar had ever known. He himself felt twice as fit as he had when he came here and maybe ten times as competent.

He sighed reflectively. He had learned so much in the intervening months it staggered him. He could identify all the edible flora and fauna in the surrounding hills. He knew how to built shelters and fires. He could even make small igloos from the winter snows in which to huddle, protected from the ice-storms which would otherwise surely freeze the skin from his bones. He knew how to treat wounds and frostbite. He had learned to fight with his hands and was as proficient now in unarmed combat as Sven or Strybjorn. He had always been good with a spear or harpoon but now he doubted there was any man in his old village who could have matched his present skill, not even the master harpooners.

It had not been easy. Half of the aspirants were dead now. Of the two score from the time of his arrival only about twenty were still alive. Some had fallen from the cliffs on which they practised climbing. Some had vanished while out hunting, taken by wulfen or trolls or by the wolves. Two had been killed during weapons practice with the axe or spears. One had been executed by Sergeant Hakon for some unmentionable crime.

Of course, new recruits had arrived, fresh-faced and full of wonder and fear. Ragnar wondered at his own feelings of superiority to these newcomers. The few months since his choosing might as well have been a lifetime. There seemed to be a gulf of age between him and the newcomers greater than that which had existed between Wolfbrother and gnarled ancient back in his home village. He wondered where those who had been here when he arrived had gone. Many of them had vanished, carried away to some unknown destination by skyship. Only Sergeant Hakon knew where they went exactly, and no one had ever dared ask him.

During this time, Ragnar had somehow mostly managed to hold his hatred of Strybjorn in abeyance. It had not vanished, it was simply waiting for an opportune killing time. And in a strange way, while Strybjorn yet lived, and Ragnar's hatred burned cold within him, he had a tenuous link to his old life on the island. Ragnar did not want Strybjorn to die while part of his Claw. He was prepared to spare him now until he was no longer part of Ragnar's responsibilities.

'Let's hurry it up,' he said. 'There are hungry mouths to feed back in Russvik.'

'Try not to eat it all before we get there, Sven,' shouted Kjel. Ragnar had noticed that along the way Sven had been stuffing portions of raw meat into his mouth and chewing them as he worked.

'Yes, you've had enough already,' Ragnar said.

'Bloody have not,' retorted Sven and belched loudly.

The aspirants laughed aloud, spirits lifted, before continuing down the hill towards the flickering lamplight of Russvik.

'I'M TELLING YOU, there were more than a hundred of them,' Nils said. He was a smallish youth but quick-witted, the leader of another of the aspirant Claws that had been formed on the day of Ragnar's arrival. So far he had lost two of his people although it seemed to be through no fault of his own. Just bad luck really. Ragnar looked at him with interest, as did all the others eating their venison and turnip stew in the long hall. This was the first definite sighting of a large body of newcomers anyone had made.

'Where did you see them?' Strybjorn asked.

'Coming over the Axehead Pass. We were up the valley from them, looking down out of the trees. Been trailing a big buck and his two does for a couple of hours when we saw them. Thought we'd better come back and tell Sergeant Hakon.'

'A hundred or so,' said Kjel. 'That's a lot.'

Ragnar knew they were all thinking along the same lines as himself. With the new intake of aspirants there were at most forty warriors in Russvik, not counting Hakon or any of the armoured visitors. Those were not good odds if it came to a fight. On the other hand, there were always the magic weapons the sergeant and his kind carried. A hundred or a thousand, it would not matter against the sorcery that could tear a full-grown sea dragon to pieces.

'What did the sergeant say?' Hakon asked.

'He just laughed and told us not to worry. It was just the winter migration of the Outlanders. He said they would give us no trouble if we left them alone. Not unless they were very hungry, anyway.'

Ragnar considered this information. A winter migration made it sound like this group was part of a much larger movement of people. Once again, he felt his own ignorance about the land in which the skyship had set him down. He wished he knew more. He wished someone would give him the chance to find out more.

One thing was becoming increasingly obvious, however. The newcomers were killing a good deal of game as they passed through the area. The deer that Ragnar's Claw had brought in was the first meat any of the aspirant groups had managed to

catch in some time. It might well be the last with winter
descending. And that was not the worst of it. The food stores in
the halls were slowly becoming exhausted. There were still
sacks of grain left, and some stringy vegetables, but not much
else. Ragnar wondered how much longer they would last and
when their supplies would possibly be replenished. He also
wondered what it was that Sergeant Hakon and the other
Wolves ate. He had never seen them share the aspirants' food.
Come to think of it, he had never even seen them eating. There
was something supernatural about that.

He shrugged and pushed the thought aside. Of course it was
always possible that the sergeant ate where no one could see
him. Maybe he had a secret cache of foodstuffs on which he
gorged himself. That thought too seemed ridiculous. Sergeant
Hakon was not the sort to do anything in secret. Why would he
need to? He was the absolute lord and master of this camp.

Still, Ragnar was worried. Winter was deepening. Food was
getting scarce. More aspirants had joined them. It was a recipe
for disaster.

'KILL HIM! Kill the swine!' the crowd of hungry aspirants cried.
The fight in the long hall erupted swiftly, toppling the wooden
tables, spilling steaming bowls of gruel. Kjel had accidentally
bumped into Mika and Vol, two of Nil's Claw, in the line for
gruel. A bowl had been spilled, splattering the lads with food.
Tempers frayed by weeks of hunger, harsh training and abuse
from Sergeant Hakon flared. In moments the two swarmed
over Kjel. Mika held him pinned to the table while Vol kicked
and punched.

Ragnar cursed. Both Mika and Vol were big and burly and
both were very good wrestlers. Neither Sven nor Strybjorn were
here yet. There was nothing else to do. If no one else interfered
it looked as if Nil's two clawbrothers would happily beat Kjel
to death. No one else looked like they wanted to interfere. They
were all too busy cheering the attackers on.

Ragnar raced forward. He sprang onto a bench, sprinted
across a table and leapt. The weight of his body and the
momentum of his jump carried him into the fray. He grabbed
Mika and Vol by the necks with his arms and bore them to the
ground. Mika's head smacked the hard-packed earth of the hall
floor. Ragnar rolled free and sprang to his feet, twisting as he

did so to face Vol. With amazing speed the aspirant was already rising to his feet. Ragnar lashed out and caught him just under the jaw with his foot. He kept his toes curled up as he had been taught so that it was the ball of his foot that connected. The force of the kick sent Vol's head snapping backward and he tumbled back onto another table, spilling food and gruel everywhere.

'You can't do that and expect to stay standing!' said a burly newcomer who Ragnar didn't recognise, as he vaulted over the table to attack him.

'Can't I, stripling?' Ragnar growled, dropping him with a punch below the chin. The newcomer's friends obviously didn't like this and moved to the attack. Grinning fiercely as he looked around for a new foe, Ragnar felt a cold draught of air hit his back. The long hall door had opened, and Ragnar heard Sven and Strybjorn's howls of joy at the developing brawl. Two heavy bodies ploughing into his attackers told Ragnar of their arrival.

It was as if a signal had been given for a general melee to begin. Tempers frayed to breaking point snapped. For no good reason bowls of gruel started flying everywhere. Benches were broken as some of the aspirants improvised weapons from the wood. Comrade lashed out at comrade, friend against friend in the madness. It became every man for himself.

Ragnar stepped back and bumped into someone. He whirled fist ready to strike and saw that it was Kjel. The Falconer looked just as ready to hit him but seeing who it was shrugged and smirked.

'Duck,' he suddenly shouted. Ragnar only just had time to throw himself flat as a chunk of broken bench flew above his head. Not even bothering to look round, he lashed out with his foot and was rewarded with a high pitched shriek as it impacted on his assailant's groin. He rolled to one side to avoid someone's flashing boot and found himself lying below a table, temporarily out of the whirlwind of the brawl.

It was madness out there. Roars and screams and shrieks of pain filled the air. Blood splattered on the floor. The aspirants fought each other with a fury that would have terrified any enemy. And in some strange way they seemed to be enjoying themselves. Fighting and brawling had always been part of the culture of Fenris, and it seemed to be doing the lads good to be able to vent their frustrations in this way. Ragnar felt the tug of excitement himself and sprang out back into the fray, just in time to take a punch in the face from Nils.

The force of the blow sent stars flying before Ragnar's eyes. He gave a grin of savage joy that froze Nils on the spot, before Ragnar dropped the man with a flurry of blows to the head, then bounding forward into the melee, laughing like a maniac.

'Enough!' bellowed a voice like thunder. Instantly the violence ceased. Ragnar froze as if pinned to the spot. Sergeant Hakon hove into view. The grin on his face was not a pleasant sight to see.

'So,' he said, 'you've nothing better to do with your time than brawl, eh? And you like the food so little that you use it for a weapon. I'm not surprised. Asa cooks the porridge so lumpy you could use it for slingstones. Still, it's a waste.

'Who started this fight?'

No one answered. The sergeant stared around the room. His gaze met Ragnar's. He forced himself to meet Hakon's eye. 'Nobody, eh? Well I guess that means you can all do two runs up the hill to work the aggression out of you before you sleep. That's after you muck out this sty.'

Loud groans echoed round the room. Nobody was happy with the thought of trudging through the dark and the snow before rest. Kjel strode forward.

'It was me, sergeant,' he said. 'I did it.'

'How, boy?'

'Well...'

Mika spoke up. 'He bumped into me, sergeant, but I threw the first punch.'

'Then what?'

'Then I joined in,' Ragnar said. He said nothing about Mika and Vol ganging up on Kjel. That was not something for the sergeant to punish. It was something that had already been settled in blows.

'You did, did you?'

'Then I joined in,' Nils said.

'And so did I,' another voice shouted. Suddenly there was a roar around the hall as all of the aspirants claimed their share of the blame. You'd think the idiots were claiming credit for killing trolls, thought Ragnar, but he felt strangely proud of them all just the same.

'Well then, you all deserve the run, don't you?' Hakon said.

'Aye!' they shouted back.

'Well, best get started then,' he said. 'Except Kjel, Ragnar, Mika and Nils. They can tidy up here first.'

With that Hakon turned on his heel and strode out of the room. The aspirants followed him out into the snow. The remaining four looked at each other.

'Best get the buckets,' Nils said sheepishly, as if expecting Ragnar to hit him again. Ragnar nodded. Kjel glanced over at him and grinned.

'Thanks, Ragnar, for coming to help me,' he said.

'Think nothing of it,' Ragnar said. 'You'd do the same for me.'

'Aye, I would.' They clasped hands and shook vigorously.

'Thanks for the black eye, Ragnar,' Nils said. 'But not much.'

'Oh well,' Mika said, grinning. 'Was the best fight I've had in ages. We must do it again sometime.'

With that they started to work.

RAGNAR'S FINGERS were bleeding, which was dangerous. He had no doubt of that fact since he was hanging from a frozen ledge almost a hundred strides above the ground. He had wrapped them in deer hide against the cold before he began the climb but the tough fabric had frayed as he had ascended the rock face, and now the sharp stone dug into his fingers.

The wind plucked at his tunic and the deerskin overcoat he had made for himself. It pushed his long black hair into his eyes at the same time as it made them water. His heart pounded. Cold sweat felt as if it were freezing on his face. He tried to tell himself not to be frightened, that there was nothing to worry about, that he had survived worse things. Under the circumstances, with the abyss below his heels and the storm winds clawing his body, this did not seem all that convincing. Aspirants had died on this rock face. Only yesterday Vol had plunged to his doom. Ragnar did not want to think about the way he had lain there for long minutes, his back broken, his innards mush, his blood reddening the snow as his life drained away. In mere seconds that same fate could be his.

Ragnar tried to shift his grip, but his fingers could find nothing to grip on the smooth, icy cold stone. Frantically he sought for purchase with his feet but the frozen rock resisted him. He was beginning to slip to his death. In his mind's eye he was already picturing the fall. He could almost feel the short plummet through space, the triumphant wind whistling in his ears, the agonising blaze of pain as the cold earth embraced his body and then the long darkness of death. Part of him almost welcomed it.

After the torture of the past few weeks, it would be almost a relief. Since the brawl things had got worse. Food had become even scarcer and the training had intensified. There had been more brawls and beatings. One of the new aspirants had been found kicked to death outside the long hall and no one had come forward to take the blame this time. Sergeant Hakon had not even investigated very hard. He said that the truth would out eventually and the guilty could not hide forever. Ragnar had not found the thought particularly reassuring. He wished that he shared the sergeant's confidence. Others had simply been unable to take the strain any more and had walked out into the snow. Their frozen bodies had been found near the camp. Sven had jokingly suggested that they might prove to be a source of fresh meat. At least Ragnar hoped he was joking.

He shook his head. What was he thinking about? As always in moments of extreme danger his mind seemed to be working at incredible speed but he was simply using it to daydream and recall the past. He needed to save himself and he needed to do it now, before his fingers skidded right off the ledge and he fell to his doom.

He frantically lifted one hand off the ledge and felt himself begin to tumble backwards. He twisted, throwing his weight forward, stretching out his free hand for purchase on the cold stone. His frozen fingers refused to respond but he brought all the force of his will to bear on them and made them work. Triumphantly he felt something under his fingers. It was almost like human hair. It must be moss or lichen, he thought. His triumph swiftly turned to despair as he felt the stuff give way. His weight must be pulling it out by the roots. His fingers lost purchase and he began to fall.

For a brief dizzying instant he felt his body part company from the cliff face. His back arched as he began the long tumble through space. In that instant he knew that he was about to die and, and no magic or sorcery would bring him back this time.

Then strong fingers clasped his wrist and his downward progress was halted for a moment. He looked up and saw Kjel looking down at him. He gave praise to Russ that Kjel had noticed his difficulties and returned. Relief flooded through his body and he felt weak. He noticed the look of strain on the Falconer's face, an instant before he felt Kjel's grip start to slip.

No, Ragnar thought, gritting his teeth and scrabbling for purchase once more, fearing as much that he would pull Kjel to his doom as that he would drop to his own. This time, with the additional leverage provided by Kjel's grasp, he managed to get a grip and flop up onto the ledge.

'That was too close,' Ragnar gasped after a moment's rest. Fear and emotional reaction had reduced his voice to a whispering croak.

'Yes,' said Kjel, his face still white with the strain.

'I owe you my life,' said Ragnar.

Kjel looked up at the remainder of the rock face. It loomed a long way above them. Ragnar could tell he was measuring what little strength they had left against the rest of the climb. The expression on Kjel's face told him the conclusion was not hopeful.

'Thank me when we both make it out of here,' Kjel said.

Wearily they began the long climb. When they reached the top, limbs trembling from weariness, breath rasping from their lungs, Sergeant Hakon stood waiting for them. There was a thoughtful expression on his face.

'Ragnar, be in the great hall with all your Claw at dawn tomorrow.' Ragnar was unsure from his tone of voice whether showing up would be a good or a bad idea.

THE DULL early morning light filtered in through the slits that served as windows in the great hall. The air smelled of wood smoke and stale sweat. Sergeant Hakon loomed over Ragnar's Claw. Ragnar felt like a pygmy standing in his huge shadow. There was a strange glint in the sergeant's eye but no readable expression on his stone-like face. He seemed to be considering them, perhaps with a view to killing them, perhaps with something else in mind.

'You have done well,' he said eventually. 'At least, you have done well to get this far. You have all survived, and you have not disgraced yourselves. There's little else that you can learn here in Russvik and you're as hard as your sorry bodies are going to allow you to be.'

All eyes were locked on the sergeant now. This was something new. His words hinted at a change in their status. Perhaps they would get to join the other Claws that had already left. Ragnar wondered about that. None of those aspirants had ever returned. His heart hammered against his ribs with nervousness.

'You are being given a chance to move on from here,' Hakon continued. 'Don't think it will be easy. Where you're going you will look back on your days in Russvik as a pleasant little carnival.'

He paused for a moment to let his words sink in. From anybody else Ragnar would have assumed the words were an exaggeration meant to frighten them, but coming from Hakon he knew they were a cold simple statement of fact.

'You may be selected to move on to the next stage of your training. That's assuming you can pass through the Gate of Morkai.'

Ragnar did not like the sound of this at all. In the legends of his people Morkai was the two-headed hound of Russ. He guarded the gates of the lowest hell. A glance around at his clawbrothers told him the significance of the name was not lost on them either.

'How will we get there, sergeant?' Kjel asked. Ragnar could tell he was doing his best to sound cheerful but could not keep the leaden tones of fear from his voice.

'You'll find out soon enough.'

NINE
THE GATE OF MORKAI

ONCE MORE Ragnar found himself inside one of the great sky-ships. He knew now it was called a Thunderhawk. Perhaps it was *the* Thunderhawk but somehow he doubted it. The way Hakon and the others talked of it he got the impression there was more than one.

Kjel, Strybjorn, Sven and himself were not the only ones clambering aboard and strapping themselves in. He noticed that Nils and Mika too had been summoned. He also recognised Lars, Hrolf and Magnus from his initial intake of aspirants. It looked like they were the only survivors. None of them looked particularly cheerful, and Ragnar guessed that they too had been on the receiving end of the sergeant's speech. Nils at least tried to smile at them but his expression was more thoughtful than happy. Like Ragnar he was wondering what waited for them at the Gate of Morkai.

There was a roar as the Thunderhawk came to life and shook itself from the ground. Looking out of the round porthole Ragnar could see that the snow was steaming off the skyship's wings as it lifted straight up into the air. Once again he was pressed back into his seat by the force of acceleration. He kept his eyes glued to the window though, determined to get a last glimpse of Russvik. Insane though it seemed after the hardships they had all endured there, Ragnar felt an odd sense of nostalgia for the place. For the past few months it had become the closest thing he now had to a home. Brutal though his life there had been he had become used to it. Now he was once more being sent off to face the unknown and that in itself was frightening. Nothing he had encountered since arriving in the frozen wastes of Asaheim had been pleasant, and he doubted this was going to change any time soon.

Thinking about home made him glance over at Strybjorn. Once more he felt a surge of hatred when he looked on the Grimskull's brutal features. Disturbingly, Ragnar recognised that his enduring hatred gave him a grim sense of satisfaction. It alone was perhaps his only constant and dependable companion.

Strybjorn caught Ragnar's glance and returned it with a glare. 'Frightened, last of the Thunderfists?' he asked.

'No,' Ragnar said. One day soon he would take his vengeance, he knew. Of that he was certain. The truce which had held while they were in Russvik was over. He would deal with Strybjorn soon provided they both survived their passage through the Gate of Morkai.

THE THUNDERHAWK raced across the snow-covered land. This time it did not leap so high it threatened to touch the stars. This time it roared down the long valleys between the mountains, and the thunder of its passage startled the beasts far below on the ice fields.

Ragnar had no idea how fast they were flying but their speed was incredible. It seemed as if they were covering as much ground in an hour as a fit man might cover in a month. Their shadow sped across the wilderness below them faster than that of any bird of prey.

All the land below them was white with snow save where the green of the pine trees covered the hills. Here and there a fast flowing stream rushed over a crevasse dropping in a long fall of spray to the earth below. Strangely, the mountains seemed even larger from their vantage point aloft in the speeding Thunderhawk. They rose in endless frozen waves to the horizon, mighty sentinels standing shoulder to shoulder against the endless assault of wind and rain and erosion.

Now the craft passed over the rock strewn surface of a glacier, glittering coldly in the sunlight filtering through the clouds. Looking down, Ragnar caught sight of a party of men passing over its frozen surface. They were not garbed in furs as all the other people he had seen were. In the brief glance he got Ragnar would have sworn they were armoured as Sergeant Hakon was, and equipped with the same weapons. They seemed to be waving at the skyship as it passed, and then in the blink of an eye were gone.

Tattered ribbons of clouds passed beneath the Thunderhawk now, and it shook slightly as it passed over them. Once again Ragnar felt a secret thrill in his heart. This must be how the gods felt when they looked down on the world, he thought. It came to him then that Hakon and his brothers were mighty mages and were privileged with the secrets of a sorcery strong enough to rule this world if only they wished to.

Then the thought occurred to him that maybe already they did, and that the world was ordered as it was because they wished it so for their own unguessable purposes. Maybe all the clans of Fenris were but the cattle of the cruel gods. No sooner had the idea flickered through his brain than some subtle instinct told Ragnar that it was the truth. Was he not riding on a vehicle such as was used by the Choosers of the Slain, and were not they the messengers of the gods? Perhaps that meant they dwelled alongside the gods, or perhaps it meant that they were in some way gods themselves. Certainly Ranek and Hakon possessed many of the legendary attributes of Russ. They possessed his strange wolf-like eyes, and his long fangs, his mighty thews and his enormous physical strength. That they were his undoubted kin was surely obvious, or so it seemed to Ragnar.

Ragnar did not doubt that he would soon find out more. The Thunderhawk was bearing him ever deeper into the heart of mystery. As long hours passed, the terrain they passed over was becoming more and more savage and bleak. Here and there mighty geysers of lava jetted up into the sky and the snow melted away in hissing clouds from the steaming surface of the black rock. It struck Ragnar that if ever there was a land fitted to holding the entrance to hell, then this was surely it.

The mountains were becoming ever higher and more barren. Here and there monstrous figures loped through the lichen-covered rocks. Packs of gigantic wolves raised their heads and howled in salute as the Thunderhawk passed. The mouths of enormous caverns pitted the barren slopes. What little vegetation there was was sere and stunted.

The valleys became ever deeper, their unfathomable depths black and forbidding, the mountains ever higher. Indeed now the craggy giants made the peaks around Russvik look like mere foothills, unfit even to be called mountains, although in truth they had been the highest Ragnar had ever seen. The mountains through which they passed were truly awesome in their scale, like a wall made by the gods to imprison daemons. Their sheer size was mind numbing. Pinned in their seats by the speed of the Thunderhawk, they hurtled through long dark valleys filled with scree, over glaciers that sparkled like rivers of ice where the probing fingers of the sun touched them. The sky-ship's fast-moving shadow fell on frozen lakes and dropped away into the clouds beneath towering crags.

The voice of the Thunderhawk roared even louder as it passed through the mountains, as if even this chariot of the gods was struggling to climb through the thinning air. The sky was becoming darker as they rose, and Ragnar was convinced that he could see the cold glitter of the stars.

Then the skyship banked sharply, and as his stomach lurched, Ragnar saw it: the largest mountain of all, the largest mountain he had ever seen or ever would see, what could only be the largest mountain in the history of creation. It towered over all the other peaks as a grown man might tower over small children. Its lower slopes tumbled for leagues into the clouds below them. It was a mountain on an epic scale, a mountain fit to be the dwelling place of gods. Ragnar knew without being told that it would be their destination, and looking around the darkened interior of the Thunderhawk, he could see that the others were similarly stunned into awe-struck silence by the magnificence of the great peak before them.

He knew now, looking at that towering mountain in the light of the morning sun, that he would never forget this moment for as long as he lived. He would never forget the wonder and the fear that the sight of this mighty pinnacle evoked in his heart.

THE TONE OF the skyship's voice changed as they made their approach to the peak. As they closed in they slowed and descended. As they came closer to the surface of the peak, the view of the mountain in all its immensity was lost, to be replaced by individual details of the land below them.

Ragnar saw that the side of the mountain was pitted with great caves, and within each of the great caves was an enormous metal door, large beyond his ability to comprehend. Until that moment, Ragnar would not have guessed that enough metal existed in all of Fenris to clad just one of those immense doors in iron. He had no idea what might lurk beyond such portals and he had no desire to find out. Ragnar simply could not imagine anything large enough to need such vast exits. He shuddered, overcome with awe.

There were other things: huge complexes of metal linked by monstrous snaking pipelines. At first Ragnar thought that the world serpent itself held the mountain in its coils but as he looked closer the idea was replaced by the no-less-shocking one that the enormous metal structures were the work of men, or perhaps of gods. They linked the steel buildings from which mighty jets of fire flared. He had no idea what purpose these eldritch engines served but he sensed that it was a mighty one. Why else would they be here on the mountain of the gods?

As they dropped further, he saw that each of the gigantic metal buildings was as large as a small island, a veritable hill of precious steel. Enormous dishes which reminded him of the one on the Temple of Iron he had seen a short lifetime ago, rotated atop those mighty structures. Several of them seemed to turn and look at the Thunderhawk as it approached. Ragnar blinked, clutched his restraining harness and gasped for air, unable to take in all the wonders and terrors he was witnessing.

The Thunderhawk came to a halt in the air near one of the vast metal doors. Looking down Ragnar could see that there was what appeared to be a huge stone bull's-eye on the ground beneath them. Even as he watched the Thunderhawk began to descend on top of it. Ragnar noticed that as the craft touched down they landed in the exact centre of that enormous target. The astonishing precision of what they had just done struck him like a blow from a sword. They had crossed hundreds of leagues of land, flown over a vast continent and somehow the helmsman of the flying ship had managed to find this exact spot and dock his craft there. He was sure that this precision was no accident but the product of a mighty sorcery, the like of which he could not yet understand.

Even above the dying groans of the engines, and through the thick metal skin of the Thunderhawk, Ragnar heard a strange pumping grinding noise and terror gripped him as he saw that the ship was sinking into the ground. Stone walls seemed to rise from the ground around the Thunderhawk as the earth swallowed him. His stomach leapt and his heart sank until a moment's consideration told him that this whole procedure was intentional, and that the stone disc was some sort of platform intended to carry the skyship down into the bowels of the earth.

He squinted out of the window, looking up, and was rewarded with a last glance of the peak receding vertiginously into the sky, like a spear pointed directly at the belly of heaven.

THEY DESCENDED from the skyship into a vast cavern that seemed as large as the vault of the sky. The walls had a glassy sheen as if they had been fused in immense heat. Clouds drifted under the great arches and obscured the enormous murals that filled the ceiling. Ragnar gaped in awe at the partially obscured scenes of battle between beings that could only be gods and daemons. Around the walls of the huge chamber enormous statues occupied titanic niches. Each was a hundred times as tall as a man, each depicted a figure armed and armoured like Sergeant Hakon or Ranek the Wolf Priest. Here, Ragnar thought, was sorcery on a scale that numbed the mind.

Ragnar had never seen anything quite like it before. The whole huge space was lit by magical lanterns which gave off a glare brighter than a thousand whale oil lamps, making the whole enormous space almost as bright as day. All around strange and mysterious figures moved about on unguessable errands.

Ragnar saw figures dressed in the same armour as Sergeant Hakon and their helmsman moving through the cavern towards other skyships, weapons held in postures of readiness. He saw men who appeared more than half machine prodding the skyships with long metal poles from which sparks and flames flared. He saw similar figures attaching long pipes to the underbelly of the skycraft. He saw humanoid figures that looked to be made entirely of metal performing maintenance on the vehicles. As they went about their duties they reminded Ragnar of the shipwrights back on his former home. They had the same air of men totally absorbed in their task.

The noise was deafening. The roar of the skyships mingled with the clash of metal on metal and the shouts of a thousand voices. The metal men clanked and whirred. The machines on which they rode rumbled like thunder. Ragnar listened carefully and realised the language in which these people bellowed did not in the slightest resemble his native tongue. It was even harsher and more guttural, and yet at the same time some of the words flowed smoothly.

The air tasted of chemicals. Not in the same way as the tanneries back home or the stink that surrounded the town of the Iron Masters. It smelled clean and minty with a hint of oil and other substances that Ragnar associated with machinery.

The air in his lungs and the ground beneath his feet seemed to vibrate with the hubbub. All of his senses were assaulted by things the like of which he had never before experienced. He suffered a moment's disorientation and then his eyes focused on the one thing in all this strangeness that he recognised.

From out of the shadowy distance the Wolf Priest Ranek strode towards them. Ragnar felt a sudden shiver of fear. The appearance of the sorcerer had always presaged mighty changes in his life.

'Welcome to the Fang! To the abode of the Wolves!' he bellowed. 'I hope you are ready to face the Gate of Morkai.'

RANEK LED THEM through long dark corridors deep into the bowels of the mountain. He strode with the purposeful confident stride of an old wolf. He knew exactly where he was going and how to get there. For this Ragnar was glad, for the whole complex was a maze on a scale which he could never have imagined. All of his home island could fit into one of the smaller chambers in this vast place.

There were times when he had to fight down the terror that filled him. Frightening thoughts constantly assailed his mind. What was keeping this vast honeycombed mountain from falling on them? What if it were to collapse burying them all alive? How would he ever find his way out again? A glance at the pale faces of the others told him that they shared his fears.

Machines and warriors and the other things, part man, part machine, moved alongside them. They were overtaken by huge wheeled carts which had no visible means of propulsion and which carried burdens too heavy to be moved by twenty strong men. Truly, Ragnar thought, mighty magic was at work here. The inhabitants of the Fang possessed engines which made the greatest machines of the Iron Masters look like child's toys.

He felt that at last he had arrived at the secret heart of the world. It was as if a curtain had been pulled away to reveal the place where the Dark Weavers spun out the fates of men. The mechanisms of destiny were being laid bare. He could see now how the gods lived, and it was an awesome sight.

Ranek led them to two cave-like openings in the side of the mountain. From inside came a strange whooshing noise. Over both openings were carved the sign of a great two-headed eagle. In its claws it held a disc which showed the wolf's head emblem of Russ. Alongside one opening was painted a fluorescent arrow indicating up. Beside the other an arrow indicated down.

'Step inside,' Ranek said, gesturing towards the left opening with one metal-clad hand. Without thinking Kjel stepped through. There was a sound like a scream as he promptly dropped from view. The others froze on the spot. Was this a trap, Ragnar wondered? Was there a huge pit there? Was this the Gate of Morkai?

Had they been brought all this way simply to be slaughtered like sheep? It was unlikely. Was this some strange form of magical sacrifice? He could not begin to guess. The things he had seen here were beyond his comprehension.

'Go!' Ranek ordered. Despite the terror which clawed at his heart, Ragnar decided that he was simply going to have to trust the old sorcerer. He stepped into the opening. For one heart-stopping moment he felt nothing but empty air beneath his feet, then he stepped out and began to fall. Even though he was determined not to scream a moan of fear passed his lips. His stomach churned as he plummeted down a long shaft. Red and yellow lights flickered past his eyes as he dropped swiftly and with ever increasing velocity. He knew now that indeed it had been a trap and his life was over. Just as he felt black rage begin to overtake him at the senseless nature of his own impending death, some unseen force grasped him in its invisible grip and slowed his descent so that he came slowly to rest on the ground at the bottom of the shaft. As he touched down light as a feather and realised that he was not going to die, laughter bubbled from his lips.

He saw another exit and Kjel standing there with a broad grin on his face.

'That was amazing,' the Falconer said. Ragnar could only nod and grin back.

'Look out!' shouted a voice from above him. Ragnar looked up and saw Sven's boots descending towards his head. He had only time to throw himself out through the exit before Sven touched down. Sven wasted no time in following him, as one by one the rest of the aspirants dropped into view.

At last Ranek appeared. He landed lightly with a flex of his knees that told he had done such a thing countless times before. His face wore no idiot grin. Ragnar realised that whatever magic there was in that shaft it had long ago ceased to hold any wonders for the sorcerer.

Gesturing for them to follow, Ranek strode on.

THE PLACE THROUGH which they passed could almost have been chosen to evoke terror, Ragnar thought, and then realised that most likely this were the case. It was dark. There were none of the glowing ceiling globes here that had illuminated the rest of the labyrinth. The only source of light was the blazing firepits and the cherry glow from the bubbling pools of molten lava that surrounded them. The air here was warm and smelled of sulphur. Clouds of scalding mist billowed across the pathways. Ragnar paid careful attention to the causeways across which they walked. To lose your footing here meant a plunge into certain death.

Ranek strode on, never looking back, confident that they were following him. He had every reason to be confident, Ragnar realised. What else could the aspirants do? None of them knew the way back or had any idea of what secrets and dangers this place might conceal from the unwary interloper.

Ahead of them loomed another massive archway. This one was carved with grinning wolves' heads and runes of an eldritch type which Ragnar had no idea how to read. Ranek stopped and turned to face them. One by one the aspirants assembled on the causeway. Subconscious discipline, drilled into them at Russvik, caused them to draw themselves up in ranks.

There was an aura of fear that hung over this place. Ragnar could sense its presence in the hot sulphurous air. Sweat plastered his hair to his brow. He knew his face was red from the heat. It felt like he was in the abode of the fire daemons. Ancient and powerful forces were at work here and Ragnar sensed invisible presences, perhaps ghosts or spirits. There was power in this archway and whatever lay beyond it.

'Behold the Gate of Morkai,' Ranek said, gesturing to the archway. 'Through it lies the path to death or glory. Beyond this there is no return save as one worthy to belong to the Wolves in body and in soul.'

'There is no other way forward for you now. You cannot leave this place alive without passing through this gate. Anyone who refuses I will throw into the firepits and the daemons will consume their souls. There is only one question here – who among you will go first?'

Silence. All eyes were locked on the archway. The sense of a waiting evil presence intensified. Superstitious fear entered all their minds on stealthy feet. Ragnar knew that they all felt the same as he did. It was no longer as if they were looking through a mist-filled arch. It was as if they were gazing into the mouth of a gigantic beast which would swallow them in just one gulp. All of them knew they should be clamouring for the honour of going first and yet none of them moved.

Ragnar knew that some powerful magic was at work here, freezing his heart with dread, sending the cold fingers of fear up his spine. With every second that passed it became harder to move, harder to speak, harder even to think. It was as if he were a small bird hypnotised by a serpent. He wanted to be able to do something and yet he could not.

But even as he stood there it occurred to him that the test had already begun, that this strange magic was part of it, that courage was one of the most important measures by which he would be judged worthy. He forced his thick tongue to move. He forced his frozen lips to open. With a sense of immense trepidation he heard himself say: 'I will pass through the gate.'

'Then go, laddie! What are you waiting for?'

Like a mechanical man or the victim of an enchantment in a saga, Ragnar strode forward on stiff legs to pass through the Gate of Morkai. As he did so a wave of dizziness swept over him. The runes on the gate glowed. The wolves' heads carved in it seemed to come alive and flow out to greet him: wolf spirits, misty and vague, dragging behind them a comet tail of ecto-plasm. In his ears he thought he heard a faint high-pitched howling such as the ghosts of a long dead wolf pack might make.

The spirits swirled around him as he strode towards the arch. They flowed into his open mouth and nostrils. He felt the vapour billow down his throat and fill his lungs. He thought he would choke on the acrid, fusty air but still he forced himself to walk forward, to come ever closer to the mighty archway…

FOR A MOMENT he thought he was through. He caught a brief glimpse of three terrible old men, clad in armour, the pelts of great white wolves draped around their shoulders then there was a sense of terrible freezing chill, a surge of agonising heat and a sense of falling far worse than anything he had endured in the dropshaft. Time and space twisted and shifted. His flesh seemed to bubble and melt and suddenly he was elsewhere.

He stood on a frozen plain. Far into the distance he could see men and machines. Some were garbed in the grey armour of the type that Hakon and Ranek wore. Others were garbed in blood red armour covered in ornate brazen skulls, yet oddly similar in design to the armour of the men in grey. The men in grey fought the men in red beneath the chill light of a pale white sun. Ragnar saw that he was standing on top of a pile of bodies. A severed head rolled away from his feet. Limbs squelched beneath his boots. He realised that he too was clad in the grey armour and it was nicked and chipped in a thou-sand places. Oil and fluid mingled with his own blood and the gore of his enemies on its once sleek surface. He held one of the strange magical swords that Hakon always carried in each hand. One had ceased to work. The blade was broken, the teeth chipped away. The other worked fitfully, coming to life momentarily, shrieking and vibrating in his hands and then stopping as if the spell animating it had ceased to function.

Looking around him he saw the dead bodies of Kjel and Sven and Strybjorn and even those of Sergeant Hakon and Ranek. He was surrounded by the men in red. Some of them had their helmets thrown back and their faces were twisted and distorted into terrible parodies of humanity. Red glowing eyes glared out with terrible hatred from within the helmets of others. He knew that there were too many of them, and that they were too strong for him. He knew without having to be told that these were the servants of Horus, the followers of ultimate darkness, the enemies of Russ. He knew that there were no deadlier killers in all the universe. And he knew that he was mere instants away from death.

One of the red-armoured ones gestured for his followers to halt. They stopped for a moment like hounds obeying the command of a master, but Ragnar knew that the reprieve was only for a moment. They still thirsted for his blood and even the will of their dreadful leader could not restrain them for long. The leader spoke now and his brazen voice was persuasive and sincere.

'You are a mighty warrior, Ragnar,' he said. 'You are a great killer. You are worthy to join us. Throw down your weapons. Partake in the ritual of blood. Offer your spirit to Khorne. Live forever and know the ecstasy of endless battle.'

Who was Khorne, Ragnar wondered? The name sounded oddly familiar, and resonant with evil. And why did his followers seek Ragnar's allegiance? Not that it mattered much. Ragnar knew that this was a genuine offer and part of him thrilled to it. The red-garbed warrior was offering him an eternity of gore-splattered combat such as was promised to the heroes who followed Russ. More, he knew that once he partook of their rituals and donned their red armour, he would take more joy in the slaughter than ever he had, and he would be rewarded for it, by a power as great as a god's. For a moment he felt the thrill of temptation. Why not join these great warriors? Why not offer up his soul to this Khorne? Why not gain immortality?

But even as he thought this, another part of him recoiled in disgust. He saw that these followers of darkness were lost and damned. Something had gone out of them, something important, and its loss had made them into something less than men. They might have honour of a sort but it was not honour as Ragnar understood it. Their twisted forms reflected their twisted souls and not all the intricately worked beauty of their ornate armour could conceal that fact.

Ragnar laughed and spat in the leader's face, then leapt into the fray smiting right and left. Not even the bite of Chaos blades into his breaking bones caused him to regret the decision. A pit of darkness opened at his feet, and too suddenly for him to comprehend the manner of his transition he was elsewhere in a different place and a different time.

All around him were walls of flesh the colour of bruised meat. Great veinous pipes burrowed through them, odd fluids gurgling within them. Yellowish arches of bone and gristle, the colour of old rotting teeth, supported the ceiling. A loathsome sticky red slime covered everything. His boots made a hideous sucking sound every time he lifted them from the tongue-like floor. The air was the temperature of blood. It felt close and sticky. He sensed life of an alien sort all around him. He felt as if he had been swallowed alive by some huge and monstrous beast.

Once again he wore the grey armour. Once again the strange and potent weapons were clutched in his fist. In his ear, at once somehow remote and immediate, he could hear the chatter of voices he recognised: Kjel, Strybjorn, Sven. Some magic carried their words, strangely flat and unemotional sounding, to his ears. He could hear them speak and their voices were hushed with wonder and fear.

Is this real? he asked himself. He was not sure of the answer. It felt real. Beneath his feet he could feel the floor vibrate in time to the bellows-breathing of the great beast. He could smell the exotic stink of its innards. The taste of odd perfumes lingered like poison in his mouth. But how could this be real? He had died under the blades of the red-clad warriors. Had he been resurrected once more as he had been after the battle with the Grimskulls? Or was none of this real? Was he trapped in the coils of some potent spell?

This one has a strong soul. The voice thundered inside his head. He could not recognise it but it sounded ancient and wise. Almost immediately after he heard the words he felt a flow of force into his mind, easing his doubts, altering his memories, forcing him to live in the moment. His doubts flowed away like blood in a mountain stream. All thoughts of anything except immediate danger vanished as he heard the distant bellowing of some mighty beast.

The voices of his fellow aspirants sounded loud in his ears. They were almost panicky. He risked a glance over his shoulder and saw fear and horror written on Kjel's face. The others straggled along behind them. Clutched in every hand were weapons

such as those Ranek had used to destroy the sea dragon so long
ago in Ragnar's other life.

He could tell that all of them were wondering what they were
doing here. All of them were looking to him for leadership just
as they had done on the night the troll had taken Henk. They
relied on his nerve, his courage, his knowledge. And the worst
of it was that he had no idea of what to do. He did not know
where they were or how they had got there or even what sort of
foe was approaching. All he was sure of was that some sort of
foe was coming, and that it was bearing down on them with
awful speed.

'Be calm,' he told them, hoping that none of them noticed
the nervousness and insecurity in his voice. Once more the bellowing sounded, and a shiver passed up Ragnar's spine.
Whatever made that noise was big. And there was more than
one of it. The sound had come from a different direction than
the other. It was answered by another strange call from the corridor up ahead. A noise that sounded like the chittering of
thousands of rats, or perhaps the clicking of hundreds of chiti-
nous claws.

The noise was coming closer. He heard Kjel cry out in fear
and he fought to control himself, to stop Kjel's horror com-
municating itself to him. In this he was only partially
successful. The sight of what sped towards him down the corridor almost unmanned him.

There were hundreds of the creatures. Monsters bigger than a
man. Each with four arms that ended in massive claws.
Nightmare faces of tiny eyes and monstrous jaws. Fast. Much
faster than a man, covering the distance between them almost
too quickly for the eye to follow.

'We're all going to die!' Kjel shouted, and Ragnar was forced
to agree with him. Still if he was going to die, he was going to
take a few of the beasts with him. And he was damned well
going to make sure that the others did the same.

'Stand and fight,' he shouted. 'Or I'll kill you myself, you gut-
less cowards!'

The roar of sorcerous weapons filled the air. The same magic
which had killed the dragon began to take effect on their
attackers. Ragnar ducked as bolts of fire passed over his head
and raked the monsters. They were dying but not quickly
enough. Heads exploded. Bodies were torn apart. Blood and

nauseating fluids streamed out onto the living carpet. Still their assailants came on, an unstoppable tide of alien hunger and hate. Despair threatened to overtake Ragnar. What use was fighting? Why not simply lie down and die?

He refused to give way. Screaming with rage and hatred he leapt forward into the mass of monsters, lashing left and right with his blades. A few stopped to engage him, more swept past to get to his comrades. He was surrounded by a whirlwind of jaws and claws that tore through his armour and his flesh. Still fighting, still trying to kill, he fought the agony that threatened to overwhelm him as he descended into darkness.

Once more he awoke unharmed. His eyes took in his surroundings at a glance. It was dark. The sky was lit by enormous bursts of light. A noise like thunder made the air shiver. All around were the ruins of a massive city, larger than anything Ragnar had ever seen except, perhaps, the Fang. The blackened stumps of towering buildings loomed over him. Each seemed almost as large as a mountain.

In the distance, at the end of the street, he could see huge metal beast-machines moving. They were shaped like men, but maybe ten times as high. In their fists were enormous weapons that sent beams of light lashing across the sky like the lightning of the gods. From their shoulders thunderbolts flashed. For a few moments the air was filled with high-pitched whining, and then in the distance could be heard the world-shaking roar of an explosion. The ground trembled underfoot like a whipped beast. A cloud of black smoke and debris leapt into the sky before settling back to earth in a surprisingly slow seeming motion.

Ragnar surveyed the scene. Once again he was in the grey armour with the wolf-sign on it. He was used to it now. It fitted him like a second skin, and made him faster and stronger. Once again he had those odd potent weapons in his hands. For a moment, he wondered what he was doing here, but once again he sensed the powerful presence of those ancient minds and all doubts were swept away.

He looked around. He was on his own. He had become separated from his comrades. For the first time in Russ alone knew how many months he was by himself. There was no one around to back him up, to help him if he fell, to watch over him while he was injured. He had no idea where the others were or how he had got separated from them in this vast and terrifying alien place. He noticed that the sun was a huge bloated red orb, and the sky was a shade of cobalt blue the like of which he had never seen before. He had a sense of remoteness, of being so far from home that he could not comprehend the distance.

He knew that he must find the others, that they were out there somewhere in need of his leadership, but he had no way of knowing where or why. He felt suddenly insignificant, lost and alone like a child in the wilderness. He fought down the feeling of blackness and despair and strode off in the direction of the battlefield. As he moved he became more aware of his surroundings, and more filled with wonder.

Men had built this place. He could tell by the artefacts he found lying amid the rubble. Pictures of families painted with a detail that made them seem almost real, imprisoned in crystals that showed the scene from different angles as you rotated them. Books in a language he could not understand printed with an odd mechanical regularity the like of which it was impossible to produce on Fenris. Children's toys made from exotic alien substances that were smooth and chill to the touch.

Slowly the scale of what he was witnessing here dawned on him. This was war fought in a way that was unimaginable among his people. This city must have held more people than his entire world, and it had been levelled by the forces unleashed here as surely as if the gods had leaned down from heaven and smashed it flat. Perhaps that was exactly what had happened. His mind reeled as he tried to picture the sheer destructive power which had been focussed on this city. Power beyond the scope of his imagination to even begin to comprehend.

Ragnar sensed that perhaps he was being challenged and tested here, and that part of his trial was to be able to adapt to what he was seeing, to understand it and to continue functioning. He knew that some of his kinfolk would have been paralysed by fear, by the sheer dread of walking amid these titanic ruins. He decided swiftly that it would mean nothing to him. He was Ragnar and he would fight just as well here as on the deck of a dragonship and he would continue fighting regardless of the presence or absence of any companions.

He was congratulating himself on his fortitude when the ground shook and he heard the menacing thump, thump, thump of approaching footfalls. One of the distant giant figures he had seen earlier turned the corner and hove into view. It was nearly ten times his height, proportioned somewhat like a man only taller and more slender. The head was long and sleek and ovular and from the way it turned alertly he could tell it was aware of him. Red and yellow pennons implanted on its shoulders fluttered in the wind. Its mighty talons gripped strange elongated weapons.

It bounded forward, covering the ground far quicker than a man. Ragnar felt himself frozen with horror. There was nothing he could do against this thing. His sword seemed as pitiful as a splinter wielded by a child against a grown warrior. This thing could crush him to jelly beneath its enormous boot without even slowing down. In fact it appeared that was exactly what it intended.

Displaced air whipped past Ragnar's face. A huge shadow flickered across the sun as the monstrous foot descended. At the last moment, he mastered himself, determined to do something. He tried to throw himself to one side, out of the area covered by the descending limb but it was too large. There was no way he could avoid it. Howling with frustrated rage, determined to do something to the thing that was killing him, he raised his sword in a last futile gesture of defiance. Sparks flared as the blade's teeth encountered metal. It was the last thing he saw before an enormous weight descended and crushed his bones to jelly.

Still screaming he sat bolt upright and found himself in a new scene. This was hell, he was convinced. He was doomed to spend eternity dying a thousand deaths in places which he did not understand, fighting against forces he could not comprehend. No, he told himself, screaming in tormented defiance, this was all an illusion, a spell woven by those bitter ancients who waited beyond the Gate of Morkai, and he would not let it defeat him.

This one is strong indeed, brothers, said the thunderous voice inside his head. *If he lives he will be numbered among the mighty.*

Once again Ragnar felt an enormous wave of power sweeping through his mind, numbing his will, draining his resistance. This time he fought against it, using every ounce of his savagery and hate. He was not going to be forced back into those alien worlds against his will. He was not going to be the puppet of some ancient wizards. He was not going to give way to…

What? He was not going to give way to what? He could not remember. There was no need to remember. He stood on a beach watching the sunset. Odd looking trees swayed in the soft breeze. The air was warm and scented with strange perfumes. Flowers more lush than anything that ever bloomed in the bleak wastelands of Fenris swayed under the wind's probing fingers.

'Ragnar.'

He turned. The most beautiful woman he had ever seen walked towards him. But 'walked' was not a lovely enough word to describe the swaying grace of her movements. Her skin was amber. Her hair was liquid jet. There was something about her features that reminded him of Ana, only an Ana with no flaws, an Ana out of which all defects had been subtly erased. She smiled and Ragnar felt his heart skip. It was a smile that warmed his surroundings like the sun might. He felt drawn to her by a subtle force, even though her smile revealed small sharp fangs like those of some vampiric beast.

'You have decided then,' she said. Her voice was musical, thrilling as sin. The mere sound of it made him drunk as a skinful of wine.

'Decided what?'

'Do not toy with me. You have decided to join us? To bond with our coven and offer up your soul to our great master Slaanesh?'

What was she talking about? Who was Slaanesh? He had no real idea but once more the very name evoked a sense of evil on an almost cellular level in him. More, he sensed there was some deeper meaning behind her words, just as her tainted beauty signified some deeper reality. Was that a hint of petulance in her tone? Was she mistaking his misunderstanding for refusal? Just what was going on here?

'I have decided nothing yet,' he said, to give himself time.

'That is unfortunate,' the girl replied, and leaned forward to kiss him. His lips tingled from her touch. Her skin seemed to exude subtle narcotics. Her very touch caused pleasure so intense it was almost painful.

As the kiss continued, he felt as if something was being drawn from him, the very essence of his personality, his soul. It was not painful. It was pleasurable, rather like falling asleep on a soft downy bed with a beautiful woman by his side, having sated himself on all the pleasures imaginable. And yet, something was wrong. This was not how he had felt with Ana.

Suddenly, Ragnar realised that he did not want to submit to this gentle destruction of all that he was, any more than he would welcome being crushed by the steel foot of a mighty war machine. He fought against it, and in doing so came to realise its strength. It was like being pulled down in the undertow of a powerful current. You could struggle all you like and still you would be dragged down to meet the sea daemons. He tried to resist and still his life force was drained away and blackness clouded the corners of his vision.

Again he woke into nightmare. This time he stood before a vast black altar. All around weird figures capered. High overhead a horned sorcerer on a great glowing disc floated, defying gravity by the strength of his magic. Even as Ragnar watched he floated down. A nimbus of light played around the sorcerer's clawed hands but so far he had made no threatening move. Ragnar raised his weapon but did not strike for he wanted to see what would happen.

'What can my master grant you in exchange for your soul?' the sorcerer asked in a voice molten with sorcerous power. 'What is it that you wish? You need but think of it, and it will be yours.'

Instantly and unbidden the image of Strybjorn's corpse sprang into his mind. Before he could even try and cover his thoughts, Strybjorn appeared bound on the altar and a huge sacrificial knife was gripped firmly in Ragnar's hands.

Hatred twisted his guts. He saw again his father lying dead in the burned out ruins of his home village. He saw his people being led away as thralls in the Grimskull dragonships. He relived the duel in which he thought he had slain Strybjorn and in which the Grimskull had come so close to slaying him. The urge to strike down at his enemy's unprotected breast was there, and almost he brought the knife down. He wanted to feel the blade plunge into Strybjorn's chest, wanted to feel the shock of steel against bone, wanted to feel blood spout forth. The only thing that stayed his hand even for a moment was the fact that Strybjorn wore an amulet that bore the same wolf's head icon that was inscribed on Ragnar's own grey armour.

'Go ahead! Strike!' said the sorcerer. 'Take your vengeance. The souls of your ancestors clamour for it. Strike and it shall be yours.'

Ragnar's hand trembled with his urge to bring the blade down. He had wanted nothing more in his entire life than to strike. Even though he knew his soul would be forfeit to the sorcerer's god the moment he did so, the urge to bring the dagger plunging down was almost too much for him. Even though he knew it would be a betrayal of the armour he wore and the people he had trained alongside, still the desire filled him.

Subtle knowledge flooded into his head. He knew that if he struck now, he would become a traitor to all his people, that he would return to the Fang and betray the servants of Russ to their enemies. If he struck, all of Fenris and all of his people would fall into the pit of destruction and slavery. He stood for a moment balanced on a knife edge with hatred on one side and duty on the other. The fate of the world teetered in the balance. In one scale was his own all-consuming hatred. In the other scale was the knowledge that his name would live forever in infamy.

What did that matter? said a still, small voice. What did all of the people of Fenris mean to him? All of his blood kin were dead, slain by this man and his people. All the inhabitants of the Fang had ever done was force him to endure pain, humiliation and privation. If by slaying Strybjorn he caused his world's destruction, what of it? In the ensuing universal death the Grimskulls would be swept away in a tide of blood and final vengeance would be his. A vengeance so complete that it would never be exceeded.

His hand trembled and the blade began to descend. He fought against the urge. This was not the sort of vengeance he had wanted. This was not a clean kill in the hot blood of mortal combat. This was the slaughter of a bound foe whose soul would be devoured by a dark power. This was not a worthy manner of vengeance.

'Take your vengeance how you like,' the sorcerer said. 'But take it!'

He gestured and the chains fell away from Strybjorn. The Grimskull sprang upright.

'Traitor!' he shrieked and launched himself at Ragnar. Ragnar dropped him with a blow of his fist and reflex action almost sent the knife plunging into Strybjorn's breast. Once again he stopped himself.

Once again he became conscious of being a pawn of forces greater than he. Once again the vision of those terrible old men who lurked beyond the Gate of Morkai sprang into his mind. He knew they were out there somewhere, toying with him, examining the innermost secrets of his being, sifting his very thoughts and judging his worthiness.

The thought filled him with an anger hotter than his hatred. Who were they to judge him? Who were they to mould his mind to their will? He would have no more of it. He bit his tongue until pain seared through him. He took the knife and plunged it into his own stomach.

'No more of these games!' he shouted, falling to his knees and watching his own blood as it pooled at his feet. Agony seared through his veins. His lips twisted in a snarl of rage and pain.

The world trembled. Rocks tumbled down from the ceiling. Everything seemed to shift and dance and melt.

'I am Ragnar and I defy you!' he raved, as darkness complete and utter took him for the last time.

TEN
THE CUP OF WULFEN

RAGNAR AWOKE slowly and painfully. He felt tired as a man might who had risen once more from the dead. All of his energy, all of his life-force seemed spent. He could remember very little of his ordeal. It was an endless-seeming nightmare of violence and death where every weakness of his psyche had been probed and exposed. When he looked down at his body he was surprised to see that there were no marks on it, no wounds or bruises. He could not help but feel that there should be.

He was naked. He lay on a cold slab of stone in a cave. The light came from one of the strange sorcerous globes. On the other slabs lay other aspirants. He recognised Sven, Strybjorn and Kjel. Cold misty breath escaped from their mouths, congealing into clouds when it encountered the chill of the cave. Ragnar shivered and realised how cold he was. He picked himself up from the slab and inspected the other bodies. One of them, an aspirant he did not recognise, did not appear to be breathing.

Ragnar walked over, the icy coldness numbing his feet, and checked the body. He laid a hand on the youth's breast. It was cold and there was no heartbeat. The limbs were already stiff with rigour. So it was true then, Ragnar thought, you could die when you passed through the Gate of Morkai. He shivered again, not sure whether it was from the chill or from fear. He felt sure that he had narrowly evaded the same doom as this poor soul.

He felt a calm icy anger being born within himself. He was angry that anyone should rifle through his thoughts and memories like a reaver ransacking a house. What gave these people the right to do such a thing, he wondered? Or rather, what made them feel as if they had the right to do such a thing?

Something made him pause to consider. Whoever they were, they surely must be doing it for some purpose. Behind this relentless testing and winnowing, behind this unending weeding out of the weak and the unworthy there must be some great plan. It made no sense otherwise. It could not simply be a form of cruel amusement for the gods, could it?

He did not know. He only knew that he was cold and tired and hungry and that he wanted out of this terrible place. He stalked over to the cave mouth and saw there was another cave beyond. In it were more stone slabs, but these ones were empty. One of the strange creatures, half man, half machine, stood watching him. One eye was human and blue. The other was of glass and steel and reflected the light like a tiny sun. It turned to look at him, and as it moved its head there was a strange whirring noise. Ragnar could see its neck was partially covered in metal, and a collar of steel fitted into the metallic breastplate that covered its chest.

'Come with me,' it said, in a strange emotionless voice, in an accent that Ragnar could not recognise. He followed it through several metal doors. Passing through each the air temperature grew warmer. In the last chamber there were robes of the same stretchable material as the tunics the aspirants had been given in Russvik. These ones though had claw-like stripes on their chest as well as the wolf's head emblem. Ragnar paused and without being told put one on. He then followed the man-machine into a large chamber where Ranek waited with the three terrible old men who had watched beyond the Gate of Morkai.

He looked at Ragnar oddly and then smiled coldly, showing those massive fangs. 'You've set us a puzzle, laddie.'

Ragnar just looked at him, then let his eyes slide beyond to take in the old men in their armour and wolf pelts. They looked only slightly less grizzled than Ranek and there was about them an aura of power and strangeness. These ones had a touch of the weirdling, Ragnar thought, and no mistake. He had often suspected Ranek of being a sorcerer but he could see now that he was mistaken. These were the true sorcerers, the runeweavers, the seers who could see into men's minds. He felt his anger and his fear focus on them.

If they sensed it they gave no sign. They looked at him as a man might look at a dog they were considering purchasing. Ragnar gave his attention back to Ranek.

'No one has ever come closer to being failed,' Ranek said. 'There is a flaw in you, boy, and it might yet be your undoing.'

'A flaw?'

'Hatred. You have a capacity for hate that is so strong.'

'Since when has hatred been a flaw in a warrior? Hating his enemies makes a man strong.'

'Aye, but hating his comrades is an indulgence that a warrior cannot afford.'

'Oh?'

'You hate the Grimskull and you want revenge on him.'

Ragnar saw no point in denying it. 'Yes.'

'You are not the first to come here that way, laddie. Often we choose warriors from both sides in a struggle. Often old enemies join our ranks at the same time. They learn to fight together side by side.'

'That surprises me.'

'It should not. The process of being aspirants creates strong bonds. Only in your case it has not been quite successful.'

'I cannot be expected to let my enemy live.'

'You must decide what is more important. Killing your enemy or living your life with honour in the service of a great cause. The greatest. Believe me, in the future, if you live, you will have enemies enough to slake your lust for battle.'

'So I must spare Strybjorn or I will fail your tests?'

'No, you must spare Strybjorn or you will die.'

'Why are you telling me this?'

'Because you have it in you to be a great warrior, laddie. And we have desperate need of great warriors. But those warriors must be loyal and true to their comrades or they are useless both to themselves and to us. Beware, laddie, the path for the darkness to your heart lies through your hatred. Bear that in mind, always.'

Ragnar looked at the old man thoughtfully. He could think of no reply so he kept silent. He glanced at the others but their seamed faces were unreadable.

'Go to the antechamber and wait,' Ranek told him. 'Soon enough you will learn what this is all about.'

RAGNAR STOOD on the edge of a huge amphitheatre on the side of the Fang. It was so large it might have held tens of thousands instead of the meagre few score aspirants who waited there. Shafts of sunlight broke through the turbulent clouds. The air was chill and small snowflakes drifted on the wind. In the centre of the arena was an enormous dais on which was inscribed the wolf's head symbol. Huge wolf-headed statues guarded the entrance. Ranek stood in the centre looking at them. His chill gaze made Ragnar feel small.

'You have done well to get this far,' the Wolf Priest said. His calm, gruff voice carried effortlessly across the arena. He was a good speaker and the acoustics were perfect, Ragnar realised. His words affected Ragnar oddly. He felt a swelling of pride in his breast. This was the first praise the aspirants had ever received from him or any of the other masters. 'You have come from Russvik, Grimnir and Valksberg, all places where aspirants are judged. You have survived where others have died. You have proven yourself worthy of consideration to join our ranks.'

He paused for a moment to let his words sink in. Ragnar could see the smiles on the faces of the others, and he could tell that Ranek's words had affected them in exactly the same way as they had him. As they had been intended to, he thought sourly.

'Yes. But that is all you have proven. Everything you have undergone so far has been but children's games compared to what you must go through now. The real testing is just beginning.'

Groans escaped the lips of all the aspirants. Ranek smiled evilly before continuing. 'Do not whine. Once you understand why this must be done, you will see our purpose. You will know what it is you endure and you will know the reason why you endure it. You have come this far and you deserve to know this much.'

All were silent now. They sensed that they were about to become party to a great secret. Ragnar found that he was leaning forward, his ears pricked for the Wolf Priest's least word. Like all of them, he desperately wanted to know what this was about.

'Who do you think we are?' Ranek asked. 'Who do you think lives in this vast mountain?'

'Russ's warriors!' Strybjorn bellowed.

Ranek laughed and his laughter was chilling. 'Aye, that is what we are. We are indeed the Chosen Ones. Just as those who came before us were chosen. And those who came before them. And so on. And so on back to the dawn of time when Russ walked among men, and the All Father, the Emperor, fought his great wars against the powers of darkness.

'You stand indeed in the place of the chosen. This is the Fang. It is a mighty fortress in a vast struggle that is waged endlessly between the forces of mankind and the forces that would destroy it. It is a place from which great warriors set forth to walk among the stars, and perform missions that will affect the destiny of millions.

'You have no idea how momentous those missions are. There is no way you possibly could. If you survive it will be many years, perhaps many lifetimes as men measure these things, before you have the faintest inkling of it.

'You think you have been chosen to join the ranks of the immortals, to fight alongside Russ on the Day of Wrath. This is nothing less than the truth. The Fang is the home to a brotherhood of warriors, a Chapter as we call it. We are the sons of Russ, drawn from his people. We call ourselves the Space Wolves, and some day you will come to understand why.

'Let me tell you of Russ. Some of you may think of him as a powerful spirit, a god who watches over you. He was not. At least not in the sense you think. He was a man. Aye, and something more than a man. He was a primarch, a superhuman being raised above the level of normal mortals by the power and technology of the All Father. He was stronger, faster, tougher, more resilient, more potent than anything you can imagine. He founded our Chapter to follow him into battle. He chose our people, the folk of Fenris, to be his warriors. He chose only the hardiest and the best of our ancestors, for only they were worthy of this ultimate accolade. This is a tradition that we keep even in these lesser days.'

He paused for a minute and gazed at them. His eyes caught the light and seemed to burn like fire. None of them could meet his gaze. 'I bear within me the mark of Russ. All of the Wolves you will meet in this fortress do. It is a thing that has changed me. Made me different from mortal men. It has extended my life for centuries, made me faster, stronger, more powerful than any mortal man you have ever met or ever will meet. It may do the same for you.'

He paused again. All of the aspirants looked at each other. They were all wondering what he meant, Ragnar knew. His own mind reeled from what he had heard. How could this old man know what Russ was like? How could he speak with such certainty about the ancient times? He was not mad, as far as Ragnar could tell. He sounded convinced of his rightness. And of course he was different from all of the mortals Ragnar had ever met. He was larger, stronger, faster. He possessed those terrifying fangs and those odd wolf-like eyes.

'I say "may" because there is another possibility. It may kill you or it may do worse than kill you. It may transform you into a monstrous beast, a wulfen, a thing more than animal and less than man. Other things may go wrong too.'

The old man gestured and suddenly the chamber went dark. He alone was illuminated, standing in a pool of light. Ragnar heard some of the aspirants mutter about sorcery but he wondered. He had seen many things since he came here. It was just as likely that the old man had some hidden means of controlling those ever-burning lanterns. It seemed possible that they were simply machines, vastly more complex versions of the lamps he had seen at home. What happened next caused him to doubt his complacent assessment.

'Pay attention now,' Ranek said. 'You are about to take the first step along the path of knowledge.'

He gestured again, and suddenly floating in the air above him was a naked youth of about the same age as the aspirants. He looked so real that at first Ragnar suspected that he had materialised, been summoned like a spirit out of thin air. As he watched though he saw that there was no movement of any sort, and that if you looked very, very closely you could see through him. He was translucent as a spirit indeed. Ragnar wondered at the magic of it.

'This is a human youth. A lad very much like yourselves. Watch what happens next. You will see what happens when the canis helix is added; this is the mark of Russ.'

As Ragnar watched, the youth began to change. His body became more muscular and hairy. The fingernails thickened and became talon-like. The eyes took on the odd wolf-like look that Ranek's and Hakon's had. Fangs began to protrude from the gums. He took on the aura of strangeness and power that Ragnar had come to associate with the masters of the Fang. He could hear gasps of amazement from the other aspirants as they watched.

'At the end of the transformation, if all goes well, you will be many times stronger and faster than you are now. You will heal quicker. Your senses will be much keener. You will be braver and more ferocious than ever you were. If all goes well.

'If the change goes badly worse things may befall you.'

A look of idiot ferocity and madness came into the projection's eyes. It slumped forward in a disgustingly feral way. All intelligence drained from its face. 'You may go mad or become an idiot.'

The change continued. The thick growth of hair continued to sprout until it covered the whole body like an animal's pelt. The features of the face were obscured as if by fur. The talons on the fingers and toes grew longer until they became full claws. The fangs became so large they distended the face. A look of utter ferocious hunger distorted the youth's features. Ragnar remembered the creature he had once dreamed about. It had looked exactly like this except that the colour of the fur was slightly different. He did not doubt now that he had looked upon a wulfen.

'Or you may become a wulfen. Why is this, you are wondering? It is because the mark of Russ unleashes the spirit of the beast that is within us all. Some men are strong enough to control the beast. Others let the beast control them. When they do, a wulfen is born.

'All of these things are things that might happen once you drink from the Cup of Wulfen. If you survive this first transformation you will be well on your way to becoming a Space Wolf. The question that faces you now is do you have what it takes to face the beast within you? Or will you fail utterly and be consumed?'

Ragnar looked at the old man and wondered at his words. It seemed that they were not being given a choice. This was yet another test they must pass. Would they never end?

IN THE FANG he had no way of telling night from day. They were shown to individual cells and locked within them. A meal waited for him in the small chamber. It consisted of hot meat, fresh cooked bread and ale which tasted slightly metallic. He gulped it all down as if the meal could be his last. It tasted better than anything he had ever eaten.

As soon as he had finished it he stalked up and down his cell. He tested the door but it was locked and beyond his strength to open. Moments later the light went out and the room was plunged into darkness. Unable to do anything else he lay down on the pallet and within moments was asleep.

His dreams were dark. He was stalked through a maze by a monster. No matter how hard he ran and how cunningly he hid it was always there, a few steps behind. And he knew he did not dare look behind him, for if he did, he would see that the monster's features were his own.

His body was covered in cold sweat when he woke.

THE TEMPLE WAS elaborate, intricately decorated with finely worked stone worn with passing ages. Yet for all its splendour, Ragnar found the place gloomy. Artificial glow lamps threw their sodium glare into a carefully directed pool of yellow light, in which stood the centrepiece of the ancient chamber. Wolf heads decorated the altar, which appeared carved from a single rock. On its intricately carved stonework rested a chalice of some unknown metal, which also bore the wolf's head symbol of the Space Wolves. Ranek was there, looking old as the mountain itself. He was flanked by two masked warriors in similar armour to his own. Ragnar could see that one of the masked warriors had an arm that was made all of metal. Exposed bits of it clicked and whirred as it moved. Each of them held a device that looked like a hammer. Ragnar thought immediately of the hammer of Russ, the Lightning Bringer. Perhaps these weapons were its kin.

Ranek glared at them all then strode forward to the altar. He raised the great chalice with his massive gnarled hands then raised it aloft almost as if he were about to dash it upon the ground.

'Behold the Cup of Wulfen,' he said. There was hoarseness in his voice that took Ragnar a moment to work out was reverence. 'Look upon it and wonder. You look at an object older than this fortress: an artefact forged in the dawn of time by the servants of the All Father. This chalice was carried by the Chapter all through the Great Crusade. It was part of our heritage during the dark times of the Great Heresy and the war with Horus. The hands of Russ himself were clasped around this chalice in the dim dawn of time. Look upon it and think upon my words.'

Ragnar looked again. If what Ranek claimed was true, and he saw no reason to doubt the Wolf Priest, this was an artefact which had once been held in the hands of the god of his people. It was older by far than anything else he had ever encountered. At first glance it did not look like much, but even as he watched, he thought he could see glittering runes of light appear in its side. And a nimbus of strange energies played about it.

'We call this the Cup of Wulfen for a reason. The ancients who made this vessel imbued it with potent magics. Whoever drinks from this vessel will, if they are worthy, take upon themselves the mark of Russ, and with it a portion of the man-god's powers. If they are unworthy, they will pay a terrible price. Listen then to the tale of the wulfen, and know why.

'Back in the days when Russ first came to Fenris to recruit his warriors, there was a jarl named Wulfen. He was a mighty man, fell and strong, proud in his power. He was a man gifted beyond all others in the art of war and he was bested only once in his life, and that was by Russ, who humbled him before all his people but seeing a worthy warrior spared him, and offered him a place among his warriors.

'Russ spoke to the assembled men of Fenris and told them of his plan. He offered them power and a vast span of years if they followed him to make war among the stars. They roared their acceptance, and hailed Russ as their chief. He told them that they must drink a potent brew from the great cup and thus would their transformation begin. Wulfen was the first to step forward and he swigged the glorious mead of Russ from the chalice.

'But evil lurked still in Wulfen. He was consumed by a secret gnawing hatred of Russ and he planned to take treacherous revenge upon the man-god. The guardian spirit within the cup saw this the moment Wulfen put it to his lips, and it worked a spell on him, making his outer self match his inner evil. To the horror of those who looked on, the great chieftain changed. He turned into a dreadful thing, half-man, half-wolf and he sprang on Russ with a howl of hatred. But Russ was not dismayed. With one blow, he crushed Wulfen's skull and slew the beast that had been revealed.

'He looked upon his followers and told them that Wulfen was unworthy, and that this would be the fate of all those who drank from the chalice with evil in their hearts. He told them that those who wished could now depart without drinking. To our ancestors' credit, no man departed, and all drank and all gained the power that Russ had made their due. And thus began the founding of our Chapter. Those men strode forth to write their name in the history of all the worlds of men. Those who drink from this chalice now will do likewise. If they are worthy. Think on this for a moment.'

Ragnar thought. Was this just a story? Somehow he doubted it. So far they had been told nothing without a purpose, and Ranek did not look like the sort of man who was going to start making things up now. Even as he watched the two armoured warriors had begun to empty a strange brew into the chalice that Ranek held before him. The ingredients came from two separate flasks and as they mingled in the chalice, they began to bubble and steam. All the while they did this, Ranek spoke words in the strange tongue that Ragnar had heard before.

It seemed that if he drank from this chalice with evil in his heart, he was doomed to become a monster, and doubtless to be killed like the original Wulfen. He wondered though where the monsters they called wulfen came from then. If they were unworthy aspirants, why were they still alive? How did they escape from the Fang? Yet again he sensed a mystery here. One he was in no position to answer yet.

Another question nagged at him. Did he have evil in his heart? Would the terrible fate that befell Wulfen be his? He considered what he had been told earlier about his hatred for

Strybjorn. Was that evil? He did not think so. It was simply the way any warrior of Fenris would feel about one of the killers of his clan. Still, why had they warned him then?

The priests had finished mingling the contents of the flasks now. Ranek set the cup down on the altar. Inside it they could see the brew bubbling like a devil's broth. The Wolf Priest glanced around at all of them, then reached within his pouch and produced a handful of wooden straws.

'Each of you must drink. You are not asked to volunteer. It would be pointless. We will let Russ decide the order. In my hand are a number of spills of wood. On each is cut a number of notches. Each of you will take one spill. Starting with the one whose spill has the highest number of notches, you will drink. You will come forward in order, kneel before the altar and take a mouthful of the holy mead from the chalice. Is that clear?'

All of them yelled their assent. There was a nervous quality to every voice, Ragnar thought. And no wonder. Each of them must be thinking about the possibility of becoming a ravening beast. Ranek advanced towards them with his hands outstretched. One by one the aspirants took a piece of wood from his hand. Ragnar watched their faces for a response. He was gratified to see Strybjorn's twist with something like dismay. When his own turn came, his hand was steady when he reached out to take the small splinter of wood. Before he even looked at it his fingers had felt its side and he discovered only one notch. It appeared that he would be going last. He did not know whether to be glad or sorry.

Ranek told them all to open their hands, and looked at the spill they had chosen. He arranged them in order of their numbers and then returned to the altar. Ragnar saw that Strybjorn was at the front, then Sven, then Kjel. There were others between him and his comrades. As he had suspected he was going last.

'Advance to the altar,' Ranek said.

Strybjorn walked forward. His face was pale but determined. He knew that all eyes were upon him, waiting to see his response. He was not going to show any fear. Hatred warred with admiration for the Grimskull's courage within Ragnar as he watched Strybjorn's firm stride. Strybjorn knelt before the altar then rose proudly to take the Cup of Wulfen with a firm hand. He raised it to his lips, threw back his head and drank. Ranek had to reach forward and pull the cup down to stop him drinking it all.

Strybjorn stood there for a moment. All of them watched with baited breath to see what would happen. Ragnar could hear the beat of his own heart, feel the sweat on his palms as he waited. He was ready to leap forward and strike Strybjorn down with his bare hands if he showed the slightest sign of a change. He doubted that he would have time to do anything before Ranek but he would at least try.

Moments passed. Nothing happened. Ranek gestured for Strybjorn to step back, and the Grimskull backed away. Sven strode forward next. His movements were jaunty; his chin was held high. He forgot to kneel, though, and Ranek brought him to his knees with a blow. Sven shook his head, grinned at the Wolf Priest without malice and rose to drink from the chalice. He even smacked his lips when he finished and managed a belch. Ragnar was surprised that Ranek did not hit him again. Instead he merely laughed and told Sven to move away. Once again no change occurred.

Kjel moved forward. He looked pale and shaken but he took the chalice and drank. He grimaced as he finished the mead and looked as if he wanted to spit it out but somehow he forced it all down then he too backed away. No change swept over him.

One by one the aspirants advanced. One by one they drank. None of them became monsters. Then all too quickly it was Ragnar's turn. He marched forward, feeling the eyes of all the others burning into his back. They were all watching him now, wondering if he would be the one to fail. They had all passed. They were secure. He was not.

He kept his tread steady as he marched towards the altar. He kneeled before it, offered up a silent prayer to Russ and then rose to take the Cup of Wulfen from Ranek's hands. It was heavier than he expected. The metal was cool to the touch and his hands tingled with the contact. Yes, there was indeed magic here, he thought. He raised it to his lips and paused for a moment. He paused and the warning he had been given after he had passed through the Gate of Morkai flashed through his mind. Did his hatred of Strybjorn represent the kind of flaw which would unleash the beast within him?

A momentary urge to drop the thing passed through him, to throw it away as if it had turned into a poisonous serpent in his hands. If the fluid was spilled he would not have to drink it, he could not become a monster. Had the others all felt this way, he wondered. Had they been tempted to cast the chalice away? Had they considered their own flaws before drinking? He steeled himself. He was not going to disgrace himself now. None of the others had, and he would not bring shame to the Thunderfist name. He was the last of them. If it were his destiny to become a hideous beast, so be it. He would face the doom the fates wove for him like a warrior.

He raised the cup to his lips and drank. From the smell he expected it to taste terrible. It did not. In fact, he could not detect what it tasted like at all. His tongue tingled and the roof of his mouth became numb. The back of his throat felt like he was downing a draft of ice cold water. He kept drinking and drinking until eventually he felt the chalice being pulled gently from his hands by the Wolf Priest.

Now his skin felt like it was tingling. His whole body felt cold. Was this it, he wondered? Was this the prelude to becoming a beast? Was he about to become a monster and be slain? He glanced up and looked into the eyes of Ranek. He saw nothing there. No sympathy, no horror, no alarm. He felt a little dizzy and it seemed as if the strength were going to drain out of him. He could hear his heartbeat loud as thunder now, and he felt certain that at any moment he was going to feel his muscles twist and tear as the transformation overtook him.

ELEVEN
THE SPIRIT OF
THE BEAST

IT WAS THE dream again. He was running down a dark corridor, in an endless maze, beneath a mighty mountain. Behind him the beast came on. It was huge and it was fierce and he knew that if it caught him it would devour him. His feet were like lead. The floor stuck to his soles like tar, slowing him down, but leaving his pursuer free to run at full speed. Its howls echoed through the darkened halls. Its breath was hot on his neck. Its foul slaver dripped on his flesh and when he turned to face it, it had his face, yet terribly altered, just as he'd known it would. He raised his hands to try and protect himself but it was no use. It reached out with mighty claws. They pierced his flesh and drew blood. The pain was like red hot irons in his side. He woke, his mouth wide open and only just managed to stop himself from shrieking.

For a moment, he saw one of the ectoplasmic wolf spirits that had entered him at the Gate of Morkai drifting just out of reach. As he breathed it shimmered and vanished, seemingly drawn back into his lungs with the intake of air. A hallucination, Ragnar told himself. Just a trick of his fevered brain.

His whole body ached. He felt like he had been stretched upon a rack. His head was sore. His gums bled. His hands hurt.

He felt alternately too hot and too cold. Sweat beaded his flesh for no reason that he could think of. It was hard to think. His thoughts felt slow as molasses. The pain made thinking difficult. He was numbed. Cold. Devoid of feeling.

Ragnar gazed down at his hands in wonder, squinting to make things clearer. His hand looked different. It was broader and flatter. The muscles had more definition. The nails were becoming thicker and sharper. Actually, the whole world looked different. His eyes were watering again. At least it was better than the searing pain that sometimes made it feel like someone had stuck a hot needle through his eyeball. He sniffed the air. There was that strange scent again. What was it? He shook his head. He had no idea. For the past week his nostrils had been assaulted by a tidal wave of scents so strong they threatened to overwhelm him.

The smooth sheets below him stuck to his skin. He peeled himself off. The friction of parting skin from silk felt like someone was going over his skin with a rasp. He had become far too sensitive. Somewhere, far in the distance, he could hear someone muttering. From the next cell he could hear Sven's breathing. The noise was appalling, like someone working a bellows. He shook his head again and waited for the sensations to subside.

They didn't. This did not surprise him. Sometimes they did. Sometimes they didn't. In fact, most often they didn't. He sometimes thought that it was not the sensations that subsided but his ability to endure them that increased. He was not sure though. He was not sure of anything. He was sick all the time. He felt nauseous but he also felt hungry. It was a torment almost beyond enduring.

Wild anger surged through him. He bit the inside of his cheeks until the salty tang of blood touched his lips. He battered his hands against the wall in blind rage until the blood flowed. The pain was almost unendurable to his heightened senses but in some strange way it helped to calm him, to bring him back to reason.

He rubbed the interwoven stretchable links of the metal bracelet on his arm, stopping when his fingers came to the metal disc that had been inscribed with his rune. It had been put there by the Iron Priests after he had drunk from the Cup of Wulfen. Every aspirant had one. There was nothing magical about it as far as he could tell although it did have a rune inscribed on it. Every aspirant's rune was different. He and Kjel and the others had compared them. Ragnar's bracelet bore a rune like the figure of a man with two wavy lines above it. The lines might denote clouds or nothing at all. Kjel's rune showed a stylised hawk. Considering that it bore a slight resemblance to the double-headed eagle emblem they saw everywhere this might be considered a good sign.

His mind slipped in and out of focus. Think, he told himself. Remember! Your name is Ragnar. You are the last of the Thunderfists. You are a human being. Not some mindless beast. You are not ill. You are changing. The mark of Russ is upon you. He looked at his hands again. Yes. There was definitely more hair there now than there had been yesterday. There was more hair on his chest. On his whole body. He rose unsteadily to his feet, fighting off a wave of dizziness. He stood there for a moment, weak and shaking and feeble, and then as quickly as it had come the weakness passed, and he felt strong, strong beyond belief, strong enough to rip steel, to tear through stone. He raced out of the chamber and down the corridor, determined to find food to assuage the hunger that burned in his belly.

The corridors were comfortably darkened. It did not matter. His eyes could see in the dark now better than they once could. He did not need them anyway to find the food. He could smell it. He could smell the raw fresh meat even though it was hundreds of yards away. He bounded along past the cells where the others lay. None of them looked any better than him. In fact many of them looked worse. All of them looked different.

As he passed Kjel's cell he saw the Falconer lying there. His eyes were open and they reflected the dim light like a dog's or a wolf's. They were becoming just like the eyes of Ranek and Hakon and all the others they had seen here in the Fang. Ragnar guessed his own were too. Kjel looked bigger, more muscular too. He seemed to be sprouting like a weed, gaining height and muscle mass. They all were. Part of Ragnar's mind which was still functioning wondered whether that was one of the reasons the world looked subtly different. He had gained so much height in the past few days that his eyes were further above the ground. His whole perspective had altered. It was a source of wonder to him.

Another part of him did not care at all. It only wanted meat. It wanted to slake its hunger and then its thirst and then it wanted to throw itself on the floor and sleep. And it was prepared to kill anything that sought to prevent it from doing so. The part of Ragnar that was still human wanted to shudder. He knew the bestial part of him was getting stronger, was becoming so strong at times that it submerged his consciousness, drove out all rational thought. He tried to fight against it, knowing that the more this happened, the easier it would be for the wolf spirit to gain control again. Eventually it would gain control permanently and then to all intents and purposes Ragnar might as well be dead, for he would no longer exist as a man.

He made himself think. It was as if he had two souls now, one human and one beast. No, it was more like his soul had been split into two, one part animal, one part human, and they were fighting for control. He knew now that they had been wrong to think they had triumphed when none of them had changed after drinking from the Cup of Wulfen. The change was not like that in the tale Ranek had told. It was not instantaneous. It was slower, more subtle. It had taken days for the beast to begin to emerge and for the evidence of the internal changes to begin to become visible on the outside. They had all been too quick to think they had won. Ranek and the others, the two Iron Priests as he had called them, had known differently.

Ragnar forced himself to remember being led through the corridors of the Fang to these cells. At first it had seemed strange that the area had been sectioned off with barred metal doors. It had seemed like a prison, not a place for aspirants who had just passed an initiation test, and that was just what it was – a block of secure prison cells. They had been locked in these shadowy corridors to endure the changes and, it seemed, to go mad. At first they had not realised what was going on. Then they had started to feel ill. Then the fights had broken out as they had become aggressive and hungry and the craving for meat took them.

Ragnar shook his head as a wave of feral anger passed through him. Just the thought of anyone trying to stop him from getting his food filled him with rage. Let them try, he thought. He would tear their flesh from their bones with his bare hands and he would consume it. Stop, he told himself. That is not the way a man behaves. That is not the way a warrior behaves. A warrior has pride. A warrior has control. Somewhere deep within him, the beast howled mockingly.

He reached the area where the food lay. The bloody carcass of a huge deer had been thrown down onto the cold stone flags. He was lucky. None of the others were awake yet. No. Wait! What was that?

Ragnar was suddenly aware of the sound of padding feet behind him. Bare flesh slapped the stone. He turned to see Strybjorn racing towards him. Face twisted with hatred and hunger, Strybjorn looked different from the youth Ragnar had known back in Russvik. His features were broader, harsher, even more brutal. His eyes were wild. His nose was larger, nostrils wider. He was taller, broader, more muscular with the rangy strength of a full-grown warrior.

'Mine,' he shrieked and dived forward, fingers outstretched, nails like raking talons. For the barest of moments, Ragnar stood frozen. The part of him that was still human was horrified. If the Grimskull had been taken possession of by daemons it could not have been more horrible. There was a transformed, bestial expression painted on his face that was appalling to behold. His face was bright with anger. At that moment, he looked as if he fully intended to kill Ragnar. Part of Ragnar did not mind. Part of him welcomed it. Now was his chance to take final vengeance on his foe.

At the last second Ragnar sprang to one side. Strybjorn's nails raked his ribs, drawing blood. The salt tang of it assaulted Ragnar's nostrils and somewhere deep within him, the beast stirred. Suddenly he was furious again, filled with anger and a black brooding rage. Conscious thought faded, to be replaced by a desire to tear and rend. Animal savagery flooded his brain. It seemed like his mind would be drowned like a dragonship foundering in a stormy sea.

He fought back, trying to hold the wave of animal emotion in check, knowing that he would need his intelligence as well as animal cunning and ferocity to survive the coming struggle. Strybjorn sprang again. This time Ragnar bent double and allowed him to pass over his head. As he did so, Ragnar straightened, grabbed him and threw him to the ground. Strybjorn tumbled away. Ragnar twisted in time to see him land badly but keep rolling, dissipating the momentum of the fall, and eventually rise to his feet once more.

Part of Ragnar was aware that if this struggle was fought out to its logical conclusion then one or the other of them was going to die, or at least be seriously hurt. The beast within howled and jabbered. It did not care. It wanted only to fight. To kill or be killed and then, if it survived, to eat its fill. And part of the human Ragnar desperately wanted to do the same.

Ragnar was aware now that he was fighting this battle on numerous levels: not just with Strybjorn but with himself, with the thing that lurked within him. He knew now that if he gave way to the beast it would only become stronger, and that in the end would lead to a destruction as inevitable as anything that Strybjorn could mete out to him.

Already Strybjorn was returning to the attack, moving forward with swift padding steps, mouth open, teeth bared in a hideous grin that revealed his emergent fangs. In that moment, he truly looked daemonic. He lashed out, fingers flexed, hands become talons to rake and rend. Once more he drew blood. Once more Ragnar found himself fighting not just against the pain but against the near irresistible tide of anger and hate that urged him to leap forward and bury his teeth in Strybjorn's throat. The warning Ranek had given him after the Gate of Morkai flickered through his brain. He saw now that his hatred was indeed a weakness, one that would allow the beast within him to over-power his human self. Giving way now would merely lead to his soul's destruction. Revenge now was not worth the loss of his self. He would wait, and take it later, if he could.

Instead of attacking in bestial frenzy, he balled his hand into a fist and lashed out, catching Strybjorn a blow just above the heart. As the Grimskull reeled backwards, Ragnar struck again. His fist caught Strybjorn just beneath the jaw, hitting so hard that he rose onto the balls of his feet before slumping back-wards unconscious upon the ground. Ragnar fought down the urge to leap upon his recumbent body, to rend and tear until he drew blood, to kill and devour. At that moment he felt as if his sanity, his soul, teetered on the edge of a vast precipice, a misty gulf into which his spirit would fall, never to return to the world of men.

He knew that if he gave way to this urge, he would forfeit his humanity, finally and forever. Eating human flesh was one of the strongest taboos of his people, giving way to it would make him ashamed of himself, would be another way to make Ragnar the beast stronger and Ragnar the man weaker. He could not afford to let this happen. And yet part of him wanted to do it anyway, wanted to give in, to surrender the constant heavy burden of thought and become less than a man, yet more than a beast. He knew that there was a traitor in him that wanted simply to give way, to get it all over with, to end this one-sided struggle and enter a world where everything was simple and basic, where there was no need for reason or thought or honour. Part of him wanted to give way to the forbidden urge and drink human blood. And worse, he realised that dark thing had always been there, waiting only for the stuff within the Cup of Wulfen to bring it to light, to make it strong. And now Ragnar was not sure if he could stop it consuming him, even if he wanted to.

For a dozen heartbeats he stood there, at war with himself, struggling for control. It was a fight as swift and fierce and deadly as the one he had just had with Strybjorn and he knew the outcome was just as important. He fought for control, looked for a way of binding the beast. He forced himself to remember all the unfinished business he had that would not be dealt with if he surrendered to the beast. He would never penetrate the secrets of the Space Wolves. He would never understand their magic. Slowly, a breath at a time, he calmed down. His heart ceased to race. He managed to focus his eyes on the food that had been the initial cause of his brawl with Strybjorn.

He reached down and ripped out a huge chunk of raw bleeding meat with his fingers. He forced it into his mouth and began to chew the cold moist flesh hungrily. He swallowed quickly, and gulped more down, determined to eat his fill before anyone could stop him. He bit and chewed until his hunger was assuaged and only then did some semblance of sanity return.

He walked over to the drinking fountain where cold water poured down into a stone trough. By some magic it never overflowed. The water ceased to emerge as the trough was filled. He lowered his head to drink and froze as he caught sight of his reflection. He saw himself and it was not a reassuring sight. His hair was wild. His eyes glowed strangely. Blood had dribbled from the corners of his mouth and covered his hands and his clothes. His face was gaunt as a madman's. He opened his mouth and saw that his teeth were longer and sharper. His canines were becoming fang-like. He looked monstrous and feral. Thus must a wulfen look, he thought, when it emerges from its nighted lair to feast. Quickly he dropped his hands into the water and cupped them to drink. He told himself that it was because he was thirsty. In his soul, however, Ragnar knew that the real reason was to smash his reflection with the endless ripples.

RAGNAR FELT CALMER NOW. He had no idea how much time had passed, only that it had done so. At first he had tried to keep track of the number of days that had gone by, or at least the number of times the lights had dimmed and brightened, by scratching marks on the walls of his cell. He knew that this had not always worked. He knew that long periods had gone by while he lay in delirium or submerged in bestial frenzy, and he had been unable to make his mark.

He got up and made his way down to the feeding pit, for such was how he now thought of it. He was hungry still but not now with the ravenous burning hunger that had threatened to consume his soul. The beast was still there, he thought, but he had its measure now. It was part of him but he was in control of it. His senses no longer seemed so keen they hurt. He knew they were far better now than ever they had been before but he had grown accustomed to them. He could sift through the information they presented him with and understand it. In a way it was little short of miraculous. He could see things in the darkness, track people by scent, hear a feather drop.

And he felt faster and stronger than he ever had. He did not doubt that most normal people would seem to be moving like slugs to him now, if ever it came to combat. He was broader too. He could lift the great stone bench in his room, a feat that would have broken his back during his time in Russvik. He felt as if he could run for leagues now without tiring, and he was sure he was much tougher and healthier. He had never felt better in his entire life.

Not everyone had been so lucky. He squirmed when he remembered some of the things that had occurred. They were like dimly recalled scenes from some terrible nightmare. Some of the aspirants had gone mad. He remembered Blarak dashing his brains out against a wall, and someone else trying to eat them. He was only glad that it had not been him. It could so easily have been when the madness was upon him.

He shivered, wondering if truly it was all over, whether he really was his own master once more, or whether the madness had merely abated temporarily. In the feeding pit, he knew, fresh raw meat awaited him.

THE IRON PRIESTS pulled Ragnar from the sensor coffin. It was just as well, he thought. He was not sure that he could have stood it for much longer. The metal walls enclosing him in their cold grip, the sensor probe wires wriggling like snakes across his skin, the strange jolts of sensation as the Priests invoked their magical engines had all conspired to drive him to the edge of sanity. Had he been incarcerated in this cold tomb for hours, days or perhaps years? He had no way of telling! The beast within him had howled and raved, sickened by its imprisonment, desperate to escape, and for once Ragnar had found himself in complete agreement.

He knew now that this served a purpose, that the Iron Priests were testing him, seeing how his body was adapting to the changes, monitoring him to see if anything had gone wrong. He knew that the blood samples they drew from his body with their brass needles were sent somewhere to be analysed with ancient machines, and that the reflex tests administered with jolts of chained lightning were carefully assessed by the priests. Even so, knowing that this rigour, this testing, was for the good, somehow did nothing to allay the maddening claustrophobia which Ragnar experienced as it felt like he was about to be crushed in a confined space, and his mind cried for the wide open spaces of the outside world.

And, of course, he thought sourly, none of this was for his benefit. Their magic could allow the priests to predict what was going to happen to him. It seemed that once their changes had begun they could tell who was going to descend into madness, who was going to mutate, and who was going to descend into the monstrous condition of being a wulfen. They just would not do anything about it. They seemed content to let these things take their course and inscribe the results in their great musty leather-bound tomes. Their attitude seemed to be that there were plenty more aspirants to choose from, and if an individual failed, well, it was the will of the gods.

He shook his head and gazed around the chamber. It was huge and lit by the flickering light of ancient glowglobes. All around, massive machines hummed and whirred. They seemed incomprehensibly ancient, and in places they were rusted. Huge clumps of wires bound by copper coils and inscribed with hoary runes ran from engine to engine and connected them to the massive control altars behind which the Iron Priests sat and prayed and invoked the strange electrical spirits which they worshipped. The air smelled of ozone and oil and the unguents used to polish the machinery. Halos of luminescence played around the active engines showing the presence of the spirits they had summoned. From where he stood Ragnar could see Strybjorn strapped into a monstrous copper circle. His arms and legs were splayed as if he had been crucified. The circle floated inside another circle and slowly rotated first to the left then to the right then upwards so that Strybjorn was suspended upside down and then back to its normal position. As it did so, in the air next to the machine an image formed. It was roughly the same size as Strybjorn and had his outline made all of glowing lines of light. In some areas, mostly around the head and chest the lines were a deep angry red; in most other places they were green or yellow. Ragnar guessed that the individual colours indicated the areas in which most changes were taking place in the aspirant's body, but as with every new thing he experienced here, he did not know for certain. After a moment's hesitation, Ragnar resolved that there was only one way to find out.

'What do the lines on that glowing figure mean?' he asked pointing in Strybjorn's direction. The Iron Priest turned to look at him, his features covered by his expressionless metal mask. He fingered one of the runes inscribed on the ingots of iron around his neck and stared at Ragnar as if considering whether to reveal one of the secret mysteries of his order. Ragnar noticed with a faint shock of recognition that the rune was the same as one of the runes inscribed on the sides of the Temple of Iron on the Islands of Fire. Was there a connection between the two orders, he wondered?

'The red areas on the holoshadow indicate places within the aspirant's body where great changes to its internal chemistry are still taking place. The yellow areas are the ones which are either stabilising or beginning to change. The green areas are stable.'

Ragnar had no idea what the word 'chemistry' meant but he saw that his general idea had been correct. He was surprised that the priest was telling him this too. In the past these servants of Russ had been terse and uncommunicative, but now perhaps a change seemed to be coming over them. This one still did not quite seem to regard him as an equal but at least now appeared to consider him to be someone of some small merit. A brief surge of excitement passed through Ragnar. Perhaps he could see how Ragnar's change was going and whether the omens were favourable. Or perhaps it would be better not to know, to sink in ignorance into raving bestiality, if that was to be his fate. He decided to see if he could find out.

Once more the Iron Priest considered his question for a long time before responding in his slow cold voice. This time Ragnar was quite certain he recognised the accents of the Island of Fire in the man's speech.

'Your transformation is proceeding slowly and in a controlled fashion,' he said eventually.

'Is that bad?' Ragnar asked, worry gripping his bowels.

'Negative. Generally it is a positive indicator. A body which adapts in a slow, steady fashion usually adapts to the genetic implants favourably. Normally it is when change occurs in rapid, uncontrolled spurts that we see unfortunate degradation in the subject.'

'So I'm going to survive.'

'We did not say that. There is always some room for error in these auguries. Sometimes an aspirant appears fine for months and appears to successfully complete the transformation, then devolves at the last second. Sometimes aspirants begin to degrade and then recover. Nothing is certain. All of it is chance and down to the will of Russ and the blood spirits.'

Ragnar shivered. He might have guessed how the priest's answer was going to sound. It seemed there was still every possibility that he was going to fail.

WEEKS PASSED. Ragnar felt a lot better now. He felt the same way he had when he recovered from the purple fever as a child. While he was sick it had seemed as if he were never going to feel well again. Now that he had recovered, he was profoundly grateful for the feeling of health and strength that he possessed. Everything looked brighter, more colourful. The air smelled sweeter. Food tasted better. The feeling of the strange fabric against his skin was no longer a torment but a pleasure.

Of course, he told himself, that too might not simply be to do with his feeling better. It might well be because of the changes wrought by drinking from the Cup of Wulfen. All of his senses seemed much keener now, and in terms of strength and fitness he felt better than he ever had. The Iron Priests had pronounced themselves well satisfied with his transformation, although they had, as ever, managed to add a few cryptic warnings, saying there was still a danger of something going wrong.

Ragnar did not need their warnings to tell him this. He could still sense the beast spirit waiting within himself, although to tell the truth every day he was becoming more comfortable with its presence. It was simply part of him now, a thing that would give him strength and ferocity when called on, and which enabled him to understand the information his altered senses gave him. He felt now like he was part man and part wolf, or perhaps something greater than either. Just from looking at the other Aspirants he could tell that not all of them felt the same way. Perhaps they were finding it more difficult to adapt.

Kjel looked haunted. There was a strange fey look in his eyes and his face was gaunt and strained. He constantly glared about him like a cornered beast. When he sensed Ragnar's eyes upon him, he growled and spat as if sending a warning. Ragnar noticed that Kjel was beginning to sprout hair all over. It covered the backs of his hands and protruded from the collar and wristbands of his tunic. His posture had changed too. He hunched forward with his hands held low and his fingers hooked like claws. Ragnar found it hard to see the bright, cheery Kjel he had once been in this wild-looking creature. Kjel scratched at the bracelet on his wrist, clawing around it until he drew blood from his own flesh. There was something about him that reminded Ragnar of a wolf with a paw caught in a trap.

Sven, on the other hand, was less changed in appearance, perhaps because he had always been more savage to begin with. He grinned at Ragnar, showing his new fangs, and his eyes caught the light of the glowglobes, reflecting it eerily. If anything Sven had become even broader and more muscular. His arms were now the size of Ragnar's thighs and his chest was round as a barrel. Ragnar sensed that Sven was enjoying the transformation now and almost at peace with the beast which undoubtedly raged within him.

Aware of a burning gaze upon himself, he turned to look at Strybjorn. Now there was a man who was not at all relaxed. The Grimskull was taut as a hawser drawn tight in the wind. There was something wild about him; a mad rage ran amok in his eyes, and it was evident in his posture too. Strybjorn looked as if he were ready to leap into action at any second, at the slightest provocation. Looking into his deep, cave-like eye sockets it was all too easy for Ragnar to perceive the beast lurking within.

Ragnar still found it odd, almost uncomfortable how he seemed able to sense the others' moods and perhaps glean something of their thoughts. Perhaps that was another effect of the transformation. Perhaps they were becoming more like wolves in a pack, able to understand each other by means other than words and gesture. Perhaps he was reading things in his fellow aspirants posture and scent. That was partly it, Ragnar realised. He felt as if he could almost smell their moods. Kjel's strangeness had an odd acrid odour. The smell of Strybjorn's restrained wrath reminded him of smouldering wood. Sven's cheeriness of the scent of ale. He knew these were imprecise ways of describing the things even to himself, but he did not have the words to do otherwise. There was nothing in his language to express the ideas, to describe the smells or to distinguish the million subtle alterations in the scents which Ragnar now knew happened with every heartbeat.

Ragnar looked around at the others and his heart fell. So few remained. Nils was still there, and a stranger called Mikal. There was no sign of any of the others. He had no idea what had happened to them. Somewhere in the fever-dream madness that were the memories of his transformation, he thought he could discern images of the Iron Priests entering and carrying away aspirants who had become slinking monsters or who had descended into gibbering madness, but he was not sure. He knew that for as long as he lived he would never be entirely certain of what had happened during this period of his life, and in a way he was glad. He was sure there were actions in there that he would rather not recall.

The metal door swished open magically, parting into two distinct sections. Ranek stood there in his full mystical regalia. He surveyed them for a moment and then smiled grimly. What he said next sent a shiver of fear to Ragnar's core.

'Not many now,' Ranek said. 'Not many at all. And soon there may be less. It is time for the ultimate test.'

TWELVE
THE ULTIMATE TEST

RAGNAR SHIVERED. It was cold and it was dark and he was alone. He looked out across the chill landscape and the titanic peaks and realised that he could quite easily die here. For the first time in months, he was really and truly on his own. There was no one around for a hundred leagues. Already the Thunderhawk was receding into the distance, vanishing into the heavy grey clouds in the direction of the Fang. He had been the last to be dropped into the snow. The others had been set down already somewhere off in the far distance among the isolated peaks. Ragnar had not realised that there were quite so many aspirants until he had seen them all troop aboard the gunship. All told, he had counted over a score of them on the Thunderhawk. Obviously, Ragnar thought, Space Wolf candidates were brought in from places other than Russvik and kept in many separate areas of the Fang. He had no idea why this was, he just knew it must be so. It was the only explanation he could think of. Swiftly he dismissed the thought as irrelevant to the matter at hand. He had his survival to think of.

Ragnar glanced around him at the bleak and dreary landscape. Huge boulders had tumbled into the valley and obscured much of it from view. Some of the massive rocks were covered in lichen, which showed that it was at least possible for plant life to survive in this barren wilderness. Many of the boulders were already partially covered in snow. Large flakes were starting to fall, slowly, softly but inexorably. After a moment or two contemplating the dismal scene before him, Ragnar shook his head to clear his befuddled thoughts, took a breath of the chill air and took stock of his situation.

All he wore was the grey tunic of an aspirant and the leather belt that held his scabbard and dagger. That was it. He had no supplies of any sort. Nothing else to help him survive in this deadly place. Ragnar knew that at first glance, his task might seem a simple one: he had to return to the Fang and present himself to the Space Wolves. If he survived, he would be initiated as a true Space Marine. If he failed, he would most likely be dead. It was as simple as that.

Things were not so bad, Ragnar told himself. It could be worse. At least his aspirant's tunic, woven as it was from some strange grey material, was uncannily warm. And he had his knife. It did not sound like much even to Ragnar, standing alone in the darkness in the snowy wastes high in the mountains of Asaheim. However, at least the Fang was easy to find. It towered above every other peak in the range and was visible on the horizon. But even as he thought this, another part of his mind whispered that he was doomed. There was so much that could go wrong. Warm though his tunic was, he doubted that it would prove warm enough if the winds really started to blow and the temperature began dropping. And there was always the possibility of it being ripped and torn as he travelled. Ragnar wondered whether it could maintain its miraculous warming qualities then.

Yes, the Fang was visible, but from his time in the far lesser mountains around Russvik, Ragnar knew that clouds and freezing fog could descend at any time, reducing visibility to zero. These valleys were most likely a maze and it would be all too easy to get lost if that happened. And what was he going to do for food? This landscape was as stark and bare as the plains of hell. He doubted that he would find anything edible here. And if he did, it would perhaps find him just as edible.

There might well be packs of the great iron grey wolves at large in these peaks, or trolls, or nightgangers or cannibal tribesmen or, worst of all, there could easily be wulfen. Not even his knowledge of how wulfen were born could shake him of his fear of the monsters.

Well, Ragnar thought, there would be time enough to worry about these things when or if he encountered them. Right now, he had better start moving. Perhaps he could find a cave before it really got dark.

AHEAD OF HIM was a stunted tree. Ragnar was strangely reassured and cheered by the plucky tree. It was small and warped, but at least it was growing, clinging to the hillside with its roots. It was defying the mountain, and it showed that living things could survive here. More, if he were clever, it would help him survive. He knew that soon, if he continued to descend, he would see other trees. He had been among mountains long enough to know now that there was a line above which trees did not grow, and that the highest ridges and peaks were bare of all vegetation except moss.

He took up another handful of snow and stuffed it in his mouth. At least he would not die of thirst as long as it lay on the ground. From the things Hakon had told them back at Russvik he knew it was possible that disease spirits might lurk in the unpurified water but right now he did not care. Thirst was a far more real and imminent danger, and he had no way yet of making fire nor any pot to boil water.

The snow froze his gums and chilled his tongue, but it melted and he gulped it down. In his hand Ragnar held a chunk of flint which he had picked up amongst the treacherous banks of shale and scree on the mountainside. He wished he had a pouch to carry it in, but he did not, so holding it in a clenched fist was his only option. The rock would serve two purposes, Ragnar hoped. The first was that he could throw it at any marauding beasts. And with his new-found sheer muscle power, Ragnar was utterly confident that he could throw a sharp stone very hard indeed. The thought brought a wolfish smile to his face. The second use for the flint was that he could strike it with his knife to create sparks, and thus make a fire.

Some hope, Ragnar thought, strength draining out of him as he looked at the damp bark of the tree. Now he had wood aplenty, but it was wet and cold, and Ragnar knew that there was no chance of getting it to catch fire under these conditions.

Ragnar shivered again, and briefly wondered how the others were doing. Had their past few days been as hard as his, a long weary trudge through the snow and cold, trying to follow the valley paths and to always keep the great peak of the Fang visible ahead of them? Had they shivered at the wind's chill blast as they passed along narrow and slippery ledges which hung out over awful rock strewn gorges? Had they kept their ears peeled for the calls of the great beast, the wulfen which they all feared so? Had they watched in awe as a mighty rock eagle passed overhead scanning the bleak landscape for prey with eyes keen enough to spot a mouse moving from a thousand feet up? Had they too survived by chewing edible moss, and eating eggs stolen from the nests of mountain birds?

Ragnar shivered. It was possible that the others were already dead. He had seen so many ways to die on his march so far, and he was only a few days in. In the storm-wracked mountains, there was the constant possibility of avalanche and rock falls. There was the strength-sapping chill all around that made you just want to lie down and die. There were the narrow paths where a single misstep would cast the careless down into a great abyss. Perhaps they had been eaten by beasts. Perhaps they had gone mad. Perhaps the delayed effects of the transformation had taken them and they had become monsters themselves, even now hunting for Ragnar to rend him limb from limb.

Of all the possible fates which preyed on his mind, this was the one that affected Ragnar the most. He knew that there was still the possibility that something might go wrong even now. The Iron Priests had told him that no aspirant was safe for at least a month after the transformation and possibly not even then. The beast that lay deep in his mind might still leap forth to devour his soul. Perhaps this wild place was all it needed to leap out and possess him utterly. It was not a reassuring thought.

Ragnar forced himself to put one foot in front of the other, knowing that soon he would have to find a place to rest for the night once more. Even with his newly altered eyes, travelling in darkness in these mountains would most likely prove suicidal. There was always the possibility of missing something, of stepping on a patch of scree and tumbling downslope, of stumbling into an unseen pit. Besides, at night the temperature would soon drop even further and he had no wish to test the heat-retaining abilities of his tunic any more than he had to. One thing Ragnar had learned during his time at Russvik was that survival in these circumstances was mostly a matter of doing nothing to provoke the Fates. Rather like playing a game of chance, the trick was to keep as many of the odds in your favour as you could. This meant not taking risks unless you had to. Even if you were strong and capable and confident, as Ragnar most certainly was with his new found strength and combat skills, a slight mishap would be enough to end your life under these harsh conditions. Even a minor accident, a sprained ankle, a twisted limb, a minor ailment could be enough. Ragnar knew that such an accident would bring weariness, numbing the mind, sapping the strength, making the toughest warrior easy prey to other dangers. Over time such minor scrapes or injuries could grow gradually worse until eventually they immobilised even the strongest amongst the Space Wolves. Ragnar resolved that the trick, then, was not to fall victim to the slightest avoidable mishap in the first place. Easier said than done, he thought.

He looked around for a place to rest and saw that near the tree there was a small indentation with an overhanging ledge which protected the hollow from the worst of the wind and falling snow. Ragnar decided that this was as good a shelter as he was likely to find this night. He began to hack at the tree, collecting twigs and needles and cones for firewood and a long heavy branch that would serve as both club and walking stick. After some effort, he even managed to cut off a longer, straighter, narrower branch which Ragnar hoped he might be able to sharpen and use as a spear.

It took Ragnar some time to collect his booty and return to his resting place. It took him a longer time yet to give up trying to get a fire started using sparks from his knife and flint over a pile of needles and cones. The needles were damp and in no condition to catch light. At least such activity kept him awake, and Ragnar thought that this was probably a good thing in this frozen and desolate landscape. Eventually, chilled and weary, he made a carpet of needles to provide some insulation from the cold rock and then lay down and fell asleep. His last thought was to wonder whether he would ever awaken.

* * *

RAGNAR DREAMED of wolves. He dreamed of beasts that were half-man, half-wolf. He dreamed they were stalking him through the endless stone canyons that lay in the shadows of the mountains. In his dream he was cold. In his mind he sensed the presence of the other, of the beast that had awakened within him when he drank from the Cup of Wulfen. It too responded to the howls. For once it did not seem to want to struggle against his control. It seemed to realise that they shared a body, and that if Ragnar died then its existence too would end. It was just as wary of any threats as he was, and for the first time Ragnar began to see the possibility of something other than an uneasy truce between him and his darker more feral side.

In his dream, Ragnar began to stalk his enemy, rather than slinking away, and guided by the wolf spirit within him, he knew that he would find prey within the stone valleys, that soon he would be able to bury his own fangs into hot, blood-soaked meat.

HE AWOKE IN darkness to bone-chilling cold, shivering, unsure whether the sound he was hearing was something from the shadow world of his dream or from the harsh, flinty realm of reality that surrounded him. He did not have to wait long to find out. The howl sounded again, louder and closer now. Surely it was the wail of a storm daemon summoning its brethren. A cry of unutterable hunger and pain and weariness. Ragnar recognised it as the howling of one of the great wolves of Asaheim. He shivered, knowing that if any of the creature's kin were near, his life would soon be over. Assuming surprise, he might be able to overcome one of the great beasts in combat but there was no way he could defeat a pack. Ragnar knew that acting en masse the wolves of Fenris could drag down a troll or even an ice dragon. In all the wastelands of Asaheim there were no more fell creatures.

He strained his ears to listen and tested the night winds with his nostrils. He thought he smelled something, the tattered remnants of a sour odour fragmented by the wind's cold fingers. It was a smell that he instinctively recognised as belonging to one of the great wolves. He pulled himself low in his lurking place and considered his options. There was at least one good thing about his situation. At the moment he was downwind of the wolf. He could smell it but it could not smell him. Of course that could change as quickly as the wind could shift direction but there was nothing he could do about this, other than pray to Russ that it did not happen. And there was something else about the wolf scent too – a taint, a stink, an odour as of sickness or disease. Ragnar was not yet experienced enough to know exactly what such a smell meant but he hoped that it indicated the creature was merely ill and not the carrier of some plague taint.

He checked his weapons. He held his knife in his left hand and his spear in his right. The club lay nearby, ready to be seized up after the sharpened stick was cast. Ragnar did not hope for much from it; he had intended to harden the point in the flames of the fire he had never managed to start, so he had no idea how effective it would be. Still, it had to be better than nothing. Ragnar thought it a pity he had no shield. He shrugged. He might just as well wish for one of Ranek's magical weapons. Both things were just as unavailable to him.

Ragnar stilled himself. The hair on the back of his neck rose as he heard the faint scraping of talon on stone, and then loping down the long track the Fenrisian wolf came into view. Marvelling at the ability of his eyes to pick out detail even in the dark of night, instantly Ragnar could see that the wolf was old and wounded. Its fur was white and mangy, an old wound going gangrenous in its side was the source of the rotten stink. It was limping a little and favouring its right front foot.

Ragnar held his breath. It was an old wolf, perhaps a pack leader that had lost its struggle against younger more fearsome wolves and had thus been driven out. It was obviously weakened and starving, and yet it still looked like a fearsome foe. It was as high at the shoulder as Ragnar was and even in its weakened state must outweigh him by almost two to one. Its fangs were like daggers and its eyes burned with red madness. Even as Ragnar saw all this, it appeared to notice him for the first time. It opened its mouth and let out another long lonely howl of rage and hatred, and then it sprang.

Ragnar reacted instantly, casting his spear directly at the mighty beast's breast. The point of the weapon struck home driven by the full power of Ragnar's steely muscles. Blood flowed where the fur parted. The wolf tumbled and the shaft broke. Ragnar hoped the tip was left embedded in the wound.

He did not wait to pick up the club, but seizing his advantage leapt forward himself. The immense wolf snarled and lunged at him. Ragnar sprang to one side and caught the enraged brute around the neck, avoiding its deadly fangs. He had no doubt that one bite would rip his throat out or smash a limb to a bloody pulp. Ragnar intended to wrestle the beast down, confident of the power in his superhuman muscles to overcome any mere wolf. As the beast growled and strained to best the aspirant, Ragnar quickly learned that his blind confidence was misplaced.

It was like trying to hold back an avalanche. Enormous cable-like sinews bunched beneath the matted fur. The scent of the wolf's foetid breath stung Ragnar's nostrils. With the cunning of years, the great wolf hurled its weight against Ragnar, smashing him against the sharp rocks which lay strewn about the valley floor. Razor shards cut his arms in a dozen places, and his hands soon ran slick with his own blood. With the weight of the old beast on his chest, Ragnar felt the breath being forced out of his lungs. Soon he was gasping, and lights danced before his eyes. The wolf growled deep in its throat. He hooked his arm around its throat and struggled with all his strength to hold the beast in place. It turned and snapped up at him. The horrid jaws closed like a bear trap mere inches from Ragnar's nose. With his breath coming in ragged gasps, Ragnar swiftly brought his knife up and stabbed it repeatedly and frenziedly into the warm yielding flesh of the wolf's throat. He pulled the knife crossways, feeling the drag of muscle, sinew and artery. Blood spurted as the beast's throat was cut. Warm and crimson fluid jetted out onto the cold grey stone. As the blood steamed in the cold night air, Ragnar held the wolf in place until its thrashing struggles lessened, became feeble, and then finally ceased.

Then he set to work butchering the creature.

RAGNAR WAS WELL pleased with his night's work. He had a new cloak of uncured wolfskin hide. Granted, the scraped fur stank, but it served as another layer of insulation around his body. The raw meat of the creature's flesh and innards had assuaged his aching hunger and drinking its warm blood in his cupped hands had refreshed him. Better yet, the wolf's sinews would provide him with cord to bind his knife to the tip of a spear, turning it into a really formidable weapon, once he found another suitable branch. A tattered scrap of fur had already provided him with a pouch to carry his flints in. He had used a final strip to create a makeshift sling with which he could hurl jagged fragments of rock at great speed and distance. As he marched along he practised with it, achieving a tolerable proficiency.

Ragnar studied the sky, not liking the look of it. Huge black sooty clouds obscured the Fang and the southernmost portion of the heavens. He thought he could hear the distant rumble of thunder. Still, there seemed to be nothing else he could do except push on. Munching on a still moist strip of wolf flesh he set out at an easy lope down the slope.

USING HIS newly-made spear like a staff, Ragnar continued on through the wood. He was happy with his new weapon. The long branch was strong. The dagger was fixed firmly in place at its tip. He felt ready now to take on almost anything.

He liked it better here, he thought, looking at the mass of pines that surrounded the trail. The forest seemed endless but it was warmer and he was now far below the barren ridges above the tree line. Streams raced downwards, carrying meltwater and rain from the peaks. Birds whistled and sang and there were signs of small animals everywhere. He knew now that at least he was not going to starve or die of thirst.

Already he had clambered into the trees and recovered some eggs, sucking the contents out through a small hole he had punched in the top. The stream water was cold and refreshing and he wished he had something to carry it in. If he stayed in this forest, it would be possible to live here, Ragnar thought. Perhaps he should try. After all, he did not have to go back to the Fang, and he owed nothing in particular to the Wolves except a lot of pain. Ragnar doubted that anyone would ever find him if he chose to remain here in isolation. In fact he quite sincerely doubted whether anyone would even try. The Space Wolves' attitude seemed to be that they did not want anyone who could not meet their standards anyway, and simply by not returning, Ragnar knew he would fail that test.

Looking around as he walked, Ragnar saw more and more evidence that in truth a man could live in these woods quite well. He could build a lean-to as he had been taught, which he could use until he found a suitable cave. He could dry out wood. He could build a fire. He could hunt, and find edible vegetables. He could have a long life here, living by his own rules in a land which would be his own small kingdom.

And yet, Ragnar knew in his heart of hearts that he could not abandon his quest. It was not simply a matter of pride, either, although that most certainly played its part. He had unfinished business back at the Fang with Strybjorn, if the Grimskull bastard was still alive. But more than that there was something else. Ragnar did not want to exist alone out here in the mountain forests. Something at the Fang called to him, as the fellowship of the pack might call out to a wolf. Ragnar had been changed when he drank from the Cup of Wulfen, he knew. He had become something more than and less than a man. It was as if the beast that had awakened within him had made him at least part wolf, and the wolf within him craved the company of the pack. He craved to find a place in it. He craved to carve out his own position within its hierarchy.

More than that, Ragnar knew now that there was something back at the Fang itself he also craved. While he had taken nothing but hard knocks from Ranek and Hakon and their ilk, he knew now that they were supermen worthy of respect, and that they considered their tasks in this life to be worthy and honourable. Ragnar knew that he wanted what they had: their certainty, their pride, their power, their magic. He wanted to become one of the secret masters of this world, and more than that he wanted to be worthy to be one of them. And Ragnar knew he would not do so by remaining here among the woods and mountains no matter how appealing the thought might be.

Ragnar knew that since he had been chosen, he had changed, and not simply because he had drunk of the Cup of Wulfen. A whole new world had opened up for him, a place wilder and vaster than anything he had ever imagined back on his home island. He had done things that none of his people ever had: he had ridden in flying ships, passed through the Gate of Morkai, looked upon the cloud-capped spires of the Fang. He had begun to understand that the world was not as he had always thought it was, and that there were greater and more terrible things in the universe than tribal wars and long sea voyages. He had begun to sense that the Space Wolves had a great and terrible purpose, and that all these tests that seemed so threatening to him were in a way necessary to that purpose. In the visions he had seen at the Gate of Morkai he had begun to get some inkling of the mighty and terrible nature of their other-worldly foes, and of the destiny that might await him should he prove worthy. Ragnar was certain that it was no accident that he seen what he had. He was certain that his possession of this profound knowledge was intentional on the part of those ancients who tested him, and he felt that what he did with that knowledge might even be part of the test. Ragnar knew from talking with his fellow aspirants that some of them simply refused to believe the terrible visions, never mind accept them, and he felt sure that this was a mistake.

In a strange way, Ragnar was even pleased to be here, now, amid the towering mountains. He knew that he was looking upon nature's wild and terrible beauty in a place he felt sure no man had ever seen before. Like sailing the ocean storm, or seeing the red sun sink below the sea at the end of a hard day at the oar, that in itself was thrilling. He even felt something like gratitude to the Space Wolves for putting him here, where he might experience the awesome loneliness of this place.

Shaking his head, Ragnar exhaled, his breath fogging in the crisp air. He knew that he needed to push on. He intended to find his way back to the Fang. And he intended that he would not be the last.

THE MIST WAS thick and clinging and reduced everything to a shadowy outline. The rocks around Ragnar were phantoms. The path was barely visible just a few strides ahead. Sometimes the clouds would shift and billow and he would be able to see a little further but mostly he was shut in by dim, insubstantial walls that muffled sound and sight and made the way ahead invisible.

Ragnar was reminded of his people's idea of hell – a cold and misty place where the shades of the dead roamed a dry and rocky land. This place met that description almost exactly and at that moment it seemed all too possible to Ragnar that somehow he had died without knowing it and stumbled through the gates of death. He listened to the soft movement of the wind currents, tested the air for scents and prayed that this was not true. If it was, at least it seemed that even in death he was able to keep his new found powers. Still, Ragnar felt that it would not be fair for him to have come so far and to have died without knowing it.

He pushed the thought aside as a figment of his overactive imagination. He yet lived. Blood still flowed in his veins. His skin still tingled with the cold. Condensation glistened on the fabric of his tunic and he could feel the moist droplets as he wiped it away. This was real. Truly he might die here, but he was not dead yet. He grinned grimly to himself.

The mist was dangerous. Of this Ragnar had no doubt. He was following a long ridgeline between two mighty peaks and the path was a hard one. In places it was exceedingly narrow and threatened to crumble underfoot. Often it was a mere ledge alongside a drop that Ragnar had no idea of the depth of. He merely knew that he did not want to test it by falling into it. Perhaps the worst of it was that the path continually twisted and turned so that there was always the threat that it would veer away suddenly to left or right and Ragnar would place his foot on emptiness before tumbling to his mist enshrouded doom.

Ragnar used the butt of his improvised spear as a staff and tested the way as he inched along the ledge. He had no idea at all whether he was going in the right direction or not, but was simply convinced that he needed to press on. Suddenly, and only for a moment, the mist parted, and Ragnar had a clear view along the ridge. For a moment he felt as if he were soaring on wings above the clouds. Far, far below him the valleys and ridges were obscured by the gloom but all around him the peaks emerged from the clouds like islands from the seas of Fenris. The shrunken sun sent spears of light into the mist. Ragnar gasped aloud, as ahead of him he saw the mighty column of the Fang, rearing with sinister majesty through the swirling grey clouds. Truly it was a sight of wondrous beauty.

Ragnar felt he was scaling the very walls of heaven, that he walked upon the clouds. This must be what it was like to be Russ, he thought, or to be a god. It was, in a strange way, by far the most impressive sight he had ever seen, and it moved him deeply. Ragnar's heart swelled within his breast and a fierce joy overcame him. He would survive! He would return victorious to the Fang, to take his rightful place amongst the wolves!

Then in a moment the clouds rose again, like huge breakers throwing themselves onto a storm-wracked beach. The wet mist and cloying fog closed in once more. The vision disappeared. Suppressing a shiver, Ragnar pulled his stinking wolfskin cloak tight around his shoulders and trudged forwards into the realm of shadows.

FOR SOME TIME NOW, Ragnar had sensed something out there in the dark grey of the clinging fog. He was not sure where or what it was, but he was sure that there was something watching him. He imagined he could feel its burning gaze boring into his back like a blade. Ragnar looked back over his shoulder into the gloom for the tenth time in as many minutes, and saw nothing. He tested the air constantly, and was sure he caught the scent of something at once familiar yet somehow strange, a bitter tang in the air, a scent that made him shudder.

Ragnar knew that he was getting close to the Fang now. After a troubled night asleep on a high ridge, this very morning he had caught sight of the Fang's lower slopes from the ever rising hills. At dusk as the darkness closed in, he saw the regular patterns of light on the hillside that marked the presence of human beings. He could picture in his mind's eye the enormous structures he had seen when he had first arrived, and he could make the lights conform to the outlines of those gigantic machines with very little effort. Now they seemed as welcoming as they once seemed terrifying and strange.

It had been a long trek. Seven hard days from the place where he had been dropped to this ultimate mountain. He was weary, hungry and cold but he felt a sense of achievement such as he had never known before. All the lessons he had learned at Russvik he had put to good use. He had found shelter and food and water. He had preserved his health and his sanity. He had used his newly honed senses to the maximum extent. He had kept himself alive with nothing and no one to help him save the blessing of Russ. And the truth was that until a few moments ago he had rarely felt better about himself or the world. Now, however, he felt a shiver of fear pass through him at the sense that some inhuman evil presence dogged his steps.

Ragnar guessed that another day's march would bring him to one of the outposts of the Space Wolves, barring accidents, and he had been keen to rest this evening and press on at dawn. Now, he simply felt the urge to keep moving while the full moon beamed down. It was all he could do to keep from breaking into a run, like a hare pursued by a fox. His human logic told Ragnar that he had no proof that anything followed him at all, that his nerves were simply frayed by his long ordeal. The animal instinct of the beast within him told a different story. It screamed at him to flee or fight, to run or stand his ground. And Ragnar had come to respect the beast.

He sensed that running would be no good. Running over broken ground in uncertain light would be sure to lead to an accident, one that would most likely prove fatal if he were then attacked. Ragnar knew it would be best to make camp, to build a fire using his pouch full of dried leaves, twigs and sticks and try to rest. Perhaps the flames would frighten off whatever it was that watched him. Perhaps not. It might be worth a try.

Somewhere deep within him he felt the presence of the beast. It watched and waited and in it a furious anger was building up. It did not like being hunted. It did not appreciate being prey rather than predator. It wanted to turn at bay and confront whatever followed it with tooth and nail. Ragnar was strangely reassured by that, and found himself in agreement. Running through the dark was not going to help, neither was worry or fear. They would only paralyse him and sap his energy. With a fierce grunt, Ragnar realised that he had come to a decision of sorts. Nearby stood several huge boulders, enormous shadows in the gloom.

In their lee would be some shelter from the wind and the elements. He moved in their direction, determined that he would build a fire. And wait.

THE FLAMES FLICKERED. The smell of woodsmoke reached Ragnar's nostrils. He munched on the nuts and berries he had collected earlier and wished that he had some water to moisten his mouth. Tomorrow he would find a stream, he told himself. If he still lived.

He avoided looking directly at the flames so as not to ruin his much enhanced night vision. He was still keenly aware of that sense of presence. Ragnar listened keenly to the sounds of the night, and sniffed at the cold air. The hairs on the back of his neck rose now as he heard the sound of pebbles rolling down the scree, disturbed by the approach of something heavy, something that moved with furtive care. Ragnar reached for his spear and rose to a crouch, placing his back to the largest of the boulders, a stone half again as tall as he. At least in this way he would not be taken by surprise from behind. Whatever it was would have to face his wrath. And if he had to, Ragnar knew he would die with his wounds to the fore, as his father had taught him. He licked his lips, his hands clenching and unclenching on the rough shaft of his spear.

The stink he had smelled earlier became stronger. In it was a hint of something human, and of something animal. There was a smell like that of a wolf's fur. Now he could hear a faint snuffling sound, as of a large beast sniffing the air. His fingers tightened even harder around the spear shaft, his body tensed like a coiled spring as he made himself ready to strike at the unseen enemy.

Fear boiled in the pit of his stomach. The small hairs of his body rose. He recognised the outline of the thing that appeared in the firelight. It was tall and heavy and manlike. Its torso was covered in the remains of a ripped grey tunic that now appeared far too small for its massive muscular form. Its hands ended in long talon-like claws. Its head was still human but covered in thick, matted fur, and its snarling mouth revealed massive fangs. In its eyes burned hunger, rage and a startling intelligence. It opened its mouth and gave a low feral growl. An answering growl was torn unbidden from Ragnar's lips.

It was wulfen. Ragnar knew now what had been stalking him, knew that he had suspected it all along and this had been the source of his fear and his unease. The beast within him had recognised the wulfen. That the thing intended to kill him and feast on his flesh he had absolutely no doubt. It was going to be a matter of kill or be killed. He knew he would have to strike quickly and without mercy if he were to have any chance to live. He brought his improvised spear up and braced for the killing stroke. Within himself the beast stood ready to strike.

And in that moment his hand was stayed. He found that he could not bring himself to make the cast. This wulfen had once been a man just like him. It had been an aspirant. It had drunk from the cup. It had undergone the same changes and torments that he had. In Russ's name it could so easily have been him, if the beast had gained control. Indeed, it was all too possible that this creature was someone he knew. It might be Kjel or Sven or even Strybjorn. Could he really just kill it out of hand?

It appeared the creature felt something like the same emotion. It halted for a moment. Its eyes moved from Ragnar to the fire and then back to Ragnar again. It growled once more. Ragnar could see its muscles tensing. He could see now that a bracelet similar to the one on his own arm glittered on the thing's wrist, and knew with a thrill of horror that it was most likely one of his own former companions. But which one, he asked himself. Was it a friend or foe?

In a moment all such considerations became moot. The wulfen sprang. By instinctive reflex action Ragnar sent the spear hurtling into its chest. The long blade pierced its ribs and buried itself in the monster's heart. The shaft bent and then broke under the creature's weight and the force of its leap. Ragnar was slammed back into the boulder and for a moment found himself gazing into the creature's eyes. Human intelligence seemed to flood back into them.

The twisted lips formed a single word, 'Ragnar,' then the wulfen died.

Ragnar looked down on the slumped form, filled with both horror and triumph by what he had done. He had killed a wulfen. Alone. But he had also known it as a man, a good friend. Ragnar bent down to inspect the bracelet on the creature's arm to find out who it had been, hoping against hope that it was Strybjorn.

In the flickering light the rune etched onto the metal was clearly visible. It showed the sign of the hawk. Ragnar vented a long howl of rage and grief into the cold, uncaring night, knowing that he had just killed Kjel, his only true friend.

THIRTEEN
ACCEPTANCE

RAGNAR LAY ON the surgical altar once more. He looked up to see the masked faces of the Iron Priests. He could hear the dim thrum of their machinery, the odd soul-chilling music of their ritual chants, the occasional scream or howl of a warrior in pain as the razorsaw circular knives of the priests bit into their flesh.

The table beneath him was sticky with his own coagulated blood, the smell of it and of various chemicals assaulted his nostrils. His fingers bunched around the metal grips on the side of the altar. He took a deep breath and willed himself to be calm.

Since he got back to the Fang there had been many strange medical rituals performed over him. He had been put in various technical engines and scanned. Iron Priests had prodded him with sensor wands, encased his head in scanner helmets, clipped monitoring filaments to his limbs. He had been fed a diet of meat and ale containing the chemical taint of many strange drugs. His enhanced senses had told him of their presence, but he assumed that they had been put there for his own good so he had not worried. Not that worrying would have done much good anyway, since he was entirely at the mercy of the Iron Priests.

At least he was still alive. Not all of the other aspirants were. Sven had returned. So had Strybjorn. So had many of the others but not all. At least five, including Kjel, had not come back from the ultimate test. A full month had passed and it seemed unlikely now that they ever would.

Ragnar forced the thought of Kjel to the back of his mind. He did not like to think about it. Kjel had been the closest thing to a friend he had possessed among the aspirants, and now Kjel was gone. Many times recently Ragnar had lain awake wondering what it must have been like for the Falconer, wandering alone through the great wilderness while his body altered into something other than human, and the beast within devoured his mind and his soul. Had he been aware of what was happening the whole time? Or had he fallen early into merciful oblivion? Ragnar realised that he would never know.

The Iron Priests assured him that the changes wrought by the Cup of Wulfen were complete, that his body had now fully integrated the magical thing they called the canis helix, and that he was ready to move on to the next part of the process that would turn him into one of the Wolves. He was ready to have the thing they called the geneseed implanted.

Ragnar took another deep breath and strove to remain calm. The beast, the animal side of his nature, did not like this. It hated being strapped down, caged, subject to the will of others. It did not like this business at all. There was nothing he could do. He turned his head fractionally and saw that one of the high Iron Priests was approaching. He held a glass chalice reverently in both hands. In it was a pulpy fleshy thing from which emerged various nodules and tubes of tissue. The chanting of the priests around Ragnar's altar grew louder and more rhythmical as the warrior approached.

This was the geneseed, Ragnar knew, remembering the things he had been taught over the past few weeks. This was the master component that controlled all the others and would enable his transformation into a full Space Wolf. It would enable his body to adapt and it would control the host of other implants the Iron Priests were going to place within his flesh. It did not look like much, but it was a sacred thing. This scrap of bloody flesh had been borne by many Wolves before Ragnar, had originally been taken from the flesh and blood of Russ himself. It was a direct link with the ancient times and with the god of his people. It was a staggering thought to Ragnar that soon within his own body would be part of his god. However, it was something that all the other Space Wolves possessed, and went a long way towards explaining the superhuman attributes they possessed. In a very real sense they were kin to the gods. And soon, Ragnar thought, if all went well, so too would he be!

The Iron Priest came ever closer. Ragnar felt a needle spike going into his arm. In his hyper-sensitised conditioned it felt like a stab from a sword. There was brief flash of agony and then coolness flowed through his veins, spreading from the point where the needle went in. In moments he was relaxed and numbed and aware of his body as a remote and distant thing. It was as if his soul floated on a cloud of ice and looked down upon the things that happened to his flesh.

He felt his skin shake and a soft pressure on his chest as one of the Iron Priests reached forward and cut him with a ripsaw. Flesh parted. Blood flowed. Ragnar doubted that more damage could have been inflicted with a blow from an axe and yet he was aware of it only as a passing discomfort. He saw the high Iron Priest make a complex gesture over the vessel in which the geneseed rested before reaching in with one gauntleted hand and pulling the fleshy thing out. He heard an odd sucking sound as the geneseed was placed within his ribcage and began the task of grafting itself to his nerves and veins and sinews. It was an odd sensation the like of which he had never endured before. It was as if a living thing were crawling about inside his chest cavity. He imagined tentacles of flesh emerging from the thing's carapace, of veins sprouting from it like roots from a seed, of bits of nerve binding themselves to his own. The image filled his mind as another needle was driven home. Molten pain flashed through him, dispersing the coolness, and his spirit toppled forward into a black abyss.

RAGNAR KNELT IN the meditation chamber. He felt better now. His chest no longer felt swollen and constricted by the presence of the geneseed. The scars of the ceremony were already fading even though only days had passed. He was aware only of a slight sensitivity around the whole area where it was tender to the touch. He had found himself poking at it daily like a man touching a cavity in his tooth with his tongue. It seemed inconceivable to him at this moment that the scars and the tenderness both were marks of the favour of Russ, yet he knew it must be so. The things he had learned over the past few days made that all too clear.

He forced the thoughts from his mind and concentrated on Ranek. The Wolf Priest stood before the aspirants once more and bade them begin the ritual. Ragnar cleared his mind as he had been taught and began to intone the strange prayer. He felt himself relax as he reached forward and picked up the crown of knowledge. It was a mysterious and age-old thing of brass and iron, connected to the engines of knowledge by pulsing cables of copper and glass. Ranek had told them the crowns were connected to great knowledge machines where all the history of the Chapter was stored, and much ancient lore. By donning the crowns, that lore could be pumped directly into his head at a rate far beyond that at which a person could normally memorise it. Ragnar found the whole process a frightening and magical one. Once the crown was in place, and the correct litanies intoned by the priests, then the knowledge came. Not only in the forms of words and memories, but also of sounds and pictures and emotions. Ragnar knew his own feelings were being subtly altered by the machines, but he did not care: the possession of the lore was worth the price. He had learned so much in only a few days. It was an enlightening experience in its own way. The more he learned, the more he understood the Space Wolves, and the more he understood the Chapter the more he longed to serve them and be a part of them.

He knew now that the world was a far greater and more complex place than ever he had believed. Indeed there was not just one world but many. Fenris was an orb that circled the Eye of Russ. It was merely one of many such worlds that floated in the space around that huge sun. And in turn the Eye of Russ was just one of millions of suns that made up the galaxy and around many of which orbited other inhabited worlds. Strangest of all, not all of these worlds were inhabited by humans. Some were ruled by green-skinned monsters called orks. Some were the homes of a tall beautiful yet utterly alien people called the eldar. One whole sector of the galaxy was the home of daemons and those who served them.

The vast bulk of the human worlds were ruled by the Imperium, which the Space Wolves served. The Imperium was ruled by the Emperor, the All Father, the crippled god who had given life to Russ and his brothers and whose shattered shell now existed in a great machine on the ancestral world of Terra. The Emperor was served by an enormous corps of priests and magistrates and rulers and tax collectors. In his name massive armies moved across the galaxy carried by huge ships capable of sailing between the stars. All the other races and nations and kingdoms Ragnar had learned of were the enemies of the Emperor and of humanity, and would do anything to undermine the All Father's rule and destroy his realm. Across the galaxy, savage wars raged between the Emperor's legions and those of his foes, and in the forefront of many of these wars were the Wolves.

He saw the founding of the Wolves all those long ages ago when the All Father was young and walked among men. He saw the coming of Russ to Fenris, and then the arrival of the All Father seeking his lost son. He saw Russ recruit his honour guard of warriors and name them the Wolves of Space. He saw too that the All Father had many strong sons, called primarchs, who founded their own Chapters, just as Russ had done. He learned that these warriors, who all shared the geneseed of their primarchs, were known collectively as Space Marines.

Ragnar saw the founding of the Imperium, and then the terrible war with the arch-heretic and traitor Horus which tore the new-born empire apart and resulted in the crippling of the All Father and the death of Horus. He saw that many of the Space Marines and their primarchs followed Horus in his folly and betrayed their oaths to the Emperor. He saw them depart for the strange warped area of the galaxy known as the Eye of Terror and watched them devolve into things less than human. Ragnar knew now that he was being made privy to knowledge kept secret from the vast majority of people, and that he must never divulge this lore to anyone who did not already know of it. He shuddered when he found out about the four great powers of Chaos, the ultimate arch-daemons who were forever at work to undermine the empire of humanity.

There was Khorne, the Blood God, lord of slaughter, whose followers went laughing into battle filled with an unslakable thirst for carnage. There was Tzeentch, the Great Mutator, who transformed his worshippers and made them privy to the darkest secrets of sorcery. There was Nurgle, the Plague Lord, whose followers spread blight and disease to the furthest reaches of the cosmos. There was Slaanesh, depraved god of unspeakable pleasures. He knew enough now to recognise some of their worshippers as the beings he had encountered in his visions beyond the Gate of Morkai. Ragnar prayed most earnestly that he need never learn more.

He learned of Russ's disappearance on his great quest to find the seeds of the tree of life which would cure his Emperor. He learned of the long and honourable history of the Wolves unto the present age. More and more knowledge poured into his willing brain and he soaked it up like a sponge.

He saw how vast and terrible the enemies of mankind were, and how great was the need for mighty warriors to oppose them. He understood now why the testing of the aspirants had been so savage and brutal. In these dark times no flaw could be allowed in those who were to stand between humanity and its enemies.

Chants and litanies and prayers filled his mind. He understood many of them now. They were to focus a warrior's mind, to keep his faith as strong as his arm. He knew that others were to help him use the new abilities he was gaining daily as the Iron Priests did their work.

He understood the changes that were being wrought in his body better now. He was being given the knowledge to help him do so. He knew that he had been given a second heart, and augmented muscles and glands that would enable him to breathe poisoned air and eat poisoned food without coming to harm. His senses had been made even keener and his body far more resilient. He knew that he could now recover from almost any wound that did not kill him outright, even without medical care, given time. He learned the basics of field medicine for cauterising amputations.

Most of his body was enclosed in a flexible black metallic carapace. He knew that the various plasteel nodes protruding from it were contact points that would enable his body to interface with the armour that all Space Marines wore like a second skin. He was astonished that he now possessed the vocabulary and the knowledge to understand these concepts. Truly the power of these ancient engines was great.

More and more knowledge flowed into his mind. He learned of weapons and their use. He learned of tactics and organisational structures. He learned the ten basic offensive manoeuvres and the four strong defences. And he smiled as he did so, the pleasure centres of his brain stimulated by the awesome intricate subtle mechanisms of the old machines.

He saw the organisation of his Chapter. He saw that it was arranged into twelve great companies, each led by a mighty warleader from whom the company took its name. He saw that there was a thirteenth great company belonging to the Chapter's leader which consisted of all the priests and other types of warrior. He saw the progress that he would need to make through the Chapter. He learned that if he were accepted he would become a Blood Claw, part of a pack of similar youthful warriors struggling to tame the unruly beast within. If he lived he would become first a Grey Hunter, then a Long Fang, growing older, wiser, mightier and more cunning.

On and on went the endless flow of knowledge, burning itself into his memory, making him wiser, and causing his brain to glow with love of his Chapter and Russ and the Emperor.

'LIFT YOUR ARM,' the Iron Priest said. Servo-motors whined as Ragnar did so. The priest nodded his masked head, and then tightened a joint with his power wrench. Ragnar felt him do it. The sensation was an odd one, not painful exactly, but it let him know that something was happening with his plasteel carapace. The knowledge implanted in his brain told him that over the coming months and years he would get better at recognising the meaning of these sensations.

'Now move your fingers.' Ragnar did as he was told. Once more the priest made a few adjustments. Immediately his hand felt better, more flexible, stronger. The priest intoned a litany to the machine spirits and then bowed his head once more. It appeared the work was complete.

'You may rise,' the priest said. Ragnar raised himself from the altar. As he did so the various cables and attachments the priest had fitted retracted back into the sacred stonework. He was free to move. Ragnar smiled and looked down at his body. The entire length of his massive frame had been encased in plasteel and ceramite yet he did not feel too much different. There was no sensation of being encumbered by heavy armour. In fact, if anything he felt lighter, fitter and stronger. He knew now that the powerful servo-motors within the armour were doing their work, helping support his weight, make him mobile. The Iron Priest obviously recognised that smile and knew its meaning.

'You must be very careful over the next few days, for you do not yet know your own strength.'

Ragnar looked at him, not quite following his meaning. A small servitor robot moved closer at the priest's gesture. A compartment in its chest opened and a long telescopic arm stretched out and placed a stone in the priest's hand. Ragnar was amazed by the seemingly mystical manner in which the priest and his machine communicated. Not a word had been spoken.

'Take this stone,' the Iron Priest said. 'Do not worry; it has no significance at all. It is merely to demonstrate a thing.'

Ragnar took the stone, marvelling at the sensitivity of the gauntlets that let him feel its texture despite being thick enough to stop the blow of an axe. It was not quite like touching the stone with his bare flesh. It felt more as if he were wearing thin gloves. The Iron Priest was right. This was going to take some getting used to.

'Crush the stone,' the Iron Priest said.

Ragnar looked at him, not quite able to comprehend what he was saying. He knew that it was theoretically possible for the systems in his gauntlets to generate enough pressure to do so, yet something instinctive in his brain rebelled against the concept. It was not possible. Human beings could not crush rocks with their bare hands.

'Do it,' the priest said. There was a note of command in his voice that could not be disobeyed. Ragnar closed his fist. Instantly he felt resistance and instinctively he began to loosen his grip but the Iron Priest merely repeated his command. Ragnar closed his fingers once more. There was a cracking sound as the stone broke like an eggshell crushed by a strong man. Ragnar opened his hand to see that the hard stone had been reduced to several small chips of rock.

He let out his breath in one long slow exhalation. Now he truly began to understand the power that had been granted to him.

'THESE ARE YOUR own personal weapons,' the armourer said. 'You are responsible for them. Each has been stamped with your

rune-sign so you will know them, and we will be able to identify them in the event of your death.'

Ragnar picked up the weapons reverently. There was a pro-
jectile weapon, called a bolt pistol. It was like the magical
weapon with which Ranek had dispatched the sea dragon, only
smaller. And there was a chainsword, one of the potent
weapons that Sergeant Hakon had carried. In the belt on which
the pistol was scabbarded was a dispenser of other small but no
less potent weapons known as microgrenades.

'Be careful with these,' the armourer said. 'They are as dangerous to fools as they are to enemies. Now follow the servitor
and report to the training ranges.'

Ragnar looked around and saw Sven, Nils, Strybjorn and the
others all standing inspecting their weapons. They all looked
different now, taller, heavier and more burly with their heads
shaved save for one long strip of hair, and their bodies encased
in armour.

On their faces was the same look of pride and wonder that
he knew must be on his. They all looked as if they had just
been given enchanted weapons out of legend, and in a way
they had. He gave Strybjorn another long hard look. It was just
possible, he thought, that the Grimskull might have an accident on the training ranges. Strybjorn looked up and met his
gaze, and Ragnar felt that it was all too possible that his enemy
was thinking the same thing about him.

THE BOLT PISTOL kicked in Ragnar's hand. Even with the
enhanced strength granted by his armour and his altered body,
the recoil was something fierce. The gun moved like a wild
thing he held trapped in his vice-like grip.

The shell blazed past the target and hit the stone wall
behind, blowing a huge chunk out of the cavern wall. Ragnar
was exhilarated by the sheer sense of power using the weapon
gave him at the same time as he was frustrated by his inability
to hit the target. Not for the first time he became aware of the
difference between the theoretical knowledge the ancient
engines had placed in his head, and the actual practical ability
to do something.

He knew all about this weapon. He knew how it worked. He
knew that it fired caseless self-propelled ammunition capable
of piercing armour up to several hundred strides. He knew the

magazine capacity. He knew in theory how to disassemble, clean and repair it. He knew all about firing it. He knew about relaxing as you took aim, breathing out gently as you fired. Unfortunately there was a big difference between knowing this stuff and being able to do it.

'Do not worry, lad,' said Sergeant Hengist, their weapons instructor. 'Just keep at it. It will come eventually. Anything can be mastered with practice. And you do need to master this. Believe it or not, there was a time when I couldn't hit the side of a barn door. Now...'

In one smooth fluid action, without seeming to aim or concentrate, Hengist drew his own pistol, seemed only to extend his arm, point it and pull the trigger. A cluster of three shots hit the bull's-eye directly over the heart of the man-shaped target.

Ragnar watched in awe. 'You make it look so easy, sergeant,' he said.

'Nothing is ever as easy as it looks, lad. And it's the mark of a master that they make difficult things look easy.'

Ragnar nodded. He enjoyed listening to Hengist talk, and he enjoyed learning from the grizzled veteran. It was one of the most pleasant things about his new status. He and the other aspirants weren't exactly accepted but at least they were not treated as simply expendable things. They had value to the Space Wolves now. They might become part of the Chapter at some future date. Or maybe Hengist was simply more pleasant than the other Space Marines. One thing Ragnar was becoming aware of was that all these awesome fearsome characters were different. They were people in and of themselves, as distinctive as all the folk back in his home village. His former home village, he corrected himself. In another, far distant, life.

He did not know why this surprised him. Perhaps it was simply that he had become used to seeing all of the Space Wolves as the same. They certainly all looked similar. They were all far taller and stronger than mortal men, and they all possessed those odd wolfish eyes and frightening fangs. And they all had a similar fierce and feral manner in some ways. And, of course, they all wore the greyish armour, which sometimes made them look more like machines than men. Still, Ragnar was coming to realise that for all that they were men just like he was. And he was also coming to respect them, for he knew that all of them there had come through everything he had done, or worse, and had survived years of terrible warfare besides.

'Try again, lad,' Hengist said, not unkindly. 'And this time don't think so hard about what you're doing. Just relax and do it. Do it a thousand times if need be, but keep doing it. One day your life and the life of your comrades will depend on your accuracy. Sure as Russ was a drinker, that's the truth.'

Ragnar nodded and raised the pistol once more. He turned to see if Hengist was watching him, but the sergeant had already walked down the line of aspirants and was talking quietly to Sven. Ragnar closed one eye, breathed deeply and as he exhaled pulled the trigger. The bolter shell sped past the target and buried itself in the wall.

Ragnar let out a long sigh of frustration. This was going to take a lot of practice.

RAGNAR CHARGED through the jungle thicket. The air was hot and humid. Green fronds whipped his face. Carnivorous plants snapped at his knees. He ducked a strangler vine, skidded onto his knees and rolled forward through the leafy mulch into cover behind the toppled remains of some titanic fallen tree.

He heard a disturbance in the undergrowth ahead of him. He wiped spores from his face, sighted along the barrel of his pistol and whipped off a shot. It smashed through the leaves and exploded sending a cloud of paint and dye over the crouched figure of Sven. 'Got you,' Ragnar cried.

With a groan, Sven put his hand over his heart, pushing the button that would deactivate his comm-links then toppled theatrically back onto the ground. Ragnar smiled with satisfaction. That was the third of the Red team he had picked off this exercise. One more and his squad would have won. He would have wiped out all the rival team. He was enjoying himself. He liked this strange place and he enjoyed these training exercises. This vast cavern full of alien flora was the place where the recruits were inducted into the basics of jungle warfare. It was a controlled environment deep below the Fang, where the heat and the humidity were carefully controlled to create a place just like the real thing. He was pleased with himself. His shooting had improved greatly with practice, just as Sergeant Hengist had promised him it would.

'Got you,' he murmured, knowing all he had to do now was find Strybjorn, the last member of the Red team.

'And I've got you, Ragnar,' a voice said from behind him. Ragnar twisted around striving to bring his pistol to bear but he was too late. Strybjorn stood there his pistol already pointed. He squeezed the trigger and the impact of the shell knocked Ragnar over. A cloud of paint covered his armour. Briefly Ragnar considered ignoring the hit and firing back at Strybjorn but his sense of honour would not let him. Well, that and his knowledge that Sergeant Hengist was probably watching him through one of the camera eyes of the floating drones that moved through the caves. Frustrated, he punched the button on his chest comm unit and cut himself out of the link.

Ragnar cursed. It was going to take a long night of scrubbing to get his armour clean again. Still, he was grateful that it had been only a paint shell and not live ammunition when Strybjorn fired.

He wondered whether the Grimskull would have been so quick to pull the trigger if he had been firing a real bullet. Ragnar knew that he himself would have been.

RAGNAR LOOKED DOWN on Vrotwulf's corpse. Things looked like a mess. The whole back of his head was gone and a pulpy mass of blood and brains decorated the wall over the aspirant's bunk.

'Bones of Russ,' Ragnar breathed. It had all happened so quickly. One moment Vrotwulf had been sitting there laughing and joking and polishing his bolt pistol. Then there had been a bang and a roar and his head had disintegrated. It had all happened so quickly that the youth had not even had a chance to scream.

Sven came over and looked down at the corpse. He picked up the gun and looked at it. 'Idiot!' he muttered. 'The magazine was still in it.'

Ragnar looked closely. 'And the safety stud wasn't pushed in,' he added. They looked at each other. Ragnar guessed that they were both thinking the same thing. Deaths in training still happened, and most of the time through sheer carelessness. He was coming to recognise the signs. This was indeed part of the problem with the way knowledge had been imparted to them. All of the aspirants knew things but the knowledge was not yet fully part of them. They all knew the procedures for cleaning their weapons but they had not yet learned the total respect that the firearms demanded. It was that way with much of the lore they had learned. As always there was a huge difference between knowing the theory and being able to implement the practice.

'I suppose someone better go tell the powers-that-be,' Sven said. He looked meaningfully at Ragnar hoping that he would volunteer.

'Off you go then,' said Ragnar. Sven snarled, showing his developing fangs but did not argue. He and Ragnar had clashed often in the past few weeks, establishing their positions within the pack, and Ragnar had always come off the best. The others were learning not to challenge him whether in a simple contest of wills or an exchange of blows. Ragnar returned to contemplating the body. He offered up a prayer to Russ.

Well, he thought, they were learning respect, the hard way. He just wondered how many more of them would die before the training was over.

ONLY TWO MORE DIED, to Ragnar's knowledge. An aspirant known as Logi managed to blow himself up with his own krak grenade during live ammunition training. Another aspirant, Hrald, had simply keeled over and died while eating one day, and his body was carted off by servitors to be dissected by the Iron Priests. No one really understood what had gone wrong, although word went around that his body had rejected either the geneseed or the new organs that had been implanted. Ragnar was not quite sure how this could happen but the new lore implanted in his brain told him that sometimes human bodies simply would not accept implants, that they rebelled against any alteration, and the subject simply died. This was not a cheering thought to Ragnar or to any of the other aspirants but there was nothing they could do about it except lie awake at nights in their cells and wonder whether it would happen to them. After a few days Ragnar simply quit worrying. He had not died and wondering about it seemed like a needless waste of energy.

Besides, there was so much to learn and to do that his entire mind and spirit were kept occupied. Each day at dawn he rose and entered one of the great meditation chambers, where he busied himself reciting the litanies that had been placed in his brain the previous day. After three hours of contemplation of the religious mysteries and honing his spirit for war, he ate a hearty breakfast. While his body digested this he was hooked up to one of the ancient tutelary engines and more knowledge was pumped into his brain, along with an unquestioning adoration of Russ and the Emperor. By noon, stiff but unwearied, he was unhooked from these ancient cryptic devices and went to the chambers of armaments. For the remainder of the day, depending on the schedule set for him, he either exercised, or practised unarmed combat, or trained endlessly with the weapons he had been issued. Every few days, they would be sent to one of the environmental chambers, sculpted to resemble some alien landscape, and practise the disciplines of war and survival in those strange places. Ragnar came to recognise quickly what days those would be, for some knowledge of them would have been placed in his brain the day before.

After this they would retire to the refectory for the evening meal, and then another session either with the tutelary machines or with the Iron Priests. The things they learned now were always technical in nature, usually concerning the maintenance of their weapons and armour, or the new organs that had been implanted in their bodies. The day would conclude with several hours in the meditation cells and then to bed where Ragnar would drop into an exhausted sleep.

Every seventh day, they would assemble in the Chamber of the Aspirants where Ranek had first explained their purpose to them. The Wolf Priest himself would arrive and preach to them, telling them old tales of the Chapter's glory, stirring their hearts and minds with the deeds of those who had gone before them. They were then taken around the Fang, always to places they had not seen before. The nature and purpose of the great devices which they were permitted to see were explained to them, along with their glorious places in the Chapter history.

Ragnar looked with awe upon the sites of ancient battles with the forces of Chaos from those dark periods when the Fang itself had been invaded. He watched in wonder as mighty sky-ships took off, destined he now knew to pierce the envelope of air that surrounded Fenris and rendezvous with those mighty vessels that plied the unimaginable distances between the stars. He stared at the vast automated factories where the weapons and munitions of the Space Wolves were created from the very bones of the planet, from deep mined metals and minerals and oil.

As the days became weeks and the weeks became months he found himself becoming more and more comfortable with his new role and his new position. He got to know many of the people around the Fang by name, and he saw that slowly, as he learned and grew and survived, that they were coming to accept him as one of them. He became more aware of the rhythms of the place and of the fact that it was more or less empty of the Space Wolves themselves who were forever on the move around the galaxy on the Emperor's business.

He knew more now of how the Chapter was divided up into a number of great companies, the armed retinues of mighty warleaders, and that it was rare indeed for more than one of those great companies to be at the Fang at any given time. Sometimes the companies would return home briefly to be re-armed and re-equipped and to replace losses taken in battle with new recruits from among the aspirants. He knew that there was a constant steady flow of aspirants passing through the Fang, and that one day it would be his destiny to be chosen to accompany one of those great companies out to the stars.

He saw many new aspirants arrive, brought in from Russvik and other places like it scattered around Asaheim, and bound for the Gate of Morkai. He started to recognise those who had arrived before him. Sometimes, in the meditation chambers, he would see true Space Wolves. Grizzled warriors returned from their incredible adventures, and pausing for a moment's peace in the sanctuaries of the Fang before returning to their duties. At such times he wanted nothing more than to join them, and to be on his way to the great battles in far flung parts of the universe, but in his heart, he knew he had a long time to go before that day would come. Ragnar had talked to the older aspirants and learned that sometimes years could pass before they were shipped out to join their more experienced brethren. Still, he told himself, this was no bad thing; it would mean he had plenty of time to hone his skills and ensure that he did not disgrace himself when that great day came.

His hatred of Strybjorn became a dull ache that gnawed at him, but even so the Grimskull had become part of his new life, like Sven and Nils and the others. They all trained together as a team now, and they all realised that they were part of one warband and would be shipped out together when the time came. They had still not been made full Blood Claws or been assigned a warleader, but they knew the day would come when that would happen. No one doubted any more that they were good enough, or that they would make the grade. All of them realised that it was just a matter of time.

RANEK LOOKED DOWN on them from the dais. His scarred face was filled with a pride that was reflected in Ragnar's heart and on the features of all the aspirants present.

'You have done well,' he told them. 'You have learned all that was set to you and you have lived through trials that it is not given to many men to endure let alone survive. You have a right to be proud.

'But not too proud, for all that you have learned here should point your thoughts in the direction of one great truth. The life of a Space Wolf is one long trial and there are many ways still a warrior may fail that trial. He might become cowardly or lax in his duties or he might fall into error or sin. He might let some small chink of doubt or hate…'

Was it Ragnar's imagination, he wondered, or had the Wolf Priest looked directly at him when he said this.

'…or taint of weakness through which our daemonic enemies may enter his soul and corrupt him. We must never forget that this happened to some of our forebear Chapters in ancient times, and that they were in many ways mighty men, greater even than us. We must never forget that the wars we fight are in many ways as much spiritual struggles as physical battles, and that our faith in Russ and in the All Father is our shield.

'And we must never forget the purpose of this long life of tribulation and testing. It is to see if we are worthy to stand beside our primarch in those last days when the powers of Chaos emerge like dragons to swallow the universe, and the end of all things is at hand. For in those days, the chosen ones will stand beside Russ and make war on the evil ones, and thus will the fate of everything be decided. Bear this in mind in the future when you are asked to lay down your life for your comrades and your Chapter. If you prove worthy, it will be your reward to stand alongside the greatest of all heroes in the most important of all battles, and surely no warrior can ask for more than that.

'Now you have been judged worthy to pledge yourself at the sacred Altar of Russ and to join the ranks of the Wolves. Advance, kneel before the altar and swear that you will serve this Chapter in all ways and at all times, unto death and beyond, with body, mind and soul.'

It was the proudest moment of Ragnar's life when he did so.

RAGNAR AND SVEN clashed steins of ale. Ragnar raised his lips and threw the foaming brew back in one long pull. He wiped his lips with the back of his armoured forearm and let out a long belch. He was drunk and he knew it. This ale must be potent indeed he realised to be able to affect him despite his body's ability to metabolise poisons. Perhaps this was the source of the legends of those who died after drinking the ale of the gods. Not that it mattered much to him now.

He glanced around the hall. The place was full. It seemed like everyone in the Fang had been assembled for this feast of acceptance. Long trellis tables filled the chamber. The newly accepted aspirants had one massive bench to themselves. Creatures half man, half machine brought them an endless supply of ale, and platters of fresh venison taken from the enormous spits at the end of the room. On the table in front of him were plates piled high with bread and butter and cheese. He thought he had never tasted food so good. Perhaps that was simply because of his improved senses or maybe it was all much better provender than Ragnar had been used to.

'One more, Ragnar,' Sven said, his face red and flushed with happiness and booze, 'and then we arm wrestle.'

'Fine!' Ragnar swigged more ale and felt the eyes of Ranek upon him. He raised his tankard and toasted the Wolf Priest. Ranek returned the gesture heartily. It was echoed by the armoured figures that flanked him on all sides. Suddenly and spontaneously the assembled Wolves burst out into a roaring lusty song. Even though he did not know the words, Ragnar joined in, bellowing out the tune wordlessly, pausing only to stuff more food and more ale into his mouth.

The only thing that clouded his happiness was the presence of Strybjorn at the table. Soon there would be a reckoning, he thought. He had put off his vengeance too long. After that realisation dawned within Ragnar's befuddled mind, somehow the evening did not seem so bright, the beer did not taste so fine, nor the songs so rousing.

FOURTEEN
IN THE FIELD

RAGNAR GRIPPED the hilt of the chainsword tighter as he watched the Thunderhawk take off. The skyship's exhaust flared as it accelerated away over the mountains. Within seconds there was a sound like a thundercrack and the vehicle had vanished. He glanced around at the others to see how they were taking things.

No one in the pack looked nervous or out of sorts which was good considering this was the Blood Claws' first active mission. All of them were looking at Sergeant Hengist and waiting for his commands. Ragnar glanced at the sergeant but the older Space Wolf seemed lost in thought at this moment, so Ragnar gave his attention back to his surroundings.

The pack was in a bleak place. Not quite as wild as the mountains he had trekked through before being accepted, but still rugged enough to give most people pause for thought. They stood in a clearing in a wood in a long valley. All around them massive peaks raised their snow-capped heads to the sky. Somewhere in the distance he could hear the sound of fast-flowing water. It must be the river they had seen from the air earlier, he thought, racing down the slope to join the lakes below.

The woods around were dark and gloomy. He could smell pine and greyleaf, and other tough and hardy types of tree that could grow at this altitude. He could hear the scuttling of small animals in the undergrowth and birds singing. Spears of early morning light pierced the clouds, and lightened the overcast morning. Off in the distance he could see soot-black thunderclouds gathering, and he realised that before nightfall there would be a storm. This did not trouble him. He had become used to the infinitely variable weather of the mountains. Or at least he hoped he had. A small cautious voice within him argued that no man was ever completely accustomed to the climate here, and any man who thought differently was destined for a fool's early grave. It was always best to respect the elemental forces of nature.

As far as he could tell there were no immediate threats, but that meant nothing either. He had been taught to be always ready for trouble. Who could tell? Anything might lie in ambush out there. Maybe that was what had happened to the previous pack.

Ragnar sighted along the barrel of his bolt pistol looking for targets. Nothing sprang into view except some squirrels gathering nuts at the foot of one the nearest trees. No dark and sinister forces were evident. Perhaps the pack had simply got lost, or been delayed, or perhaps their communications equipment had failed. Ragnar smiled to himself. He doubted that such simple explanations were likely. A pack of Blood Claws led by an experienced Space Wolf sergeant were unlikely to have got themselves lost in the mountains of Asaheim. They had compasses, and locators and all manner of reliable equipment the use of which still astounded Ragnar. Of course, rad storms could disrupt the locator beacons and communications nets, and magnetic vortices could impair compasses. But what were the chances of both those things happening at once? And for a fog to spring up that made dead reckoning impossible? Not likely he thought, but still, was it possible? The fact remained that the other pack was overdue, and had not made its rendezvous with the Thunderhawk. Something had undoubtedly happened, and it was Hengist's pack's task now to find out what.

Ragnar glanced over at the sergeant. He was casting about at the many trails leading from this clearing. Ragnar doubted that he would find any sign. Scents would be over a week old and the rain most likely would have washed away any tracks. On the other hand, they would never know unless they looked.

The other Blood Claws seemed just as impatient to be about their task as he was. There were a dozen present, the survivors of all the groups of aspirants with whom Ragnar had been inducted. There was Strybjorn, and Sven and Nils. He could see the strange fey youth Lars who everybody said was destined to be a Rune Priest one day. There was Snori and Wulf and Kezan and several others that Ragnar did not know too well. They were all keen to be off, wanting to take this opportunity to prove themselves in Sergeant Hengist's eyes.

Ragnar was glad that Hengist was their leader. The old warrior's presence was immensely reassuring. He seemed to possess a wisdom and a self-control they all lacked. Perhaps it came with the scars and the long fangs, Ragnar thought. There was an air of sadness about Hengist, of a man who had lived on beyond his time. Ragnar knew that like many of the instructors in the Fang and places like Russvik, Hengist was the sole survivor of his pack. All the old comrades he had gone through his basic training with, and whom he had fought alongside throughout his career were dead and gone, leaving Hengist to live out his last days alone. Ragnar looked around him, and, seeing all his companions, realised that it was perfectly possible that one of them would end up in this position. He just prayed to Russ it wasn't him.

Now and again the sergeant would pause and consult with the small locator unit he held in his right hand. Ragnar realised that the sergeant was not simply looking for a sign, he was exercising his logical faculties, deciding which trail it was most likely their quarry had taken from here to their last known position.

After about five minutes the sergeant nodded with satisfaction and gestured for them to follow him as he strode along the trail he had chosen. As they entered beneath the shadows of the trees, a bird called somewhere far-off. Ragnar did not recognise its cry but there was something about it that was disturbing. He shivered, touched momentarily by a premonition of disaster. He looked around and saw that Lars apparently felt the same way. His lean ascetic face was twisted and his eyes briefly held a wild expression.

Ragnar looked away. Even by the standards of Blood Claws newly adapted to the effects of the Cup of Wulfen, Lars was regarded as a wild one.

RAGNAR'S ARMOUR whined as he strode purposefully up the hill. The servo-motors and gyrostabilisers were working hard to keep him balanced on these long slopes, and his armoured feet dug great clods out of the earth as the Space Marines powered onwards. Ragnar for one was exhilarated by the cold clear air and the beauty of their surroundings. His augmented muscles did not feel in the slightest tired. It seemed like the armour was doing most of the work of marching for him, and that he could keep going forever if he wanted to.

Ahead of him he could hear Sven grumbling as he walked. The canis helix seemed to have warped his mind strangely. He talked to himself more, griped a great deal, and generally wore an aura of gloominess. That was just the way it was, Ragnar thought, shrugging to himself. It would take more than Sven being miserable to break into Ragnar's sense of well-being today. Of course, Ragnar reminded himself, none of them had remained untouched by the awakening of the beast within them. He fully recognised that he himself had become shorter tempered, more ready to snap with little provocation. Any time anyone questioned Ragnar or tried to put him in his place, he felt an urge to fall on them and show his mastery by pure physical strength. At its worst he felt the urge to tear out their throats with his teeth. At such times he needed all his willpower to restrain the beast, and all the calmness that repeating the ancient litanies granted him. The worst of it was that he hardly noticed these fits until they passed. They simply seemed a natural response. And these were just the changes he had noticed. He often wondered if there were other deeper ones that he was simply unaware of. He knew this was the case with some of the others.

Sven simply did not seem to notice that he talked to himself. Nils was unaware that he constantly sniffed the air as if testing for the presence of enemies. Strybjorn was even more silent and grim and brooding than he had ever been before. It seemed that there was a price to be paid for the great powers they had gained, and that they were all paying it in their different ways. It was a disturbing thought. He had been told that with time they would all adapt, but, right at this moment, Ragnar found this hard to believe.

To distract himself from these gloomy reflections, Ragnar considered their mission. The original pack had been dispatched to this remote spot to investigate the falling of an odd meteor shower. Apparently, this was something that happened quite often in this part of Asaheim. But such an occurrence still had to be looked into, for sometimes enemies tried to infiltrate their way onto the planetary surface using meteor showers for cover. Ragnar was not sure what these enemies might do once they got here but he had learned that the Space Wolves rarely did anything without good reason.

Thinking of the awesome powers of the enemies of humanity, Ragnar realised that his Chapter had good reason to be wary. There were all manner of strange magics and technologies that could be deployed from these remote locations. A spy could perhaps learn all the secrets of the Fang preparatory to a full blown invasion. He knew such things had happened in the past, and could easily happen again.

In any case, the unit was to find the survivors of the previous patrol, if there were any, and render all assistance possible. If there were no survivors they were supposed to locate the bodies and recover the sacred geneseed as well as find out what had killed the first pack. Assuming that whatever had done it did not wipe out Hengist's pack as well. That was always a possibility, Ragnar thought. After all, the previous unit had been just as numerous and as well armed as they were.

The difference was, Ragnar told himself, that we are prepared for something to happen. He was forced to smile at that. A Space Marine was always prepared. Every mission was to be performed as if it were a matter of life and death. After all, sooner or later that sound premise was bound to be revealed as the painful truth.

THEY MADE CAMP that night not so much because they needed the rest but in case they missed something when they searched in the darkness. They were much closer to the last known location of the ones they sought. Ragnar could now understand the wisdom of dropping the aspirants some distance away, and getting the Space Wolves to walk the rest of the way on foot. They were in long narrow wooded valleys with no obvious place for a

Thunderhawk to set down. The only reasonable way in was on foot. Plus they had discovered some traces of the missing pack: discarded food tubes, areas where the undergrowth had been hacked away with chainswords. In a way these were signs of carelessness or overconfidence. Hengist's band were taking care to leave no trace. Ragnar had no idea what the sergeant feared they might encounter, but he was obviously taking no chances.

No fires had been lit. Sentries had been posted at strategic points around the camp. All communication was on directional scrambled links in the comm-net. It would be very difficult for anyone to eavesdrop on their communication. Ragnar was still getting used to the fact that a small bead in his ear and another one on his throat could let him talk with other Blood Claws at a distance without shouting, but he was profoundly glad this was the case. A sentry could warn them quickly and nearly silently as soon as he spotted something. Anything hoping to sneak up and surprise them would swiftly find the tables turned.

Ragnar looked over at Sven. The muttering fit seemed to have passed and he was his old self again. He sucked food paste from a self-sealing tube with a grimace. 'I wonder if they put this dog excrement straight into the tubes or whether they add some cat puke into the mix first,' he said, grinning ruefully even as he sucked his tube dry. Ragnar knew what Sven meant. Field rations might well be nutritious, containing everything a warrior needed to live on in the field, but they did not taste anything like real food.

'If you don't want yours, give it here,' Nils said. Ragnar could never understand how someone so gaunt and skeletal could eat so much. It was a sentiment Sven obviously shared.

'You want more of this?' he asked.

'There's nothing wrong with this stuff. I like it.'

A disbelieving look flickered over Sven's face. Ragnar noticed that despite his protest he made no attempt to hand over his food tube.

'Is there nothing you won't eat?' Sven asked.

'I don't know. I haven't found anything yet. Apparently with my new and improved stomach there's very little I can't eat.'

This was true. They had been schooled that all manner of 'enzymes' and 'glands' had been added to their stomachs along with the geneseed. They could eat wood if they had to now, and poison, they had been told, would have no effect on them. Personally Ragnar was glad that he'd never had any call to test any of this yet.

'I saw him eating a bunch of twigs earlier,' Strybjorn said.

'There was a nice fat slug on one of them,' Nils said with a look of relish on his face. Ragnar was not sure whether he really had done this or was just making it up to disgust the rest of the Blood Claws. 'Anyway, I don't know why Sven is always going on about what I eat. I've never seen anybody put away as much food as he does.'

Sven grinned. 'Yes, but that's real food. Venison and bread and cheese and ale. Not this stuff.'

'I would kill for a bit of cheese right now,' Lars said. Ragnar agreed with him. Just talking about real food made his mouth water. The food paste suddenly tasted even worse than usual.

'Get some sleep,' Sergeant Hengist said. 'Who knows – you might well get a chance to kill something soon.'

RAGNAR WATCHED the dawn break over the mountains. It was the end of his watch and he was not even slightly tired. The beauty of the thing was breathtaking in its own way. At first the mountains were only slightly more than invisible. Their outlines were like a jagged hole cut in the fabric of the night. As the sky lightened they began to come into view but yet appearing flat, like painted scenes on a stone wall. As the light intensified, they acquired more substance, more depth, more detail until they suddenly sparkled, as if newly made, in the sun.

Mist rose like smoke from the trees below them. It was as if the mountains were giving birth to clouds in the morning light. Or as if some wizard had used a spell to set the forest alight with some arcane trickery which created smoke but not flame. Ragnar knew that such was not the case, that soon the mist would evaporate like a ghost in sunlight. Still he enjoyed looking at the reborn world and listening to the chorus of birds greeting the sun.

In the distance he heard Sven and Nils begin to bicker over food once more. Sven was accusing the other Blood Claw of stealing his food tubes in the night.

THEY PACED DOWN the slope towards a strange warped area of the forest. All of them were silent now, and all of them were wary.

As they picked their way down the trail they had seen the area below them. The forest looked deeper and darker and more tangled. The trees looked blotched and sickly. Sergeant Hengist studied them through magnoculars before speaking.

'This is different,' he said. 'This was not in Urlek's report.'

'Looks like those trees have got the plague,' Ragnar said.

'Don't say that,' Sven said. 'Nils will want to eat them.'

It really did look as if the trees had caught some sort of plague, Ragnar thought. They were stunted and hunched over like sick men. They all looked as if they were rotting and dying. Strange luminescent fungus clung to their sides, its faint glow visible even in the watery daylight that broke through the forest canopy. Ragnar had never seen anything even remotely like this.

He looked around. Lars's face was again twisted in a grimace. Ragnar could understand why. He too had a very bad feeling about this. Something smelled wrong. The whole area gave off an odour of corruption or decay, and there was a very slight yet disturbing tang to the scent in the air which made the hairs on the back of his neck rise. It was obvious that Sergeant Hengist felt the same way. He opened a broad band channel to the Fang and began to speak his report. There was a crackle of static. Some phenomenon was interfering with his comm-signal. For a moment Ragnar had the eerie premonition that the sickness of the trees had something to do with the interference, but he dismissed the thought as ludicrous. How could that be? Somewhere deep within his brain, the ancient engines had placed the knowledge that far stranger things had been known to happen.

Ragnar wondered what the sergeant would do. He could order them back to the high ground and hope to get beyond the range of the interference, or he could order them to push on. For a moment it seemed like Hengist himself was undecided, but then he gave the signal for them to move out. It looked as if they were going to carry on.

THEY STOOD NOW at the last recorded position of the missing pack. This was the final reference point where the Fang's sophisticated location systems had been able to detect them. Ragnar now understood why. The trail through the tainted woods ended in a sheer rock face. The only way forward was through a cave mouth which gaped in the mountain side.

Sergeant Hengist gave a hand signal that told Ragnar to advance and investigate. Holding his weapons ready he loped forward cautiously, as if the cave were some dragon's mouth that might snap shut and devour him. As he moved closer the odd stink became somewhat stronger and Ragnar's unease intensified. Somehow, he sensed that there was something in the inky darkness of the cave that he really did not trust or like, a hint of rottenness far greater than anything in the corrupt forest that surrounded them.

Carefully, Ragnar picked his way up to the cave mouth and peered into the gloom. He saw nothing except a long trail leading down into the darkness below the mountain. He felt as if he were looking down the gullet of some vast beast.

+ See anything?+ Hengist was using the comm-net.

'Only a tunnel,' Ragnar replied. 'What now?'

+We go in.+ Hengist said.

Ragnar had been afraid Hengist was going to say that.

FIFTEEN
IN THE DARK

RAGNAR GLANCED around into the gloom. The shoulder lamp on his armour sent a bright finger of light out to pierce the stygian darkness. At the moment it revealed only the clammy wall of the cavern, but Ragnar had a distinct feeling that was likely to change soon. The walls glittered, pearlescent in the torch beam. Something just wasn't right. Every augmented and supertrained sense which Ragnar possessed screamed this fact at him. On edge, he listened on the assigned communicator channel, but all he could hear was the crackle of static. Some force, perhaps background radiation from the surrounding rocks, interfered with the comm-net. That was not good. All the training missions Ragnar had been part of had stressed how much good communication was essential to a unit's effectiveness.

'What's that?' Sven asked. Ragnar could see that Sven, who was on point, had stopped moving and was bending down to inspect something in the wet sand of the tunnel floor. Ragnar kept his eyes focused on the area beyond his comrade just in case something unexpected and doubtless threatening should emerge out of the darkness. He kept moving, until he had passed Sven and took up a position where he could cover the rough cut corridor. As he did so he caught a quick glance of the thing Sven was studying. Ceramite glinted up from the sand in reflection of the blue-white gleam from Sven's shoulder lamp. It appeared to be a piece of Space Marine armour, half covered by sand. Perhaps a chunk of chest plate. An isolated part of Ragnar's mind almost absently noted that the fragment of insignia visible could easily be extrapolated to complete the Wolf Head rune.

Mentally filing this fact away, Ragnar stared down the tunnel, staying on the balls of his feet, doing his best to keep alert while his mind wrestled with this information. This new development was not good. Very few natural forces could fracture ceramite armour. Ragnar assessed that it probably wasn't a rock slide or an animal which had killed the armour's wearer. If indeed the bearer was killed, and not simply lying injured or imprisoned somewhere within these seemingly endless passages.

All of which led to another disturbing thought. Ragnar wondered if he had known the person who had worn that armour? Had it belonged to one of the older Blood Claws who had been accepted into the chapter ahead of him? He had seen many of them within the Fang. Ragnar began to silently recite one of the old litanies in his mind, as he had been trained. Turning the words over in his mind, they felt like old friends, reminding him to stay in the moment, to focus on his surroundings, and not to let memories distract him. In this dark place all of these well-learnt instructions things seemed like very good advice.

Ragnar tried to estimate how far they had come. It seemed like they had wandered for leagues through these tunnels following the faintest hint of a trail. According to the pedometer built into his armour they had covered exactly five point zero six Imperial kilometres, but that still did not give him any idea how deep they were underground. The corridors had wound and twisted like a drunken serpent. They might be deep within the bowels of Fenris, or they might only be a hundred strides from where they started. It was impossible to tell.

He was certain of one thing. He did not like the smell of this place. There was a taint of something like corruption in the cool, clammy air, and the hint of a scent that made him want to bare his fangs and strike at the first thing that came within range. It was something unnatural, and the beast within him instinctively revolted at its presence. Only the presence of his battle-brothers gave Ragnar any assurance.

'Ceramite armour,' he heard Hengist say in his gravelly, matter-of-fact voice. 'Clean fracture too. Looks like someone used a magsteel blade judging by the break. Very interesting.' Hengist could have been describing the salient features of one of the automated combat drones in the training pits of the fang for all the emotion in his voice.

'I never knew the Outlanders had magsteel forges,' Sven said.

'Maybe they don't,' Hengist replied.

'What do you mean?'

'We'll see. Let's push on. Ragnar, you seem to have taken over point. Might as well stay there.'

'Yes, sergeant.'

Ragnar pushed on, deeper into the all-enclosing darkness.

'LOOKS LIKE some sort of storage place,' Ragnar said, staring around the vast cavern. Roughly hewn walls of a grey-green hue arched away above them, rearing up into complete darkness overhead. Rust marks from mineral ores stained the walls like old blood. Ragnar doubted that this cave was entirely of natural origin. The ruddy sand beneath their booted feet was dryer here, and crunched as they walked. Bat-winged creatures flickered away from their lights like torn scraps of shadow. Search beams flickered out inquisitively from a dozen or so shoulder lights, casting long shadows in the gloom. The faint whine of armour-servos and the flapping of the bat-creatures was the only sound. All around the walls were clay urns. Ragnar walked over to the nearest one, wondering whether he should lift off the lid. Hengist strode past and smashed it with his fist. A stale odour of old grain and mould immediately assaulted Ragnar's nostrils.

'Looks like you're right,' Hengist said. Ragnar gazed around as the rest of the pack moved into the cavern. There was something very strange about this place, he realised. Parts of the cavern were natural and parts definitely did look somewhat man-made. Ragnar would have sworn that he could see a part of a plasteel girder almost entirely enclosed in rock. He pointed this out to the sergeant.

'Take a look,' Hengist said. Ragnar looked for handholds in the wall and began to pull himself up. As he did so, a foul smell of excrement wafted into his nostrils. This was obviously where the bat-like creatures made their lair. Soon he had climbed far up the walls, past many niches that looked like nests. The rest of the pack was a long way below him, illuminated by the flickering finger of his shoulder light.

Then he reached the cavern roof, and was not entirely surprised to find that his initial supposition was correct. These were girders of plasteel, partially corroded. The knowledge the Fang's teaching machines had placed in his head told him that they must be immeasurably ancient. It took millennia for plasteel to begin to corrode. He lowered himself back down to the ground and reported his findings to Hengist.

'It looks like we've found one of the Ancients' sites then,' the sergeant said. 'And obviously we're not the first.'

Ragnar looked at him questioningly.

'Mankind is old on Fenris. People were here long before Russ and the Imperium. The original settlers were supposed to have sheltered from the elements in these caverns, and hid here during the Age of Catastrophe.'

Ragnar nodded. That made sense. These caves were the perfect place to hide from the cold, the storms, the meteor showers. And this part of Asaheim was stable. No quakes. Of course, that only begged the question of why they had been abandoned. Ragnar asked Hengist. The sergeant grimaced and shook his head.

'There are only legends now but it is said there was some ancient force present in the rocks which caused mutation and made the inhabitants susceptible to the influence of Chaos. Some say that this was a natural thing, others that it was the result of ancient forbidden weapons being unleashed. No one knows now. All that is known is that the cavern cities were abandoned, and that Russ himself forbade any to make their homes there.'

'It looks like Russ's edict had been disobeyed,' Ragnar said.

'Yes,' Hengist agreed. 'There are always those who will do forbidden things, simply because they are forbidden. It is part of the folly of mankind.'

Ragnar was surprised to find himself at least partly sympathetic to the views of those who would inhabit the caves. After all, they made a perfect shelter from the wild storms of Asaheim. He knew that present necessity was often stronger than ancient taboo. While these thoughts flickered through his mind, he held his tongue. Briefly suspicion flared that such self-questioning thoughts might not have been his own, but the product of some outside influence insidiously playing on his mind, but Ragnar dismissed the idea as irrational.

'We'd best push on, if we're going to find any trace of our missing brethren,' said Hengist.

AHEAD OF HIM Ragnar could hear the constant drip-drip-drip of moisture condensing on a cavern ceiling and then dropping into some deep underground pool. He was surprised to round a corner and see a faint pale yellow glow ahead of him. He dimmed his shoulder lamp, made a hand signal for the Blood Claws behind him to hold their position, crouched down and advanced slowly towards the source of the illumination.

The tunnel narrowed and the floor of the passage rose slightly as he moved. He was forced to use one hand to balance himself as he moved up the slope. He held his bolt pistol ready in his right hand. As his head rose above the level of the passage, a strange vista came into view.

He saw that he was looking down from an opening high in the side of another vast cavern, and that far below him, cupped in the bowl made by the floor of the cave, was a huge body of water. Phosphorescent algae swirled like trapped nebula in the water's black and oily surface. It was this that gave off the greenish-yellow glow. Ripples expanded from the places where moisture beads, like saliva dripping from the giant stalactite fangs of the ceiling, disturbed the surface. It almost seemed to Ragnar that he and his fellow Blood Claws were being consumed alive by some huge beast. It was as if the mountain were alive and he was being dragged ever deeper into its stomach for digestion. The sensation made him shiver. A ramp of collapsed rock and sand led steeply down to the pool.

Ragnar turned and gestured for Sven and Strybjorn to advance. His two comrades moved up and past him. While he covered them from his perch, they scuttled crab-like down the slope towards the surface of the water. Ragnar waited tensely, half expecting some monstrous head to emerge from the pool and snap at them, but nothing happened. The only sound was the faint dripping of the water and the scuff of the two Blood Claws' feet on the slippery rock surface, punctuated by the occasional hiss or whirr of a compensator struggling to adjust as rocks slid away under the weight of Space Marine armour.

Sven and Strybjorn stood for long moments waiting, heads cocked to one side as they tested the air, then they gave the all clear signal. One by one, the remainder of the Blood Claws advanced into the chamber, to be joined by Sergeant Hengist. Once they were all within, Ragnar moved down the slope to join them.

'This is hopeless,' he heard Sven mutter. 'We'll never find them.' He emphatically spat a gob of phlegm into the lake. 'That is, if they were ever here.'

Hengist's keen ears caught even these faint words. 'We will continue until we have established the fate of our Wolfbrothers,' the old sergeant growled. 'That is our duty and our way.'

'Aye,' Sven said. 'Fair enough.' He kicked absently at a rock with his booted foot. It arced into the pool, disappearing with a dull splash. 'Still, this is a fell-looking place right enough. I half expect to see a den of trolls any minute.'

For himself, Ragnar would almost have welcomed the presence of such monstrous creatures. It would have helped dispel the strange tension he was starting to feel, and would have helped him forget the weird sensation of being watched by hostile eyes, a sensation that was starting to make the flesh between his shoulder blades crawl. Maybe this was just his overactive imagination playing tricks. Somehow, this time, he doubted that.

'It's like a bloody sea,' Sven said with a trace of ironic humour. 'Maybe we can catch some fish for our supper.'

'I would not dine on the flesh of anything plucked from those foul waters,' said Lars. 'Nor would I drink of them.'

Ragnar was forced to agree. There was something deeply disquieting to him about this huge underground lake and its glowing surface. He could not see the far shore from where he stood. His fear of it had not in the slightest decreased. Nor did the suspicion that at any moment a monstrous head was going to break the surface. Ragnar wondered if the great sea dragons perhaps had kin which dwelt beneath the waters in these deep caverns? Every few heartbeats he caught himself shooting swift nervous glances at the water's surface before glancing back to make sure nothing was sneaking up behind him. Something about the other Blood Claws' scent and stances told him that they felt the same way, despite all their efforts to conceal their nervousness.

None of them could forget that another pack of their brethren had become lost and had perhaps died down here. Every now and again he felt sure that he heard the faint padding of feet behind him, but when he glanced back he could discern nothing in the dim, boulder-strewn immenseness of the cavern. It surprised him when Sergeant Hengist began to move back down the line, pausing occasionally to mutter instructions to each Blood Claw. When he got back to Ragnar he moved alongside him and whispered.

'Switch off your shoulder lamp. You and I are going to wait here, and surprise whoever is sneaking along our trail.'

Ragnar nodded and obeyed. Now he knew his instincts served him well. That knowledge gave him some small, grim satisfaction.

RAGNAR'S EYES swiftly adjusted to the gloom. The faint glow of the lake gave him just enough light to see by. In the distance he could see the lights of the rest of the pack receding into the distance. He could hear their faint footfalls on the rock. Excitement and fear churned in his stomach. He knew the others would turn and race back at the first hint of trouble, but he wondered whether they would be in time.

The presence of Sergeant Hengist crouched behind a nearby rock was very reassuring. Hengist was a long proven and battle-tested warrior, for whom Ragnar had every respect. At such a time as this, with his first real battle since the struggle in his home village impending, that was an important consideration. He forced himself to concentrate on the litanies he had learned back in the Fang, to clear his mind of fear and worry and all other emotions that might reduce his chances of survival. He prayed to Russ and to the All Father to make his arm strong and his eye sure and to guide him through the coming conflict. Ready icons flickered across his senses, as his power suit told him that all his battle systems were fully function. Ragnar was prepared for the coming fight.

That was, if there was to be a conflict. Ragnar was still not entirely sure that there would be. So far his keen senses had been unable to detect any sign of anyone or anything following them. Perhaps Hengist was simply imagining things. At the same time, he knew this was mere wishful thinking. Hengist's senses were much keener than his own, and the sergeant had many more years of experience at interpreting the data they absorbed. It did not seem at all likely that Hengist had made a mistake. Furthermore, Ragnar's own dire foreboding and keen instincts spoke to him at some deeper level, telling him that danger was near. Somewhere in the depth of his mind, the beast stirred, responding to the threat. Suddenly Ragnar was glad of its presence, glad of all the implants and the training he had received back at the Fang. He felt strong and powerful and capable. He knew that no ordinary mortals could possibly prove a match for him, and the potent weapons he carried. The more cautious part of his mind reminded him that a pack of his brethren, equally capable and equally well equipped, had already gone missing down here, and his foreboding returned redoubled.

The flicker of a hand signal caught from the corner of his eye told him that Hengist had spotted something. A moment later Ragnar heard a faint soft padding, as of unshod feet on the wet sand – and he knew that the sergeant was right, that they were being followed.

He clutched his weapons tight and steeled himself for action. His body tensed and coiled like a great spring, and he made himself ready to move and strike at a heartbeat's notice. Nearby he sensed the sergeant also had made himself ready. Ragnar peered out into the gloom and became aware that a wave of shadowy humanoid figures was moving towards them, as quiet, stealthy and inexorable as a tide moving up a beach.

His heart sank when he saw quite how large the crowd was. There must be hundreds of people following them. It seemed to him in that moment that the odds must be insuperable. He shook his head, commended his soul to Russ and to the Emperor, and made himself ready to die. Then suddenly he sensed Hengist move, heard the sound of something whip through the air close by. A moment later, light blazed through the cavern, and there was a roar like thunder as something exploded in the midst of the oncoming crowd.

Ragnar had a second to realise that the sergeant had thrown a grenade before the full horror of the scene illuminated by the terrific detonation etched itself on his brain. In that brief blazing instant, in that hellish light, he caught his first real glimpse of the denizens of the terrible under caverns deep beneath the surface of Fenris. From the descriptions he had heard, he saw that they were undeniably nightgangers.

They were bestial. They had bodies roughly humanoid in outline but slouching and ape-like. Huge saucer eyes evolved to capture the slightest hint of light dominated their ape-like faces. Their skins were pale white and leprous, blotched in places with bizarre birthmarks and the stigmata of mutation and disease. Ragnar was reminded in an odd way of the twisted forest outside the cavern's mouth, and he realised that in some way these people were probably the human equivalent of those disfigured trees there.

And yet the most horrifying thing was that these creatures quite obviously were, or had once been, people. They, or their ancestors, had been as human as his own clan. How long had it taken for this to happen, Ragnar wondered? How many aeons spent in slow devolution underground had been needed to produce this race of monsters? Had the stigmata of mutation been passed on from generation to generation growing slowly worse as the cavern folk became more bestial and unknowing? Or had it all happened at once, the product of some strange magic unleashed in this dark world deep below the mountain peaks?

Not that it mattered much at this moment. Even as he watched, the nightgangers recovered from the shock of the explosion that had rent through their midst. They milled around looking for a cause. Hengist chose that moment to lob another grenade. Once again the mighty flash rent the age-old gloom. Once more the misshapen folk of the underworld died, flesh torn, blood raining down on the survivors. Blinded by the unaccustomed light of the explosion, they recoiled, clawed and webbed hands clasped over saucer-like eyes.

The scent of the blood combined with the tension of the wait goaded the beast within Ragnar to fury. He leapt up from his hiding place, bolt pistol spitting death. He unleashed shot after shot into the crowd of pursuers. They were so close packed that every shell found a home more often than not. Sometimes they blasted through the tightly packed mass of flesh and buried themselves in another target. Screams of pain mingled with roars of bestial fury.

And yet, misshapen though they were, the nightgangers were not lacking in courage. Either that or they were over-blessed

with stupidity. Ragnar knew his own people would most likely
have broken and fled at least momentarily before the torrent of
supernatural death raining down on them but these denizens
of the underworld did not run. They were made of sterner, or
perhaps madder, stuff. Swiftly Ragnar realised that opening fire
had been a mistake. The muzzle flash of his gun and the blazing contrail of his bolter shells unmistakably gave away his
position to the nightgangers. They could not help but notice
where he was, and with a mighty roar of frenzied rage they
raced towards him.

Ragnar answered their war cry with a wolfish howl of his
own, and was reassured to hear it echoed back from the throats
of the approaching Blood Claws. He pulled the trigger again
and again as the frenzied mass of mutants approached, sending bolter shell after bolter shell rocketing into his targets.
Heads burst, chests were torn apart as the shells exploded in
their targets. The nightgangers had no armour capable of resist-
ing those terrible shots. All they had in their favour was sheer
weight of numbers, that and an insanely ferocious courage.

Hengist lobbed grenade after grenade from his own hiding
place, and every one exacted a hideous toll on the nightgangers. It seemed to Ragnar almost as if a giant hand was
reaching down into the middle of his foes and tossing them
about like leaves before the wind.

The nightgangers were close enough now so that he could
make out details of their individual appearance. He was
shocked to discover the extent that mutation had affected
them. Some of the miserable creatures were covered in fur,
some of them had horns protruding from their heads, some of
them had hooves and claws and shark-like rows of teeth in
their hideously distended jaws. They were like aberrations from
the wildest depths of nightmare. It was as if the gates of hell
had opened to let a horde of gibbering misshapen things flop
through into the world.

Even as he fired, a detached and calculating part of Ragnar's
mind find itself wondering if the nightgangers were really so
different from him. After all, he too now possessed an excess of
body hair verging on fur, and he had fangs, and his eyes had
altered. He swiftly pushed these thoughts aside. They had nothing to do with the fight in which he was engaged, and they
verged dangerously close to heresy. The alterations to his body

were signs of his kinship to Russ, marks of the Emperor's favour and blessing. They were products of an ancient mystical process that dated back to the Dark Age of Technology. The stigmata shown by these nightgangers were signs of something else. Perhaps they were the badge of Chaos, of those whose souls had been as corrupted by its warping influence as their bodies had been.

The nightgangers were almost upon him now. Ragnar leapt atop the rock behind which he had been waiting. The night-gangers had not responded with missile fire and he had no need of cover. In hand-to-hand combat, occupying the higher ground would give him a temporary advantage. With a swift mental command he upped the magnification of his shoulder lamp so that it would dazzle any nightganger who looked directly at it. A touch of a switch activated his chainsword. It vibrated angrily in his hand as the serrated edges of its blades accelerated up to their maximum cutting speed. Ragnar laughed aloud, feeling the full battle rage come upon him. The beast roared within his soul, demanding to be unleashed.

The nightgangers were almost upon him. Hengist tossed a last grenade that tore another apart and then Ragnar heard the sergeant's chainsword activate as well. He looked down into the sea of mutant faces, let out a long angry howl and then dived into their midst like a swimmer leaping into a turbulent sea.

Even before he landed he lashed out with his chainsword. It passed through flesh like a cleaver through meat. The smell of friction-heated bone reached Ragnar's nostrils as the scream of the chainsword hit a new high note cutting through bone. The moment passed as the chainsword took the limb clean off. Blood gouted from the stump. Ragnar took off a head, severing vertebrae cleanly and easily before taking the top off another. As he did so he kept up a steady stream of shots from his bolt pistol against bodies too closely packed for him to miss. The screams and howls of his victims echoed in his ears, goading the beast within him to ever greater fury and lending ever more strength to his frenzied limbs.

In moments the nightgangers recovered from the shock of his charge, and leapt to meet him. They were armed only with crude hatchets, stone-tipped clubs and spears. They struck at him wildly at first, and their blows, unable to make proper contact with his fast moving form, slid harmlessly off the smooth curved ceramite of his armour. He was aware of their strikes in much the same way as a man would be of rain striking his cloak. The sensation was at most uncomfortable, but certainly not painful.

He moved through his foes like a whirlwind of death, leaving dead and dying nightgangers in his wake. For a brief triumphant instant he felt like nothing could stand against him. He was invincible, unstoppable, a god of death reaping the lives of his enemies. In that ecstatic instant he had some inkling of how Russ must have felt after his apotheosis. He whirled and struck and kicked, feeling bones crunch beneath his blade. He stamped down and reduced the fingers and skulls of fallen enemies to jelly. He howled long and exultantly and his bloodlust was echoed in the calls of his comrades. At that moment Ragnar felt as if he did not need them, that he was capable of routing and killing all the nightgangers on his own. It did not matter how many of them there were or how brave. There was simply no way for them to overcome him. The struggle was going to be so one-sided.

Then he felt a bite of pain in his ribcage. He looked down to see an axe blade lodged in the hardened ceramite of his armour. It was made of black iron and yet it had cut through one of the hardest substances ever produced in the foundries of the Fang. How could this be? Then he noticed the red glowing runes that blazed on its surface and he had his answer. Evil sorcery was at work here.

For a moment he felt a surge of panic. He half expected to feel evil magical power flow through his body like poison. He knew of such fell weapons, tales of their power had been implanted in his brain by the teaching machines of the Space Wolves. They could have all manner of dreadful powers, built into them by their daemonic makers. Who knew what this one would be capable of?

He stood frozen for a moment and the nightgangers took advantage of his confusion to swarm over him, striking and rending as they came. A blow from a stone club sent his pistol to the ground. Another blow from an axe grazed his forehead drawing blood. Some nightgangers grabbed his legs, others grabbed his arms. They howled with triumphant bloodlust convinced that they had captured their prey.

'In the name of the Emperor, fight boy!' he heard Hengist shout. The words stirred him from his daze and he suddenly realised that it did not matter if he were poisoned or cursed. If he did not start to fight back he would be dead in a matter of moments anyway as the nightgangers' weapons buried themselves in the joints and chinks of his armour. With a roar he flexed his limbs. Servo-motors whined with the strain as he cast the nightgangers off, hurling them aside as if they were made of straw. He whirled around, wielding his chainsword with both hands, lopping limbs and heads off everything within his reach.

From the corner of his eye he caught sight of a nightganger chieftain or shaman lifting another of the cursed axes to throw at him. Snarling with rage Ragnar bounded forward bringing his chainsword down in a mighty arc of death. It took the shaman on the skull and cleaved it in two, passed right through his neck, his chest, his stomach, his hipbone. With one blow he clove the shaman clean in two sending entrails and internal organs toppling out onto the stone floor of the cavern. In that moment, he saw that he had cleared the whole area around him. He reached down and plucked the axe from his armour, casting the foul thing as far away from as he could.

Looking around he saw that Hengist had left a trail of destruction right through the nightgangers and had now turned at bay to confront them. Even as the sergeant braced himself to strike once more there was a howl of dismay from the nightgangers as the other Blood Claws ploughed into their ranks. Together Hengist and Ragnar leapt into the fray once more.

It was all too much for even the nightgangers' courage. This time they turned and fled, leaving the corpses of their many dead strewn across the floor of the cavern.

SIXTEEN
THE TEMPLE OF CHAOS

RAGNAR LOOKED AT the scene of carnage. He could not begin to count the dead nightgangers. He could only guess that at least a hundred had died. All around he could hear sporadic fire as the other Blood Claws blazed away at their retreating foes. He would have carried on shooting too but he was more interested in what Sergeant Hengist was up to.

Hengist had bent over the body of the dead shaman and was inspecting his throwing axe without touching it. Ragnar moved over to beside his leader.

'What is it, sergeant?' he asked.

'These weapons have been touched by the power of Chaos,' Hengist replied.

'I thought as much. One of them pierced my armour during the combat.'

'What? Let me see.' Hengist bent forward and looked at the place where the axe had smashed through ceramite. He inspected the break closely then sniffed.

'No blood,' he said. 'It did not break flesh. You were lucky.'

'Lucky?'

'Sometimes these weapons bear a poisonous power. Sometimes they carry the taint of Chaos itself. That alone can be enough to drive men mad.'

He tapped the utility belt at Ragnar's waist. 'Best use repair cement on that break. It should at least hold your armour together until we get back to the Fang.'

Ragnar did as he was told, smearing the quick-hardening paste into the gaps in his armour and waiting for the few moments it took to harden on contact with air.

'What now?' he asked.

'We go on,' Hengist said.

THE BLOOD CLAW pack pushed on deeper into the mountain. As they progressed, Ragnar became more and more aware of signs of occupation. Here and there bones cracked for marrow lay scattered through the passage. Close examination showed that they had once belonged to someone human or near-human.

'What do these people eat?' Sven asked.

'Always thinking about food, eh?' Nils replied.

'When they're not eating each other, you mean?' Strybjorn added.

Ragnar nodded. Try as he might it was difficult to picture what the nightgangers subsisted on. Unless they ate the huge roaches that occasionally scuttled away from the light. Perhaps they ate the bats or the eldritchly glowing fungi that spotted some of the walls. Or perhaps they made forays onto the surface to hunt. Strybjorn's words conjured up another image of warring clans of the hideous mutants fighting each other in the dark and consuming their dead victims.

Was that what had happened to the previous pack, he wondered? Had they had their armour split and their flesh winkled from it the way Ragnar used to get crabmeat from a shell? But if so, how had it happened? It did not seem possible that the nightgangers could overcome a fully armed and prepared pack of Blood Claws. By Russ, he and Sergeant Hengist had routed what must have been a whole tribe of them virtually on their own. Their weapons were too primitive, their tactics too simple for them to have overcome a whole unit.

And why had the other pack come here in the first place? Their mission had been to conduct a routine investigation of the area in which the great meteor shower had fallen. Had they somehow been lured down here to their dooms? Was that what was happening to Ragnar and his comrades even now? He wished he had answers for these questions, but he did not.

Still, he told himself, he would doubtless find out the truth soon enough.

'LOOKS LIKE THIS cave complex has just been abandoned,' Lars said.

'You're right,' Ragnar said with a quick glance around the area. Pots and pans, small stone statues, necklaces of finger bones, leather sacks full of unidentifiable stuff lay strewn everywhere as if they had just been abandoned. Ragnar sniffed the air. The scent of the nightgangers was still everywhere, fresh and strong. Some of the scent traces were subtly different. Women and children, most likely, Ragnar thought.

'Must have known we were coming,' Sven said, a nasty grin twisting his ugly face. 'Maybe the survivors of our last battle came here to warn them not to cross us.'

'Or maybe they just wanted their womenfolk out of the way before they collapse the roof on us,' Lars suggested.

Sven bared his teeth in a snarl. He had not liked the other Blood Claw's tone. Hengist moved between them, to break up any potential brawl. Now was not the time for a squabble over precedence in the pack. Instantly Sven and Lars moved apart.

'I don't think that's what's going to happen,' Hengist said. 'No, I think we're in for something different.'

'Like what?' Ragnar asked.

'I wish to hell I knew. Whatever it is, one thing's for sure. It won't be pleasant.'

Ragnar was forced to agree. Like the sergeant, like all of them, he could sense the presence of something else in the air, could sense the gathering of forces to oppose them. There was a power here, deep beneath this mountain. He was certain of it. And he was certain that this power was strong and ancient and evil. He decided that he had better give voice to a thought that was obviously on the mind of every Blood Claw.

'Perhaps we should turn back, sergeant,' he said.

'Not yet,' Hengist said. 'We haven't found what we came for yet.'

'And I doubt we're going to,' muttered Sven.

Not unless what we came to find was death, thought Ragnar.

'WHAT WAS THAT?' asked Lars. Ragnar looked at him. There was no need to ask what the blond-haired Blood Claw had meant.

He had heard it too. Somewhere off in the distance a great drum was beating. Its vibrations could be felt through the walls like the throbbing of a massive heart.

'It's our subhuman friends letting their kinfolk know that dinner will soon be served up. And that it consists of tender young Blood Claws,' Sven said in his surliest voice.

Nils shook his head. 'Food. Always thinking of food,' he said mockingly.

THE CORRIDOR descended downwards. The way was illuminated by glowing fungi. Vast mushrooms blotched the damp floors and walls and sent an eerie greenish glow shimmering through the air. Ragnar could taste their spores on his tongue, and their scent almost overpowered all others. It was sweet and sickly and smelled of rot and corruption. There was something about it that reminded him of corpses. Here and there trails of luminescent slime threaded their way between the growths and vanished into holes the size of a man's head in the walls of the tunnel. The image of loathsome slug-like creatures fastened itself in Ragnar's mind and would not depart. Perhaps such creatures were what the nightgangers ate.

He knew that there were tunnels running parallel to the one they were in. He could sense that those tunnels were filled with vast hordes of nightgangers. Occasionally he would catch sight of their forms fleetingly as they passed the mouth of a side tunnel, but the mutants kept their distance and did not come within striking distance. Either they had learned their lesson, or they were waiting for something they knew was to happen.

Ragnar suspected that it was the latter. Hengist pushed on oblivious, following a trail that seemed obvious only to him. Ragnar was not sure whether this was because of the sergeant's keener senses and greater experience of tracking or because the sergeant's weird was upon him, and he was following his death-path. Ragnar had heard of this happening to others back in the island. Men would hear the siren call of their doom and rise from the table to march to their deaths in a troll's lair. He did not see why a Space Wolf should necessarily be exempt from such a thing, although at the moment he thought it best to keep his suspicions to himself.

Ragnar risked a glance over his shoulder. Far, far off in the distance he thought he caught the glimmer of glowing eyes. He hurried on to catch up with the rest of the pack.

SUDDENLY THE trail ended. Ahead of them was a long stone bridge over a vast chasm. Ragnar stood on the chasm's edge. Somewhere far below he thought he heard the sound of water. Sven picked up a pebble and tossed it into the abyss. They both stood there counting but there was no sound of the stone hitting bottom.

On the far side of the chasm was an archway in the wall. It was of dressed stone, and even at this distance Ragnar could see each block had been carved with a leering daemon head. It seemed that Hengist's tracking skills had not led them false, and that they had indeed found what they had come for.

The sergeant turned and looked back at the Blood Claws. His ancient, lined face looked pale and drawn in the light of their shoulder lamps. His eyes glittered feverishly in their sockets.

'As I suspected,' he said. 'A temple of Chaos.'

'Maybe we should go back now, and report it,' said Lars.

Hengist turned on his heel, readied his weapon and strode towards the bridge. He paused at the edge, knowing that it was not the leader's duty to place himself unnecessarily at risk. He halted for a long moment, and then said: 'Ragnar, advance and scout out the doorway. Be careful. The bridge might not be safe.'

As if I needed anyone to tell me that, Ragnar thought as he paced forward. In the distance, behind them, he was sure he heard the murmuring as of a great crowd.

WIDE ENOUGH for just one Space Marine at a time, and stretching several hundred paces across the chasm, the stone felt solid beneath his feet, but Ragnar was taking no chances. He advanced cautiously, placing one foot slowly in front of the other, only gradually placing his full weight on his leading foot. It would not do to forget how heavy he was now in his power armour, despite his agility and speed. Also, there could be traps or deadfalls on the bridge. Ragnar knew that anything was possible where the devilish minds of Chaos worshippers were concerned. The stones looked solid but if there was even a slim chance of them giving way and sending him plummeting down into the abyss below, Ragnar wanted to be prepared. If he was going to die here, he wanted to die in battle. That was the only way a warrior should go.

Now where had that thought come from, Ragnar wondered, feeling the beast stir warily within him. Had it come from whatever was in the temple ahead? He could feel the presence of something there, just as surely as he could feel the cold moist breeze on his brow. It pulsed outwards through the gloom like an invisible, spectral beacon. He offered up a prayer to Russ and to the Emperor for the safety of his soul, and pushed on, his armoured feet scuffing dust from the narrow causeway.

Ahead of him, the archway grew larger. He realised that it was immense. Just as this bridge was longer than it had first appeared, so was the opening correspondingly more huge. He began to appreciate how much labour had gone into the creation of this obscene place. This whole structure was no recent work. The flagstones over which he passed had been worn down by many feet. The thing was centuries, if not millennia old.

In the gloom and distance his eyes had been fooled. Now he was starting to realise the scale of the deception. He guessed that the arch was maybe ten times his height, and that each of the blocks making up part of it was at least as tall as he was. The hideous twisted heads chiselled from the stone looked large enough to swallow a grown man at a bite. In a way, the artistry that had gone into their creation was wonderful. They looked like the heads of real living monsters about to emerge full-grown from the stone. He half expected those yawning mouths to gape wider and snap at him as he approached.

From up ahead, through the towering black archway, Ragnar thought he heard a faint murmuring or chanting, but he could not be sure. He moved across the flagstones up to the archway itself. He paused there for a moment, and glanced through, and what he saw took his breath away.

He looked down a vast flight of marbled steps into an enormous chamber carved from the very heart of the mountain. At the far end of the chamber stood a massive statue of what Ragnar perceived could only be an enormous daemon. The statue appeared to be made of some form of crystal and inlaid with bone. Each scale of its shimmering skin was a jewel. Colours constantly shifted and moved across its surface, mingling and shifting endlessly. The statue was perhaps five times the height of a man but such was the aura of power that surrounded it that it seemed much larger still. Its eyes flickered like flames. There was something about the glow of its skin that made it hard to focus on, that baffled Ragnar's eyes, seeming to suggest that at any moment the statue might change form into something else, or spring into sorcerous life.

Great metal wings were folded round the statue's shoulders like a cloak. Its head was curiously bird-like. It stretched out monstrous talons in a gesture that was at once curiously human and supremely menacing. The thing gave the impression of something at once bestial and god-like, of being at the same time something far greater and far worse than human. And from it, waves of dark power seemed to pulse like the malicious heartbeat of an insane god. Ragnar knew without having to be told that this was an effigy of some aspect of Tzeentch, the Great Mutator, the daemon lord of vile sorcery. His implanted knowledge gave him absolute certainty of that awful fact. Ragnar's skin tingled from the sorcerous emanations the thing projected.

So great was the impression of the statue, and so much did it draw his eye, that it was several heartbeats before Ragnar could begin to take in the rest of the chamber. It was as sickening as the statue was impressive. Multi-coloured flames jetted from the walls of the chamber casting their hellish illumination to the furthest corners. From the way they danced and from their pungent smell Ragnar could tell that these were jets of natural gas.

It was what their light revealed that was so daunting. Scattered across the floor were piles of hideously mutated corpses, bloated and twisted but immediately recognisable as having once been human. It looked as if their flesh had been heated unto liquefaction and flowed into new and bizarre shapes. Heads had swollen like balloons to twice their previous size. Fingers had fused together to form flippers. Masses of entrails had exploded from stomachs, become twisted tentacles which looked to have strangled their owners. In some cases the small fangs in their mouths had become huge tusks. Fur had sprouted from some of their skins. In other cases the skin had become transparent to reveal the mass of internal organs. One poor wretch had sloughed away his skin like a snake to reveal the pink mass of muscle and vein beneath. Here was an awful example of the true power of Tzeentch.

At last Ragnar knew the fate of the previous pack. Hanging from great structures of carved bone were their armour and their weapons. A howl of horror and rage was drawn from Ragnar's open mouth. In the flickering light of the gas jets the great statue of Tzeentch seemed to smile mockingly.

He turned and beckoned for his comrades to follow him across. They came over far more quickly than he had, loping from flagstone to flagstone.

'By Russ!' he heard Sven mutter. 'This is a foul place.'

'A Temple of Tzeentch,' Hengist said. 'The Great Mutator. One of the All Father's four greatest enemies.'

'We must destroy it,' Strybjorn said.

'Excellent idea,' Lars said. 'But how?'

'Use grenades,' Nils said.

'That will not work,' Hengist said. 'Unless I miss my guess, that evil thing is bound with foul sorcery. It will take greater weapons than we possess to destroy it. We must inform the Chapter of what we have found here.'

'I think you will have other things to worry about, false marine,' said a cold and mocking voice.

Ragnar looked up. A figure had appeared before the altar of Tzeentch. He was not quite sure how it had come to be there. He had seen no one enter the temple. Ragnar found his eyes drawn to the speaker. It was hard to resist the impulse to stare.

The newcomer was garbed like an odd parody of a Space Marine. His armour was bulky and appeared to be of archaic design. More, it looked as if parts had been removed, and replaced or repaired or modified with bands of gold or black iron. Red glowing eyes burned out from within a massive and intricately horned helmet. It held a bolt pistol of equally antique design in each hand.

Ragnar could see that its armour was impossibly ornate. Glittering jewels and daemon heads were inlaid all over its surface and shimmered in the light of the gas jets. Perhaps it was just a trick of the light but some of those heads seem to leer and yawn and wink, stretching in a manner no natural metal could. From the memories placed in his brain by the Fang's teaching machines, Ragnar knew he looked upon one of humanity's deadliest foes, a Chaos Marine.

'It is you who are the false Marine,' replied Hengist. 'It was your kind who broke your vows to the Emperor and to humanity.'

'It was your senile god who broke faith with us. He was too weak. And humanity proved itself ungrateful and unworthy of our rule.' The voice carried a taint of arrogance, perhaps even boredom.

'The rule of daemons and daemon worshippers. The rule of those who bent their knee before our most ancient enemies. You are scum, worse than scum.'

'And you will have a long time in which to repent those words, and to whimper prayers of mercy to He who will soon consume your soul. And believe me, your prayers will not be answered.'

'You will not talk so proudly once I have taken your head and cast your foul corpse into the abyss.'

The Chaos Marine laughed. It was not a pleasant laugh, Ragnar thought. It was too mocking and too full of confidence by far. No warrior should be able to laugh that way when confronted by a full pack of Space Wolves. The blue and gold armoured warrior appeared to read his thoughts.

'You and all your yapping puppies could not manage that.'

'Could they not? The least of these Blood Claws is a better and truer warrior than you, oathbreaker.' Hengist spat on the polished floor of the Chaos temple.

'I admit they were handy enough against ignorant superstitious subhumans but as you can see I am armed and equipped at least as well as you.' The sorcerer-marine gestured theatrically about him.' Perhaps I should remove my weapons and fight you with a spear. That way you might at least have a chance. But no, that would still be too easy for me. I could use my bare hands.'

'You talk a brave fight, for one who hides in the darkness below the world!' Ragnar interjected, feeling his anger mount.

'I have nothing to prove, slave to a false god. For ten thousand years the name of Madok had caused his enemies to tremble.'

'Only if they were weak-willed fools cowed by empty boasts.'

'Your prattle wearies me, youth, and since you have been good enough to give my brethren time to arrive, I think we should proceed with the slaughter.'

As Madok spoke doors in the side of the temple slid open and more Chaos Marines were revealed. Hengist raised his gun to fire but Madok was quicker. Both his pistols leapt up and began blazing away. Bolter shells clipped the sergeant's armour as he dived into cover behind the archway. Two of the pack were not so lucky and were cut down by a blaze of fire from the Chaos Marines.

Ragnar followed Hengist's example and leapt out of the line of fire. Strybjorn and Sven and several others of the pack held their ground and responded. Their shells flashed across the temple but some evil power seemed to send them astray, and they exploded harmlessly on the flagstones around the Chaos Marines. Ragnar looked across at Hengist for orders. The sergeant raced across the archway and rolled into position beside Ragnar.

'There must be a full squad of Chaos Marines in there, maybe more. They will prove too much for a pack of Blood Claws. The Chapter must be warned of this. Take Sven, Strybjorn, Nils and Lars and head back to the surface. The rest of us will hold them off for as long as possible.'

Ragnar wanted to protest. The beast within him was strong. The smell of blood made his hackles rise and filled him with the lust to kill. More than that he felt it unfair that he should be denied the chance of a hero's death. Hengist seemed to sense the emotions passing through his mind.

'Sometimes the life of a Space Marine is not easy,' he said. 'Now take the others and go.' He bellowed for the Blood Claws who were to follow Ragnar to fall back. Even as he watched, Ragnar, saw Kraki and Volgard go down to the Chaos Marines' fire. He saw too that they had yet to take a casualty even though they were advancing slowly and relentlessly as automatons across the open floor of the temple. He could hear their other-worldly, unnerving laughter as they came on. Surely indeed they were protected by some malign power, Ragnar thought. Then he knew for certain that it was time to go.

SEVENTEEN
FIGHTING RETREAT

'LET'S GO!' Ragnar yelled and raced back across the stone bridge away from the temple. He did not need to look back to see if the others were following him. He sensed their presence behind him and caught their scared, angry scents. Like him, he guessed they were frustrated and furious at being forced to leave the combat with the Chaos traitors. He cursed that such a blasphemy had been perpetrated on the holy soil of Fenris at all, and wondered how long the Chaos scum had been lurking below the surface of Asaheim. He guessed that they had come under cover of the last meteor storm, but part of him gagged at the thought that perhaps they had been here for months, years, decades even. Impossible! Ragnar refused to countenance such a thought. And now, having uncovered such a nest of vipers in their midst, they must flee!

Not that they were going to be spared any fighting, Ragnar knew. Up ahead of them he could see that the way was blocked by a horde of nightgangers, led by what looked to be a rune-weapon wielding shaman. The creature pointed a long, skull-tipped staff at Ragnar. He saw a halo of eerie reddish light crackle around its tip and then a bolt of searing mystical energy arced towards him. The Space Wolf sprang to one side just in time and it shattered the stones where he had been.

Without thinking Ragnar raised his bolt pistol and snapped off a shot. All the long hours of practice on the ranges proved their worth. The bolter shell flashed straight and true towards its target. The shaman's head exploded like a jellyfish hit with a blacksmith's hammer.

The nightgangers set up a bestial roar and began to race forward onto the bridge. They waved their clubs and axes furiously and chanted the name of Tzeentch. Ragnar was not so much worried by their numbers and weapons as he was by the fact that the sheer mass of bodies might slow them down and prevent them making their escape before the Chaos Marines behind overtook them. He was determined that Sergeant Hengist's message would reach the Chapter.

'Grenades!' he ordered. 'Now!'

As one the Blood Claws took microgrenades from the dispensers on their utility belts and began lobbing them at the oncoming horde. A wave of explosions passed through the crowd killing as they went. Gobbets of flesh and gallons of blood flowed everywhere. The sheer cataclysmic fury of the onslaught stopped the nightgangers' charge. The whole vast mass of them wavered for a moment.

'Pour it on!' Ragnar yelled and the Blood Claws hurled their grenades with redoubled fury. More and more nightgangers fell. The smell of blood and shattered bodies filled the air. Then at the last second Ragnar realised his mistake. The sheer force of such a large number of detonations concentrated on one spot had begun to weaken the bridge. Even as he watched huge chunks began to crumble and drop away into the chasm below. He realised that if the pack did not get clear soon the whole bridge would collapse and they would tumble into the great abyss.

To make matters worse, a bolter shell chipped the wall of the bridge close to his arm. He glanced backwards to see if anyone was firing at him from the temple entrance but he saw only the remnants of Hengist's force still firing away from the position where they were pinned down. He glanced back at the nightgangers and his keen eyes saw what he sought. A few of the mutant leaders brandished bolt pistols. Some of them were of a familiar design, exactly the same as the weapon he held.

Doubtless they had been looted from the corpses of the dead Space Wolves back in the temple. A few more were of a similar archaic design to those carried by the Chaos Marines. They must have arrived on the planet with the heretics, Ragnar thought. Not that any of this would matter if he did not get off the bridge soon.

He glanced around to see that all the others had noticed what he had. He knew at once from their scents and their posture that they had. He had not needed to order them to stop throwing grenades. With the independence of true Space Wolves they had made the decision for themselves. Still they stood and kept up a hurricane of fire on the enemy, killing with every shot. Ragnar saw at once that there was only one thing to do.

'Forward!' he cried. 'Quickly! Come on!' He raced forward, feeling the bridge begin to shudder and tremble at his every step. It was obviously only a few heartbeats from total collapse. Ahead of him more and more of the flagstones were tumbling into the chasm below. The yawning gap between the still stable part of the bridge and the ledge on the other side grew ever wider. As he ran he wondered whether even his enhanced muscles would enable him to leap so wide a distance. Well, he thought, gritting his teeth in a feral grin, there was only one way to find out.

Each step brought Ragnar closer and closer to the edge. He heard his heartbeat loud in his ears, smelled his own tension and excitement. He knew that he would have to time things just right. A single misstep could take him over the edge and send him tumbling to his doom. Leaping too early would be just as fatal if he could not cover the full distance. Gripping his pistol and sword tight, he ran as close to the edge as he dared and then sprang.

Instantly he was vividly aware of the enormous gulf beneath his feet. Wind tugged at his hair. He felt as if he were moving in slow motion. He could pick out every detail of the mutants' features ahead of him. See every wart and boil that disfigured their twisted faces, count the pores on their skin. He had never been so aware of anything in his whole life. All of his superhuman senses were keyed up to a new level of awareness that was positively astounding. So close to death, Ragnar had never felt so alive.

He let out a long howling warcry. Even as he hurtled forward through the air Ragnar raised his pistol and snapped off a shot at a nightganger at the front of the precipice's edge. The mutant clutched his stomach and slumped forward tumbling down into the gloom and the darkness. Ragnar fired another shot and dropped another of his foes, then with a surge of relief he felt the solid ground beneath his boots once more. His knees flexing at the impact with the rocky edge of the far cavern, Ragnar shouted his defiance into the assembled mass of nightgangers. He was alive, and now they would pay! Now they would know first hand the true wrath of a Space Wolf! He surged forward, chainsword swinging, trying desperately to clear a path through the tightly packed nightgangers before his brethren landed on top of them. He knew it was all too possible under these circumstances that they might get entangled and overbalance and fall together into the gloom.

Flesh parted, bones splintered under the impact of his chainsword. He simply pulled the trigger of his bolt pistol knowing that every shell would find a home in this mass of bodies.

Ragnar cleaved his way through the nightgangers like a ship crashing through a stormy sea. He became a living engine of destruction, a whirlwind of death that twisted and howled and writhed its way through the massed ranks of mutants. Behind him he could hear the chanting of his brethren as they did the same. Soon a fine red mist of bloody droplets filled his sight from where his chainsword had split flesh and severed tendons and veins. The screams of the dying were almost deafening, even with the sonic dampeners within his helm. Deep within his soul, urged on by the scent of carnage, the beast grew stronger.

Ragnar fought now by pure instinct. He did not need to think. The beast was in control. Reflexes, nerves and sinew were in perfect harmony. He reacted to any threat perceived by his hyper-keen senses with the speed of thought. At that moment his combat ability far transcended that of any mortal. Nothing could or did stand in his way. Behind him, the other Blood Claws ripped through the mutant line like a good sharp axe through rotten wood.

Nightmare faces leered, jaws wide to scream, as he chopped them down. Twisted bodies gave way under the impact of his blade. The blows of stone clubs ricocheted off his armour. He ducked a whirring stone from a slingshot. His senses were so keen that it appeared to be moving towards him in slow motion, and he seemed to have all the time in the world to get out of its way. He shifted his head and was rewarded by the scream of a nightganger behind him who got in the stone's way. With a swift snapshot, he shattered the skull of the slinger and continued to hack his way towards freedom.

A blast of sorcerous energy cleaved through the air, a multi-coloured serpent of purplish-blue light that writhed its way towards him. He smelled ozone and a bitter perfume as it drew closer. Ragnar tried to leap to one side, springing clean over the head of a nightganger, but the crackling bolt altered its course and came straight at him once more. He raised his blade to parry, but faster than thought the finger of writhing, hideous energy swerved around and struck Ragnar's armour full on the breastplate.

Instantly his whole body was bathed in agony such as Ragnar had never known or guessed was possible. Every nerve ending screamed its pain. Ragnar felt his armour blister and begin to melt. Sparks flew outwards as systems started to short. Mad interference patterns flashed across his visor and crackling static roared in his ears. His hair stood on end. Surges of energy caused his power-assisted limbs to judder and spasm of their own accord. Ragnar felt like his eyes would boil in their sockets. He could smell his hair burning. He staggered like a drunk, engulfed in purple fire.

With a huge effort of will, Ragnar forced himself to concentrate and search for his foe. Gritting his teeth, he tasted the coppery tang of his own blood in his mouth. Looking up he saw a cackling, subhuman shaman capering madly on a floating disc of light, high above the crowd, towards the very roof of the cavern. More cursed sorcery, Ragnar thought. The serpent of energy writhed from the end of a skull-tipped staff held in the heretic's claw-like hand. Desperately, Ragnar tried to bring his pistol to bear, but tears of pain filled his eyes, and blurred his vision. It was becoming difficult to focus. Black and purple stars danced across his eyes and his tongue was stuck to the roof of his mouth. Ragnar knew without a doubt that in mere moments he would be dead.

Then suddenly a bolter shell flew straight and true and buried itself in the shaman's heart, knocking the fiend off the already fading disc. As he fell, the shaman spread his arms wide

and the serpent of light flickered and faded. Even as he tumbled down, another shell blazed towards the nightganger
mage, temporarily averting his downward progress through
sheer force of impact. The bolt round entered one eye and
exited the back of his head in a fountain of brains and blood.
Ragnar looked around to see who had shot his enemy, and to
his surprise saw that it was the hated Strybjorn. His sworn rival
raised one hand in a salute and then gave his attention back to
smiting the mutants.

Ragnar fought the dizziness that threatened to overwhelm
him. His armour was already running automated system
checks, and endless lines of icons flashed and flickered in the
periphery of his vision. Out of the corner of his eye he caught
sight of a grenade hurtling towards him. Judging from the
direction it had not been thrown by any of his comrades. It
must be one of those weapons the nightgangers had taken
from the dead Space Marines. One thing was certain, whoever
had thrown it cared nothing for his comrades' lives. Ragnar was
surrounded by howling nightgangers, all of whom would die if
a grenade exploded anywhere nearby.

Even in his semi-stunned state Ragnar knew his armour was
in no condition to take a direct hit from a krak grenade. He
could hear the damage in the atonal whining of the servos, and
the flashing red icons in his read out told their own dismal tale.
He knew he had only one chance and that depended on how
short a fuse the hurtling explosive was on. As it swept closer he
reached up with the flat of his chainsword and batted it away,
hoping against hope that the shock of the impact did not trigger the detonation he feared. For one brief heart-stopping
moment, Ragnar half expected to feel his arm wrenched from
its socket by the explosion but then the grenade was flying
backwards into the packed mass of nightgangers. A moment
later came the blast that sent subhuman forms blown into myr-
iad pieces tumbling through the air.

Ragnar reeled onwards. The nightgangers sensed his weakness and swarmed over him. Stone hatchets and clubs smashed
into the fracture lines on his damaged armour. Chunks of
ceramite fell onto the stone floor. Ragnar lashed out with the
butt of his pistol, smashing a skull, drove his chainsword point
first through the chest of the nearest nightganger, then split his
body in two with a swift up and down motion. The nearest

mutants, seeing the stalwart determination written on his face, started to back away. This gave Ragnar the space to send his chainsword in a swirling berserker circle around him, cleaving heads and bodies in twain. He whirled through the mass like a razor-edged cyclone and then in a moment realised that he was in the clear. There were no more nightgangers around him.

Panting and out of breath, Ragnar glanced backwards and saw Sven, Nils, Lars and Strybjorn all hacking their way through the mass of struggling mutants. They seemed to be swimming through a sea of raw flesh and spurting blood. All around them, nightgangers fell like wheat before the scythe of a reaper. The Blood Claws seemed inhuman, invincible, unstoppable. But then Ragnar caught sight of another grenade hurtling towards Strybjorn and Sven. He howled a warning, saw the Blood Claws begin to react and knew instinctively that his cry had come too late.

Sven managed to throw himself to one side, just in time. He dived headlong into a mass of nightgangers, howling and chopping as he went. Strybjorn was just a fraction too slow. He was grappled by several nightgangers all intent on pulling him down so they could bludgeon his exposed head with their cudgels. At the last moment, he threw them off with a mighty roar and attempted to evade the grenade. He almost managed it, but began his leap just as the detonation erupted, catching his armour and sending him tumbling through the air like a rag doll tossed aside by a cruel child.

Ragnar stood momentarily paralysed, overwhelmed by strangely mixed emotions. It seemed his hated enemy was dead, killed by the explosion, robbing Ragnar of his vengeance. But that was not the worst of it. Suddenly it seemed to Ragnar that his revenge was a small thing to consider indeed compared with the menace of the Chaos Marines and the evil god they worshipped. That was a threat to all humanity, and Strybjorn had fallen in battle against it. More than that, he had saved Ragnar's life from the shaman's evil spell, and there was no way now Ragnar could repay that debt. He howled in rage and frustration, suddenly aware after all these months of dull hatred that he did not want Strybjorn to die this way, that possibly he did not want the Grimskull to die at all. Compared to the menace that was unleashed deep below this mountain, their old tribal enmities seemed petty and foolish.

He noticed that Sven had turned and was making his way through the mass to where Strybjorn had gone down. Even as Ragnar watched he saw Strybjorn suddenly emerge from the sea of stinking bodies and reel to his feet. His armour was cracked. Internal machinery was visible. Half the skin of his face was peeled away and teeth and jawbone were visible. One arm hung limp and bloody by his side, but still he fought on, chainsword flashing, killing as he went. By Russ, if nothing else he was a mighty warrior, Ragnar thought, then the paralysis left him and he leapt into action, chopping and hewing his way through the nightgangers towards where Sven and Strybjorn made their stand.

In moments, he had cleared a path, and he and the other Blood Claws were clear. He grabbed the reeling Strybjorn by the arm and helped support him as he moved on. Turning to Sven and Nils, he shouted, 'Grenades!'

Sven grinned evilly and began to hurtle grenade after grenade into the press of nightgangers. Heartbeats later, Nils did the same. The caves echoed with the thunder of explosions, the flash of detonation lit the air like lightning. Once more it was all too much for the nightgangers. Leaderless since the death of their shaman, they turned and began to retreat in the direction of the chasm. The sheer weight of numbers and press of bodies carried them over the edge. Ragnar could hear their screams as they fell down into the eternal darkness.

Swiftly he pulled the medical pack from his belt. Ragnar knew he would have to act quickly to save Strybjorn's life. He knew it was only a matter of minutes, if that, before the Chaos Marines were in pursuit. He looked up to see Sven standing over him. His armour was spattered with blood, gore and congealing brains.

'Good fight,' Sven grunted. Ragnar looked at him and nodded, wondering how long they had before the Chaos Marines swept over them. He knew that it was imperative to warn the Chapter of what they had found here, yet he also knew that he was not going to leave Strybjorn here wounded and alone to face the coming of those evil ones. He remembered what the old wizards beyond the Gate of Morkai had told him about how his hate was a weakness that would allow evil into his soul. He knew now they had been correct, and that there was only one way for him to rid himself of that hate.

Swiftly he came to a decision, praying that it was the right one.

'Sven, take Lars and Nils and the others and get out of here. Get to the surface. Get as far from this cursed place as you need to for your communicator to work, and then summon the Chapter.'

By way of answer, Sven reached up and released his helmet claps. The helm fell away onto the wet sand with a dull thud, revealing the Space Wolf's feral face, contorted with rage and looking for all the world like a daemon in the stuttering light of Ragnar's shoulder beam. 'And leave you and Strybjorn here all alone to hog the fighting and all the glory?' Sven shook his head violently. 'Are you mad, or do you think I am?'

Despite the dire situation they were in, Ragnar could not suppress a smile. He clasped an armoured hand onto Sven's shoulder. 'Get your helmet on and go now, you idiot, or I'll rip your throat out with my teeth. Can't you see that it is more important that the Space Wolves find out what's going on here than for you to die heroically?'

'So you say! I notice that you're staying.' Sven glared at Ragnar through eyes which were narrowed to mere slits, his voice a menacing whisper.

'That's because Strybjorn saved my life, and I'm not going to leave him here.'

'You go! I'll stay!' The fever of battle was bright in Sven's eyes, and he nervously fingered the teeth of his chainsword.

Ragnar lost his patience at Sven's obstinacy. 'I'm not going to tell you again!' he roared. 'Go now or I'll kill you myself.' Their eyes locked. Their teeth bared. The stink of anger and confrontation was in the air. Ragnar felt the hair on the back of his neck rise. A moment later, Sven apparently sensed Ragnar's determination, in some instinctive way, and like a wolf giving ground before the pack leader, he backed down.

'All right,' he said, picking up his helmet and brushing blood flecked granules of sand from the ceramite visor. 'I'm going. But next time it will be my turn to stay behind with the wounded.'

Ragnar grinned at him. 'Fair enough,' he said. Sven looked away for a moment, then barked orders to Nils and Lars.

'Right you two, you heard the hero. Let's get moving. And no argument or I'll rip your hearts out and eat them before your eyes.'

'Always thinking about food,' Nils muttered. He gave Ragnar the thumbs-up as he moved past.

'We'll meet again,' Lars said. 'I know it.'

'I pray to Russ that you are right,' Ragnar said, watching as the trio retreated into the darkness and then were gone.

RAGNAR TOOK OUT a canister of synthi-flesh and sprayed it onto Strybjorn's face. It congealed instantly to cover the bare bone and teeth. It did not look pretty but at least it would keep the wound clean and sterile. He took the repair cement and just as quickly plugged the cracks in Strybjorn's armour, but not before reconnecting and splicing the power-fibres. Lastly, after a quick glance to make sure everything was in place, he injected the wounded Blood Claw with a powerful stimulant. Strybjorn's eyes opened and he let out a howl of pain and rage.

'You're still here, Thunderfist. I am surprised.' His voice was violent and ragged, coloured by the pain coursing through his injured frame.

'You saved my life. I'm paying my debt.'

'I don't need your help,' Strybjorn hissed through gritted teeth, and tried to rise. He managed to get to his knees, but then started to topple. Ragnar reached out and grabbed him, putting his hand under Strybjorn's left arm. His chainsword was holstered and he held his bolt pistol in his left hand. Blood trickled in rivulets through the cracks in Strybjorn's armour and stained Ragnar's arm red.

'We'd best get going. It's only a matter of time before the nightgangers find their courage again. Or the Chaos Marines find it for them.'

Even through his pain, Strybjorn managed to look thought-ful. 'I wonder how Hengist and the others are doing.'

Ragnar strained his ears to listen. He could hear no sounds of conflict in the distance. It appeared Hengist's force was dead or worse yet, captured. Ragnar hoped that the tumbled bridge would hold back the Chaos Marines for a little while but somehow he just knew it would not stop the pursuit for long.

Strybjorn leaned against Ragnar as they moved off into the gloom.

* * *

RAGNAR TRIED TO retrace the steps that had brought them down to the temple. It was difficult. He could catch scent traces of the Space Wolves but they were overlaid by the acrid stench of the nightgangers to the point where it was difficult to pick out his Claw brothers at all. Ragnar realised now how they had been sucked into a trap, allowed to move ever deeper beneath the mountain while a huge force of nightgangers assembled all around them. They had been allowed to reach the temple, and they had walked in like living sacrifices to the Changer of Ways. It was not a cheering thought.

Ragnar's shoulder lamp probed the gloom ahead. He bent down and saw recent traces that Sven and the others had been here. That at least was reassuring. A groan from behind him told him that Strybjorn was not in a good way. Ragnar turned to see that the Grimskull was pale-faced, his skin taking on a yellowish pallor that Ragnar had come to associate with death during his former life on the islands. He only hoped that Strybjorn's super-human strength would make the difference and pull him through. Ragnar wondered how he could discern what was wrong. Perhaps there had been internal injuries that he did not have the skill or the equipment to treat. He knew that was all too possible. Often it was not the obvious wounds that killed war-riors. When he was a lad, Ragnar had heard tales of men taking what appeared to be a light tap to the skull, fighting on through a battle, and then keeling over stone dead in their moment of tri-umph. Maybe that was going to happen to Strybjorn.

'You go on without me, Thunderfist,' Strybjorn said. The words sounded strange coming from his mangled jaw. 'I'll wait here. If any are pursuing you I will hold them off.'

'You are coming with me, Grimskull, if I have to knock you down and carry you. You've come this far. Be man enough to go the whole way.'

Their eyes locked. As with Sven he sensed the resistance there, and as with Sven he beat it down. He felt that had Strybjorn been at his full strength, he might not have obeyed, but in his weakened condition, he did not have the willpower to defy Ragnar.

'You win,' he said. 'Onwards.' The motors in Strybjorn's armour wheezed asthmatically as he moved, and ruptured feed pipes vented steam from his backpack, but the Grimskull moved off at a limping stagger along the tunnel.

Ragnar could see that it was all he could do to keep on his feet.

RAGNAR BREATHED a sigh of relief. He recognised this place. It was the great underground lake. He had never imagined that he would be glad to see its foul waters, but certainly he was now. Sighting the waters around his home island would not have made him any happier at that moment. No matter how bleak and foul this place, it was a landmark Ragnar recognised, and he knew he was on the right track.

There had been times over the last few hours when he had thought he was lost. The way looked very different on the way back up to the surface. Ragnar understood only too well why. It was simply that he was now going in a different direction, experiencing the tunnels and caves from an opposite point of view to that of a few hours ago. As if that was not enough, he knew he was tired. He was alone except for Strybjorn. All of these things had conspired to alter his perceptions of the place, rendering it unfamiliar, menacing and hostile. He shook his head and reminded himself that in truth it was all of those things.

'Is this the lake of the dead?' Strybjorn asked, his voice a bubbling whisper. Ragnar realised that his fellow Blood Claw was hallucinating. 'Are we here at last?'

'No,' Ragnar said. 'It is not. It's just that foul, Chaos-tainted pond Sven spat in on the way down.' Ragnar tried to smile, but the best he could manage was an exhausted grimace.

'It's you, Thunderfist. I killed you then, and you killed me, and we've come to hell together.'

Ragnar shuddered. For a moment, it seemed quite possible. His mind reeled with the concept. Perhaps Strybjorn was right. Perhaps their corpses lay back in the ruins of the Thunderfist village. Perhaps the whole trip to Russvik, the whole process of induction into the Wolves had been merely a hallucination, a last dream-like fantasy conjured up by his pain-wracked brain as he fell forward into death. Perhaps now they really were dead. Mutually slain, maybe they had entered hell together.

Ragnar fought for a hold on sanity. He breathed deeply of the foul air, catching the scent of stagnant water, and mould and fungus. He saw the trails of blood where the corpses of the nightgangers they had slain earlier had been dragged away, most likely to be devoured. He felt the cool ceramite gauntlets encasing his fingers, and the hilt of the bolt pistol in his hand. He scanned the area, senses keener than those possessed by any mortal man.

No, he told himself. I am not dead. Nor is Strybjorn. Not yet anyway. We are Space Wolves, chosen of Russ, and we will not give up.

He unclipped another vial of painkiller, and pressed it against the induction valve in Strybjorn's armour. With a hiss the vial emptied as the chemicals entered the Blood Claw's system. Strybjorn let out a long groan, shook his head, looked around, his cavernous eyes filled with pain, but no longer perhaps quite so feverish.

'Let us go on,' he said. Ragnar nodded his agreement. In the distance, he thought he heard the sounds of pursuit.

'WHAT WAS THAT?' Strybjorn asked. Ragnar was surprised that the Grimskull had heard anything. For the past hour he had become increasingly feverish, barely able to stand on his feet.

'It was nothing,' said Ragnar. He was lying. It was the sound of metal-shod feet moving up the corridor behind them. The echoes rang harshly on the stone. It was difficult to guess the distance that separated them from the source of the noise but Ragnar could not believe it was far. Whoever was following them was confident. They were making no attempt at stealth. They were coming on with all speed.

Ragnar cursed. He realised that they were in the long gallery where he had climbed to spot the ancient girders. It seemed to Ragnar as if days or weeks had passed since they were last here. The surface was not too far away now, as far as he remembered. They had almost made it. Almost. Still, he consoled himself with the thought that Sven and the others seemed to have escaped. He had come across no sign that disaster had overtaken them or that they had been captured. They must have reached the surface by now, Ragnar thought. They might even have got clear of the zone of interference and been able to summon help. They must have made much better time than him on the long climb from the dark heart of the mountain. They had not been burdened by the wounded Strybjorn.

'Let's get going,' Ragnar said. 'Not much further now.'
Strybjorn nodded and limped onwards.

They had almost crossed the gallery when Ragnar heard a familiar melodious yet sinister voice ring out behind him.

'Where are you going, puppy? Do turn around, please. I want to look at you, for I never like shooting anyone in the back.'

Ragnar recognised the voice. It belonged to the Chaos Marine who had taunted Sergeant Hengist. Slowly he turned around, letting Strybjorn slump to the ground as he reached up to draw his chainsword.

Ragnar almost flinched as he faced his enemy. He had half expected to see a full squad of dreaded Chaos Marines and a horde of nightgangers. All he could make out was a solitary figure.

'Madok!' he spat. Ragnar noticed that some of the icons on the Chaos Marine's armour were glowing, doubtless with malign energies. The hairs on the back of Ragnar's neck prickled. What was going on? Was there a cursed spell being cast here?

'You remember. I'm flattered. That's good too. When your soul reaches hell, you will be able to tell everyone who killed you.' The words hissed flatly through the dank air of the cavern.

'I'm not dead yet.'

'Believe me, it's only a matter of moments before I change that.'

'Where are your brethren? All dead?'

'No. They are hunting down the few survivors of your little party who fled the battlefield like the cowards they are.'

'I don't believe you.' Ragnar could feel the beast within his soul snarl at the insult and begin to rise to the fore.

'What you believe or don't believe is irrelevant.' Once again, Ragnar thought that he could hear a hint of boredom in the Chaos follower's voice.

'Then why are you telling it to me, filth?'

The armoured sorcerer sighed, as if wondering at the sheer ignorance of the whelp before him. 'Because it's been a long time since I've had the pleasure of taunting one of your kind from so close. And I intend to savour it. It's one minuscule speck of revenge for the burning of Prospero, but these days I take my pleasures where I can.'

'You are of the Thousand Sons then.'

Ragnar knew now that Madok was one of his Chapter's most ancient and feared foes, devilish magicians as well as fearsome warriors. The Space Wolves had cleansed the Thousand Sons' homeworld of Prospero in the aftermath of Horus's rebellion thousands of years ago. The Traitor Marines had never forgiven them for it. Several times since they had attacked Fenris, apparently with the intention of repaying the favour. Ragnar wondered if Madok's presence now was indicative of another such plot. Of course, he thought, it had to be. That was why it was so imperative that someone get away to warn the Space Wolves. Ragnar gleaned a small crumb of solace and confidence from the thought of Sven passing on the message, and the retribution which would swiftly follow.

'Bravo. The idiots in the Fang still teach some aspects of the ancient truths then.'

'They told me enough about your treacherous kind to recognise a twisted and irredeemable foe of humanity when I see one.'

To Ragnar's surprise, Madok laughed. His mocking voice took on a scholarly tone. 'They told you nothing. It was not us who attacked your Chapter. It was you who treacherously attacked our home.'

'After you had forsworn your duty to humanity and the Emperor.'

Madok shook his head. 'So much certainty. So little knowledge. We did not forswear the Emperor. He forsook us. He sent his Wolves to attack us simply because he did not like the path our primarch, the revered Magnus, had uncovered: the path to knowledge and limitless power.'

'Limitless evil, you mean.'

Madok shook his head sorrowfully.

'Truly it is said that it is foolish to argue with those whose minds are closed. And no Chapter has ever had minds more closed or uncivilised than the Space Wolves. I don't know why I have wasted my time trying to enlighten you.'

Ragnar wondered that too. Was the Chaos Marine waiting for something, he wondered? Perhaps he was hoping that his companions would arrive and help him capture Ragnar. At that precise moment Ragnar did not care. Every moment he delayed Madok was a moment more for Sven to bring word to the brethren at the Fang.

'We may be uncivilised but we are loyal to our oaths,' Ragnar growled.

'You're certainly persistent in your folly.'

Ragnar wondered what Madok meant. He was starting to detect something now, some enchantment that tugged at his senses and compelled him to listen to what the Chaos Marine had to say. Was this some subtle spell designed to make him vulnerable to heresy?

He decided he'd better do something. Yet something prevented him from acting. His mind felt as if it was snagged in a net. Were the glittering jewels on Madok's armour glowing more brightly? Were they the cause of his caution? Shaking his head to clear his thoughts Ragnar asked the Chaos sorcerer, 'How did you get here?'

'We came in answer to the prayers of those who worship the Great Mutator. We came in under cover of the meteor swarm that your childish brethren came to investigate. We came in answer to those who worship us. The temple below was consecrated by one of my brethren left on this world after our last attack on the Fang. He taught the true way to those mutants. He led them out of error and into freedom.'

Ragnar nodded. The last piece of the puzzle was in place. He forced his arm to move, to fight the spell that he was sure Madok was placing on him. Slowly, as if fighting against a great weight, he raised his bolt pistol until it was almost aimed directly at the Chaos Marine. As if Ragnar had broken their spell, the gemstones on the Chaos Marine's armour ceased to glow.

'You are stronger-willed than I thought, puppy,' Madok said, his voice dripping scorn and hatred. 'I suppose now I will have to kill you. A pity. It would have been pleasing to have you march willingly to the altar of Tzeentch and have you offer yourself up to the Changer of Ways. Still, I suppose we can't have everything.'

With eye-blurring speed, Madok brought up his weapon and fired. Ragnar's sluggish reflexes were not up to matching him. Before Ragnar could even react the pistol was blown from his hands with one shot. It was an awesome feat of marksmanship. Knowing now he had but once chance Ragnar raised his chainsword and rushed forward. The barrel of Madok's bolter moved to cover him. It appeared huge as the mouth of a cave. Ragnar's keyed-up senses saw the barrel was indeed shaped like a daemon's head whose mouth would spit bullets. He knew at that moment he was going to die. There was no way at this range that a warrior like Madok was going to miss.

He flinched as he heard the roar of a shot, before realising that somehow, impossibly, he was not hit. Instead he saw a great chunk had been bitten out of the Chaos Marine's armour, forcing the sorcerer to stagger back. Of course, Ragnar grinned, Strybjorn still had his pistol; he must have regained conscious-ness and opened fire. Madok reeled backwards and then regained his balance in an instant, almost casually sending a shot past Ragnar. The shriek of shattering armour and a groan of pain told Ragnar that the shell had found a home in Strybjorn's body.

Still, the Grimskull had given him a chance, and Ragnar fully intended to take it. As he ran, the last trace of spell-induced lethargy fell from him. Ragnar knew he was himself again; a Space Wolf in full battle frenzy. With a howling warcry he sent his chainsword through a vast arc, intending to drive it clean through the heretic's body. Madok swivelled desperately, trying to bring his gun to bear. He almost made it. Instead, he just managed to interpose it in the way of Ragnar's blade.

There was a shriek of metal on metal. Sparks flew as the two weapons came into contact then the chainsword cleaved clean through the Chaos Marine's gun. Still Madok had time to drop it and step back. The sorcerer extended his hand with a grasping gesture and a runesword flashed from the scabbard at his side and leapt into his hand. Its blade was black. Red runes gleamed with pent-up sorcerous energy along its length. Ragnar knew without having to be told that its touch would be deadly. He chopped again using two hands to drive his blade home. Madok's daemonsword rose to parry. Blade rang against blade with a clangour like a hammer hitting an anvil.

Madok struck back at Ragnar. The Blood Claw leaped clear and sent a counterstroke hurtling at the Chaos Marine. Once again Madok parried easily. They circled each other warily now, weapons held at the ready. Ragnar's hair stood on end as Madok's blade emitted a low eerie moan. It was somehow alive and sentient, Ragnar sensed.

'That is correct,' Madok purred, guessing the chain of Ragnar's thoughts. 'This daemon weapon will consume your soul even as it drinks your blood. It thirsts, you see.'

'First it will have to hit me,' Ragnar said, a low growl emerging from his throat as he lashed out at the Chaos Marine. Madok ducked below the stroke and lashed out with a lightning-quick counter.

'I don't think that will be a problem,' he said, unleashing a flurry of blows which Ragnar strove desperately to avoid. He parried, ducked barely managed to spring aside from the onslaught. The speed and power of the Chaos Marine were incredible. Ragnar knew how strong he himself was, but compared to Madok he might as well have been a child.

And why not, Ragnar thought, as he managed to turn aside another thunderous blow? The shock of the impact left his arm feeling numb. Compared to the Chaos Marine he was but a child. Madok had millennia of experience and all the gifts that the powers of Chaos could lavish on him. Fighting against such a man was more than madness, it was sheer folly. There was no way to overcome such a fell foe. Ragnar felt that he might as well just give up. It would be less painful in the end.

Once again Ragnar became aware that these thoughts were coming from outside himself, that he was being subjected to the influence of some external power. The woeful dirge being sung by the runesword was affecting him. The effect was subtle and demoralising. Its hellish shrieking sapped the courage and strength from Ragnar's arm and will. Once more he steeled himself and threw off the spell, parrying Madok's blade and throwing himself into a furious offensive that sent the Chaos Marine backwards step by step until Ragnar had regained all the ground he had lost to Madok's onslaught.

He could sense the Chaos Marine's chagrin at this unexpected resistance. His lips twisted into a wolfish grin as he hammered another blow down. This one made it past Madok's guard and sheered one of the leering daemon heads from his armour. For a moment Ragnar thought he had struck flesh but then he saw that some sort of red-hot liquid metal was pouring forth. It bubbled like magma then evaporated into a silverish poisonous cloud. Hastily Ragnar stepped back, knowing instinctively that to breathe the foul stuff meant death. He knew that such was the magic surrounding the Chaos Marine that not even his own body's superhuman ability to adapt to poison would be good enough to save him.

'A good blow,' Madok said sardonically. Suddenly and unexpectedly he lashed out with his boot. It caught Ragnar in the groin, and he felt the codpiece of his armour crumple under the sledgehammer force of the impact. The sheer power of the blow sent him tumbling through the air to sprawl headlong on the stonework next to the recumbent form of Strybjorn.

Ragnar let the momentum of his fall carry him, and he rolled backwards, got his feet beneath him and sprang upright. Pain surged through him from the area of his groin. He felt barely able to stand upright and he shook his head in a desperate effort to clear his senses. While he had been tumbling Madok had closed the ground between them with appalling speed. His howling runesword was held high, ready for the final stroke.

At that moment, Ragnar felt a mind-numbing weakness spread through him. He knew he did not have the strength to stop the killing blow, and that his life was surely over. All Ragnar could do was watch the Chaos Marine come ever closer. He was fascinated by the glowing runes and the wailing song of his deadly blade. He knew that in mere moments, he would feel its chilly bite, and if what the heretic had said was true, he would feel his soul sucked from his still-living frame.

As Madok strode past Strybjorn's mangled form, the Grimskull's eyes came open. With a gasp of effort and willpower, he reached out with his one good arm, and with the last of his strength grabbed the Chaos Marine's ankle, pulling him off-balance. Not expecting an attack from this quarter, Madok started to tumble and fall. Instinctively, Ragnar raised his chainsword to protect himself from the falling warrior. There was the wail of metal on metal as the rotating blades bit home. Sparks flew as he sliced through the hellmetal of Madok's armour. Ragnar just had time to roll clear as the poisonous gas spurted forth and Madok hit the ground, driving the whirring, chewing blades still deeper into his chest until it passed all the way through his torso and emerged from his back. A great, roiling geyser of foul smoke erupted towards the ceiling and slowly dispersed, as a long wail of aeons of despair assaulted Ragnar's senses.

Madok's helmet rolled clear from the chest plate of his armour, and Ragnar could see that it was as empty, as if no one had been wearing it. Perhaps that was the case, he thought. Perhaps the physical form of the Chaos Marine had faded long ago, leaving his armour animated only by some foul residue, or the vile essence of his evil soul.

Briefly, Ragnar stood panting heavily in the cave. Pain wracked his body. He felt no sense of triumph right at that moment, though he knew he should have. Between them, he and Strybjorn had overcome one of the most powerful foes a Space Marine could face. Against all odds, they had won. Yes, Ragnar thought, more by luck than skill. That, and their enemy's overconfidence. Under the circumstances, Ragnar was happy with a victory whatever the reasons. It was the best that could be hoped for.

Ragnar reached down and drew his blade from the recumbent form of his enemy. He picked up Strybjorn's fallen pistol and stuck it in his holster. He bent down and hoisted the body of the Grimskull onto his shoulders and then, bracing himself against the weight, began to make his way slowly towards the surface. His damaged armour creaked and groaned under the pressure, and Ragnar reminded himself to personally thank his artificer for tending so carefully to the ages-old suit. It had served him well on his first real mission.

Feeling the heavy weight across his shoulders, Ragnar grinned. That's three times this day I owe you my life, Strybjorn, he thought. And that is a debt I will repay if it kills me.

Now, though, Ragnar resolved that he could only do that if they both made it alive to the surface. His mouth set in a determined grimace, Ragnar strode off up the tunnel towards the surface once again. He hoped it was not far.

THE COOL NIGHT AIR hit Ragnar's face as he emerged from the cave mouth and with it came a strange chemical taint that smelled like oil and naphtha. It took a second for it to register in his pain-soaked mind that he had made it to the surface. It took another second for it to register that the whole area around the cave mouth had been cleared of foliage. It took another split-second for it to register that the muzzles of half a hundred weapons were pointing at him. His nostrils flared and he caught the scent of Chapter brethren. Lots of them.

'It is me, Ragnar,' he said, just to make sure that they understood he was not hostile. He felt certain that they had already recognised him, but under the circumstances it was impossible to be too careful. It would be a foolish death to survive the long perilous trek under this daemon mountain, and then be mown down by his own battle-brothers.

Spotlight beams fell on Ragnar, throwing him into brilliant illumination. His altered pupils instantly contracted to compensate for the stark light, but even so for a moment he was blinded. An instant later he felt the touch of powerful minds probing carefully through his thoughts, and he was sure he could sense the presence of the three ancients who had waited so long ago beyond the Gate of Morkai. This time, Ragnar opened his mind to them, wanting to make sure there was not the slightest possibility of a misunderstanding. Ghostly fingers tugged at his thoughts, and he felt that he was recognised and acknowledged.

'It is Brother Ragnar and Brother Strybjorn,' a voice said. 'And there is no taint of Chaos upon them. Russ be praised.'

'Step forward, lad, and give Brother Strybjorn into the care of the priests,' said a voice from the gloom. Ragnar recognised it as belonging to Ranek. The searchlight beams winked off and overhead he made out the running lights and ghostly outlines of several Thunderhawk gunships. It seemed that the Chapter had got the warning and responded to it instantly and in great force. Ragnar knew that it was a measure of the seriousness with which they must view the threat of what waited below the mountain.

Mustering his last reserves of strength, Ragnar strode forward towards his battle-brothers, forcing himself to walk proudly upright, despite the pain, his damaged armour and the numbing weight of the Grimskull across his shoulders. Several hurried forward to take Strybjorn from him. He saw they wore the insignia of the healers. One of them looked at him and gestured for him to follow down the slope. He did so, and within a few dozen strides stood at the entrance of a field hospital tent. The healers had already connected their strange devices to Strybjorn's armour and were beginning to utter the chants of their arcane rituals. Ragnar saw that one of the medics was attaching machinery to him as well.

'How is Strybjorn?' he asked. 'Will he live? He saved my life, you know.' The words seemed foolish even as they left his lips but the healer only smiled, showing his fangs.

'And you have most likely saved his by getting him here in time. Now be silent. I must see to you.' The words were a command, but they were gently said and held no rancour, so Ragnar obeyed. He heard the whoosh of air as chemicals were injected into the appropriate vents in his armour, then a click as the panels of his chest plate swung open. In an instant he felt relaxed. He shook his head to clear away the slight blurring of his vision, and then noticed Sven standing in the doorway of the tent.

'So you made it out, brother,' Sven said. 'I am glad.'

'It appears you did too, and that you got the message through.'

'Yes, and what a time we had of it. I thought we were never going to get far enough away to be out of the zone of interference. We must have covered a good two leagues or so before I could make contact with the Fang over the comm-net.'

'Then what happened?'

'Then all hell broke loose. About five minutes after I delivered the message I saw the fire-trails of Thunderhawks in the sky. They swooped low and began firing chemical rockets into the forest. Within another two minutes they had cleared the area around the cave entrance for a thousand strides. A few heartbeats after the alchemical fires subsided the Thunderhawks were on the ground and what looked like every Wolf in the Fang poured out. They're all here – Ranek, the Librarians, the Iron Priests. There's a huge monster-machine they call Bjorn the Fell-Handed. They say he's one of the Ancients, that he walked beside Russ. All the full brothers who were in the meditation cells. A mass of support equipment. It looks like we walked into a real hornet's nest, and they intend to clear it out good and proper.

'Me and Nils and Lars just got back from where we put in the word a couple of minutes ago. I thought I'd come and see how you were before we head below the mountain.'

'You're going back in?'

'Try and stop me! The first squads have already started. They're laying sealed comm-wires, checking for deadfalls, making sure it's not a trap and the whole ceiling won't fall in once we're all down there. The Thunderhawks are scanning the mountain looking for any other exits. Once we get the all-clear we're going back down in force to clear the Chaos scum out.'

'We killed one of them,' Ragnar said. 'Strybjorn and I. We killed the leader, Madok.'

'So I heard. The Librarians told everyone. The whole Chapter is talking about it. Seems it's a long time since any Blood Claw won a fight with a full-blown champion of Chaos like Madok. Seems like you performed a mighty deed.'

'We were lucky.'

'Given a choice between a leader who is lucky and a leader who is wise, I'll take the one who is lucky,' Sven said. 'Anyway, don't say that too loudly or you'll spoil things for everybody round the camp. It's the first time since I got to Russvik that anybody round here has treated us as if we mattered.'

'I don't think that's true. They always treated us as if we mattered. That's why they were so hard on us.'

'Whatever. When you get your wounds dealt with come down and join us. Nils has found us something to eat.'

'I am in no way surprised by that,' Ragnar said and smiled. A sense of elation finally filled him. He had come through his baptism of fire without disgracing himself. He knew that soon they would clear out this nest of vipers and avenge their fallen brethren. And Ragnar was looking forward to playing his part in the brutal revenge to come.

EPILOGUE

'Brother Ragnar,' said a cold clear commanding voice. 'Brother Ragnar, awake.'

Ragnar's eyes snapped open. He was suddenly aware of his surroundings, of the cool minty tang of medical incense, of the chill marble feel of the surgical altar beneath his back, of the way his breath congealed into clouds in the cool air. He looked up and saw a lined and scarred face smiling down into his own. The two fangs revealed by the grin told him he was in the presence of his battle-brothers. The pain in his chest warned him he was back among the living.

'I cannot be in hell, Brother Sigard. You are too ugly to be allowed through its gates.'

'And you are too mean to die, Brother Ragnar. Although to tell the truth, it was touch and go there for a while. There was a point when both your hearts stopped, and your spirit wandered free from its body. We thought we had lost you then for sure, but something brought you back. I'm not sure what.'

'I still have business among the living, brother. I have enemies to slay and battles to win. I am not yet ready to die. How goes the war?'

'Well. We have cleared the dropsite, and Imperial forces are moving in to secure the perimeter. We've made a good beginning here but the battle will go on. These heretics are tough ones, and rumour has it that the forces of Chaos have reinforced them. Indeed it may be that the Thousand Sons are present once more. There are rumours that Madok has been sighted leading their troops.'

'And there is my unfinished business, brother. Twice I have thought I killed him. Third time will be the charm.'

'I wish you well in your quest, brother. And it may be that your wish will be granted soon, for our enemies are mounting a mighty counter-attack against us.'

'How soon may I leave here?' Ragnar asked.

'In another few days, brother.'

'Not good enough,' Ragnar said, ignoring the pain and lifting himself from the altar. The life-support tubes automatically withdrew from the induction points in his armour. 'The Chapter will need every man in this coming conflict.'

'As you wish, Brother Ragnar,' Sigard said.

Ragnar nodded and moved slowly towards the door. From outside he could hear the welcome thunder of battle.

**There is more Warhammer 40,000
action coming soon in
GHOSTMAKER, a new Gaunt's
Ghosts saga from Dan Abnett.**

**Here is a preview of the
mayhem to come...**

From GHOSTMAKER:
A BLOODING

Day Sixty, Voltemand Mirewoods

THEY WERE A good two hours into the dark, black-trunked woods, tracks churning the filthy ooze and the roar of their engines resonating from the sickly canopy of leaves above, when Colonel Ortiz saw death.

It wore red, and stood in the trees to the right of the track, in plain sight, unmoving, watching his column of Basilisks as they passed along the trackway. It was the lack of movement that chilled Ortiz. He did a double-take, first seeing the figure as they passed it before realising what it was.

Almost twice a man's height, frighteningly broad, armour the colour of rusty blood and crested by curving brass antlers. The face was a graven death's head. Daemon… Chaos Warrior… World Eater!

Ortiz snapped his gaze back to it and felt his blood drain away. He fumbled for his radio link.

'Alarm! Alarm! Ambush to the right!' he yelled into the set. Gears slammed and whined, and hundreds of tonnes of mech-anised steel shuddered, foundered and slithered on the muddy track, penned, trapped, too cumbersome to react quickly.

By then the Chaos Space Marine had begun to move. So had its six comrades, each emerging from the woods around them.

Panic seized Ortiz's convoy cluster, the ten-vehicle forward portion of a heavy column of eighty flame- and feather-painted Basilisk tanks of 'The Serpents', the Ketzok 17th Armoured Regiment, sent in to support the Blueblood push. They had the firepower to flatten a city, but caught on a strangled trackway, in thick woodland, with no room to turn or traverse, and with monstrous enemies at close quarters, far too close to bring the main guns to bear, they were all but helpless.

Panic alarms spread backwards down the straggled column, from one cluster of vehicles to the next, in a discordant howl of protesting gears and roaring, smoking engines. Ortiz heard tree trunks shatter as some commanders tried to haul their machines off the track.

The World Eaters started baying as they advanced, wrenching out of their augmented throats deep, inhuman calls that whooped across the trackway and shivered the metal of the tank armour. They howled the name of the bloody abomination they worshipped.

'Small arms!' ordered Ortiz. 'Use the pintle mounts!' As he spoke, he cranked round the autocannon mounted on his vehicle's rear and angled it at the nearest monster.

The killing started. The rasping belch of flamers reached his ears and he heard the screams of men cooking inside their superheated tank hulls. The Chaos Marine he had first spotted reached the Basilisk ahead of his and began to chop its shell like firewood with a chain axe. Sparks blew up from punctured metal. Sparks, flames, metal shards, meat.

Screaming, Ortiz trained his mounted gun on the World Eater and fired. He shot long at first, but corrected before the monster could turn. The creature didn't seem to feel the first hits. Ortiz clenched the trigger and streamed the heavy tracer fire at the red spectre. At last the figure shuddered, convulsed and then blew apart.

Ortiz cursed. The World Eaters soaked up the sort of punishment that would wreck a Leman Russ. He realised his ammo drum was almost empty. He was snapping it free and shouting to his bombardier for a fresh one when the shadow fell on him.

Ortiz turned.

Another Chaos Marine stood on the rear of the Basilisk behind him, a giant blocking out the pale sunlight. It stooped and howled its victory shout into his face, assaulting him with concussive sonic force and wretched odour.

Ortiz recoiled as if he had been hit by a macro shell. He could not move. The World Eater chuckled, a deep, macabre growl from behind the visor, a seismic rumble. The chainsword in its fist whined and swung up.

The blow didn't fall. The monster rocked, two or three times, swayed for a moment. And exploded.

Smeared with grease and ichor, Ortiz scrambled up out of his hatch. He was suddenly aware of a whole new layer of gunfire – sustained lasgun blasts, the chatter of support weapons, the crump of grenades. Another force was moving out of the woods, crushing the Chaos Marine ambush hard against the steel flanks of his artillery machines.

As Ortiz watched, the remaining World Eaters died. One was punctured dozens of times by lasgun fire and fell face down into the mire. Another was flamed repeatedly as he ripped apart the wreck of a Basilisk with his steel hands. The flames touched off the tank's magazine and the Chaos Space Marine was incinerated with his victims. His hideous roar lingered long after the white-hot flames had consumed him.

The column's saviours emerged from the forest around them. Imperial Guards: tall, dark-haired, pale-skinned men in black fatigues, a scruffy, straggle-haired mob almost invisible in their patterned camo-cloaks. Ortiz heard strange, disturbing pipe music strike up a banshee wail in the close forest, and a victory yelp erupted from the men. It was met by cheers and whoops from his own crews.

Ortiz leapt down into the mud and approached the Imperial Guardsmen through the drifting smoke.

'I'm Colonel Ortiz. You boys have my earnest thanks,' he said. 'Who are you?'

The nearest man, a giant with unruly black hair, a tangled, braided beard and thick, bare arms decorated with blue spiral tattoos, smiled jauntily and saluted, bringing up his lasgun. 'Colonel Corbec, Tanith First and Only. Our pleasure, I'm sure.'

Ortiz nodded back. He found he was still shaking. He could barely bring himself to look down at the dead Chaos Marine, sprawled in the mud nearby. 'Takes discipline to ambush an ambush. Your men certainly know stealth. Why is it–'

He got no further. The bearded giant, Corbec, suddenly froze, a look of dismay on his face. Then he was leaping forward with a cry, tackling Ortiz down into the blue-black mud.

The World Eater lifted his horned skull out of the muck and half-raised his bolter. But that was all. Then a shrieking chain sword decapitated him.

The heavy, dead parts flopped back into the mud. One of them rolled.

Ibram Gaunt held his keening chain sword in front of his face like a duellist making a salute, then thumbed it to 'idle'. He turned to Corbec and Ortiz as they picked themselves up, caked in black filth. Ortiz stared at the tall, powerful man in the long dark coat and cap of an Imperial Commissar. His face was blade thin, his eyes as dark as space. He looked like he could rip a world asunder with his hands.

'Meet the boss,' chuckled Corbec at Ortiz's side. 'Commissar Gaunt.'

Ortiz nodded, wiping his face. 'So you're Gaunt's Ghosts.'

Day Sixty, Imperial Planetary Headquarters, Voltemand

MAJOR GILBEAR poured himself a brandy from the decanter on the teak stand. 'Just who the hell are these awful scum?' he asked, sipping from the huge crystal balloon.

At his desk, General Sturm put down his pen and sat back. 'Do help yourself to my brandy, Gilbear,' he muttered, though the sarcasm was lost on his massive aide. Gilbear reclined on a chaise beside the flickering amber read-out displays of the mes-sage-caster, and gazed at his commander. 'Ghosts? That's what they call them, isn't it?'

Sturm nodded, observing his senior adjutant. Gilbear – Gizhaum Danver de Banzi Haight Gilbear, to give him his full name – was the second son of the Haight Gilbears of Solenhofen, the royal house of Volpone. He was nearly two and half metres tall and arrogantly powerful, with the big, blunt, bland features and languid, hooded eyes of the aristocracy. Gilbear wore the grey and gold uniform of the Royal Volpone 50th, the so-called Bluebloods, who believed they were the noblest regiment in the Imperial Guard.

Sturm sat back in his chair. 'They are indeed called Ghosts. Gaunt's Ghosts. And they're here because I requested them.'

Gilbear cocked a disdainful eyebrow. 'You requested them?'

'We've had nigh-on six weeks and we can't shake the enemy from Voltis City. They command everything west of the Bokore Valley. Macaroth is not pleased. All the while they hold Voltemand, they have a road into the heart of the Sabbat Worlds. So you see I need a lever. I need to introduce a new element to break our deadlock.'

'That rabble?' sneered Gilbear. 'I watched them as they shambled off their stinking dropships. Hairy, illiterate primitives, with tattoos and nose rings.'

Sturm lifted a data-slate from his desktop and shook it at Gilbear. 'Have you read the reports General Hadrak filed after the Sloka took Blackshard? He credits Gaunt's mob with the decisive incursion. It seems they excel at stealth raids.'

Sturm got to his feet and adjusted the sit of his resplendent Blueblood staff uniform. The study was bathed in yellow sunlight that streamed in through the conservatory doors at the end, softened by net drapes. He rested his hand on the antique globe of Voltemand in its mahogany stand by the desk and span it idly, gazing out across the grounds of Vortimor House. This place had been the country seat of one of Voltemand's most honoured noble families, a vast, grey mansion, fringed with mauve climbing plants, situated in ornamental parkland thirty kilometres south of Voltis City. It had been an ideal location to establish his Supreme Headquarters.

Outside, on the lawn, a squad of Blueblood elite in full, resplendent battle dress were executing a precision synchronised drill with chainswords. Metal flashed and whirled, perfect and poised. Beyond them, a garden of trellises and arbours led down to a boating lake, calm in the afternoon light. Navigation lights flashed slowly on the barbed masts of the communications array in the herbarium. Somewhere in the stable block, strutting gaudcocks whooped and cried.

You wouldn't think there was a war on, Sturm mused.

He wondered where the previous owners of the mansion were now? Did they make it off-world before the first assault? Are they huddled and starving in the belly hold of a refugee ship, reduced overnight to a level with their former vassals? Or are they bone ash in the ruins of Kosdorf, or on the burning

Metis Road? Or did they die screaming and melting at the orbital port when the legions of Chaos first fell on their world, vaporised with the very ships in which they struggled to escape?

Who cares? thought Sturm. The war is all that matters. The glory, the crusade, the Emperor. He would only care for the fallen when the bloody head of Chanthar, demagogue of the Chaos army that held Voltis Citadel, was served up to him on a carving dish. And even then, he wouldn't care much.

Gilbear was on his feet, refilling his glass. 'This Gaunt, he's quite a fellow, isn't he? Wasn't he with the Hyrkan Eighth?'

Sturm cleared his throat. 'Lead them to victory at Balhaut. One of old Slaydo's chosen favourites. It was decided he had the prestige to hammer a new regiment or two into shape, so they sent him to the planet Tanith to supervise the Founding there. A Chaos space fleet hit the world that very night, and he got out with just a few thousand men.'

Gilbear nodded. 'That's what I heard. Skin of his teeth. But that's his career in tatters, stuck with a understrength rabble like that. Macaroth won't transfer him, will he?'

Sturm managed a small smile. 'Our beloved overlord does not look kindly on the favourites of his predecessor. Especially as Slaydo granted Gaunt and a handful of others the settlement rights of the first world each conquered. He and his Tanith rabble are an embarrassment to the new regime. But that serves us well. They will fight hard because they have everything to prove, and everything to win.'

'I say,' Gilbear said suddenly, lowering his glass. 'What if they do win? I mean, if they're as useful as you say…'

'They will facilitate our victory,' Sturm said, pouring himself a drink. 'They will not achieve anything else. We will serve Lord Macaroth twofold, by taking this world for him, and ridding him of Gaunt and his damn Ghosts.'

Voltemand Mirewoods

'You were expecting us?' Gaunt asked, riding on the top of Ortiz's Basilisk as the convoy moved on.

Colonel Ortiz nodded, leaning back against the raised top-hatch cover. 'We were ordered up the line last night to dig in at the north end of the Bokore Valley and pound the enemy fortifications on the western side. En route, I got coded orders, telling us to meet your regiment at Pavis Crossroads and transport you as we advanced.'

Gaunt removed his cap and ran a hand through his short fair hair. 'We were ordered across country to the crossroads, all right,' he responded. 'Told to meet transport there for the next leg. But my scouts picked up the World Eaters' stench, so we doubled back and met you early.'

Ortiz shuddered. 'Good thing for us.'

Gaunt gazed along the line of the convoy as they moved on, the massive bulk of the Basilisks as they ground up the snaking mud-track through the sickly, dim forest. His men were riding on the flanks of the great war machines, a dozen or more per vehicle, joking with the Serpent crews, exchanging drinks and smokes, some cleaning weapons or even napping as the lurch of the metal beasts allowed.

'So Sturm's sending you in?' Ortiz asked presently.

'Right down the river valley to the gates of Voltis. He thinks we can take the city where his Bluebloods have failed.'

'Can you?'

'We'll see,' said Gaunt, without the flicker of a smile. 'The Ghosts are new, unproven but for a skirmish on Blackshard. But they have certain... strengths.'

He fell silent, and seemed to be admiring the gold and turquoise lines of the feathered serpent design painted on the barrel of the Basilisk's main weapon; its open beak was the muzzle. All the Ketzok machines were rich with similar decorations.

Ortiz whistled low to himself. 'Down the Bokore Valley into the mouth of hell. I don't envy you.'

Now Gaunt smiled. 'Just you keep pounding the western hills and keep them busy. In fact, blow them all away to kingdom come before we get there.'

'Deal,' Ortiz laughed.

'And don't drop your damn aim!' Gaunt added with a threatening chuckle. 'Remember you have friends in the valley!'

TWO VEHICLES BACK, Corbec nodded his thanks as he took the thin, dark cigar his Basilisk commander offered.

'Doranz,' the Serpent said, introducing himself.

'Charmed,' Corbec said. The cigar tasted of liquorice, but he smoked it anyway.

Lower down the hull of the tank, by Corbec's sprawled feet, the boy Milo was cleaning out the chanters of his Tanith pipe. It wheezed and squealed hoarsely. Doranz blanched. 'I'll tell you this… when I heard that boy's piping today, that hell-note, it almost scared me more than the damn blood cries of the enemy.'

Corbec chuckled. 'The pipe has its uses. It rallies us, it spooks the enemy. Back home, the forests move and change. The pipes were a way to follow and not get lost.'

'Where is home?' Doranz asked.

'Nowhere now,' Corbec said and returned to his smoke.

ON THE BACK ARMOUR of another Basilisk, the hulking figure of Bragg, the biggest of the Ghosts, and small, wiry Larkin were dicing with two of the tank's gun crew.

Larkin had already won a gold signet ring set with a turquoise skull, which he kept glancing at admiringly. Bragg, on the other hand, had lost all his smokes and two bottles of sacra. Every now and then, the lurch of the tank beneath them would flip the dice, or slide them under an exhaust baffle, prompting groans and accusations of fixing and cheating.

Up by the top hatch with the vehicle's commander, Major Rawne watched the game without amusement. Velaz, the Basilisk commander, felt uneasy about his passenger. Rawne was slender, dark and somehow dangerous. A starburst tattoo covered one eye. He was not… likeable or open like the other Ghosts seemed to be.

'So, major… what's your commissar like?' the commander began by way of easing the silence.

'Gaunt?' Rawne said, turning slowly to face the Serpent. 'He's a despicable bastard who left my world to die and one day I will slay him with my own hands.'

'Oh,' the commander said, and went to find something important to do down below.

ORTIZ PASSED GAUNT his flask. The afternoon was going and they were losing the light. Ortiz consulted a map-slate, angling it to show Gaunt. 'Navigation puts us about two kilometres or so short of Pavis Crossroads. We've made good time. We'll be on it before dark. I'm glad, I didn't want to have to turn on the floods and running lights to continue.'

'What do we know about Pavis?' Gaunt asked.

'Last reports were it was held by a battalion of Bluebloods. That was at oh-five-hundred this morning.'

'Wouldn't hurt to check,' Gaunt mused. 'There are worse things than rolling into an ambush position at twilight, but not many. Cluggan!'

He called down the hull to a big, grey-haired Ghost sat with others playing cards.

'Sir!' Cluggan said, scrambling back up the rocking Basilisk.

'Sergeant, take six men, jump down and scout ahead of the column. We're a couple of kilometres short of this crossroads.' Gaunt showed Cluggan the map. 'Should be clear, but after our tangle with the damn World Eaters we'd best be sure.'

Cluggan saluted and slid back to his men. In a few moments they had gathered up their kits and weapons and swung down off the skirt armour onto the track. A moment more and they had vanished like smoke into the woods.

'That *is* impressive,' Ortiz said.

**The story continues in
GHOSTMAKER by Dan Abnett,
the next instalment in the saga of
Gaunt's Ghosts, coming soon
from the Black Library.**

Also from the Black Library

FIRST & ONLY
A Gaunt's Ghosts novel
by Dan Abnett

'THE TANITH ARE strong fighters, general, so I have heard.' The
scar tissue of his cheek pinched and twitched slightly, as it
often did when he was tense. 'Gaunt is said to be a resourceful
leader.'

'You know him?' The general looked up, questioningly

'I know *of* him sir. In the main by reputation.'

GAUNT GOT TO his feet, wet with blood and Chaos pus. His
Ghosts were moving up the ramp to secure the position. Above
them, at the top of the elevator shaft, were over a million
Shriven, secure in their bunker batteries. Gaunt's expeditionary
force was inside, right at the heart of the enemy stronghold.
Commissar Ibram Gaunt smiled.

*IT IS THE nightmare future of Warhammer 40,000, and mankind
teeters on the brink of extinction. The galaxy-spanning Imperium is
riven with dangers, and in the Chaos-infested Sabbat system,
Imperial Commissar Gaunt must lead his men through as much in-
fighting amongst rival regiments as against the forces of Chaos.
First and Only is an epic saga of planetary conquest, grand ambition, treachery and honour.*

Also from the Black Library

TROLLSLAYER
A Gotrek & Felix novel
by William King

HIGH ON THE HILL the scorched walled castle stood, a stone spider clutching the hilltop with blasted stone feet. Before the gaping maw of its broken gate hanged men dangled on gibbets, flies caught in its single-strand web.

'Time for some bloodletting,' Gotrek said. He ran his left hand through the massive red crest of hair that rose above his shaven tattooed skull. His nose chain tinkled gently, a strange counterpoint to his mad rumbling laughter.

'I am a slayer, manling. Born to die in battle. Fear has no place in my life.'

TROLLSLAYER IS THE first part of the death saga of Gotrek Gurnisson, as retold by his travelling companion Felix Jaeger. Set in the darkly gothic world of Warhammer, Trollslayer is an episodic novel featuring some of the most extraordinary adventures of this deadly pair of heroes. Monsters, daemons, sorcerers, mutants, orcs, beastmen and worse are to be found as Gotrek strives to achieve a noble death in battle. Felix, of course, only has to survive to tell the tale.

Also from the Black Library

SKAVENSLAYER
A Gotrek & Felix novel
by William King

'BEWARE! SKAVEN!' Felix shouted and saw them all reach for
their weapons. In moments, swords glittered in the half-
light of the burning city. From inside the tavern a number
of armoured figures spilled out into the gloom. Felix was
relieved to see the massive squat figure of Gotrek among
them. There was something enormously reassuring about
the immense axe clutched in the dwarf's hands.

'I see you found our scuttling little friends, manling,'
Gotrek said, running his thumb along the blade of his axe
until a bright red bead of blood appeared.

'Yes, Felix gasped, struggling to get his breath back
before the combat began.

'Good. Let's get killing then!'

*SET IN THE MIGHTY city of Nuln, Gotrek and Felix are back in
Skavenslayer, the second novel in this epic saga. Seeking to
undermine the very fabric of the Empire with their arcane
warp-sorcery, the skaven, twisted Chaos rat-men, are at large
in the reeking sewers beneath the ancient city. Led by Grey
Seer Thanquol, the servants of the Horned Rat are
determined to overthrow this bastion of humanity. Against
such forces, what possible threat can just two hard-bitten
adventurers pose?*

Also from the Black Library

DAEMONSLAYER
A Gotrek & Felix novel
by William King

THE ROAR WAS so loud and so terrifying that Felix almost dropped his blade. He looked up and fought the urge to soil his britches. The most frightening thing he had ever seen had entered the hall and behind it he could see the leering heads of beastmen.

As he gazed on the creature in wonder and terror, Felix thought: this is the incarnate nightmare which has bedevilled my people since time began.

'Just remember,' Gotrek said from beside him, 'the daemon is mine!'

FRESH FROM THEIR adventures battling the foul servants of the rat-god in Nuln, Gotrek and Felix are now ready to join an expedition northwards in search of the long-lost dwarf hall of Karag Dum. Setting forth for the hideous Realms of Chaos in an experimental dwarf zeppelin, Gotrek and Felix are sworn to succeed or die in the attempt. But greater and more sinister energies are coming into play, as a daemonic power is awoken to fulfil its ancient, deadly promise.

Also from the Black Library

EYE OF TERROR
A Warhammer 40,000 novel
by Barrington J. Bayley

Tell the truth only if a lie will not serve

'WHAT I HAVE to tell you,' Abaddas said, in slow measured tones, 'will be hard for you to accept or even comprehend. The rebellion led by Warmaster Horus succeeded. The Emperor is dead, killed by Horus himself in single combat, though Horus too died of his injuries.'

Magron groaned. He cursed himself for having gone into suspended animation. To be revived in a galaxy without the Emperor! Horrible! Unbelievable! Impossible to bear! Stricken, he looked into Abaddas's flinty grey eyes. 'Who is Emperor now?'

The first hint of an emotional reaction flickered on Abaddas's face. 'What need have we of an Emperor?' he roared. 'We have the Chaos gods!'

IN THE DARK and gothic future of Warhammer 40,000, mankind teeters on the brink of extinction. As the war-fleets of the Imperium prepare to launch themselves on a crusade into the very heart of Chaos, Rogue Trader Maynard Rugolo seeks power and riches on the fringe worlds of this insane and terrifying realm.

Also from the Black Library

INTO THE MAELSTROM

An anthology of Warhammer 40,000 stories, edited by Marc Gascoigne & Andy Jones

'THE CHAOS ARMY had travelled from every continent, every shattered city, every ruined sector of Illium to gather on this patch of desert that had once been the control centre of the Imperial Garrison. The sand beneath their feet had been scorched, melted and fused by a final, futile act of suicidal defiance: the detonation of the garrison's remaining nuclear stockpile.' – **Hell in a Bottle** *by Simon Jowett*

'HOARSE SCREAMS and the screech of tortured hot metal filled the air. Massive laser blasts were punching into the spaceship. They superheated the air that men breathed, set fire to everything that could burn and sent fireballs exploding through the crowded passageways.' – **Children of the Emperor** *by Barrington J. Bayley*

IN THE GRIM and gothic nightmare future of Warhammer 40,000, mankind teeters on the brink of extinction. INTO THE MAELSTROM is a storming collection of a dozen action-packed science fiction short stories set in this dark and brooding universe.

Also from the Black Library

REALM OF CHAOS

An anthology of Warhammer fantasy stories, edited by Marc Gascoigne & Andy Jones

'MARKUS WAS CONFUSED; the stranger's words were baffling his pain-numbed mind. "Just who are you, foul-spawned deviant?"

'The warrior laughed again, slapping his hands on his knees. "I am called Estebar. My followers know me as the Master of Slaughter. And I have come for your soul."' – **The Faithful Servant** by *Gav Thorpe*

'THE WOLVES ARE running again. I can hear them panting in the darkness. I race through the forest, trying to outpace them. The trees seem to throw themselves in front of me, to slow my progress as I crash on. Behind the wolves I sense another presence, something evil. I am in the place of blood again.' – **Dark Heart** by *Jonathan Green*

IN THE DARK and gothic world of Warhammer, the ravaging armies of the Ruinous Powers are howling down from the savage north to assail the lands of men. REALM OF CHAOS is a searing collection of a dozen all-action fantasy short stories set in these desperate times.